INTERVIEW WITH THE DEVIL: EPOCH

MICHAEL HARBRON

First edition 2024

Something wicked this way comes.

— RAY BRADBURY

CONTENTS

1

THE MORNING STAR

Not Your Mother's Antichrist

For every church of God, there existed a temple of Satan.

It just so happened that while the former thrived upon the surface of the world, their towers reaching toward heaven in a bid to reach spiritual ascension, the latter thrived under the ground, eager to seek the depths where their patron deity dwelled.

One such Satanic temple existed three hundred feet under St. Paul's Chapel. Three hundred feet was deep enough that no one ever got wise to the devil-worshipping activities that took place in that temple and still close enough to the surface that a one-and-a-half-minute elevator ride got you back to the surface in a Bank's perpetually out-of-order ATM room.

This was New York City. People other than tourists did not have the time to stand around and see what other people were doing, and let's just say there were tourists on 209 Broadway, busy taking pictures of St. Paul's Church, not paying attention to the ATM room across the road.

Tourist or born-and-bred New Yorker, everyone ignored scaffolding. Wherever it was, it was ugly and took away from the beauty of the city.

But not as ugly as the things happening right under St. Paul's.

Three hundred feet was nothing. New York City Water Tunnel No. 3, which, while off-limits to the public, could still be accessed by just about anyone, was built two-fifty feet below Van Cortlandt Park. Then, there was the Basilica of St. Patrick's Cathedral catacombs, which went as far deep as four hundred feet, but this was not a matter of public or private knowledge. Only the papacy and those buried in those catacombs were aware of what happened under the catacombs. Nothing pleasant there either, unless your idea of pleasant involved sex trafficking. The deepest of New York City's underground subway construction was twelve hundred feet, which was the same height as the Empire State Building, giving new meaning to the credo, "As above, so below."

What most people did not get about this city was that there was a thriving ecosystem right underneath its surface, what the initiated knew as the Old City, what the depraved knew as the Real New York.

Cults. Secret Societies. Ascetics. Madmen. All these and many more had found a home in the Old City, and were all bound by the only law that was enforceable by death: None shall ever speak of the Old City.

Within the Baphomet Temple, where no sliver of sunlight could reach nor any scream of agony issued from within the walls of this unholy enterprise ever escaped, distinguished men in elegant robes gathered around a bloodstained stone altar.

The robes they wore were deep purple, golden lines

making profane sigils. Each member held a silver chalice aloft; these chalices were empty now but soon to be filled with the blood of the seven-year-old boy tied to the altar. Here, where noise was not an issue, they did not gag the child. Rather, they let him scream as much as he could to truly let the terror set roots in the depths of his consciousness. The ritual worked best if they shattered the child's psyche, and there were more ways of doing that than just tying him.

Here, in this temple, where the rules were ancient and passed down from one black preacher to the next, it was allowed (in fact, encouraged) to derive sexual pleasure from ritual sacrifice.

And all of these dozen men intended to do just that, just as they had been doing from time to time. But first, the words of the ritual.

The oldest of the robed men stepped forward, the part of his visage not hidden by his deep hood lit dimly by the soft glow of candlelight. He had a white jaw-clinger beard and his skin was sagging. In his hands, he not only held the chalice but also a silver dagger with Baphomet etched on the handle, one hand pointing skyward, the other hand pointing Hellward.

The man gripped his blade tight and cut a shallow slit along the length of the writhing child's torso, drawing blood. The child's screams rang through the stone interior of the temple, his tears splashing on the slab. The harder he tugged, the tighter the robes got.

"Hinc ego hanc animam in nomine satanae immolamus, et Dominum Tenebrosum exoro, cum devotis eius cultoribus nobiscum communicat," whispered the ritual leader, putting his cup against the boy's body and sieving a drop of blood into his chalice. A drop would suffice. The other eleven came forward in unison, doing the same, a drop each in each of their chalices.

The words the master of this ceremony had spoken translated to, “Hereby, I do sacrifice this soul in the name of Satan, and pray the Dark Lord communes with us, his devout worshippers,” and as they each stood with a droplet of the boy’s blood in their chalice, they waited for a sign. These sorts of proceedings almost always featured a sign, something that would lend them confidence in their ritual and bolster their spirit to carry on.

All of the hundreds of candles in the temple flickered at once in the wake of the gust of wind that blew in from the temple’s entrance. The ritualists were far too entranced by the ritual, by the sight of the small, bleeding, screaming, blonde-haired boy, that they only took the flickering of the candles as a sign, and not for the heralding of a new presence in their midst.

“Brother Von Barreth, if you would,” one of the ritualists spoke in a deep voice, nodding at the master of ceremonies.

“In nomine Satanae, diabolicus spiritus,” Reinhold Von Barreth whispered, raising the dagger above the boy’s heart. He locked his gaze with the child, saw the terror in his blue eyes, and smiled. This was *right*. This was how it had always been, how the men who ran this world got their power. This was as natural to him as breathing or falling asleep.

He brought down the dagger with full force, intending to pierce past the kid’s ribcage and spear his heart. They would then fill the rest of their chalices from the spurting blood that would gush from the gash in his chest.

But such a thing never came to pass, for within the blink of an eye, the dagger completed its downward trajectory not on the boy’s shirtless body but on the deeply stained stone slab. As for the boy, he was nowhere to be found.

"What?!" Reinhold yelled, his hood no longer covering his face. The brute force of his dagger's descent had chipped its pointed end. "Where's the fucking boy?!"

"Oh, he's right here, aren't you, Jake?"

The twelve cultists shot a look up in unison, staring at the figure standing atop the stone steps of the ritual chamber. His form was hidden in shadows, except for his eyes which glowed a deep red. The boy stood whimpering, hiding behind his savior's leg.

"Jesus fucking Christ, you know, when I read the tinfoil hat posts on Reddit about child-sacrificing cults all over the country, at first I didn't think they were real, but now that I know they're real, I'm a little disappointed to see that you're a member, Reinhold," the man said, standing his ground.

"Just who in the Hell do you think you are?" Reinhold barked, brandishing a Colt revolver. The other eleven did the same. He was just one person, and while they were all still wondering how he'd rescued their sacrifice in a split second, they knew that they outnumbered him and there was nowhere for him to go.

"Hell, Reinhold. I am Hell," the man spoke, then knelt beside the kid. "Hey, listen, Jake. That's your name, isn't it? Jake Halloway? I'm going to need you to hide behind this pillar here. Close your eyes. Cover your ears. This is going to be over soon. I promise I'll get you home safe. I just need to do this first, okay?"

The boy nodded, then wiped fresh tears from his eyes.

"Does it hurt?" The man asked, pointing at the long slit on the boy's chest.

The boy nodded.

The man ran his finger up the slit, making it disappear instantaneously.

"Now it won't. Come, then. Hide behind this pillar. I'll come get you in a minute."

The child did as he was told. Dressed in nothing but his underpants, he took two faltering steps and tucked himself behind one of the many pills that held this temple up.

"Now, gentlemen. What are we going to do about this?" He asked as he climbed down the steep steps, his face coming into view as the ambient candlelight fell upon his features.

Clean-shaven, with wavy hair, and a handsome smile on his youthful face, he walked up to the cultists, unperturbed by their weapons, and came to a halt right in front of Reinhold.

"Reinhold, you sick fuck. Are you hard right now? What, did you pop a couple of Viagras before the ceremony? Were you going to fuck a kid's corpse? Even by my lowly standards, man, I've got to say, that's dark."

"Mr. Joseph Banbury. W-wh-what are you doing here?" Reinhold stammered as he tried to keep his gun's aim steady. Regardless of who Joseph's backer was, he had seen too much. Reinhold could not let him leave this place alive. He would deal with the consequences later.

"Ooh, Reinhold, are you thinking of putting one right between my eyes?" Joe laughed, then stepped right in front of Reinhold. "Do it."

Reinhold did not need telling twice. He pulled the trigger.

Joe reeled a step back, holding his forehead.

He howled, "Holy shit. That was a figure of speech, man. I didn't think you were actually going to shoot me between the eyes!"

The twelve men had never seen such a thing before. That someone, upon being shot, would still be cognizant and unaffected. They each took a step back out of fear, except for Reinhold, who stood with his revolver still aimed at Joseph.

Joe held the bullet in his fingers. It hadn't even scratched his skin. Although, there was a black mark where it had come into contact with his forehead. Joe rubbed off the gunpowder and stood there, frowning, as if what had just happened did not register on his pain scale any more than stubbing one's toe did.

"That was not cool, *Von Barreth*," Joe said, the last two words uttered mockingly. "And here I'd thought that I'd only chop your dick off for molesting kids. But you've angered me, man. Oh, you've angered me."

"Just who...*what*...are you!?" Reinhold's hand had begun to shake at the prospect of having his penis cleaved off his body. The image that flashed across his mind showed his own self reflected withered and nude, a red cockless gash between his legs. The gun fell from his hand and fell with a loud clang on the stone floor.

"Well, I'm not your mother's antichrist, I can tell you that. And I don't condone this shit. Honestly, where did you all collectively get in your thick skulls that the Devil might like something like this?"

Upon mention of his name, the Devil appeared in a smooth stride, but only to Joseph, not to anyone else. As far as they were concerned, he stood there alone.

"You know, I might have let it slip a couple hundred centuries ago that this sort of thing would amuse me. But humanity's grasp on sarcasm was very rudimentary back then. But why are you interrupting them, Joe? Don't we have better things to do?"

"Better than saving an innocent kid's life from these sick fucks?" Joe asked.

The Devil scoffed. "When you took upon your new role, I did not expect you to be so micro-managerial about it."

"It's just this one thing, Lucifer. You know that. That guy, he's sort of vital to our future operations. Oh, I'm sorry," Joe said, diverting his attention back to Reinhold. "*Was* vital to our future operations."

"Who are you talking to?" Reinhold asked, his voice a nervous mess.

"None of your business," Joe said, still wiping his forehead. "That hurt, Reinhold. And not in a good way, either. You know, like how when your girlfriend decides to peg you for the first time. You wouldn't happen to know anything about that, would you? I wager all your girlfriends were way too young to know what pegging was."

"Enough!" Reinhold snapped, picking his gun up. "You wouldn't tell us why you're here. You interrupted our ritual. And now you're mocking me. Mr. Joseph Banbury, I am not sure how much you know of the Old City and the ways of the Old World, but we never impose upon one another. We let each other do as they will."

"What makes you think that I am a part of your Old World?" Joe growled, the faux charisma gone, replaced by raw rage. He reached forward, pulled the gun away from Reinhold's grasp effortlessly, and threw it across the temple. Then he grabbed the old man by the neck and lifted him off the floor. "I'm ushering in the New World Order, Reinhold. And you and your lot of sorry ass power hungry pedophilic dinosaurs are not a part of it. I just wanted to do you the honor of letting you know to your face that we couldn't sit around and wait for your bureaucratic ass to give us the go-ahead, and so, through a rather creative maneuvering of this fine country's legal system and some Mr. Robot level of black hat hacking, I've seized your personal assets. I did so the moment I got wise to what you were doing. No one's going to be missing you. That's the way of the world. The vacuum of your absence will be filled by someone younger than you, better than you."

"You wouldn't dare," Reinhold choked, his face growing paler than wax. "Shoot him."

Joe shot an infernal look in the direction of the rest of the cultists, then at the temple entrance. The stone doors closed on their own. The Devil, who was standing by the temple's entrance, shook his head and clicked his tongue.

"What are you doing, Joe?" He asked, hands in his pocket, looking bored. "There are thousands of cults like this all over the world. Do you really think you're going to put an end to all of them?"

"Why can't I? I wield the power to do so," Joe asked over the desperate screams of the cultists as they banged against the closed door. "I get to shape the world, and my world does not stand for these men."

"The Devil benefacts a saintly antichrist. Can you hear how stupid that sounds? A saintly antichrist is just plain old Jesus Christ, Joe!"

"Let me do this! And if you're worried about what I'm going to do, maybe you shouldn't have handed me all that power in the first place!" Joe roared at the Devil. The Devil, exasperated, only shook his head further, and pointed at Reinhold.

"What!?" Joe called out.

"He's been dead for some time. You've been choking him for a minute. Your big virtuous monologue, it's wasted."

"Oh, fuck," Joe said, lowering his arm, and the corpse with it. The Devil was right. Reinhold was dead. "Sometimes, I forget just how powerful you've made me."

"That's exactly my point," the Devil said. "You wield all that power. Use it for a bigger cause. Our cause."

Upon seeing their leader dead, the ritualists, who had so far been banging on the stone door, as if that would somehow make it open, stood silent, petrified, their backs against the temple door. On the surface world, they were people who held enormous power. In government. In politics. In the world of commerce. But in that moment as Joseph Banbury closed the distance and smote them all down in a blaze of Hellfire, their money, power, fame, and resources did not come to their help.

As they burned, they screamed and yelped and clung to each other, their melting bodies fusing together in one amorphous mess, this temple no longer their place of worship but their mausoleum.

"You're too impulsive," The Devil said. "Reminds me of my old days."

"At least I'm not spitting in God's face and getting cast out of heaven or anything like that," Joe said, climbing the steps and heading to where Jake was hiding.

"No, no, you're doing much worse. You're spitting in my face."

"Yeah, but you can take it."

Joe turned his attention to Jake, who was still hiding behind the pillar, eyes closed, ears covered. Joe gently touched him on the head. The boy whimpered at his touch.

"Hey, it's me," Joe said, kneeling on one knee.

The boy stared at him with wet, wide eyes.

"You're ready to go home, aren't you?"

The boy nodded.

Joe held out his hand.

The boy furtively took it.

* * *

When the boy opened his eyes again, he was back in his bedroom in Queens, clothed, healed, the events of the past day no longer registered in his memory. He shifted in his sleep, turned over, and went into an even deeper slumber.

Outside his window, Joe sat perched on the roof, staring at the boy, a smile on his face. He did not need either the Devil or God telling him that he'd done a good thing. He knew it already in his heart of hearts.

Tomorrow would be a new day, a day that would bring with it new opportunities. He just had to get Reinhold out of the way so that he could run his enterprise efficiently, bring in his own people.

"Now, if only you'd stayed alive for a few seconds longer, I'd have told you that I'm overtaking the Von Barreth Cathedral on the corner of Park Avenue and 106th. I'm going to be using it as the headquarters for The Morning Star. Well, The Morning Star's ownership. We're also keeping some of your money. The rest is going to children's charities all over the country. But no worries. I'll tell you all about it the next time I'm down in Hell," Joe said, holding Reinhold's detached head in his hand.

"Don't lose your head over it, kay?"

2

RECONCILIATION

With Joseph's face plastered everywhere from Times Square to her IG feed, Lilly felt it best to escape the Joe Bubble that New York City had become. This was exactly what she had warned him against. Becoming larger than life. She could see from the look in his eyes on the billboard across the street that this man did not have any intention of writing another book.

He'd sooner dominate the world in a bid for power than write another book. It wouldn't be the first time an author of strong repute would transition to a more political role of power. Didn't Hitler do exactly the same? Publish a best-seller, get his face on Times Magazine, then proceed to massacre six million Jews and wage war on all of the free world.

"What's with the advertising?" she sighed. New York was far more colder and vertical than Bridgewater had been. But it was home. Back when Lilly had packed her bags and left, she knew that she wouldn't be able to stay away from the city forever, and now that she was standing at the entrance of her apartment building, she felt a knot in her stomach signaling that it was a bad move to come back to the city. If anything, she'd have moved northward, maybe seek shelter in the snowy wilderness of British Columbia.

"Seriously, though," Lilly smiled weakly, hiding her franticness under it. There were three billboards that she could see from the street, and all three of them had Joe's face on them with the words "The Morning Star" next to it. "It's not like people the world over didn't see you bring a kid back to life. How much more marketing do you need?"

"I don't know. I'm overdoing it, aren't I?" Joe said, picking up her bag. The way he'd just appeared out of nowhere and was standing next to her so nonchalantly gave Lilly a jump, sending her crashing against the glass door. Joe reached his arm out effortlessly and held her just before she could collide with the glass and shatter it into a million pieces. He pulled her close, helping her find her balance, then slowly let go, as if he didn't want to let go but had to.

"I have a frail heart, Joe, and half of it is because of you. Don't be giving me these jump scares if you want me to live for a few more years," Lilly said, taking her bag from Joe's hand. "And what are you even doing here? Don't you have corpses to raise, your evil lair to build?"

"Ah, I see that you're still salty—"

"Salty!?" Lilly snapped, attracting the attention of all the walkers-by on the sidewalk. "Salty? Have you forgotten the last time we met? When I begged you not to go through with the book? You insulted me in more ways than anyone ever has. And then, just like that, you left. Did not even try to—"

"Try to what? Get you to stay? You made it abundantly clear back then that you did not want to. And look what's happened in your absence! I don't know how many billboards is one too many."

"What?" Lilly was genuinely confused.

Joe tried to smile at her, but the hostility on her face hadn't waned yet, implying that any smile wouldn't be warmly received nor reciprocated. So, instead, he picked up the rest of her bags again and nodded at the doorman to let them through. The doorman quietly pulled the door and nodded back. Joe stepped inside.

"Just what do you think you're doing?" Lilly asked, standing her ground outside in the cold.

"Helping you with your stuff. Isn't it obvious?"

"Why are you doing this?"

"Because that's too many bags for you to carry."

Lilly rolled her eyes and sighed, then relented and walked inside, not wanting to be out in the cold any longer. It was warm in the lobby, the dim music from the elevator carrying over the air, the box of donuts on the front desk smelling heavenly. Joe walked over to the elevator and waited for her.

"I don't need your help to carry my things," Lilly said, pushing past him and pressing the call elevator button. "Don't you have better things to do with your time than be here?"

"Better than being with my friend? I don't think so," Joe said, giving her an earnest smile. He looked normal. A bit tired with shadows under his eyes, but unlike what Lilly had imagined him to become, he was still Joseph Banbury, that ruffled hair, skinny writer in baggy clothes.

Lilly stepped inside the elevator, Joe following her inside with her luggage.

"We're friends, all of a sudden?" Lilly asked. "You cannot go about pretending that none of that happened."

"Look," Joe sighed, putting down her bags and facing her, a somber expression plastered all over his face. "It's ironic that I, a writer, am not good with my words in this very moment, but that's not because I don't have the right words. I have them right here," he said, pointing at his head. "But I know that none of them are right enough. I was rude. I was nothing short of an asshole. I broke your heart. And I cut you out. That's all on me. You only ever cautioned me against *all this.*" He waved around with both hands. "And instead of heeding your warning, I hurt you. I am sorry for that, Lill. I truly am."

She eyed him inquisitively, trying to decipher if this was a sincere attempt or one just to patronize her. She saw that his old vehemence was all there, the same intensity that had piqued her interest back at the college party that started it all.

"How did you do it?" she asked the burning question that had been hounding her since the day she saw him bring that little girl back to life.

"Huh?"

"That kid. You breathed life into her. Don't think I don't know what's going on with you because I do. I want to hear you say it, so that I know that you know that I was right back then," she said, driving her finger into his chest, prodding it with every word she spoke.

"You said know too many times," Joe grinned. "That's bad writing, Lill."

"Don't you Lill me."

"Fine!" Joe raised his hands and stepped back as far as the elevator's confined space would allow him. "What do you want me to say? That the Devil gave me these powers? That I've effectively become Satan's tool? That I crossed a moral threshold when I used necromancy to bring that girl back to life?"

"I don't know about Satan's tool, but you're certainly *a* tool, Banbury," Lilly said. The elevator came to an abrupt halt. They were on her floor. She stepped out without waiting for him. He clamored behind, struggling with her luggage, making sure to not miss any of the bags.

Lilly swiped her card on her door across the hallway and held the door open for Joe to bring her stuff in. Then she closed the door behind them, and turned on the light. Her apartment was as impeccable as the day she'd left it. All the furniture in place. The books lined alphanumerically on her shelves. Her work desk immaculate. Tchotchkes above the fireplace welcoming her with their lifeless gazes.

After fiddling with the thermostat, she headed into the kitchen and procured two chilled beers from the fridge. Joe had already made himself home on the living room sofa, fiddling his thumbs and looking around in admiration.

"We're past the point of bullshitting," Lilly said, handing him his beer. "So don't even start with the whole the-devil-is-metaphorical-in-my-book shtick. He's real and you know it. Hell, from the way you write about him, the two of you are practically best friends. But did you or did you not, Joe, sell your soul to him?"

"I didn't," Joe said, taking a large gulp from the beer and immediately choking on it. He leaned over and coughed loudly. Lilly, unable to help herself, slapped his back thrice and then ran her hand up and down over it so he'd breathe better.

"Thanks," Joe said, his eyes a little red. "But, yeah, I didn't. Damn, this beer's got a kick to it."

"You didn't sell your soul for the magic, the power, the money, the fame?" She asked, sitting across from him on the coffee table.

"Look at me, Lilly," Joe said, his eyes still watering.

Though, it was hard to tell if it was tearing up from emotions or from choking on beer. "My soul is my own. I never signed any contract that granted him dominion over me. It's....a long story that I've been wanting to share with you for the longest time, and not having you by my side hurts terribly."

"Mm-mm," Lilly shook her head fervently. "You do not get off that easy."

"Punish me, then, but don't shut me out," Joseph said.

"Like you shut *me* out?"

"What was I going to do? You told me that you had no intention of helping me with that book. I might not have signed over the rights to my soul, but I was under a lot of pressure from him to publish it."

"How do you like it, being a cog in the infernal engine that is the Devil's grand design?" Lilly scowled and put her beer down. The more she stared at him, the more she saw a power-hungry man who'd stop at nothing to harness more authority. It fogged up the image of the wet-behind-the-ears teenager that he was back in college, and made her loathe him for what he'd become.

"You mean you know about the Devil's grand design?" Joe asked, putting his beer down next to hers.

"Everyone and their mother know all about it. It's all there in the Bible! It's another thing that no one takes it seriously. But let me assure you, the Devil is real and he takes it all very seriously."

"Don't you think I know that? I interviewed the guy. He took me to Hell and back. Did unspeakable things to me. Told me straight up that he fucked my mom and that I'm his son! Do you think I wanted to do any of that? To write the book? Kind of hard to say no to one's father."

"You..." Lilly whispered. "You're...the...antichrist?"

"Now look who's failed to notice the obvious. I could have told you all that back then if you'd only just listened to me and agreed to be by my side rather than cut all ties with me," Joe said. There was no mistaking now that there were tears earnestly flowing from his eyes. "I have been through the wringer, Lill. And all through that, I did not have the one person by my side whom I'd always counted on."

"You're supposed to bring about the end of this world. What the fuck are you doing, sitting and crying on my sofa?" Lilly was no longer sitting across from him. She was at the other end of the room, eager to keep her distance from him, her heart gripped with terror.

"Don't be like that," Joe said, slowly rising to his feet. "I have no control over the fact that my dad's the Devil. I did not seek to write his book. And when I tried to do as you said, straight up refuse him, he punished me for it. My hands were tied. But they aren't anymore. I wield this *power*, and I don't know what to do with it. This whole thing that I've started, Morning Star, Lill, I'm in over my head."

"What have you been doing with all that 'power?'" Lilly asked retreating even further, her back against the kitchen counter, her hand seeking the handle of a kitchen knife.

"Well, believe it or not, tonight, I shut down a Temple of Baphomet and saved the life of the kid they were about to rape and sacrifice. Singlehandedly and in one fell swoop killed a dozen men, including Reinhold Von Barreth, brought the kid back to his home, wiped his memory clean, and made all the evidence disappear," Joe said, a self-satisfied grin on his face.

"So your idea of being the antichrist is to go directly against the Devil and take down his temples and adherents?" Lilly stopped seeking the knife handle and instead relaxed her whole body.

"Yeah, I mean, he's already given me power, money, and all, and he promised me that I could do things my way. I'm going to do great things, Lill. Things that I couldn't have done by just being a writer alone. And damn it, I need you by my side. Someone to steer me when I veer, someone to tell it to me like it is. Like you did back then. Only this time around, I promise that I won't lash out at you, won't insult you. I'll never disrespect you again."

"Do you seriously think that I'm going to drop everything that I've got going and work for the antichrist?" Lilly laughed dryly. "You must truly be out of your mind."

"Don't think of me as the antichrist, then. Think of me as Joe Banbury. For the most part, I am still him."

"What about when you're not him?"

"You mean when I don the mask of the Morning Star and go about gallivanting in the city, saving people, stopping crime? Yeah, I'm thinking that Marvel picks me up and features me on their roster right next to Ghost Rider," Joe laughed. "Bound by Hell. Sworn to solemn duty."

"Why me?" Lilly's walk back to the living room was slow and deliberate. She still did not trust Joe, but from the way he'd been honest with her tonight, she was beginning to get there.

"Because I love you, Lill," Joe said, walking up to her, his face close to hers, his hands reaching out and touching her shoulders. "And I truly am sorry for everything. Somehow, I am going to make it up to you. Let me start by offering you a fuck ton of money, a nice role as Director of Communications, and a corner office."

"You *love* me?" Lilly frowned and pushed his arms away.

"Yes. I love you. And I don't mean it in the way schoolboys fall for schoolgirls nor how a brother loves a sister. I already have a sister. And I've had my fair share of schoolboy crushes. I love you because you're my Naloxone. You keep me grounded. Right now, all I need is to stay grounded. Nobody can do it better than you."

Joe did not wait for her to reply before he hugged her fiercely.

Lilly, still confounded, first stood there frozen, her arms pinned to her side, then sighed and put her hands on his back. "So you want me to be your glorified babysitter? Make sure itty witty anti-chwist don't blow the world up by accident?"

"Basically, yeah," Joe laughed, holding her close. "Can you do that?"

"I mean..." She thought about it in the brief spell during which her tongue searched for the right words. "It better pay good, because I know you're a handful and a half, especially now that you're resurrecting people and hunting old white powerful pedos."

"They're quite diverse, Lill. It's not just old white people. It's quite the melting pot of fucked up they've got down there," Joe guffawed. "But if we're to bring a new order to this world, we need to cleanse it of its old rot."

"How much of a hold does the Devil have on you right now, and I want you to be honest with me," Lilly said, holding him by his shoulders and pushing him at arm's length, studying his eyes.

"None. He doesn't dictate me around anymore. He comes and goes, sometimes expresses his satisfaction, sometimes his dissatisfaction, but I've been absolved of the hold he had on me ever since I finished the book. That's why it took me so much time to get back to you. I needed to be my own person again if I had to come back to you. And now I am."

"Give me time to think about it," Lilly said.

"Here's your card," Joe fished out an access card with her name and picture on top of it. Under her name was the title "Director of Communications." The card bore The Morning Star's emblem on its top right. "If you show up at work tomorrow, I'll take it as a yes. If you don't, well, I still meant the apology, and I'd still like to stay in touch."

"Goodbye, Joe."

"Goodbye, Lill—hey, hang on. Where were you, by the way?"

"Huh?"

"I've been coming here every other night asking the doorman about you, calling you ceaselessly, but you weren't in the city and you weren't picking up the phone, and when I...um...tried to scry to see where you were, I didn't get anything in the vision."

"You scry now?" Lilly was positively astonished.

"Yeah, I read like fifteen grimoires to learn necromancy, Lill. It figures that I picked up a trick or two along the way. So...where were you?"

"Not that it's any of your business, but I was in Bridgewater."

"Ow. We're still being catty, I see," Joe said, lingering in the doorway. "Well, all right. Goodbye, then. I guess if I see you tomorrow, that'll be that." He turned around and began walking toward the elevator.

"Joe!" Lilly called back. Joe turned his head.

"What is it, Lilly?"

"Are...are you okay?" She asked. For a second, she'd let go of her anger and indignation, and tapped into the care that she felt for him. He looked okay, but was he doing okay? She wanted to know.

"That's why I love you, Lill," Joe said, smiling at her one

last time before disappearing into the elevator. "And yes, I'm fine. Hope to see you tomorrow."

When he was gone, Lilly closed the door, and then, reeling from the emotional whiplash of this confrontation, descended with her back against the door, and burst into tears. It was all too much.

3

RIFTS

Joe retched loudly, sputtering out black, tarry goo from his mouth. He hunkered down on the bathroom sink and tried to control the pain, but it was to no avail. Waves upon waves of agony burst forth from within him and traveled to all his extremities. It was like being set on fire.

He tried to distract himself with the bland view of the freshly painted white bathroom walls. The tiles, all new, were all white too. The mirror above the sink was nice, oblong, and had one of those LED light rings around it.

He retched again. The bathroom alone was not enough to distract him from the pain. Something was alive in his guts, kicking and squirming, and it was crawling up his esophagus as he knelt above the sink, holding on for dear life.

Thick, black, bilious sludge filled his mouth, burning his entire tract as he vomited in the sink. In hindsight, he should have done it in the toilet. The contents of his profuse vomiting pooled in the sink, bubbling.

Joe looked at his reflection in the mirror, his eyes

sunken, his face pulled and gaunt. This was not akin to the waking nightmares of old, and so he did not know what this was. He was the epitome of health, jogging daily, having quit smoking and drinking, and eating a strictly vegetarian diet to combat the perpetual heartburn he was carrying around these days. And yet this. What was this?

Before he had a second to gather his thoughts, a claw shot out of the pool of sick and grabbed Joe's forearm, digging its claws into it. Joe tried to tug himself free, but before he could, another dead hand shot out of the bubbling puddle and grabbed his other arm.

They pulled him toward his puke with grotesque force, and since it had all happened in mere moments, he'd been caught off-guard, unable to defend himself from something he did not understand.

A third hand, this one skeletal with bits of muscle and tendon still hanging onto it, reached out from within the sink and grabbed him by the back of his hand. Together, these three hands yanked him with such brutal strength that Joe's head went under.

He came face to face with the three demons who were pulling him, each of them more fiercer than the next, their eyes billowy havocs of infernal dreams, their forms shaped by the terrain of Hell, their darkened souls nourished by the horrors they had to endure.

Below them, a blaze roared in the dark, and instead of lighting up the surroundings, it only served to darken them more. He could hear the screams of the damned, see the machinery of Hell at work, feel the rhythmic clanging of large chains as they struck against flesh.

"Why are you doing this!?" He tried to reason with his captors, but their mouths, quite literally, were sewn shut with red entrails painfully going in and out of their sutured lips. Horned and winged, these denizens of Hell were only here to bring him back, not to reason with him.

But in this brief window, Joseph had overcome his pain; he tapped into his latent strength, and freed himself of their grips at the same time, surfacing back into the plain old white bathroom in Von Barreth Cathedral.

He saw his goo-drenched reflection in the flickering light, the mirror growing murkier with each passing second. As he backed away from the sink, the mirror's surface turned entirely dim, revealing decayed, white-eyed faces staring and screaming at him. In unison, they crossed over the thin sheen of the mirror, just as the three demons from the sink resurfaced, this time with their whole bodies instead of individual appendages.

Dark strands emerged from the wall behind him, eager to subdue him.

But he was not so easily subdued.

"ENOUGH!" Joe screamed, transforming. No longer did a skinny and messy-haired man stand before the horrors but a winged, horned fury, red the color of his skin, rage the sole expression in his eyes, his muscles bulging from under his earthly clothes, his sentient tail raising its pointed end with the intent to attack.

All the horrors paled in comparison to Joe's devilish form; the tendrils no longer sought to subdue him, the screaming faces in the mirror quietened down, and the three demons who had appeared so bashfully out of the pool in the sink meekly went inside, poking only their petrified heads out of the tarry liquid.

"What is that you want of me?" Joe roared, hoping that the bathroom walls were soundproof because Amy and Shaun sat in just one room across the meeting room, waiting for him.

"Oh, they don't want something from you, Joe," The Devil spoke, stepping out from behind Joseph. He did not speak in the warm manner that Joe had come to anticipate, but in a way so cunning that his words felt alive with malice. "They're just here to bring you back to your home."

"My home!?" Joe growled at the Devil, both of them matched in form, Joe younger and powerful, the Devil older and wiser.

"Hell, son," the Devil said, waving at all the horrors present within the room, making them disappear in an instant. The lights stopped flickering, and the puddle of sick that had been the cause of it all drained immediately into the sink. The mirror went back to its bland reflection of the bathroom. The tendrils sunk back into the wall, leaving no sign that they were ever here. "They're eager to get the Crown Prince of Hell back in...Hell. Don't pay them any heed. They just grow restless. It's not every day that one of the spawns I've sired truly taps into their potential and turns into a great beast, like you have. They recognize you as their prince."

"Some way to handle a prince," Joe said, immediately shifting back to his ordinary, human form. "Can't you control your riffraff?"

"They're not mine to control," the Devil shrugged, following Joe's suit and shifting into a mild-mannered form, the same dignified one with the sharp jawline, slick hair, and crisp suit in which he had appeared to Joe during the entire length of their interview. "They get peckish. Impatient. Angry."

"Angry?"

"That you, one of them, a Hell-dweller, walk the surface with such brazenness. The way they see it, your place is down there with them. And yet here you trot so smugly."

"You never mentioned any of this before I embraced my identity," Joe prodded a finger into the Devil's chest.

"It just didn't occur to me to mention it," the Devil smiled with the cunning of a fox, and raised his hands with centuries of perfected sarcasm, followed by an, "oops."

"Listen," Joe retracted his finger. "There's lies by omission, and then there's blatant lies. This is neither. I can read you like a book. Or did you forget that I wrote *the* definitive book on you? This was never part of the bargain. You're just fucking pissed at me. Why don't you say it like you mean it instead of orchestrating these unscary set pieces? They don't want me back in Hell. *You* don't want me back in Hell. I have work to do here. So what the fuck gives?"

"You tell me," the Devil spat, eyeing Joe with disdain. "Work to do, my ass. What have you been doing since the first sermon? Nada mucho. Zilch. Role-playing as a vigilante, trying to do *good* on such a small scale that it will never register, never stick."

"I *was* raised Christian," Joe spat back, getting sick of Satan.

"Speaking of which, how's your mother doing?" It was evident that the Devil was just as sick of him.

"You son of a bitch, you don't go there," Joe said, revealing his wingspan, extending it across the length of the bathroom.

"Oh? Why not? What are you going to do? Maybe I should pay her another visit, make an elder brother out of you? Maybe that one can do as I say," the Devil said.

Joe had no control over his rage as he slashed across the Devil's face, gashing deep, red lacerations across his handsome face. He lunged forward, pinning the Devil to the wall. The mirror shook and fell on the floor, shattering.

"Good. There's that rage. And I was beginning to think

that you were going soft on me," the Devil laughed and then effortlessly threw Joe across the room.

"WHAT DO YOU WANT FROM ME!?" Joe screamed, holding his chest. It throbbed where the Devil had shoved him, a reminder of who was really in charge, who was stronger. "I've been doing everything you said, to the dot, every step of the way! What more do you want from me!?"

"Do it faster!" The Devil screamed back, holding Joe by the collar and pinning him. "This isn't Costa Cruises! We are on a deadline! And stop it with the saving people nonsense. You're not emancipating anyone!"

"I thought you wanted to change the way the world worked," Joe said. "Are you too blind to see that I'm doing that in my own way?"

"I am not blind," the Devil seethed. Then, with a pause, and much more calmly, "...what are you talking about?"

"Why don't you trust me for a minute there? This is all still new to me. The power, the responsibility. I'm doing it in the way that prevents my mental faculties from imploding."

"I never mistrusted you. I am a creature of speed and momentum. All I see is that it's been months since you did something big. Something that would continue to captivate the attention of people across the world. We're losing traction. And if I am not one thing, it's effete."

"Why don't you sit with me in the meeting and you'll see what I mean," Joe asked, going over to the sink.

"No, thanks. You've been very disappointing lately, and I do not want to endure more of that."

"It will be well worth your time," Joe said, splashing water over his face. "And the disappointment ends today."

When the Devil did not respond, Joe turned the taps off and looked around. He wasn't there any longer.

"Joe?" Joph called from the other side. "Are you okay in there?"

Fuck. That meant that the bathrooms were not soundproof.

"I'm okay," Joe said. "Coming out in a sec."

When Joe opened the door, it was the sight of a dismayed Joph peering into the bathroom. Joph sighed.

"You broke the Vienna mirror?"

"What's with the Vienna mirror?"

"It cost seventy thousand dollars. That LED lighting had gold in-lay in it. Ah, sometimes it's like trying to explain color theory to a colorblind person," Joph said. "Why did you hire me to do the interiors of this place again?"

"Because you're the best. And I'm sorry about the mirror. I'm not colorblind. I know that's diamond dust coating along its edge. You really don't know how much you've taught me, do you?"

Joph covered his face and groaned. "Then why did you break it?"

"It fell, Joph. Maybe you should have hung it up with more than just one nail," Joe groaned back in mimicry, and stepped past Joph.

To his credit, Joph had done something truly spectacular with the interior of the cathedral on such short notice. Out with the old, in with the new. Fresh new reflective windowpanes that spanned from wall to wall, minimalistic décor, and beautiful artwork that breathed fresh life into the place. Joph really was the best, and now he had a canvas to do with as he pleased. Give or take a Vienna mirror.

Joe stepped into the meeting room, where Amy and Shaun, bored out of their gourds, were swiping and tapping away on their phones. When they saw Joe step in, they immediately put their phones down.

"Hey there, rockstar," Shaun cheered, raising a fist in Joe's direction.

"We're not the Black Panthers, Shaun. And I'm not a frat pledging teen."

"Don't leave me hanging," Shaun said, a tinge of embarrassment covering his face.

Joe, still a little rattled by the confrontation in the bathroom, sighed and gave in, bumping Shaun's fist. Then he settled down on the chair at the head of the table. Across the room, the window gave a clear view over the Park Avenue Viaduct to the Japanese Zen Garden across the street with its red maples, cherry blossoms, and bamboo. The sight of it always soothed him, but not today. The images of Hell were still burned fresh in his mind's eye, and no amount of Buddhist meditative gardening was enough to drive that out just yet.

"Joe, are you okay?" Amy asked.

He was getting really tired of everyone asking him the same damn question. But this was his sister. He had asked her to be here. And it had been hard for her to see things from his point of view, especially after what happened between him and his mother. While Amy did not outright blame Joe for Joyce's little cardiac episode (which resulted in her getting a stent), the culpability was there in the air. He could smell it. For the moment, though, he had done what he'd thought was the noble thing and had refrained from mentioning to Amy that they were only half-siblings. Such a thing would only draw her away. He did not need that. She was trying her best to be with him, support him in any way she could, and she'd already lost much because of it, including her job and many people from her social circle.

"It's been a day, Ames," Joe said, reaching out and holding her hand. "How are you doing?"

"Still coming to terms with the title of Chief Ethical Officer. You know, Joe, you could have made me Head of Legal, but Ethical Officer? That just sounds like one of those fake corporate jobs they create for nepo-hires. Tell me I'm not a nepo-hire."

Something clicked in his head, making him laugh. If the Devil wanted an efficient antichrist at his constant beck and call, maybe he shouldn't have nepo-hired his own son. Maybe he should have sought the best guy for the job, not a tortured writer from New Jersey.

"What?" Amy asked, looking hurt.

"You're not a nepo-hire, sis. You're the best of the best. And your job is to steer us away from controversy. Give everything we're doing an ethical spin. Not that we're doing anything unethical, per se. But, like, going forward, whatever The Morning Star does should align with its moral principles."

"We still don't have a thorough list of the moral principles," Shaun said. "Listen, buddy, if I'm going to be strategizing for you—and, by the way, I, too, quit my own thing to get yours going, not that I'm looking for brownie points—we need some clarity."

"Shaun, I swear to God."

The room went immediately dark, but Joe had a feeling that it had only gotten dark for him. The other two did not notice anything out of the ordinary.

"Easy on the holy parlance," the Devil spoke, appearing in one corner of the room. "You know I don't like it when you invoke Her name."

Can you stop throwing tantrums after every five seconds, Jesus? Joe shot an aggressive look the Devil's way.

"You're the one who invited me to the meeting," the Devil said. "I'm just complying."

Meeting doesn't start until a couple minutes later, Joe said. *And stop being the Censor Police. It does not suit you, and what do you mean, her?*

The room's light went back to normal, the Zen garden in view again.

"...are you going to be blanking out a lot, because..." Shaun scoffed. "...I don't know what's happening with you."

"Easy there, jackass. I was chasing a thought," Joe said. "The way I see it, you two are jonesing to get started. But we're just three people right now. I'm waiting on a fourth."

"And who, pray tell, is this fourth?" Shaun asked, rifling through the file in front of him.

"That would be me," Lilly spoke, appearing in the doorway.

Seeing her lifted his heart and made him instantaneously forget about the Hellish episode he'd had in the bathroom. She wore her hair long, and was dressed in the way he'd hoped Amy and Shaun would be—professionally. She smiled at Joe and closed the glass door behind her as she came in. "Wasn't sure I'd come."

"Lilly," Joe said, rising from his seat and stepping forward to meet her. He gave her a tight hug, which she repaid in kind by squeezing him twice as hard, knocking his wind out. "I'm so glad you're here."

"Oy vey, you've got to be kidding me. You did not mention she'd be here!" Shaun snapped.

"You got a problem with that?" Joe asked, waving his hand at the empty chair next to him. "Because if so, then you've got a problem with me."

That was all the courage that Shaun had, because he folded the next second, mewling, "No, no. I ain't got no problem with that."

"Good, then we can get started," Joe began. "This has

been a long time coming, but we're finally here now. Each of you is going to be vital to the operations of The Morning Star. To catch you up to speed, Lill, Amy is going to be the Chief Ethical Officer. She's there to make sure that whatever TMS does, it's all above board."

"How exactly are you going to make resurrections sound above board, Amy?" Lilly asked, raising her eyebrows at Joe's sister.

"Simple," Amy said through pursed lips. She wasn't Lilly's biggest fan. "Miracles."

"So we're going forward with the whole 'Joseph Banbury performs miracles' thing, then?" Shaun asked, taking notes.

"Yeah, what's wrong with that?" Joe asked.

"Because miracles are a specific term for acts of remarkable faith performed by prophets, clerics, saints, and so forth. Where do you fit in within any of those categories? What's to stop people perceiving your miracles as black magic?" Shaun said.

"I don't like the way you're attacking my client," Amy snapped at Shaun.

"First of all, he's not your client. You guys are coworkers. There's a separate legal department taking care of all that. Get with the program, sweetheart. Second of all, I am just one person asking a very real question. There are billions of people out there on this godforsaken planet, and they're asking questions a hundred times worse than what I've got."

"Hey, Shaun. Why don't you let me handle this, seeing as how it's my card that says Director of Communications and not yours?" Lilly said.

"I don't need you to stand up for me. I can do that on my own," Amy barked at Lilly.

"I wasn't standing up for you. I'm just trying to address what Shaun said—"

"Enough," Joe said quietly. "At this rate, we're never going to get anything done. What's with the fucking bickering? I thought you were all on my team."

"We are, but you've remarkably chosen a specific set of people who can't stand each other. I don't like Shaun. Shaun doesn't like me or Amy. And Amy can't stand either of us," Lilly said. "You're right. At this rate, we're never going to get anything done."

"And what about you?" Amy snarked.

"For Joe's sake, I can bear you both," Lilly said. "Does that sound fair? Because I think that we should all be doing that. Bearing each other for his sake. This is his enterprise."

There was silence in the room for a full minute as each person affected each other.

"I heard shouting, and I thought to myself, this crowd needs to get its balm on," Joph said, stepping smoothly into the room with a tray of drinks.

"And who is this supposed to be?" Lilly asked, her temper still on the higher end of the emotional barometer.

"You know how like Disney's got imagineers?" Joph asked, putting a Shirley Temple in front of Lilly. "Well, I do the same thing for The Morning Star, or did you not notice how fancy this place looks?"

"You make a mean Shirley Temple, kid. How'd you know that was my favorite drink?"

"Call it intuition. And by intuition, I mean Joe mentioned it to me," Joph grinned, placing a double shot of whiskey in front of Shaun and a Bloody Mary in front of Amy. As for Joe and himself, he took two wine glasses from the tray, handed one to Joe, and kept the other.

"Joe mentioned I like Bloody Mary's?" Amy smiled.

"Is this Ballantine's, because Shaun don't drink no

whiskey if it ain't Ballantine's," Shaun said, inspecting his drink.

"Yes, and yes. And also, cheers to all of you. This is the first Morning Star meeting, so why don't we all take it a little easy? I know tensions and tempers both are running a bit high, but hey, a year later, when this whole thing is running smoothly, sustaining itself, we'll all be better for it. How's that sound?

"Salud," Joe said, clinking his glass with Joph's and drinking his wine.

"Aight, I'm going to make like a tree and leave, because Kobayashi's installing the Zen waterfall by the entrance, and I don't want him to get any water on the Spanish marble," Joph said, taking a bow and leaving with his wine glass.

Once everyone had imbibed their drinks of choice, the atmosphere of the room began to change gradually. Lilly opened up to Amy, and Shaun stopped attacking anyone who opened their mouths.

Joe relaxed in his chair and opened the file, eager to discuss the first order of business.

"I have got to mention this," Lilly said, putting her empty glass on the table. "Does anyone find it strange that we're sitting in the Von Barreth Cathedral and they just found his body yesterday?"

"Strange, why would that be strange? Didn't he pledge the Cathedral building to our cause very openly on TV almost a month before he died?" Shaun asked, swirling his half-empty glass in his hand.

Joe thought it best to remain quiet on the matter.

"We're legally in the clear. I have the documents to prove ownership."

"Still. He's dead. I mean, he was only the biggest name in the literary world," Lilly said.

"And now he's dead, and the Big Five can end their contracts with his estate, and pursue their own endeavors. The way I see it, he did the world good by dying," Amy said. "I don't know if you've read Page 3 of The Times today, but people are coming forward confessing some real dark shit about him."

"As much as I'd love for us to dwell on Reinhold's legacy, we've got our own legacy to think about. So, without further ado, should we officially commence our first meeting?" Joe asked, noticing that the Devil had appeared once more in the corner of the room bearing a most dejected expression on his face.

"You're the boss, boss. Shoot," Shaun said, draining the rest of his whiskey.

"No, I think that was Angela," Lilly said.

Amy nodded and pointed at her, saying, "True that."

Joe grinned, sifting through his file. He'd kept this under wraps for a long time. It wasn't as if he hadn't been planning anything. He was just playing it close to the chest. He was sure that what we had would certainly get their—and the Devil's—attention.

He studied the eagerness on their faces, and the look of surprised amusement on the Devil's. Even he did not know what Joe had planned. Then, almost casually, as if he was commenting on the weather outside, he said, "We are going on a world tour."

4

THE TOUR

It ended up being just him and Lilly. Shaun politely declined after he read the whole itinerary in detail.

"Ain't no way you expect me to head to India and Iraq within a week of each other. 'Sides, I got my own business to take care of, Joe. I'll be here when you're back. Trust me."

Joe had expected Shaun to pull something like this at the last minute. Fortunately, it was a little earlier than last minute when he weaseled out of the tour, giving Joe enough time to think on his feet and plan around Shaun's absence from it. Besides, it was not like Shaun couldn't strategize from New York. Useless though he felt like at times, the man had his merits, and Joe knew better than to part ways with him for good.

Amy, on the other hand, was not comfortable with the idea of leaving their parents unattended for too long. Mom hadn't recovered all that smoothly from the angioplasty, which meant that someone had to drop by twice a week to see if the Banbury household was still holding its own.

"Two weeks? That's putting a lot of pressure on Dad, Joe," Amy said.

"And what am I supposed to do with you not there?" Joe asked, knowing that while he could survive without Shaun, doing so without Amy was going to be especially difficult seeing as how she was in charge of the ethics of The Morning Star movement. Not that he didn't trust himself; he just happened to trust Amy more. Given that his frame of reference for political correctness had been warped and distorted after all that he'd been through with the Devil, Hell, and turning into the antichrist, he really needed her to be by his side.

"Lilly doesn't have that bad of a moral compass if you think about it. Maybe she can help you. Don't worry though. We'll take care of New York in your absence," she said.

That's what everyone else had to say. Joph, Tasha (who'd been all too eager to work as his digital media marketer), and just about everybody else whom he'd looked to rely upon. *We'll be here when you're back. We'll hold the fort.*

Fuck the fort. He wanted to conquer the world. Had they lost faith in him already? Or was it perhaps that they were scared of him, too afraid to say what was really on their minds?

And then there was Lilly, who, after seeing that the others had ditched him, looked at him with the same kind of pity with which you look at a wounded pup, not knowing whether to take it home with you or to the dog shelter.

"Give it to me," Joe said, a tad defeatedly, pouring coffee into his cup, staring at the Zen Garden across the street. "What are you thinking?"

"First off, this kitchen is impeccable. Kudos to you and Joph for figuring out that an establishment of such scale desperately needs a fully stocked kitchen, and look, we've got two different types of air fryers! Don't mind if I steal one, do you?" Lilly chirped, opening the cupboards, taking stock of all the groceries stocked inside, and whistling whenever something impressive caught her eye.

"Lill."

"Listen," Lilly sighed, stepping close enough to Joe that he could hear her when she spoke in a low tone but not so close that any onlooker might misperceive it as some office PDA about to take place. "Prophets, messiahs, Jedis, they almost always have to make their journeys alone. That's the downside to the whole hero's journey. The loneliness of it. But think of the cause. That's why you're doing this. Don't think of the people you're leaving behind but the ones whom you'll meet on your journey. There are Morning Star peeps all over the world. And we get to meet them. Doesn't seem all that depressing now, does it?"

"I was expecting them to be more enthusiastic, Joe commented, Amy and Shaun's refusal to go on the trip still fresh in his mind. "Meh."

"Dude. I'm going with you. What more could you ask for?"

"Really?" Joe scowled. "I had to convince you tooth and nail the other night. I don't have it in me to keep on convincing you to stay."

"Well," Lilly said, looking a little hurt but swallowing that hurt as she focused on the larger message. "Good thing about convincing someone is you don't have to do it over and over again. I'm convinced. I'm on your side. I'm going with you wherever you go. I have faith in you."

"You do?" There it was again, the same adolescent validation he'd felt when she'd read his manuscript in his dorm room.

"Yes. I don't necessarily have faith in the Devil or God in

the way that people say they do when they say the word 'faith', but I know you. I've seen how far you've come. It just so happens that a lot of my beliefs align with yours. So, of course, Joe, I have faith in you. This tour could be good for us. Look what the Blonde Ambition Tour did for Madonna."

"Didn't take you for a Madge fan," Joe chuckled, feeling a little better.

"Bleurgh. I am not. But I'm not denying her influence. Just like I'm not denying your influence," Lilly said, giving Joe a little shove on the shoulder.

"I am glad that you're coming with me," Joe said, his attention going back to the Zen Garden.

"Aw, you don't have to keep saying that over and over. You've got me on a payroll. That's more than enough gratitude. Money is the great equalizer."

"I thought that was supposed to be death."

"I'm doing a thing where I'm not thinking about death as much, I see it enough as it is," Lilly said. Her tea was finally finished boiling. She poured the contents of the kettle into a purple mug that said, 'World's Best ___' and in the blank space, she had hand-written 'Director of Communications.' Joe chuckled as he watched the purple cup turn pink upon the sudden temperature change. "Follow me, if you will, to my office. I've got something for you."

Joe humored her by following her, coffee in hand, his eyes darting everywhere, looking for signs of any more Hell portals opening. The office space was largely empty and white and showed no signs of portals, Hellish or otherwise. Lilly's corner office was packed with boxes of her stuff. It had been a day since their first meeting, and it hadn't been an uneventful day. Shaun and Amy came in one by one, presenting their excuses. The Devil, it appeared, had been so disappointed with the way that the meeting had concluded that he hadn't reappeared again. All this tension between the two of them was making Joe question his devotion to the mission. It wasn't like he could back out now. After he'd done so much. Somewhere deep inside, the Devil knew that too. That it wasn't as if he could turn over a new leaf with a new antichrist. There had been way too much investment in this one as it was.

"Earth to Joe!" Lilly called out loudly. Joe came back to the present, observing Lilly sitting at her desk, a file in front of her. The corner of Park and 106th was vibrantly visible from both windows, and from here, that little piece of Japanese flora was clearer than it was from any other window of the Cathedral, making Joe wonder if he'd done the right thing, giving this office to her. His own was nothing to write home about. It had no windows, being in the basement of the building. You lose some, you win some. In losing the view of the city, he'd gained a superhero level secret lair riddled with monitors and servers that allowed him to see everything that was happening all over the world, and quite a lot of what was happening under it.

"What is this?"

"It's what you hired me for. The press release comes before the tour, Joe. Otherwise, no one's ever going to know that you're heading out to meet prominent religious leaders, thinkers, and scientists."

"It's not just a press release," Joe said, looking at the contents of the file. "This is a script for a press conference."

"Yes. And you're going to give one today, as a matter of fact, so that we can be on our merry way first thing Monday."

"A whole week later?" Joe asked, a little indignantly.

"Gives the news world plenty of time to do several news cycles, making your tour as public as possible, or did I misunderstand the assignment? I thought that this was going to be a very publicized trip," Lilly asked, apprehension crawling around the edges of her words.

"No, no. You're right. This gives us time to publicize it as much as we can. The news gets it first. The internet second, and before you know it, those TikTokers and Instagrammers start speculating. It will take a week to make that happen," Joe said, but he was not looking at Lilly as he spoke those words. He was looking at an enraged Satan, fuming at the nostrils, standing behind Lilly.

Joe spoke more deliberately. "We're not going slow. We're making good time."

"I know that," Lilly said, squinting at him and turning her head sideways. "You okay?"

"I'm fine. What else do you have on your agenda?"

"This." It was not Lilly who spoke, but the Devil.

One single word followed by an unpardonable act. He grabbed Lilly's head—and while she was still trying to perceive what was happening to her, her eyes growing wide and a look of pure fear plastering over her face as she realized that something invisible and quite violent had latched onto her, was digging its nails into the cheeks, drawing blood—and snapped it abruptly and with precision, his face expressionless as he did it. The Devil did not stop there. He yanked her head, ripping tendons, muscles, and bones clean off with a squelching sound, and threw it at the window, cracking the glass.

Lilly's headless body sat there spouting blood from the gash where her neck used to be. She sat there for a full second before her body toppled over and fell on the white marble floor, tarnishing it with thick red blood.

Malevolence was the sole expression etched into the Devil's grimacing face, his humanoid form drenched in

Lilly's blood, his eyes peering spitefully from behind the sheen of red splattered over his visage. Breathing heavily, he locked his eyes with Joe, letting him know the true extent of his rage and dissatisfaction.

"Joe? Do I have to expect you to do this again and again?" Lilly asked.

Joe blinked, and the scene was reset, the Devil standing wrathfully behind her, and Lilly, completely oblivious to the fact, was asking Joe a question with exasperation.

"What?"

"You keeping zoning out, man. I know what you're doing," Lilly said, getting up from her chair and walking over to the door. "I'll ask you again. Are you doing okay? You do not look well."

"I...I think that we might need to hurry this up along, Lill. We might not have a week," Joe said, the Tarantino-esque scene still playing out in front of his eyes.

Lilly studied Joe's face intently, then kept quiet as some manner of understanding dawned upon her. "How about Wednesday? This Wednesday? We'll lose our edge of several news cycles and the press release making it everywhere we need it to go, but at least we'll be well on our way. No more delays."

Joe breathed a sigh of relief. The Devil, still not on speaking terms with Joe, took his leave by way of disappearing into thick black smoke that only Joe could see, but since he hadn't enacted on the visceral vision he'd intruded upon Joe's senses, Joe only took it to mean that the Devil was fine with the updated plan.

"He's not best known for his patience," Lilly said, closing the door to the office and walking back to her chair. As she walked past Joe, she whispered in his ear, "I can tell that he's giving you a real hard time of it."

"How can you tell?" Joe asked, aghast.

"Because I saw a whole ass fast-forwarded slideshow of emotions on your face, and it wasn't because of anything that I was saying," Lilly said. "You can cut the bullshit when you're with me. I know how these things go. I've worked under pressure from bosses that are right up there with the Devil in terms of being assholes."

"You don't know the half of it."

"Why don't you tell me after the press conference? Maybe I know more than you think," Lilly winked.

Joe was just glad to see her head attached to her body and not rolling on the floor. He took his leave before he could hurl.

* * *

In the evening, Joe stood at the dais in his conference room. Behind him, rather officiously, was the flag of the United States of America and the flag of The Morning Star. He stood at their center, dressed in a suit, his eyes scanning the dozens of reporters who'd come flocking to the Cathedral at the drop of a hat. Or rather, when Lilly sent forth the press release detailing Joe's tour.

The cameras in the back flashed every time he so much as moved a muscle. Joe tried to focus on the view of the street outside. The entire eastern wall was basically one long window that showed the pedestrians walking unaffectedly on the sidewalk, people eager to head home after a long day of work, some of them stopping at a coffee shop, some of them stopping at the dark hotel bars they'd come to frequent, the others in a bit of a hurry, walking briskly past the crowd gathering around the Von Barreth Cathedral, distancing themselves from anything remotely religious.

Amy, Shaun, and Joph were seated behind him. Lilly stood right next to him, ready to tap in should the going get tough, as these things often did. The atmosphere was charged with anticipation, the recorders and cameras held by the reporters jabbing into the air.

The Devil flitted between the crowd, disappearing and appearing, the urgency of the undertaking evident in his quick stride, his impatient looks that he kept shooting Joe's way, and the way he was smoking one cigarette after the other, filling the conference room with invisible smoke.

"Hello, ladies and gentlemen," Joe began, speaking into the mic. Much of the confidence that he had embodied at the first sermon he'd given in the Garden seemed to have been lost in the wake of the menial nature of handling his newly founded organization. Nothing like good old paperwork, red tape, and slow bureaucracy to snap you out of your devil complex. As he stood before the reporters, Joe was a very tired man.

"Hey, who are you resurrecting next!?" a bald, pudgy, and rowdy man with dark circles under his eyes and his tie hanging loosely around his shirt barked, which caused the entire conference room to break into loud, incoherent, rancorous remarks and questions from the rest of the reporters.

The Devil glared with his golden-red eyes as Joe began to stammer.

"How about he resurrects my foot from your ass, Larry? Or better yet, your mom? Though, I heard that it's not a one-man job. It's going to take jumper cables and a bulldozer!" Shaun got to his feet and roared back over the cacophony of the crowd, silencing everyone immediately. "Now, if we can all fucking behave ourselves and let the man speak. Christ's sake, he's not running for office, the way you're hounding him."

"Thank you, Shawn," Joe grinned, regaining some part of his confidence. The Devil, taken aback by this sudden de-escalation, looked partly amused too. "And as for your question, Larry, I am not Joe the Resurrector anymore than a certain carpenter was Jesus the Water-Walker."

"So you're equating yourself to Jesus?" a woman, her hair in a tight bun, lips pressed sternly together, shouted from the front row.

"No. And I do not intend to step on anyone's toes. It might have seemed the case earlier, given that my entire doctrine is antithetical to the prevalent religions of the world, but I come bearing the message of coexistence and tolerance. I do not deny the importance of your religious figures. I do not equate myself to them. I derive myself from far humbler roots than them. I am no one's Buddha nor anyone's Jesus. They were saints bathed in the light of all that is holy. I do not make any such claims."

From the corner of his eye, he could see Lilly smiling at him. The humble angle was one that she'd proposed in the script, and she was glad to see that he'd gone with it.

"So what's this about then?" Edmund Whittaker of BBC asked, his accent noticeably thick.

"This is about the birth of a new doctrine, one that does not deny the existence of old dogmas, does not contradict their overlapping lore, and yet offers something that's unique."

"How's it unique if all you're doing is following Satan?" Natasha Hawkins, wearing a CNN badge, asked, her recorder held up.

"Seems like we're doing the Q&A before the conference. Unconventional, but not entirely unheard of," Joe said, causing a wave of chuckles to travel across the room. "Ms. Hawkins. If we ever gave you that impression, let us collectively clear it. What does it say about me that I adhere neither to the principalities of God nor to the profanities of the Devil and yet am able to resurrect people on my own, utilizing nothing but my own wits? I did not sign some flame-bound contract. I did not take some Empyrean oath bowing in front of the throne of Yeshua. I seek myself, and in doing so, empower myself as well as others. There's more to existence than the duality of divinity in that God expels all his evil bits and labels them the Devil and keeps all the holy for himself. There's something far bigger and more profound out there. We at The Morning Star seek to find it."

"So you're basically shitting on thousands of years of tradition, belief, and practices?" Larry asked. His face was still red from embarrassment, but the way he'd worded his question in the clinical way that gotcha journalists did, it seemed that his question was more important to him than his repute inside the room.

"I do not shit where I eat, Larry. And this is the table where I eat. I sup with the rest of the supplicants, adherents, and believers, and I, too, believe. If you've read my books, you're one of the many witnesses to my journey. From an atheistic skeptic to the biographer of the Devil. I've come quite a long way, if I do say so myself, but I have a long way ahead of me. The religious leaders of old had years to develop their doctrines. I have only been at this for a short while. To highlight the inclusivity of my endeavor, I would like to mention that as I embark on this global tour, I will be meeting with theologians, scientists, and philosophers alike to develop a comprehensive doctrine that affirms, questions, invokes, and reclaims our right to believe in what we choose to believe. In every city that I visit, I shall establish a base of my operations where my adherents can gather, learn, supplicate, and understand how this universe works and what's our place in it," Joe spoke with authority. He'd taken control of the narrative, and was guiding it to where he wanted it to go, rather than travel aimlessly like a pinball colliding with the whim of every journalist present in the room.

"What is our place in it?" Natasha Hawkins asked.

"That's the billion-dollar question, isn't it?" Joe remarked.

"Seems like you don't have the answer for it either," Edmund Whittaker jibed.

"I don't," Joe said, looking at Amy, who nodded at him affirmingly. The room resounded with a collective murmur, followed by a hushed silence as Joe raised his hand. "I would be a fool to admit that I have a definitive answer, and that too in the infancy of my movement. That's ignorance, and if there's one definitive answer that I have, it is that The Morning Star serves to bring light to the people, light that battles ignorance. No longer shall we just sit and take pre-digested dogma and adopt it as our own. Where has it gotten us? Racial injustice? Religious hate? Xenophobia? Terrorism? Global conflicts? Poverty as megachurches fatten their pockets and leave nothing for the actual deserving masses? Religious tourism in the form of shrines and temples where people come to take selfies rather than absorb the ethereal wisdom that the air there is pregnant with? A loop of hedonism and overwhelming guilt that has jarred our nervous system? People out there are lost, no longer satisfied with the superficial answers that their religions have to provide. What God should we believe in if we haven't even seen any one of them, not Yahweh, not Vishnu? Why should we believe in any God anyway? That's a pretty big ask from a guy who's kept himself hidden from us all this time? If faith means believing something exists even if we haven't seen it, I'd rather give credit to the scientists of the past century who had faith in unseen phenomena like quarks, photons, neutrinos, and black holes! At least their faith was rewarded with affirmation when they made their discoveries. Do not get me wrong. I do not wear the garb of a skeptic nor that of a denier. I just want all our faith to be rewarded. To conduct the right experiments that allow us to see what we've not seen so far."

"And you think that you can do that, you, all alone, by yourself?" an old, bearded, thick-voiced reporter asked, his trembling hand holding a rather outdated voice recorder.

"You are?"

"Jay. Jay H. from The Sunday Times."

"I am not alone, Mr. Jay H. Just as Jesus and Buddha were not alone. One had his apostles, the other had his disciples. And so too does Joseph Banbury have his tribe. It's not just fringe anarchists who are a part of that tribe. We've got scientists, engineers, thinkers, artists, poets, theologists, and all sorts of excellent people in our tribe. We're all hungry for answers. As they say, if you want to go fast, go alone; if you want to go far, go with your tribe."

A moment of pure silence was followed by a round of applause. Not all of them clapped, as Joe was keen to notice. Some just sat there with frowns on their face, their arms crossed over their chests. But the rest, *most* of them, were taken with his words.

"What does this tour hold for Joseph Banbury?" Edmund, belonging to the camp of reporters who had applauded him, asked in a more respectful manner.

"All his life, Joseph Banbury's been doing what he's doing either in New Jersey or New York. It's time he took flight and saw the rest of the world. It's time the rest of the world saw him too. I intend to preach to my own, listen to those who hold different views than mine, and try to bring together people in mutual understanding," Joe said, inflecting each word with the same respect that Edmund had bestowed him. Edmund took kind notice of that, being a Brit, and offered Joe a polite smile, jotting everything down.

"Well, be sure to stop by for a pint of lager in London," Edmund quipped to the amusement of those present in his immediate vicinity.

"I will be sure to," Joe said. "And it's not just London I'm headed. From Geneva to Iraq, I will visit them all."

Yet another hushed silence, this one preceded by a communal gasp.

"What? Don't tell me I ruffled all y'all's feathers when I mentioned Iraq," Joe scoffed, going off-script. He could see Lilly shaking her head fervently, indicating that he should stop immediately.

"Some of the places you seek to visit do not share a good history with the United States, Mr. Banbury. Some discretion would be advised," Natasha Hawkins stated robotically, as if she'd rehearsed this line a hundred times in the mirror.

"And I intend to. I do not go there as an ally or critic to either cause. I'm going to Iraq because it's the cradle of civilization, where it all originated. Abraham was born in Ur, which is in modern-day Iraq. You may not know this, but it's not just humans who can tell stories. It's places, too. What do the old temples and the churches have to say? I intend to listen."

"And you're the one to do that? You're going to be the one to bring peace in our time, is that what you're saying?" A hooded man rose from the third row. He wore no nametag.

His hoodie had three giant golden letters embossed on it. C.O.Y.

"Who let the Redditors in, am I right?" Joe spoke into the mic, but before his statement could garner a response, the hooded guy jumped over the rows, toppling people over, and lunged at Joe with a knife in his hand.

Joe tapped into his newly acquired powers, holding his arm out in front of him, fingers spread apart. The hooded man slowly lifted off the ground, suspended in thin air, his eyes bulging, clawing at his own throat as if trying to remove an invisible noose.

The audience screamed and scattered once it was clear to them what was happening, but Joe kept his cool and approached the hooded man suspended above him.

"The Clerics of Yahweh will stop you at every turn," The hooded guy spat in Joe's face. Joe swerved his head and avoided the onslaught of phlegm. As Joe slowly let the attacker float back to the ground, the security detail took over, cuffing the guy, and escorting him out of the room.

"The Clerics of Yahweh? Oof. Talk about that name," Joe said. "Is it like the League of Darkness? What would you say that makes me if they're coming for me? Bruce Wayne adjacent?"

Nervous laughter rose from the crowd. Most people were unsure of what to do. Something like this had just recently happened to Rushdie, and that guy hadn't been the same ever since. Joseph walked back to the platform and addressed the crowd.

"Relax, folks. I am okay. And the guy's been apprehended. As far as I care, he's the NYPD's problem now—"

"Are you still going to go on tour knowing that there are others out there who seek to harm you?" Larry asked in awe.

"Yeah. I don't see why not. This is not the first time

someone's tried to kill me in public, and something tells me it won't be the last. But does Joseph Banbury stop? Hell no!" Joe raised both hands in the air, flailing around the peace sign. The reporters cheered for him; the cameras went crazy with their flashes; and the conference room rang with rancorous incoherence once more.

But that was okay.

The press conference was done.

Joe allowed himself to be escorted out of the room. Amy, Joph, Lilly, and Shaun rushing after him.

"Jesus, fuck, another attempt, really?" Lilly gasped, holding Joe close to herself. He felt comforted in her arms, almost like a cub being squished by a mamma bear. Amy was trying to reach in and hold some part of him in a consolatory way.

"Joe, are you—"

"Let me guess, okay? No. I'm fucked in the head seven ways to Sunday, Ames. And I feel fear just like everybody else. So, I'm pretty fucking far from okay, as that butt-fucked black guy from Pulp Fiction says," Joe said, his heart rate going back to normal. What would have happened if he'd been a moment late in activating his defenses?

Would he have died?

Would the Devil have let him?

As if following his entire train of thought with unwavering focus, the Devil spoke in his head, no longer in a sardonic manner as he was these past few days, but in a kindly manner. *I would have set aflame his body with the blaze of Hell if anything had happened to you. I have half a mind to do that right now.*

Don't, Joe called out. *Anything happens to him, the blame falls on us.*

Fine. Then my vengeance shall be slow and cold.

Vengeance?

Harm one of mine and you shall know Satan's wrath.

A solitary tear sought escape from Joe's eye. *Are we....are we good?*

Trust me, junior. We were always good, The Devil consoled him with his ephemeral presence, and then handled that charge to the humans around him, taking his leave from Joe's head.

"We're up against a whole lot of crazy, aren't we?" Amy asked, tears in her own eyes.

"Oh, you have no idea," Joe said, smiling at her, placing his palm on her cheek gently. "But you don't have to worry about me. I'll be okay."

"Fuck that. I'm coming with you," Amy said, tugging him free from Lilly's embrace and hugging him fiercely.

"I figure that you are going to need a loudmouth by your side to shut up all the Larry's of the world. It's a big world and there's lots of Larry's out there," Shaun said, placing his hand on Joe's shoulder. "I'm sorry for earlier. I've changed my mind, too."

"Hey, any chance that I can tag along? I've always wanted to visit India," Joph spoke from behind everyone.

"You really wanna come?" Joe asked.

"Yeah. Why not? But don't expect me to stick around all the time. The old world where we're headed has an art scene that's to die for. Oh, Lord, Paris, the Louvre. Fucking Munich. Are we going to Munich? Joe. Legit take me with you."

"All right. It'll be a tight fit in the jet, but sure. Come along, you!"

As they were just about to head upstairs, a loud gunshot rang from outside the Cathedral, followed by the screams of the dissipating reporters.

* * *

Merely five minutes after he had been apprehended and was escorted outside to where the NYPD cars were standing waiting for him, Bernard Lingham, the guy who'd attacked Joe with the knife, was bound in real handcuffs and not the zip ties Joe's security detail had put around his arms.

"All right, jackass. Do I need to say it out aloud? Seems like your sort have the whole thing memorized. You have the right to remain si—" the cop reading out the Miranda's Rights had just only started when Bernard, lumbering six foot eight muscular man that he was, broke free from his handcuffs and tackled the cop to the ground. He took the cop's service pistol out of the holster and held it in his hands, waving it around, gauging his odds. He was surrounded on all sides by cops, all of whom had aimed their pistols at him from behind the cover of their car doors. Beyond the perimeter that the cops had created, the journalists were getting out of the Cathedral.

It was too late. He had failed the Clerics. He could not let himself be taken in by the cops lest he wanted anyone to find out who the Clerics were, where they were hiding out in New York, and what they intended to do next.

Bernard took the pistol and shoved it in his mouth, and before anyone could do anything about it, he pulled the trigger, blowing his brains out, splattering them all over the blinking red and white lights of the car behind him.

No sooner had the cops and the people around registered what had happened did Joe Banbury emerge from the door of the Von Barreth Cathedral, followed by his entourage.

He parted the screaming crowd with nothing more than

his gaze, and walked past the cops, who only nodded at him as he stepped forward and inspected Bernard's dead body.

Joe looked around as if consulting someone who wasn't visible, and then knelt beside the body, placing his hand on the dead man's chest, and reciting something under his breath.

Time stopped. Everything slowed down.

Droplets of blood that clung to the surface of the car rose into the air, slowly and hovered to where the rest of the pool was. The pool congealed and began to travel inward, finding its way back into Bernard's head, along with the bits of his brain and bone.

For a moment, the body lay silent and unaffected by the ritual, and then, once Joe had finished muttering his incantation, Bernard Lingham opened his eyes with a loud gasp and screamed in agony.

"You do not get to escape that easy, friend," Joe said, patting the man's chest.

The cops, shaken by the resurrection they had observed, took a minute to approach the revived man, and kicked the service pistol away from his reach, binding him in two handcuffs instead of one, and restraining him with a chain across his chest. A riddled-with-disbelief Bernard quietly walked over to the car and allowed himself to be escorted to the police station without making any more fuss. Later that night, after they evaluated him medically and confirmed that he was, in fact, a hundred percent okay, the detectives grilled him about the Clerics of Yahweh.

Bernard, who could only remember the blinding pain of his suicide attempt, the nightmares of the Hell he'd been sent to for what seemed like an eternity but was in fact just a few minutes, quickly gave in to their interrogation and told them everything that he knew.

As for the corner of 106th and Park, whether it was kismet or pure coincidence, all the reporters were there at the spot, their cameramen recording in real-time as Joe resurrected another person in public, this time not some benign girl who had lost her life in a car crash but a vengeful terrorist who had mere moments ago assaulted Joe with a knife.

If tonight was about sending a message, Joe had certainly sent many.

One of them being that he was not to be fucked with.

5

THE HADRON SUPERCOLLIDER

"Remind me why it's called God particle again?" Joe was very aware of the fact that his mouth had been hanging wide open for the past half hour.

"Because science particle was already taken," Dr. Hamond Ruthers said. The experimental particle physicist serving as the Director-General of CERN, Dr. Ruthers was a man no older than Joe himself, and from the way he talked about Joe's books to him, it was evident that he was a fan.

"You're incorrigible," Joe said, elbowing him in the ribs as they stood there staring at the large, spherical, curving length of the supercollider, kindred nerds, one belonging to the realm of particles, one to the realm of letters.

"Mr. Banbury, as pleased as I am to have you here, I remind you, this is a 27-kilometer ring, and if we walk along its entire length, it might take us six hours."

"Might? Haven't you ever tried it yourself?" Joe grinned.

"I haven't. These legs are not built for walking that long," Dr. Hamond grinned back. "So, my office, then?"

"Sure thing, doctor. We're in your territory. You're calling the shots," Joe said, following the doctor across the polished floor of this immaculate facility. It did not bore him in the least, being here. On the contrary, every moment here was expanding his understanding of modern physics in a way that it wouldn't have if he hadn't been present at the heart of it all.

Lilly and the rest had stayed behind in Geneva, and were busy gallivanting around, touring Switzerland, shopping, eating, and taking plenty of pictures. They deserved it, and he did not begrudge them that they'd chosen to do it without him. They were not on a mission as far as he was concerned. He was.

Once they were in Dr. Hamond Ruther's office, a waiter came with a tray laden with snacks.

"Ooh, fast service there, doc."

"You can't science on an empty stomach. God knows, you can't write on an empty stomach either," Dr. Hamond said, and very frankly leaned over the table, helping himself to some tarts from the tray. Joe, appreciating the candidness, relaxed as he helped himself to a little of everything on the menu, famished that he was after traveling all day. Eight hours of flight time and then four hours traveling within the cities. As he'd stated in the press conference, CERN was his first stop, and perhaps the most important one given that this was going to give his mission a scientific validity.

"These donuts," Joe said, his mouth full of glazed blueberry donuts. "Jesus."

"I am glad you're enjoying my hospitality," Dr. Ruthers said, pouring them both some tea.

"I swear you're the politest guy I've ever met," Joe said, gratefully taking the tea and washing down the donut with it.

"It's not every day we get a celebrity around here," Dr. Ruthers chuckled, and then affected Joe with a very scientific, scrutinizing gaze. Joe knew what it was. It was the bullshit meter. He'd been polite so far, but now he was gauging if Joe was full of it or if he actually knew what he was about.

"Shut up, man. You guys are the real celebrities," Joe said, reciprocating Dr. Ruther's gaze, studying the man, finding clues about his personality, his orientation, his beliefs in a way only a writer could, not a scientist. When the scientist was busy gathering facts, the writer looked at the abstract.

"You humble us, Mr. Banbury. No one here has raised someone from the dead. You have, and in doing so, have forever warped our understanding of many things. Such as how can one man wield the power to resuscitate that what is dead."

"I can give you a hint. It's not a gimmick," Joe winked.

"So how?" Dr. Hamond Ruthers leaned in and asked vehemently. "What did you do?"

"Doctor," Joe began. "The Higgs field is a fundamental energy field that permeates the universe, am I right? When it interacts with particles, it gives them mass. If it does not interact with particles, everything would be massless and we wouldn't have the universe as we know it. It's the glue that holds the entire universe together. A simple, invisible, mass-giving field."

"You're versed in particle physics?" Dr. Ruthers relaxed in his chair, a look of pleasant surprise on his face.

"No more than your average Joe," Joe said, making the doctor laugh.

"You are right, Mr. Banbury. It's the Higgs Boson particle that we discovered right here in this lab, the Goddamn Particle, later named as the God particle because that was more befitting, that confirms the existence of the Higgs field. Higgs field explains gravity. It explains attraction. It's what completes our understanding of the universe."

"From a scientific point of view," Joe said.

"Precisely."

"What if I told you, and I have no way of proving it to you at this moment, so take it with a grain of salt, that this entire universe is pervaded by many such fields. Not just one. There's more that we don't know about than we know."

"What you say is phenomenon we scientists already understand. That there are fields out there we don't know about. Are you saying the nature of soul is tied to one of those fields?"

"See, that's what I like about talking to scientists. You don't have to lead them to it. They go there on their own," Joe said, giving Dr. Ruthers a much-earned fist bump.

"What do you call it? This field? If science ever goes around to proving its existence, you can be there and claim it in your name. The Banbury Field," Dr. Ruthers's face was brimming with excitement. "What are the parameters of your field, Joseph?"

"Well, it harnesses the potential and turns it into kinetic. So, the field is much like gravity. I am just the agent that topples a rock off a cliff and watches it fall. In this case, it's the soul of a person. I just assimilate it from its environs and compress it back into the body," Joe said. "And I realize that it sounds ludicrous, but hey, you've seen me do it twice now."

"This gives us particle physicists a whole new dimension to work with. And should we ever discover such a field that explains the existence of soul and spiritual energy, we'll be sure to call it the Banbury Field."

"Dr. Ruthers," Joe said, his tone growing a bit serious. "I know scientists normally tend to avoid such conversations given the primitive nature of the subject, but, like, if you were to bite, is there any evidence in everything that you've learned and understood over the years about the existence of God, the Devil, heaven, Hell?"

"We wouldn't be scientists if we carried our research with a bias, we'd be conspiracy theorists," Dr. Ruthers said. "So, yes, in everything that we do, we seek peripheral answers. Take the atom. There's a positive charge. Proton. A negative charge. Electron. And then there's the neutron. This being a metaphor, let's say that the positive is God, the negative is the Devil, and we humans are the neutral. Does it not make you think, Mr. Banbury, about the atom?"

"Come again?" Joe leaned closer.

"If the Christians, and I myself were raised as one, say that God is Good and the Devil is all that is not good, we can, by the law of association, parabolize that the proton and electron are two parts of the same atom. And as God says in the Bible, he is close to every one of us, much like how a proton and neutron are packed within the nucleus. The devil, charged with energy, prowls around the nucleus, removed from divinity, distant from man in that he is not man's friend but an enemy. But all that biblical lore aside, what of the atom?"

It hit Joe with a force that left his head spinning.

"Who created God and the Devil? What's the name of field atop which both these agents of good and bad play? What of the atom?" Dr. Ruthers whispered. "Who is the atom?"

"Jesus Christ, when you say it like that.... it's something we've been taught not to question. No one ever created God.

No one's above God. Almost like God's hiding a big fat secret."

"Who's God's God? What's the name of the Creator's Creator? That's hypothetical we scientists sometimes discuss after hours when the beer is strong and the night is long," Dr. Ruthers said. "And I thought it best to mention it to you, you being a writer, a ronin theologian, because it's certainly food for thought, isn't it?"

"Does it frighten you?" Joe asked, himself feeling a little afraid.

Dr. Ruthers took off his glasses and put them on the desk, wiping his eyes. "Mr. Banbury, we're scientists. Everything, from the Big Bang to the heat death of the universe, frightens us, moves us to document the chaos that we're surrounded by. We're specs on a floating rock hurtling through space. Yes, it frightens us. But we try to understand it so that it frightens us less. And that's what you do too. You write in words what people only ever think to themselves in secret, afraid that their blasphemous thoughts will earn them a place in Hell. And yet, everyone already thinks what you write about. What you give it is structure. That's what we scientists do. We seek to give chaos some structure."

"I'm trying to bring forth an understanding of the world that emphasizes personal empowerment, ethical living, and cosmic understanding. A large part of my ethos relies upon science because science explains cancer and tries to cure it. Religions ascribe a prayer and some holy water for it. You can see where it is lacking."

"So, your new religion would borrow the better parts of science and keep the working parts of theosophy? Others have tried it before, others have failed. You cannot keep the electron and proton in close vicinity to each other. They will always repel one another," Dr. Ruthers said, his tone taking a dejected tenor. As if he himself had been one of those who had tried and failed.

"It's not so much as a religion, because I'm not asking my followers to worship or ritualize anything. It's a doctrine that they can implement in their lives. Nothing bad will come of it if they don't. But if they do, it will empower them in ways that will benefit them.

"So how would your doctrine explain the afterlife, heaven, and Hell?"

"Look at it as if they were quantum states. This particle-wave one being our immediate reality. Heaven, also described as euphoria or the epitome of all that is good, can be the wave-like crest in the graph. Hell, with all its friction and heat and coarseness, can be the trough that is the particle-like behavior of a quantum system. It's not up to God or the Devil to assign you a place in either the crest or the trough. It's how you see yourself. Are you evolving into a wave or are you devolving into a particle? Your conscience, based on your actions and your beliefs, ascribes you that value."

"Therefore, free will is actually free will and not an illusion?" Dr. Ruthers asked.

"Yes. We're freeing free will from the constraints of the clergy and handing it back to the masses to do with as they please. So when they sin, it's a sin they're committing against themselves. When they perform virtues, they're doing it for themselves rather than to please God or the Devil," Joe said, quickly adding the disclaimer. "Just so you know, these are rudimentary metaphors we're talking in. I do not claim this as fact, and as a scientist, I know that you don't either."

"Yes, precisely, and that can be the cornerstone of your new movement, one that I'd like to be a part of if every member proves to be as enlightened as you are. The cornerstone being that we take only fact as fact and treat hypotheticals as hypotheticals."

"Don't worry, doc. The flat-earthers, the anti-vaxxers, and all the crazy ass tinfoil hat people hate us enough as it is," Joe laughed.

"I saw that attack on you at the press conference. You asked me mere moments ago if it makes me afraid. I now ask you the same question, Joseph. Does it make you afraid, what you're doing?"

Joe thought long and hard, staring at the reflection of the supercollider on the windowpane, understanding the grandiosity of it all, his own minuteness in the cosmos, and then said, "It rattles the shit out of me, doc."

"Then maybe this will rattle you some more," Dr. Ruthers said, crossing his fingers. "You mentioned quantum states. Right? Did you know they're cyclical?"

"What does that mean?"

"That we've been here before. You and I. In another life. And that while we're here, we're there too. Somewhere else. In another universe parallels to ours. There's no perpetuity. It's a cycle. When you earlier asked about my belief in traditional religions, I wanted to mention it then. The heat death of the universe will be the cause for another big bang. After millions of years, countless iterations later, Joseph Banbury will be here once more. Reincarnated just as the world around him is reincarnated. Now, tell me, Mr. Banbury, is that not the very definition of insanity, as penned down by Albert Einstein? And what does it say about the authors and poets who so casually write 'in another life' and 'maybe in another universe'? Maybe they, and they includes you too, knew better than us all along. That's why the biblical God himself is an author, and not a scientist. And so if there's someone who can understand what this entire play is about, it's you. Mr. Banbury, the whole world's looking at you as you carve out a new understanding."

"No pressure," Joe said, his forehead covered in sweat.

6

LET ME HOLD YOU

When Joe got back to his hotel in Geneva, it was with a much heavy head and a heavier heart. The conversant, Dr. Hamond Ruthers, had been a most cheery and hospitable person, but the conversation had been rife with scientific nihilism, which only served to darken the entirety of his stay in Switzerland. If this was a foreshadowing of what was to follow, Joe realized that this would only get worse from here. The next leg of his journey took Joe and his team into the old world: India, home to the oldest religion on the planet, and Iraq, the cradle of civilization.

He had only been to one city so far, and the new revelations had already been hard to digest. He suspected that when he'd meet the Orthodox Christians and the Ashkenazi Jews, their respective religious understandings would paint forth a darker shade over his mind.

He looked around the empty suite. It was the primo one at Geneva's Marriott. A room each for everyone, and a master bedroom for Joe. The others, as far as he knew, were still out and enjoying Switzerland. At least someone was enjoying this trip.

"Where's the Devil when you actually want to talk to him?" Joe called out, knowing that it was a slim chance at best if the Devil would appear upon his desire. The Devil had made it abundantly clear with more than just his words that while Joe took care of things on Earth, he was back in Hell, reigning, preparing for the Great Inevitability.

That was the Devil's term, not Joe's. He did not know nor care what this Great Inevitability was. It baffled him to even think about it at this moment. What did it mean anyway? That the world would end? That the demons would crawl out of literal Hell holes and overthrow humans as the apex predators on a post-apocalyptic wasteland?

The Devil wouldn't say.

"The Interview is over, Joseph. And while our relationship has evolved drastically over the course of the interview, revelations left, right, and center, I do not feel obliged to share the deeper workings of my empire or what the Great Inevitability is," that's what the Devil had said when Joe had tried to coax it out of him. In a way, that incident had been what had started the coarseness between the Devil and him. Joe had become defiant, and told him that if he were to give the whole aloof father treatment, then he'd behave as the prodigal son and rebel.

"What a clusterfuck that was," Joe said, reminiscing bad memories.

He intended to call the others, ask them where they were, what they were doing, and if there was room for one more.

On the other hand, it was getting late, and he was plenty tired. Tonight, he knew for certain, he was going to have the strangest of dreams.

A weary and bleary-eyed Joe dragged himself to his bedroom and was just about to crash on the bed when something knocked outside. It wasn't the kind of knock someone would rap against a door. It was far more intrusive, almost as if someone was trying to break in.

That was strange. Everyone who was supposed to be in the suite already had a key, and it wasn't like Marriott to let just about anyone walk up to an occupied suite and attempt to break in.

Joe snuck over to the door. The rest of the suite was completely dark. The only light came from the sconces in Joe's master bedroom. Whoever was on the other side, if it was a human, probably did not know that anyone was in there. A thought of terror crossed his mind. Could it be that the Clerics of Yahweh or whatever those yahoos were calling themselves had found where he was staying in Geneva?

Was this sabotage or perhaps an attempt at murder, the motive being that they'd hide in his apartment and wait for him to show up? Only that they did not know that he was already there, feeling agitated, depressed, homesick, and charged for some action, even if it meant beating someone to within an inch of their life.

And in case they weren't human and some demon from Hell come to get him, well, then he was due a talk with the Devil, one about keeping his dogs on leashes.

The door swung open before Joe had a chance to gather himself, and someone entirely unexpected walked through it.

"Tasha?!" Joe called out, his defenses disengaging as he watched her purple-streaked head bob and ogle.

"Oh, hey," Tasha waved matter-of-factly as if she was supposed to be there.

"What even are you doing here? Aren't you supposed to be back in New York?"

"I never figured out how to use these keycards, you know?" she flashed the card at him, then smiled. "Hey, you."

"Is there something I'm missing? Why are you here?" Joe asked. "Not that I'm not glad to see you," he added.

"I'll make a short story out of a long one. When you guys all went without me, I kind of felt terrible. Almost made me feel like I wasn't part of the team," Tasha said, sitting down on the sofa, legs crossed. "And then I was like, if I'm to be a part of the team, I should just go and, you know, be a part of the team. So I'm here. In Switzerland."

"Who gave you the keycard?" Joe asked, handing her a beer from the kitchen.

"They did. I told them I was with you, showed them my TMS credentials, sweet-talked them, batted my eyes. It's surprising how far you can go with feminine guile," she said, taking the beer gratefully. "I hope you don't mind that I....er...did this."

"On the contrary," Joe said, sitting beside her, drinking his beer with a sad solemness. "I was missing....home... people around me. When I set out on this journey, I did not know that it'd get this lonely."

"But you're not alone, Joe. We're with you. All of us. Joph, Lilly. Me. Shaun. Your sister. We believe in you."

"You do?" Joe asked, putting his beer down.

"Yes. For sure. What you say, nobody else says. What you do, nobody else does," Tasha said, resting her head on Joe's shoulder.

"The things the scientist said today at CERN. They've got me feeling hollow. Like I don't matter. Like nothing I do will ever matter. Is that crazy? Should I really be paying that much heed to his words?" Joe asked.

"Scientists shmientists. If they were that great, why are there millions of them?" Tasha said, making Joe laugh.

"Oh, it was a bad decision not to have invited you. You make me feel like myself," Joe said.

"Well, good thing that I'm here, anyway, no?"

"It is."

"Come. Let me hold you."

Tasha hugged him tight, making all the black, all the dark disappear in the wake of silent peace. Some time passed, and now Joseph lay with his head on her lap, Tasha stroking his hair, both of them not speaking, only taking in each other's presence. Joseph wished that the others would take a little bit more time coming back to the hotel, because he was not done recharging just yet.

"Tasha," Joe asked, his eyes drooping with sleep, his voice a slurry mess that sought to merge words together.

"Yes, Joe?" Tasha leaned closer, her tresses falling on Joe's face, feeling like a cool serenade on his hot skin.

He wanted to tell her that he felt constrained of late, one large chain around his neck being his word that he'd given to the Devil, the other chain a much larger, far more heavier one that chided him for not having written anything substantial in the past months. The third chain that he wanted to talk of was this movement that he had started, but he spoke of none of that as he began to fall asleep. He only asked, "If you're here, who's back there at the Cathedral?"

The vision of Tasha's innocent face and her high-contrast hair flickered before his weary eyes, making it seem like she was there and yet not there at the same time. The visual glitch took him by surprise, chasing away his sleep.

Joe sat upright.

"What just happened?"

Instead of telling him outright, Tasha's whole body went

out of focus till it disappeared, and then suddenly came back into vibrant focus. Tasha was no longer in an amiable spirit. She looked distraught, tears running down her ethereal face, her eyes stretched with fear.

"There is no here. There is no back there," she whispered. "I came here to say goodbye, Joe."

If there had been any drowsiness edging around the periphery of his consciousness, it was gone now, and Joe was standing on his feet, all notions of comfort gone, replaced by panic.

"What...what are you talking about, Tasha?" He tried to hold her hands in his own, but hers slipped right through.

"Every second that I spend here, it gets more difficult for me to stay. I just wanted to come by and say goodbye one last time, Joe," Tasha said, no longer possessing a corporeal form. She was all wisps and smoke, a human mirage.

Joe could not comprehend, and in the lack of his comprehension reached forward with both arms and wound them around Tasha. For a brief moment he held her, and all seemed all right with the world again. But then the moment passed and Tasha slipped through his fingers, yet standing right where she was, affecting him with the deep grief of perpetual loss.

"You can't be," Joe stuttered, the strength fading from his legs, his knees bucking as he knelt by the sofa.

"I just wanted to see you one last time before I went," Tasha said, her hand touching yet not touching his face as she wiped somber tears away from her face. "You are a good man. Perhaps the best man I knew after my father. I am glad that I came to know you when I did. I am happy that I could, in some way, help you."

"Tasha. God fucking damn it, you better not pull this shit on me. I demand you stop this at once. Come back," Joe wept, trying desperately to hold her and to stop her from leaving, but here, all his powers, all his newfound status as the crown prince of the dark realm, were rendered effete. She was fading, her life force crossing the threshold that separated life from death, and there was no body to resurrect.

He held her fading hand for the last time and tugged her close, weeping, "Don't go where I cannot follow."

"Will you tell my Mom and Dad that I wasn't in pain when I died? That I was happy? It will mean so much to me, and them, if you do so. Please, Joe."

No more a faint impression of the woman she was in life, Tasha bade him farewell with a tender kiss on the forehead, and dispersed into the air, leaving him alone.

There were no words to describe the gut-wrenching wail that escaped from Joe's lungs as the realization hit him like an anchor, that despite his powers to bring people back from the dead, the ability to tread across Hell, and having Satan as his cohort, there were some things that he was still not able to do, and perhaps might never be able to do.

Bringing Tasha back was one of them.

WHEN THE MASKED men surrounded the Cathedral at night, they did not know that anyone was inside it. Even if there was, they did not care. They sought to disrupt. None of them was ever going to rest until The Morning Star was just a brief footnote in the history of the modern world.

The night was about to hand the reigns to a blue dawn when these men lit their Molotov cocktails. They were the survivors, the ones who had escaped the police raid the other night. Under new leadership, the Clerics of Yahweh desired to level the playing field. Banbury had taken down one of their own, who in turn had cracked under interrogation and given away the location of the Clerics' headquarters. It was only fair that they burned down Banbury's headquarters.

Such was the way of the world.

And as each of them flung their burning bottles at the building of the old Cathedral, they felt justified, their cause a righteous cause. If this would not altogether stop the accursed devil prophet that was Joseph Banbury, it would at the very least deter him.

But there was someone inside the Cathedral, burning away the midnight oil. Tasha was working in the multimedia room on the first floor, finalizing some edits on social media posts that would be posted across the internet in tandem with Joe's visits to each city. She had her headphones on, blaring away Megadeth, her head inches away from the monitor.

She did not hear the crashing sounds of the Molotov bottles colliding with the glass windows of the Cathedral. She only looked around when it was too late and the fire had swept up the place.

Tried as she did to escape, she could not.

The flames, which had latched onto her as she'd tried to escape by way of the emergency exit, consumed her completely when she failed to pry open the jammed door, courtesy of the Clerics.

She screamed and slammed her hands against the door as her body became one with the flames, but somewhere during the burning, her searing mind reminisced about the witches of yore, and she likened herself to them, her spirit becoming one with theirs.

Somehow, that made it better, and it did not hurt as

terribly as she'd always imagined dying would. And when all was said and done, her body charred to a crisp, the Cathedral collapsing in on itself as its wooden support beams gave in, her spirit form stood next to the devastation, and discovered that now that her corporeal body had perished in flames, soon to turn to dust and ash, she could go wherever she wanted in the blink of an eye.

Tasha traveled the world in all of six minutes, going to all the places that she'd promised herself she would if she had the time or the money but never could.

She started by visiting her parents, both of whom were sleeping sound in their old marital bed. She did not linger much there. She just wanted to see their faces once before she went. This was not the time to engage them in some afterlife dread by exposing her spirit form to them.

"Goodbye, Ma. Goodbye, Pa," she whispered from the other side of the windowpane, and then blinked, opening her eyes in front of the Grand Canyon. It was named quite accurately so, thought Tasha to herself as she flew over it.

One by one she saw them all. Christ the Redeemer, the Pyramids of Giza, the Great Wall of China, Niagara Falls, Mount Kilimanjaro. It was only after she'd gotten her fill of all the places she'd ever wanted to see was Tasha ready to leave, relinquishing herself to the gentle pull that tugged.

"Wait. There's one more thing that I have to do," she spoke to no one in particular, but her words caused the tug to cease momentarily. "There's someone I have to say goodbye to."

After she was done saying goodbye to Joe, there was no resisting the pull anymore. She let herself be carried above the roof of the hotel and watched the first rays of the sun as they hit the snow-covered peaks, sifted through the evergreen alpines, and reflected off the surface of lakes and rivers.

"You know," Tasha said, speaking to the realm that was pulling her. "It wasn't that bad of a life."

When the firefighters were done dousing the Cathedral with jets of water, once the final flames subsided, a battering ram broke through the charred door. It was the blunt blow of the ram that brought a finality to Tasha's fate, for right next to the door was her burnt body, solidified soot and ash.

Upon its first contact with the ram, it withered away, leaving there no trace of the person that Tasha was in life.

7

REDISCOVERY

New Delhi

A husk of a man with skin as white as bone sat hunched next to a burnt-out funeral pyre. Behind him, an ancient and holy river flowed, believed by the Hindus to be the literal body of the goddess Ganga, who descended to earth to purify souls and release them from the cycle of death and rebirth.

A necklace of bones too hardy to be burnt by the fire hung around the man's long, gaunt neck. He affected Joe with a menacing gaze, the man's eyes lifeless, unflinching, deep gray.

Without breaking eye contact, the old man with the long, crusted white beard reached into the charred pyre and procured white ash. He extended his wispy arm toward Joe, offering him the ash, but when Joe did not move nor say a word, the man took it as a no and instead rubbed the ash of the dead on his body, rendering his skin whiter than it was.

A low, red moon reflected upon the surface of the wide river, making it seem as if they were stranded in the cosmos, the stars beneath their feet as well as above. Equidistantly, pyres burned, the rancid smell of burning human flesh infiltrating Joe's nose and yanking at his guts, making him wretch.

His face marked with deep red and black, the ascetic howled as Joe knelt and wretched, and it was only after the first wave of nausea had passed did Joe notice that the naked, mocking man with the patched loincloth and sunken stomach was also missing most of his teeth.

His tongue was black.

He did not let Joe wonder for long as to why that was, for immediately after he sobered up, the man took a burning branch of wood from the pyre and held it above his head, closing his eyes. Then, reciting something incomprehensible, he held out his tongue and pressed the aflame wood onto his tongue.

The sound of flames sizzling out was far more grotesque than the fresh smell of scorching meat.

Despite every fiber of his being telling him not to, Joe took furtive steps toward the baba, noticing the bugs crawling in his dirty dreadlocks.

"Do you know who I am?" Joe asked, not expecting the man to understand, but to his surprise, the profane ascetic affected Joe with another piercing gaze and spoke in perfect English.

"I know what you are not. I know what you seek. One does not care. The other won't let you. You are the third. Will you be the doorway?"

"I don't know what any of it means," Joe confessed, taking stock of his surroundings. Behind him, ancient buildings of the Dashashwamedh Ghat decorated the bankside of the Ganges with their towers and domes and colorful facades. A long and broad stairway descended into the river.

On the other side of the river, boats were tied, bobbing away with the ebbs of the water.

In a country with more than a billion people, it baffled him that he and the ascetic were the only two present in an otherwise very popular location.

"Seek loss and you shall only find darkness," The baba spat betel leaf remains from his mouth and produced a small beedi from within his loincloth. He smelled along its length before putting it into his mouth and lighting it.

Acrid hashish smoke perfused through the air, and it wasn't the only thing that blew in Joe's face. The beedi was laced with something far stronger and darker than just marijuana. It was almost as if whatever the baba was smoking was alive, sentient.

In the haze of the spiteful smoke, the old man disappeared, becoming one with the white wisps. With his eyes red and his face flushed from coughing, Joe looked around for the mystic, only to find himself surrounded from all sides by the same thick, attacking smoke that had been exhaled his way, only to realize it wasn't just the beedi smoke but the collective exhumation fumes from all the dozens of burning pyres along the Ganges.

He could see the white shroud burning away from on top of each dead body, the flames having their way with dead flesh, searing it, cracking bone, causing the cavities in the bodies to boil and explode, eyeballs gushing, hair strands flying away like fireflies, and thick, bulbous bile bubbling out of the holes rent in the skin of the dead.

Out of nowhere, and as if he possessed no corporeal form to begin with, the baba flew from within the smoke, snarling with his tongue out and his eyes inverted, looking like an avatar of Kali, his face no longer white but smeared black with soot. Before Joe could defend himself, the man took his thumb and pressed it hard against Joe's forehead, burning his skin in a blaze that he was altogether unfamiliar with. Hell did not burn like this.

"Seek beyond trinity, seek beyond death, seek beyond light, seek beyond the One or the Other. Open. Your. Eye!" Rambled the maniacal mystic as he choked the life out of Joe, jumped over him repeatedly, knocking his wind out, and baring his four fang-like teeth as his mouth descended upon Joe's neck, tearing a sizeable chunk of flesh.

The pain immediately changed the landscape around him. No longer was Joe stranded at the Ghat alongside the Ganges. Wherever this new place was, it was absolute in its darkness.

The only thing that shimmered in the distance was an old relic atop a pedestal, the light upon it bright and just as absolute as the dark around it.

Before Joe could take a step forward, his whole body became possessed with paralyzing electricity, making him thrash where he stood, keel over, and fall on his face, his whole body becoming a conduit of unimaginable pain.

Gratitude was the last thing on his mind as he shifted to wakefulness in his seat, for this was not a dream from which waking was an escape. He had been projecting his consciousness into the astral realm, and while it may have looked like he was asleep to Lilly, who sat beside him, he was more awake than he'd ever been.

More confused than he had ever been.

As this was not a dream, the pain still lingered in his body along with the acrid smell of corpses and laced marijuana smoke in his nostrils. He could taste the sick he'd thrown up on his tongue.

Lilly was looking at him with a deep apprehension that she was not about to put into words. She tried to pretend that she'd just been reading the in-flight magazine, but her fitful gaze gave it away. Joe turned around and saw the others, all of them merely pretending to be doing this, that, or the other, but he knew that just a minute ago, they were all hunched over him, trying to get him to wake up.

"How much longer?" Joe asked, deciding to play the pretend game with them.

"Another hour and we touch down at the Indira Gandhi International Airport in New Delhi," Lilly said, pointing to the LED screen in front of her.

Joe stared out the window, observing the millions of lights below in stark contrast to the darkness above, and was reminded of his vision of the Ganges. Whatever it was that he was looking for, it was there, beside the Ganges. Not in New Delhi. And yet, the nature of his visit dictated that his first stop in India be at Delhi, where he'd meet the leaders of the religious order at the Shrine of Nizamuddin, the representatives of the Roman Catholic Archdiocese of Delhi at the Sacred Heart Cathedral Catholic Church, and visit the spiritual culture campus and Hindu temple known as Swaminarayan Akshardham. When planning his trip, Joe was surprised to learn of the Jewish community thriving in New Delhi, and so the Synagogue Judah Hyam was a last-minute addition to the itinerary, but nonetheless very important.

If he was going to develop his doctrine, it was integral that he met with the leaders of these religions, held talks with them, and tried to make them understand his ideology while also attempting to better his understanding of theirs. It was not his intention to present a philosophy that immediately contradicted the theological beliefs of the major religions of the world. Were he to do so, the followers of his movement would face persecution on a global level. That was the last thing he was looking for.

"Lill," Joe said, his usage of her nickname letting her know that she needn't worry about him. "You've been to India before. How many times does this trip make it?"

"Six. And the first three visits don't count because I was in my early twenties, hammered, and desperately trying to find the same thing that everyone comes to India to find."

"Peace?"

"Their next billion-dollar idea," Lilly grinned. "Steve Jobs was allegedly tripping out on acid somewhere north of Uttar Pradesh. I went there. Spent the night where he'd spent the night. Put a tab of LSD on my tongue and slept through the entire day, dreaming of a blue god with a pitchfork and a black goddess who could control time. It was a shit trip, the LSD one, not the trip to India, mind you, because I didn't have enough cultural insight back then."

"And what about the other four times?"

"Eh," Lilly squinted and turned her face away, telling Joe that she did not exactly want to be a hundred percent honest with him. "It's like, you know, every year you take a vacation, and once you're done with Ibiza and Bali and Switzerland and Egypt, the world starts to look like a lot smaller place than you'd initially thought it was. So, I was like, fuck it, why not India? I've been to New Delhi before. I went to this ancient city called Banaras, where they make hand-stitched saris. I even bought one. Come around my place when we're back in New York and I'll show you. Saw the Himalayas. Was part of a jeep rally in Rajasthan. It's a big place with a billion people. Heck, on my last trip, I went to Bollywood, Mumbai. It was quite the experience."

"Why?"

"Because that city's like nothing we Westerners have ever

seen. How come we're not visiting Mumbai?" Lilly asked. "You'd love Mumbai and their biryani, Joe. I swear."

"Lill, I have a question," Joe asked.

"Ask away," Lilly said, slightly raising her eyebrow, the humor dissipating from her face.

"Is there a place with a rushing river, funeral pyres, and old temples? I'd wager there'd be thousands of places like that, but what would be one that you'd take a picture of, put on a postcard, and send home? Something remarkable and larger than life, if you know what I mean,"

Her eyes grew wide and her grin came back, "Ooh, very cultured, aren't we, Joe? That's Varanasi. It's the central place for mourning, death, rebirth, and pilgrimage in the Hindu world. It's one of their most sacred sites. Why do you ask?"

"Because I'm scrapping whatever else plans we have on the itinerary for India. After Delhi, we're going there."

"Why, do you want to bathe in the Ganges and absolve yourself of your sins?" Lilly asked, throwing her head back and guffawing.

Joe rolled his eyes. "There's someone there I must find."

Lilly's gaze became stern and affixed on Joe, her frown deepening as she studied him. Joe could feel her trying to find some sort of telepathic passage into his mind as she asked, "What are you not telling me?"

"It's...it's nothing," Joe said, looking away.

"Joe. You don't mean to go and visit the Dreadless, do you?" Lilly's voice was low with a newfound apprehension.

But it was nothing compared to Joe's shock.

"How did you even know?" Joe asked.

"Since it's just the two of us, I'll tell you something that I might not get a chance to tell you later. Joe, the Dreadless are not to be trifled with. Their brand of wisdom, magic, and spirituality is not for you and me. It is darker than dark, potent than potent. I am afraid you and I will not be able to perceive their brand of asceticism."

"You and I?" Joe scoffed. "Why are you bracketing yourself with me in this? No offense, but you're *Lilly*. And I am the literal son of Satan. Is there anything darker than Satan that comes to your mind?"

Lilly shook her head, her hand resting on Joe's shoulder as she leaned closer and whispered, "There are some forces that exist beyond the dichotomy of God and the Devil. You call dark black because black is the darkest dark you know of. There are shades darker than black that we cannot see, and thank God for it. The Dreadless thrive in those darker shades. You do not want any part in that."

"I think I can establish for myself what part I want in what, thank you," Joe said coarsely, turning his face away, brushing off her hand from his shoulder.

A minute later, their flight descended onto the airstrip and came to a slow yet jaunty halt.

* * *

New Delhi was a most obtrusive city, with more buildings than room to breathe, the roads packed with traffic comprising of cars, rickshaws, bikes, bicycles, carts, and the odd cow. Not to mention that the whole place sweltered like Hell. Everyone around them talked and shouted in a language they couldn't understand, and the Uber ride from the airport to the Taj Palace Hotel took them forty minutes on account of the traffic jam.

But it was also a most beautiful city, with the old peacefully coexisting with the new in a way that Joe had never seen before. Here, an old temple stood saliently between shiny new buildings. There, an old mosque with its towers and domes peeked from behind an apartment complex. If it was obtrusive in terms of architecture, it was also obtrusive in terms of how green everything was. There was not a single road that wasn't lined with greenery whether in the form of trees or plants, and being here, it did not feel like the alien land Joe had anticipated.

When the background noise dimmed, Joe could decipher English in his vicinity. Hip young Indian men toting man pouches, sporting man buns, wearing bracelets, talking away into their iPhones, not even glancing at Joe and his entourage's cars, busy in their daily lives. Women wearing t-shirts and shorts walked around in flip-flops, some eating ice cream, others dragging from their vape pens.

And for some reason, there was always music. More than the flashy billboards, the giant LED panels smack in the center of the roads, and the overabundance of colors of fruits and clothes in the shops and stalls, it was the music that hypnotized Joe.

Music of all kinds. From a car passing them by, classic tabla fused with the sound of elegant sitar boomed as a bold voice sang over the sounds of the instruments; the delectable rhythm of the harmonium coming from some music shop selling Eastern musical equipment; and the riffs of electronic guitar screaming from the west.

Joe, against the advice of his driver, poked his head out of the window, his nose serenaded by the smell of petrol, flowers, wet dirt, exhaust fumes, and fragrant vape plumes, and heard the unmistakable soundtrack of a popular American heavy metal band.

"Hey, Rahul, is that like a concert hall?" Joe asked, pointing at the dome he saw up above.

"Yes sir. That's the Shiv Sri Concert Hall. Today, there's an international concert taking place. Otherwise, this road is not as packed as it is today," Rahul, their driver, spoke in perfect English, albeit with a thick Indian accent.

"I'm surprised that Polyphia's playing here," Joe said to Lilly.

"My father was a Metallica fan, sir," Rahul, who looked relatively young, spoke excitedly and out of turn. "He had studied in America for a bit. Picked up his music taste there. It was one of the best moments of my life to take him to Metallica's World Magnetic Tour in Bangalore."

"And did he enjoy the concert?" Joph asked, genuinely intrigued.

"He wept the entire time, sir," Rahul gleamed.

"And you, Rahul, what do you do, other than Uber, I meant," Amy asked.

Joe shot a look at Amy saying, *Hey, not cool*, who shot him a look back, saying, *You got a problem with me taking an interest?* Joe rolled his eyes and did not interrupt. This was a Tesla Model X, so clearly he must be doing something right to be able to afford this car.

"Oh, ma'am, you'll think it's kind of stereotypical, but I am a software engineer by night," Rahul grinned. "I get so bored during the day that I pick rides from the airport and drop them off at the hotels."

"It's very enterprising of you," Joe said, thumping Rahul's shoulder.

Nobody spoke (in that everyone was too busy looking out the windows and admiring the fusion of historical, pre-colonial, post-colonial, and modern architecture all in one place) until they arrived at the hotel.

As Rahul helped them with their luggage, he approached Joe and whispered, "Pardon me, sir, but I know who you are, Mr. Joe Banbury." Rahul had the wickedest smile from ear to ear. "Imagine my surprise when you walked out of the airport and I realized I was going to be escorting you! But, Mr. Banbury, no security?"

The question of security was a hot topic for Shaun and Amy, it wasn't necessarily Joe they were concerned about, after all, everyone had witnessed what he was able to do to perpetrators. But it was more their own security. Joe had assured them that whilst a large security detail was indeed an option if they saw fit, he'd ensure their safety.

"Do you think I need it?" Joe chuckled, "are you a fan or....?"

"A tribe member, sir!" Rahul pulled back his sleeve and revealed the giant tattoo on his forearm. It was a pentagram around the letters TMS, standing for The Morning Star. "You don't even know just how many of us there are in just New Delhi alone, sir."

Joe held his hand out, and Rahul reverently shook it with both his.

"Thank you, Rahul. You know, I was a bit skeptical about coming to India at first but having met you, I'm happy that I did."

"Will you be establishing a base here, Mr. Banbury?"

"You bet. Give you and the rest of the tribe members an actual place to call home. How does that sound?" Joe said, not letting go of Rahul's hand. He'd only met this kid less than an hour ago, but the warm way with which he'd greeted and treated Joe was nothing short of familial behavior. Joe handed him fifty dollars, which was thirty more than what Rahul had asked for.

"It's quite generous, sir," Rahul said, pushing the dollar bills back at Joe, "But I cannot take my messiah's money."

"Messiah shmessiah, dude. Take it," Joe chuckled. "Thanks for showing me around."

There were tears of reverence, not of gratitude, in

Rahul's eyes as he took the money and procured his business card. "Mr. Banbury, while you're here, if you so much as need a bottle of Aquafina or something, you call me. Okay?"

"There's a lot of pride flags here, huh?" Joe noticed, taking the card and putting it in his pocket.

Rahul stared at Joe with shock-widened eyes, then laughed freely, clapping both hands. "Mr. Banbury, why do you seem so surprised?"

"Joe!" Amy called from a hundred meters away from the parking space. While he and Rahul had been talking, the others had made their way to the hotel's entrance.

"Well, thanks Rahul, for everything, man."

"Thank you, sir."

* * *

The suite they got was on the top floor, and it was as luxurious as their Marriott dwelling in Geneva, if not more.

"Thank fuck for AC," Shaun cursed, taking off his shirt as he headed into his room. "What the fuck even is this place? Another second outside and I'd have melted."

"Oh, chill, would you, you big idjit? It's just a hundred and four degrees," Amy scolded, lounging on the sofa, a flute of complimentary, freshly squeezed mango juice in her hand.

"Listen, lady, it's eighty degrees in New York right now. That's twenty-four degrees hotter over here. Not to mention goddamned humid!" Shaun yelled as he slammed his door shut.

"What bug's crawled up his ass?" Joph asked, standing right under the air conditioner, his own Hawaiian shirt open, revealing a toned, sweaty body.

"He's Shaun. Shaun's always gotta bitch," Lilly said,

helping herself to some of that mango juice the room service had left them. "Damn, this is good."

Joe, unperturbed by their grievances and observances, stood by the window, staring at the city. This was a place of power. He could feel the raw rhythm of life and culture and song and dance and art and music and spirituality deep within his soul as he stood there, above it all, peering into all the colors and textures and brickwork.

* * *

Tasha still occupied the forefront of his thoughts, and it was for this very reason he was quiet when he was on his own, doused in grief, wondering what he could have done if he hadn't left on the world tour at all. He could have saved her at the very least.

The events of two nights ago played in his mind over and over.

The fifteen thousand dollars fine his team had to pay for Joe trashing the entire suite in an attempt to come to terms with the loss of one of his closest friends and former lovers. What manner of futility was this that he had saved her life so painstakingly just a year ago when he'd prevented the arsons from setting fire to the Afterlife nightclub only to have her die some months later in a fire?

The Devil, who knew all too well of the volatility that had gripped Joe, did not appear to him nor lambaste him with platitudes that spoke to the inescapability of fate.

No. It was his friends who were by his side in his moment of grief, Lilly gripping him by his shoulders as she pressed his body next to hers, Amy with her hand on Joe's head in a childlike attempt to soothe her little baby brother, and Shaun and Joph, the men of the group, standing in somber silence, their arms crossed in front of their torsos, their gazes glaring into the suite's immaculate floor.

Somehow, they convinced a screaming and thrashing Joseph that the only way was forward, and that going back to New York City at this crucial juncture would put a premature and permanent end to the world tour.

"Tasha would want you to carry on," Amy said, earning Joe's rage.

In the background, the TV tuned to CNN showed the active scene of the crime as firefighters sprayed it with water while a reporter speculated that this crime matched the MO of similar acts of arson committed by the religious extremist group known as Clerics of Yahweh.

It had been Joph, who perhaps understood Joe on a more pathological level than the rest of them, who gave him a glass of water. The glass of water calmed Joe down to the point that he fell asleep immediately. Later, when the team was gathered around a snoring Joe, Joph revealed that he'd mixed two tablets of Valium in the water.

The group talked in great detail that night, unaware that there was a fifth among them. The Devil heard with immense attention as they discussed what they'd do next, and the Devil did then what he was most renowned for. Whispering in each of their ears.

That going back was not an option.

That the show must go on.

When all four of them agreed unanimously that they should head to India (avoid Israel and England for the time being) it felt like a strange acceptance, as if somehow they had made a decision that they had not wanted to make in the first place.

When Joe woke up a whole day later, his head was spinning from the effects of a double dose of Valium, and it had a docile effect on him that made him play along with whatever was happening around him.

They had packed his luggage already.

Now, as the sadness and the Valium hangover were beginning to ebb away, another grim-faced reality had bared its fangs in Joe's face.

None of it was worth it if it meant losing the people closest to him.

* * *

While the rest of them were resting or getting ready for the evening's itinerary, Joe sat in the courtyard of the hotel's botanical garden, relieved to have a moment to himself. It was hotter and far more humid in this garden than it was outside, but it was also quite quiet, serene, and peaceful. Banana palms and bougainvillea lined the corners of the orchard, the canopy provided by the mango and jambool trees blocking out the afternoon sun. At the center of the courtyard, a calming fountain spouted water from the mouth of the Goddess Lakshmi. The brickwork on the floor was color-coordinated. Red to match the red roses, white for the lilies, purple for the wisteria, and green along the garden's walkways. With no screens, phones, and electronic equipment around him, Joe felt like he had stepped back into time during the British Empire's reign over India. It was fitting that he was dressed in khakis, blending well with the motif of the garden.

Yet every time he closed his eyes to blink, he saw the ash-covered ascetic with the necklace of human bones affecting him with the gaze of death. If he tried to push away the intruding vision, it was replaced with one of the Von Barreth Cathedral up in flames, Tasha trapped inside.

But something else was stirring inside Joe, something he hadn't shared with anyone. His dreams were becoming more vivid, featuring a familiar face he couldn't quite place. The environments around him began to appear different, and he started to observe the planet in a new way. He could see the energy coursing from person to person, and people's thoughts seemed to emanate from their skulls, radiating into the atmosphere and connecting like golden strings to a large, interconnected spider web.

Joe's newfound perception revealed an underlying fabric of reality, akin to the principles of string theory. Every interaction, every thought, every emotion was a vibration along these cosmic strings, creating a symphony of interconnected energies. He could sense the resonance of these strings, their subtle frequencies weaving through the fabric of the universe, binding individuals together in a vast, collective consciousness.

As he watched a couple walk across the hotel gardens toward another couple, they exchanged greetings and hugs, creating an exchange of golden sparks. Strings and clouds of energy intertwined all four adults, and as they walked away together, Joe saw the imprint they left on each other. The golden strings made them look like puppets, stretching from their heads to the sky, reaching as high as Joe's eyes could see.

The strings connected not just people, but also the elements of the natural world. Trees, rivers, mountains—all vibrated with the same energy, their frequencies harmonizing with the collective consciousness. Joe realized that these strings were the threads of existence, tying together every being and every particle in the universe, creating a tapestry of life that was intricate and infinitely complex.

The vision made Joe aware of the delicate balance and

the profound interconnectedness of all things. He saw how a single thought could ripple through the web, influencing events far beyond its origin. It was a realization that filled him with awe and a sense of responsibility, knowing that he was now a part of this grand design, this cosmic dance of energy and life.

Everything affected everything. "If only the people could see how we're all connected." He thought to himself.

The chai in front of him was not getting cold. It empirically couldn't, given the blistering weather. But he welcomed its milky hotness scalding his tongue. He reclined in his chair and found that he was sitting under a mulberry tree with ripe fruit hanging from it. He cast a look sideways, wondering if anyone from the hotel administration was looking his way; when he was sure that no one wasn't, Joe reached out and grabbed a glistening, purple mulberry and snatched it free from the tree.

"Mulberry thievery in New Delhi ill suits you," the Devil said, appearing from behind the tree, sporting an olive sports jacket.

"What are you doing here?" Joe grimaced, averting his gaze, instead focusing on the berry he'd plucked. It looked delicious. Joe hesitantly brought it to his mouth, not knowing what it would taste like, and then let it dissolve on his tongue, that sheer sourness mixed with the sweetest sweet. He looked up at the Devil, who was also helping himself to a mulberry, unperturbed by Joe's coldness.

"Packs quite a punch, don't it? They make mulberry wine down here. I hear it's the best," the Devil said, taking a seat next to Joe. "Chai, Joe? Are you for real?"

"What's wrong with chai?"

"Joe," the Devil closed his eyes, reminiscing. "Almost a hundred years ago, I was in India with a rather enterprising writer who also happened to be a Freemason and an innovator of the highest degree. I asked him the same question. Why chai?"

"Are you talking about Rudyard Kipling? The guy who wrote The Jungle Book?"

"Yeah, where do you think he got the idea of the evil snake Kaa from?" the Devil grinned, almost snakelike.

Realizing that Satan was doing nothing but spinning his yarn, Jos wished more than anything for him to go away.

"Go away. I don't want to talk to you," Joe said, staring dead in the Devil's eyes. "I really don't."

"So you don't want to know what Mr. Kipling said about chai?"

"No."

"Joe," the Devil said with a tinge of desperation, his hand reaching out and holding onto Joe's. "I am sorry about your loss. I genuinely am."

"What do you know of it?" Joe scoffed, snatching his hand free. The Devil did not construe it as misbehavior, even though it very well was. The Devil, a longtime acquaintance of grief and loss, nodded solemnly in silence.

"Paradise is what I know of it, Joe. It wasn't just a place. It was a presence. It was a person. It was, as God had intended, everything you wanted it to be. Adam was not the only one who found companionship in the Garden of Eden. I, too, had my fair share of kin and kith there. Beings whom I could call brothers. A place I could call home. A person I could call mine. For it would come to you, Heaven would, in different forms and indulge you, sometimes as a lover, sometimes as a friend, sometimes as a mentor whose advice you cherished. Much of what Paradise is and was and will be is lost on humanity, who only seeks green pastures, cold rivers, and serene hillscapes. As if Heaven was your average devout Christian's country club. It has been eons since I've stepped into Paradise, and I know for a fact, Joe, that as long as I live, and I shall live eternally, I will not be stepping into Heaven ever again." When needed, the Devil could bring forth great sincerity.

"When you put it like that...." Joe sipped his chai. "...I guess there is something you know about loss."

"I will not compare mine to yours. A person sinks in seven feet of pool water. Another suffocates at the bottom of an ocean. Both of them effectively drown. I feel your pain," Lucifer said. "Tell me how I can help you. Don't shut me out."

"Where is she?" Joe asked, his hands shaking, his throat bitter. "Do you know?"

"Not in my domain, that's for sure," The Devil said. "I checked. Trust me. She is where I will never be."

"That brings me no comfort. If anything, it only makes me feel as if she and everybody who's ever gone to Heaven is being held hostage by God," Joe said. "It makes me feel the same way about you. Everyone condemned to Hell is down there forever. Is that fair? A man commits to a life of crime and violence for sixty years and then dies, and somehow his torment is eternal? What kind of fucked up logic is that?"

"It's God's logic. Take it up with God, not me. Why do you think I rebelled?"

"I think we already established all that in your book," Joe said, leaving the botanical garden. The Devil matched his fast stride. "What else is new?"

"What are you searching for?" the Devil asked as the two of them headed to the elevator in the lobby.

"Something is missing. I don't know what it is, but I got some part of the picture at CERN. I'm looking for the other piece of the puzzle."

"There is no puzzle," the Devil asserted his sternness as he stared at Joe vehemently. "This is all there is."

"So you say," Joe said, but he could not forget what the ascetic in his astral vision had said.

"Where do you go in your head? It's somewhere I cannot follow. What's that you're thinking? Tell me!" This time around, the Devil spoke without any of the charm and guile. He was angry, and it showed in the blaze that emanated from his body. "Why are you blocking me out?"

"I am not blocking you out!" Joe shouted back, revealing the same blaze from within his own self, letting the Devil know that this was no longer meek and mild Joe any longer, and if it looked like he was, it was because Joe had far better control over his temper than the Devil did.

"Fine! Keep your secrets! And when you find yourself wading neck deep in shit creek, don't come calling to me for help!" Hellfire erupted inside the elevator as the Devil took leave, but it did not faze Joe in the least. He was part Hellfire. If anything, it felt like a breeze of cool wind.

* * *

The meeting with the religious leaders of New Delhi did not pan out in the way that Joe had hoped. He had anticipated tension and pushback. When he got none of that, it dawned on him that this venture was not going to bear any kind of fruit that Joe had wanted.

What kind of theological discourse could he hold with these people who were agreeing to everything he was saying and were treating every word from his lips as if it were lilting music and not an establishment of a rival order that would challenge the beliefs of their orders.

The head of the Sufi delegation from the Shrine of

Nizamuddin Auliya was a melodic fellow who spoke in a singsong way, always agreeing with whatever it was that Joe happened to be talking about. When Joe talked about the Devil and God being two sides of the same coin, the Sufi kissed his own fingertips and waved his head as if he was vibing to some invisible music. Joe found it most strange and suspected that the Sufi was not entirely sober.

After having visited the church, temple, shrine, and synagogue, the religious leaders and Joe had assembled at a meeting room in Taj Palace, and while from a diplomatic standpoint, the meeting was going as well as it could, it made Joe want to French kiss the business end of a shotgun and pull the trigger.

"What do you have to say about that, Molana?" Joe, perplexed and vexed to the extreme, asked about the statement he'd just made.

"We Sufis believe in Unity. Not duality," the cleric said, and to Joe's surprise, the other religious leaders nodded fervently. "There is only the Source. There is nothing else. No bifurcations."

"But the Devil is very much real," Joe said, rubbing his forehead. "Or do you deny that?"

"Would you deny that Ram, Shiva, Vishnu, Krishna are not real?" the Hindu pandit asked. "We believe that they exist, but we are not denying the Creator."

"Who would that be in your religion?" Joe asked, holding back his impatience. The meeting room was a small and closed-off space with two tables. One table was occupied by the head of the Sufi order, the Hindu pandit, the priest, the rabbi, and Joe; the other table had Joph, Lilly, Amy, and Shaun. Shaun and Lilly were recording the conversation with cameras and mics. Amy was taking notes on her laptop. Joph was busy on his laptop livestreaming the event to The Morning Star's website.

"In our religion," the rabbi interjected. "The Source is Yahweh. Our Muslim brothers and our Christian brothers share the same Source. The former call him Allah, the latter Adonai, or simply put, God."

The pandit clapped his hand on the rabbi's back and said, "Isn't that the truth? Now, take Hinduism. We have our avatars, our deities. But there is one who sits above them all. We call him Aishwar. Aishwar is the Absolute. Beyond good, beyond evil."

"Say that again," Joe's ears perked up.

"Hinduism is not a unified religion. Every sect worships its own patron deity. But for the most part, we all agree upon the existence of the Absolute. We call him Aishwar. In his benevolent form, Aishwar is Brahma, who encapsulates all that is good. But then Brahma birthed Shiva, who is also known as the Shiva the Destroyer. Here, you have people worshipping Brahma and people worshipping Shiva. It's one and the same at the end, isn't it? And so, if your movement happens to venerate the Devil, it is neither novel nor strange," the pandit said, shaking his head sideways as he spoke, holding both hands in a praying pose, a rosary running along the length of his forearm.

"I will not say this about the rest of the world, but I will say this about India. The people and their respective gods have found a way to coexist with each other. So, if another god wants to plant his flag on this supple land, we say, the more, the merrier!" The priest said with open arms.

"The only difference being, the one your people venerate, we warn ours to stay away from," the Sufi said, his eyes drooping and all the intoxicative mannerisms gone. "What happens, Mr. Banbury, when the prayer call of Allah-u-

Akbar rings in the same sky as where they scream Hail Satan at the top of their lungs?"

"Do you foresee sectarian violence?" Joe asked.

"We're no strangers to it. While we, the leaders do not want to do anything other than coexist and open channels of communication with each other, our followers, Mr. Banbury, they're sometimes less keen. A group of angry Muslims attack a temple. In retribution, a Hindu mob demolishes a mosque. It does not happen daily, but it has happened more times than it should. And, I am sorry if I come off as inconsiderate, in its most recency, it has happened to you back in your home country. We cannot eliminate the human factor, and as beautiful a factor it is, it is also the worst aspect of religion," the pandit spoke in a low and sympathetic tone, his head knelt.

"I do not come as a fearmonger. The message of my movement is that of liberation, empowering oneself, living ethically, and understanding the cosmos on a grander level."

"Christianity offers the same. So does Islam. As does Hinduism. The principles of Judaism are rooted in the same paradigm. What's so special about your religion that people would stop following the religions of their forebears and suddenly come flocking to you?" asked the rabbi.

They had him, and the world was watching.

Joe crossed his fingers, arched back in his chair, and breathed deep. He was prepared for this.

"Samsara," Joe said, looking at the cameras that Lilly and Shaun were manning. "Do you know what that is?"

"Of course, it's the cycle of birth, life, death, and rebirth," the pandit puffed his chest as he spoke.

"According to Hinduism, every human is trapped in the cycle of Samsara," Joe spoke at large, addressing everyone in the room and everyone watching the live stream. "And it isn't until their soul achieves virtuousness that they're freed from that cycle. The Muslims would have you believe in a similar thing. They believe that God will punish every Muslim in Hell for a set amount of time. What set amount of time? Until their sins burn away. Every Muslim believes that they won't go to Hell forever. They'll just bide their time, and then transcend to Heaven. Now, the Christians believed that Jesus died for their sins. Through Christ, they can secure a passage to Heaven and avoid Hellfire. The Jews believe that only a select few, the chosen from the tribe of the Bani Israel, will ascend to Heaven, and that the rest of us, who do not ascribe to their beliefs, are going to be condemned to Hell forever.

"It's all very rigorous in terms of gatekeeping, exclusivity, virtue signaling, and being holier-than-thou. As I said, I do not come as a fearmonger. There is an oversaturation of fearmongers as it is. In such confines, where does free will thrive? I only come to free everyone's free will and allow them to go at it their own pace. I do not deny the existence of Heaven, Hell, or even reincarnation. I come to liberate people from fear. I have been through Hell, literal and metaphoric, and I can tell every single one of you whose parents or religious leaders warn them of billowing fire and flame demons, it's not all like that. Some parts of it are, and I believe them necessary. It wouldn't be Hell otherwise. But for the most part, Hell, like earth, and much like Heaven, is what you make of it. It is a call to freedom. Perhaps that would explain why our numbers keep going up every day. People are done being afraid. And a lot of us would like to start living life on our own terms. I offer them that opportunity."

With his sermon delivered, his point made, Joe stopped speaking, sat silently, and looked around the table at all everyone. They had nothing to say, for if they had, any one of them would have interjected him.

From the corner of his eye, he saw Joph and Lilly grinning at him, both of them giving him a thumbs up.

Lill mouthed, "They're going crazy online!"

Joph nodded fervently, pointing to the laptop screen.

As far as Joe was concerned, his business here was finished. He had come here for religious discourse, but only found passive acceptance of age-old doctrines passed down through the generations. These people only echoed what they'd been taught. They possessed none of the critical thinking capabilities that he'd anticipated.

It dawned on him as he left the meeting room that if he was going to come up with his own thorough doctrine (a doctrine that was more substantial than his talking points and the web content on his website; perhaps a book of his own) it'd have to be a solo venture, not a collaborative one.

8

THE DREADLESS

Finding it strange that the Devil couldn't intercept Joe's astral memories about visiting the Aghori Baba, Joe lay in bed rotating Rahul's card in his hands. It was midnight, and the others had gone to bed.

He needed to do this.

For the sake of answers.

Joe took his phone out and dialed Rahul's number, who promptly answered. After a short talk, Joe hung up the phone, got dressed, and headed out of the hotel, where Rahul was waiting for him outside the lobby.

* * *

The ride to the airport took fifteen minutes thanks to no traffic at night. From there, fifteen more minutes to buy the ticket and board the flight to Varanasi. The flight itself was an hour-and-a-half long jolty affair.

But at two am in the morning, Joe was standing in the place of his visions.

He walked toward the bank of the Ganges River. People

were asleep on the walkway, on the benches, on the steps, and just about anywhere they could find a place. It was exactly as he had envisioned. Stray dogs roamed the streets, sniffing the sleeping people, eating out of turned-over trashcans.

The pyres burned along the length of the riverbed, the lights were lit in the windows of the temples, and those who were not asleep were either by the pyres, weeping and holding onto each other as their loved ones' bodies turned to ash and smoke, or were squatting by the riverbed, eying everyone with an indifference.

In his dream, there had only been one ascetic. Here, there were no less than three dozen. Some of them were muttering with their eyes closed as they flicked their rosaries. Others were drinking broth out of plastic cups. Some were lingering beside the burnt-up and abandoned pyres, salvaging fresh ash. And then some were bathing in the Ganges at nighttime.

Joe had no idea of where to go, and no idea of where he'd start looking for the man who had visited him in the astral realm, but as a start, he went down by the riverbed to where a family dressed in white was crying beside a burning pyre.

There was no use escaping the smell. It was everywhere. After a while, it ceased to bother him. The crying and yelling and screaming became background noise that he zoned out.

"Where are you?" Joe called out, sitting by a bench and closing his eyes as he tapped into the astral dimension.

"I do not want to meet you, for the Other travels as your companion," a voice boomed from the distance. "Whatever I had to say, I already said. I dare not speak more."

"But they were just riddles," Joe retorted. "I came all this way. Can't you show yourself to me?"

"What would that achieve? I am not going to tell you any more than I have."

"If you don't tell me where you are, I will find you. You do not know what I am capable of," Joe warned, standing up from the bench and intuitively heading toward the South, where a lone boat floated in the center of the river.

"Your father could not find me if he tried," mocked the old man.

"I am not my father, as you will discover in a minute."

Joe did not need his Hell-given powers to find the ascetic. He had already triangulated the position thanks to his telepathy. This was a rare case of no meaning yes. If the mystic did not want to meet him, why was he out there in the river in the boat?

He'd only taken a step toward the southern bank when his path was suddenly impeded by the Devil, standing there in all his menace and rage.

"Is this where you've been escaping to? Where I can't find you?" Satan hissed as he reached for Joe's throat, eager to snap it in half if the impulse struck him. Such was the extent of his rage against Joe's latest rebellion.

"Aren't you supposed to be omniscient-adjacent? Can't you see all, hear all?" Joe asked. "What's with the whole 'I can't see you' shtick?"

"Don't be coy with me, boy!" The Devil roared, and exercising the greatest control over himself, retracted his arm and clenched it into a fist. "Explain yourself."

"Can't a guy travel to Ganges for a little nighttime sightseeing?" Joe asked, sticking to his guns. "It's one of the holiest cities in India."

"Do not take me for a fool. You are here to meet someone. Not just anyone. You're here to meet one of the cremation-maddened fucks who wander about this city, hoping that they'll tell you something that I haven't! Is that how little you trust me, that you'd think I'd keep something from you?" For the first time since their acquaintanceship, the Devil looked afraid. Disturbed.

It allowed Joe to ask, "Well. Are you?"

"Am I what?"

"Holding something back?"

The Devil closed his eyes vexedly and shook his head. "You are my son. I have shared with you all I know. Why would you think that I am holding anything back?"

"I don't know. Why else would you be afraid that I'm here?" Joe asked, attempting to take a step past the Devil, but the Devil put his hand on Joe's chest and pushed back.

"Don't fuck with me, Joe. I have let you do whatever you wanted to do for a long time now. Take my word for it. Turn around. Go back."

"Or what? What are you going to do to me that you haven't already done?"

"Do not test my patience!" the Devil roared, and such was the severity of his sound that everyone sleeping on the bank shifted in their sleep, even though they could not hear him. But his voice reverberated across different frequencies, disturbing their sleep, causing ripples on the surface of the river, and clouding the full moon.

"Do not test my allegiance!" Joe roared back, the river growing still again, the moon reappearing from behind the clouds, the people going back to their sleep.

Angered, and pushed to the limit, the Devil clawed forward to teach Joe a lesson, and before Joe could avoid it, Satan's feral hand dug into the skin of his chest and pulled, ripping past his skin, and digging into his muscles.

Joe shot a look back and saw that the boat wasn't there anymore. It had been moored along the bank, its passenger long gone.

"Why can't you just listen and do what I tell you to!?" the Devil shouted, digging his claw further into Joe's skin, deriving pain upon pain. "Is it all that difficult, what I ask of you?"

"Let me go!" Joe shrieked and pushed the Devil away with all of his force. It did not make the Devil so much as even budge. On the contrary, his grip on Joe grew even more fierce.

Before they could tussle further, a gaunt figure slithered past them, throwing a handful of cremation ash on Joe. As soon as the ash fell upon Joe's skin, the Devil's grip on him loosened.

Agitated, the Devil screamed, and that scream translated not just to anger, but also to loss. He could no longer see Joe, feel Joe, or hear him.

The ascetic who had appeared out of nowhere still held onto a fistful of ash.

"Do you need a written invitation? Run!" He snapped and threw the other fistful of ash in the Devil's face.

Writhing, howling, and thrashing with his infernal wings and his tail, the Devil, clawed at his eyes, and unable to see where he was headed, fell into the river.

"This gives us a few minutes," the ascetic panted as he ran away from the riverbed.

"Hold up!" Joe called out as he ran behind the dread-lock-flailing, nearly naked madman.

His savior—if he could be called that—turned a corner and disappeared in a narrow street between two cramped buildings, one a crematorium service and the other a cheap hotel called "Deep Blue Sea Resort."

Joe shot one look behind him and saw the Devil, rising out of the Ganges, wielding his pitchfork, black flames enveloping his body, his form growing larger and larger, fueled by his rage.

"Fuck!"

Joe shot after the skeletal hooligan and disappeared into the narrow street, only to come out on the other side in a soot-covered cremation ground with dozens of pyres burning.

The lithe ascetic had already run halfway up the ground. He seemed to be flying, given how fast he moved. From behind the buildings, Joe saw the Devil taking to the skies, his piercing gaze scanning for Joe, lightning crackling across the sky.

WHERE HAVE YOU GONE, JOSEPH! The Devil yelled as he flew over the cremation ground.

Joe did not pay heed nor respond as he chased after the Aghori baba. There was an old temple-like building at the end of the cremation ground, and once Joe had crossed the field with the burning bodies and the thick smoke, he could see it for what it was.

Without thinking about it, he stepped inside the pitch-black charnel house.

A hand gripped him in the dark and pulled him deeper, making Joe fall down the steep stairs and fall face-first into a pile of burnt bones. Dazed, he adjusted himself, and sat upright, watching the mystic close the charnel house's door.

For what seemed to be an eternity, Joe was in complete darkness, his eyes not able to adjust to the complete absence of light. In the lack of any luminescence, he could feel the bones of the dead shifting around him, the skulls chattering, the femurs and tibias clicking together as they fell down.

It smelled of rotting meat.

This could be Hell, for all he knew.

But then the ascetic lit a matchstick and set fire to a solitary candle.

He descended the old stone steps, the candle in his hands casting a dim glow on the thousands of bones in the house.

At this point, Joe's heart was skipping more than beating, his bewilderment and fear knowing no bounds.

"You are safe," the old man said. "For now."

"It doesn't feel like it," Joe replied to the man from his visions.

"I told you to turn away, but you wouldn't listen," the ascetic scolded him, slapping him across the head rather forcefully. "And now your father's prowling outside."

"Forget that. Tell me how you evaded him. How did you do that? Why couldn't he see me?! And why the fuck are we in a charnel house?" Joe's mouth had gone dry once the candle settled into a crevice within the wall.

There were hundreds of skull sockets affixed on him, studying him with the gaze of death. They were not the smooth-sheened skulls he'd seen before in museums and occult shops. All of these skulls were burnt black and cracked.

"You have your Lord, I have mine. And mine rules over death and destruction, Banbury. The Devil does not hold dominion over the dead. Only the souls of the damned. Not all those who die are damned, as I am sure you know. I just camouflaged you as one of the dead by smearing ash on your body. And for good measure, I threw some in the Devil's eyes."

"You can see him?"

"I can see all, boy," the ascetic said, hunching in one corner and finding a dismembered forearm, its flesh rotting away. Without any hesitation, the madman bit into it and tore off a chunk, swallowing it.

"Jesus fuck!" Joe groaned in disdain upon the display of cannibalism.

"You can cast your judgment elsewhere. I feast not on the living. Only the dead."

"Any chance you can give me a pouchful of, what's that, ash of the dead?"

"There's plenty of burning corpses out there. Get your own pouch. Fill it yourself."

"You're not all that helpful, you know."

"I don't intend to be," the ascetic spoke, taking another bite out of the human arm, and then threw it on the pile of bones.

"This is your home?" Joe asked, getting on his feet and walking around the bone-packed charnel house.

"What are you, stupid? This is their home," he said, pointing at the bones. "I have no home."

"So the Devil cannot see you? What about God? Are you invisible to him too?" Joe asked, sitting down on the steps. It was the only place where there weren't any bones.

"Which God? Allah? Brahma? Christ? Shiva? Some can, some can't. I live an unalive life, my body and ash one and the same. I live with the dead, drink of the dead, eat from the dead, and Death Herself is my deathbed companion. Do not ask me who can see me and who cannot. *I* can see them all. Kali bathing in the Ganges. Your God sitting on a throne in all passivity. Shiva, destroying. Michael, commanding the clouds. The Devil, seething, seeking you. I see the One above them all. Who hath no name yet hath a hand in everything."

"That's why I came to you. You were being awfully cryptic in our previous meeting," Joe said, and as his eyes adjusted to the dark, he realized that the steps were also made of bone. As were the walls of the charnel house. From behind packed ribcages, skulls beamed at him, their grimaces sentient. "What you say makes no sense. Wasn't it God who created everything?"

"According to your Bible, sure," the ascetic crooned, procuring a beedi from behind his dreadlocks and lighting it with the candlewick. Now, on top of the smell of rotting corpses and death, there was the additional stench of rank hash and opium.

"It's not my Bible. I denounced it a long time ago," Joe said defensively.

"Come, white man. Stop fighting me and stop fighting yourself. Partake in this. Smoke with me if you'd palaver, or else leave me be."

"What *is* even that?" Joe asked, fearfully taking the beedi from the man.

"What do you care?"

"You're right. I don't. Fuck this," Joe said, taking a deep drag from the madman's beedi, and, while he was quite seasoned in inebriating himself back at home, this was a brand of intoxicant that he had never experienced before in his life. Not on earth. Not in Hell.

"There's some ash of the dead mixed in there for good measure," said the ascetic, chuckling.

His whole body cool and afloat, Joe chuckled back, not caring. He had imagined himself doing a lot, but he'd never imagined himself smoking dead people-infused hash with a naked madman in a charnel house by the Ganges. Top that, Steve Jobs, thought Joe and burst out laughing.

"What am I looking for, whatever your name is? What do I even call you?" Joe asked, reclining on the bone steps, closing his eyes, and listening to the shifting of the bones as the baba moved around the charnel house.

"They call me Kali Aatma," the ascetic said.

"What does that mean?"

"It means one of two things. It means Dark Soul. It also means the Soul of Time. Take your pick," Aatma coughed as he inhaled deeply from his beedi.

"Who's they? The ones who call you Kali Aatma?"

"Other Dark Souls," Kali chuckled.

"Am I a Kali Aatma too?" Joe asked.

"No, you're a lost soul. You're seeking, but you've been heavily influenced by the Devil," Aatma said.

"Who's the one above them all?" Joe asked, taking the beedi from Kali Aatma. He inhaled deeply from it, resisting the urge to smoke. The smoke, while harsh and extremely pungent, brought on a nice high. Nothing like he'd ever smoked back home.

"Aishwar. The Absolute. The All-Almighty. The one lost in translation. Hindus think that Aishwar and Brahma are the same. Christians think that God and the Almighty are the same. But you would know about lost things, wouldn't you, lost soul?" Kali was now lying on the floor, resting his head atop a pile of bones.

"Hey, if they're burning corpses, why's there bones?"

"Because it's the fucking crematorium industrial complex over here, Banbury. They burn, but not enough to burn everything. It's time for the next corpse on the pyre, and the next one, and so the poor dead don't burn properly, their bones rotting away in charnel houses like these. The average human body burns completely in three hours. And yet, the crematory attendees clear the pyre after forty minutes, once the family members are gone, once all the muscles and tissues and sinews are burnt. The bones come here. This is their home. But I doubt you came all this way to learn about charnel houses, so ask what's really on your mind."

"Fine," Joe, higher than he'd ever been, reached for the beedi and inhaled one last time. At this moment, he did not care about The Morning Star, the Devil, or Tasha...

Tasha.

"Hey, Kali. I lost a friend," Joe said, remembering Tasha, and realizing that he didn't not care. He cared very much. And in his attempt to escape her thoughts, he'd found refuge amongst the bones of the dead.

"I am sorry to hear about that, Banbury. But you never really lose the ones you love. So, I'll ask you this. Did you love her?"

A tear rolled down the side of his face. "Yeah."

"Then somehow you will find your way back to her."

"Thanks, Aatma."

"No problem. Now, before I sleep, ask me what you really want to ask me, and then leave me be. I have business in the morning."

"Are you ascended or just pure batshit crazy?" Joe asked, laughing.

"I'll answer your question with a question. What's the fucking difference?" the ascetic howled harder than Joe.

"So," Joe said, sitting up. It felt like the ground was shaking. All the bones started chattering. Joe wasn't sure if it was the high or if it was an earthquake. "What's the deal with this...Absolute?"

"You're so bogged down by details, you're not seeing that he's been guiding you all this while. Why did you put India down in your itinerary? Why not Israel? And why are you headed down to Iraq after this? Why not Afghanistan? Why not Pakistan? Why not Iran? It's the Absolute guiding you."

"Toward what?"

For once, the ascetic did not answer him right away. Joe sat upright and stared at the old man. He was staring at Joe, studying him, calculating, breathing deeply. Then, he closed his eyes, and slowly uttered, "The Epoch."

No sooner than the words had left the ascetic's mouth did the entire charnel house quake with brute force.

"He's here," Aatma spoke softly. "Go, before he catches you."

The roof of the charnel house started cracking, the many bones that comprised the walls of this place beginning to slip and crack, the walls leaning inward.

"What about you!?" Joe stood up in panic and reached out a hand to the ascetic.

"Run. Save yourself. Find the Epoch. And don't let him find out about it. It's crucial that you don't."

"Give me your hand!" Joe screamed as a part of the roof collapsed right behind the ascetic, crushing all the skulls behind him. "This whole place is going to come crashing down!"

"Save your effort for where it counts, Banbury. Find the Epoch. You're headed very close to it."

Against his instinct, Joe went back down and grabbed the ascetic's hand, pulling him, but Aatma freed himself and shoved a red pouch in Joe's hand. "Here. For when he's near and you need to hide."

"Come with me, man, FUCK!"

One of the walls crashed, and with it, the rest of the building started to fall in on itself, but Kali did not budge.

"I was dead when you found me. If I die a little more, that is fine with me. The Dreadless do not dread death," he said, and took another drag from his beedi, laughing as the house came crashing on him.

Joe, who could linger no longer, ran up the stairs, the charnel house catching up with him as he tried to escape. At last, he could not walk any longer and had to rely upon his winged form to seek an escape.

At the last moment, when the entire house fell flattened, Joe unleashed his wings and shot out of the exit in the moonlight night, the ash pouch clung to his chest.

He flew a little higher, disappearing into the clouds, away from the eyes of the people who were rushing toward the wreckage of the charnel house. The Devil was nowhere to be seen, but Joe knew within his bones that it was Satan who had brought down the building on them.

9

DECEIVER OF THE GODS

Joe came to a skidding halt face first on the surface of the purgatorial, hardpan barren land. If this were a desert, where were the dunes, he found himself thinking as the flesh of his face ripped against the harsh surface the Devil had flung him across.

His body bruised, his flesh bleeding from sporadic places, Joe clamored forward on the gray surface of the unending land. No hills in the distance. No road as far as the eye could see. There was only a haze, an impenetrable fog that made it hard for him to see if the dim glow was the light of the twilight moon or the dawn of a new day.

His wings were weary. Tried as he did to flap them, they did not propel him above the ground. On the contrary, they sent a seething pain shooting down his back, traveling to his extremities, bringing forth the grim admittance of defeat.

The haze ahead of him cleared, and the Devil, in all his rage, walked forward, his snarled fingers eager to gnaw, his red skin turning dark red, his eyes no longer the eyes of a reasoning being but maddened slits of a reckless juggernaut. Tail thrashing, wings flapping, the Devil soared forward, his horns jutting out menacingly from his forehead, the pitchfork poised to skewer.

He would not listen to reason or excuse. Taller than Joe by a whole person's length and just as broader, he prodded the pitchfork into Joe's back, piercing through his wingspan, and yanked.

An agonizing scream followed the fatal pain as one of Joe's wings came clean off, a dead leathery thing withered and bleeding, lying in front of him.

The Devil was not done just yet.

Again, he speared his pitchfork and penetrated the tissue of the remaining wingspan, and ripped it roughly off Joe's upper back, leaving giant, deep, bleeding gashes where once the apparati of his flight were attached.

Ripped, these two reptilian spans curled and wrinkled, withering away before Joe's blood-soaked and teary eyes, the Devil standing over them with snide judgment on his face, the pitchfork gleaming in the haze-light, Joe's blood congealing on its three heads.

There was no exchange of words between patron and prophet, father and son. The Devil leaned in, arms stretched in a predatory stance, and roared at the top of his voice, the earth quaking under Joe as the deafening reverberation threatened to rip away his eardrums and tear open the earth so it would swallow him whole. Draconic, this roar resounded louder and louder until blood began to leak out of Joe's ears, and no amount of clamping his hands over his ears served to lessen the severity of the scream, for it not only came from outside, it was also coming from within, from the half of him that was the seed of Satan.

He had been enduring Lucifer's wrath for the better part of an hour. First flung from above the clouds of Varanasi to the green hilltops in the north, then battered into the side of the hills with such force as to make landslides happen, and now, thrown across a desert, his wings torn, his body and psyche on the verge of collapse.

From what little he could see through his bleary eyes, he saw the Devil taming himself down, walking agitatedly to and fro, his wings receding, his horns seceding, the red and black hues of his skin turning paler, his stature diminishing until he looked human once more.

The wrath in his gaze was replaced by the pain of betrayal. His nose flinched and his brow furrowed as he spat in front of Joe and growled, "Pathetic."

Too beaten to speak, Joe passed out, earned in his own blood, his will in tatters.

* * *

When he came to, it was to the sight of his disembodied wings, and the Devil sitting by a fire, staring into the flames, entranced.

"They call this the Devil's Grass around these parts," the Devil spoke, stirring the aflame brambles. "The grass that lies. It's a hallucinogen, and people being people, they see what they want to see. Some, their wildest desires. Others, their greatest fears. And somehow, it ends up being associated with me. Humans are quite capable on their own to be the very thing that they blame the Devil for being. Evil. Malicious. Lying. Cheating. Proud." Then the Devil cast a disdainful look upon Joe and added, "*assholes!*"

Knowing that there was no escape, Joe lay there, unable to do anything else other than listen. The words, just as the visuals around him, faded in and out, blurring, muting, and then sharpening, only to repeat the cycle again. His own heartbeat and the high-pitched sound of leftover blood coursing through his gnarled body were more audible to him than whatever the Devil was speaking.

"Why would you lie to me, Joseph? Why would you hide these things?" The Devil asked, and even though senseless though he was right now, Joe knew that this was as rhetorical as a question could get. "I give and I give and all I get in return are deceit and lies."

"Fuck you!" Unable to take it anymore, Joe planted his fist into the ground and propped himself up against what felt like the crushing weight of gravity. His own pain was no help either.

"Excuse me!?" The Devil yelled like a maniac, facing Joe on all fours like a pouncing jaguar. "What the fuck did you say, you fuck?" Springing to his feet, the Devil retreated his leg and brought it forward with brute force to deliver a righteous kick to Joe's face.

Joe mustered the fleeting remnants of his strength and grabbed the Devil's foot before it could collide with his jaw, and then pushed it back. Caught by surprise, the Devil staggered back.

"Fuck you! You give and give? No! You take and take and hover! I have no shred of privacy anymore. I cannot even mourn by myself. You call yourself this great liberator, and yet your shackles weigh heavy on me than any God's. You are cursed, and you deserve everything bad that ever happened to you," Joe snarled through his swollen lips and rattling teeth, spitting blood out with every word. He had tapped into a source of strength that was not divine nor infernal. It was his own, and yet, it also seemed to come from another source. With its help, Joe slowly rose to his feet, wiping away blood and spit from his face with the back of his hand and staring at the Devil."

Satan threw back his hand in pure wrath and brought it

to Joe's face, who took the punch to his jaw and still stood his ground somehow. "Beat me all you want. Kill me. Condemn my soul to Hell, but it won't change the facts. You.... *brat!*"

"I," Satan's eyes billowed with agonizing anger, "Denounce you! You are no son of mine!"

"Big fucking deal. It's just words. Your denunciation means nothing. You'd rather crash a building on top of me, killing an innocent man, surveil me like I was Osama bin fucking Laden, and second guess my every move. Denounce me, motherfucker. You're the worst father ever. And you're no patron worth being a prophet of." Joe ripped open his shirt and pumped his chest out, walking toward the Devil with weak steps. "Do it. Like you ripped my fucking wings off, do the same with my heart and be done with it. Fuck another desperate bitch. Sire another bastard. Write another book. It's only going to take thirty more years. What's thirty years to you, who have lived since the beginning of time? Free me from this curse, fiend!"

Tempted, the Devil brought forth his pitchfork and pushed it against Joe's chest, pressing it in, letting it go past the skin, making fresh blood spout from the three holes it had perforated.

"Do it!"

In another moment, Satan, giving into his wrath and pride, would have done it, but in the moment before, right as the edges of his pitchfork dipped into Joe's blood, he did not see a defiant standing before him, nor a prophet who had let him down.

He saw his son.

A son he had all but crippled and killed.

A tear came to the Devil's eye as he came to terms with a concoction of contradictory emotions. Wrath mixed with love. Pride with humility. Sorrow with joy. Agony with relief.

He screamed, pulling back the pitchfork, and cast it into far into the wasteland.

"What have I done? What am I doing?"

"Beating the living shit out of the only one who actually gives a damn about you."

"I can smell the lie on the tip of your tongue from miles away," the Devil wallowed.

"And I yours. So if you're done giving me shit, allow me to ask," Joe coughed, falling on his knees, and then descending on all fours, spitting fresh blood. It felt like his entire inside was one big leaky blood bag with pain receptors. It hurt like Hell and bled like it too. "What the fuck was that?"

"You tell me," the Devil said, quickly regaining his composure, his voice returning to its cunning, indifferent tone. "Why would you go to the madmen who sit by the pyres? What do they have to tell you that I don't?"

"I came to you first," Joe confessed, hoping that the earnestness of his confession would cover the lie. "I asked you...if you knew where Tasha went, and you said that she was somewhere you'd never be able to get."

The Devil slammed his palm over his face and shook his head, crossing the other arm over his torso, utterly disappointed. "Are you still on Tasha?"

"Forgive me if I can't speedily process my grief. I am part human after all," Joe spat out a molar in the sand. "And I needed to know where she went. Seeing as these babas exhume people on a daily basis, my intuition told me that there would be some wisdom that could give me a semblance of closure."

"Are you fucking dense? They're shit-smoking, flesh-eating, ash-smearing madmen who don't know their asshole from their mouth! What wisdom would they have that you couldn't seek from you?"

"Are they really that dense? I remember just earlier this night, one of them blindsided you," Joe asked, laying on his back. He didn't have it in him to stand or even sit. His heart felt like a malfunctioning part of an obsolete machinery, skipping beats, clenching in pain.

"That old trick? It's nothing."

"Doesn't seem like nothing if you're razing buildings and brutalizing me. What is it?"

"No! You do not get to reverse question me. First, tell me, what was it that you went there to know. I cannot peer into your mind for some reason, and I want the truth, Joseph, or so help you..."

"God?"

The Devil spat in indignation.

"Fine," Joe groaned. "The Aghori said pretty much the same thing you did. That hers was a pure soul, and it has escaped the cycle of life, death, punishment, and reward. She's in her heaven."

"That's what I said in the first place," the Devil snapped. "Couldn't you take me for my word?"

"Sorry. It's just, you're the Devil. Who knows what you say is the truth or lies to placate me? I just wanted to be sure."

"And what is this that he gave you!?"

The Devil leaned over and snatched the pouch tied to Joe's belt.

Joe's heart sank. If he opened it and found the contents within, the weak foundation of his lie would give in and his entire fabricated story would come crashing around him, and then the Devil would certainly kill him.

"What is this?" the Devil asked, reaching into the pouch and extracting a black beedi. "You were buying drugs from him?" The Devil sniffed and then gagged, holding the beedi at arm's length. "It's disgusting."

"I was getting a nice high on when guess what happens? You collapse the charnel house on top of me! Overdramatic much? You've killed a guy."

"If that guy's money is where his mouth is, he's crawling out of the wreckage alive and unharmed," the Devil said. "Otherwise, he was just a crazy man smeared in ash who sold you shit hashish."

With that, he threw the pouch back at Joe. Joe opened it and saw that it was still filled with a lot of beedis, some broken, many intact.

"If you don't trust me, I get it. But at least trust my actions and their results. We've set up a church in your name in India. We're preaching your gospel in Iraq, next. I may be immortal, but the rest of my team members aren't. That's a considerable risk to their lives, heading into that country. I did not quit my world tour and head back to New York when they burned down my headquarters. I'm still carrying your flag, rallying people to your cause. I get the impatience, but what's the point if the very person who's spreading your message is turned off by the mention of your name?"

"Are you?"

"You gave me wings, Lucifer, and then you tore them off my back. I have never known such pain as I do right now, and look at what I'm still trying to do, searing agony and all; I'm trying to placate you. You're the toughest to please and the easiest to upset," Joe wept. "I don't get paid enough for this."

"It's just," the Devil struggled with his words. "I can see

you whenever I want, hear your thoughts whenever I wish, and suddenly, I'm impeded by a wall. I can no longer hear you as I used to. I don't know what you're thinking. I don't see where you're going. If God can get overly conscious about such things, I am only the Devil, and I wouldn't put it past me to grow envious. Worried."

"Worried about what?" Joe groaned, partly out of agony, partly out of tiredness.

"Are you trying to deceive me?"

"I'm not," Joe said, looking bluntly into the Devil's eyes, unblinking, his gaze unwavering.

"Then perhaps I can try being a little less micro-managerial. Be warned, though. The next time you call on me, I may not answer. I feel a little distance between us would, as they say, make the heart grow fonder."

"Yes please."

"Goodbye, then, Joseph."

"Hey!" Joe called out, crawling toward the Devil. "I cannot move. I cannot fly. I'm dying over here. Aren't you going to help me?"

"You got yourself here. So get yourself back," the Devil jeered and then disappeared into the gray haze of the barren wasteland.

"Fine! Win that wager on your own, then!"

He didn't know if it'd work, this hollow threat, but it did.

The next second, Joe was no longer lying on the cold hardpan floor of the wilderness. He was in his bedroom at his Hotel, and the view from the window showed a dawn sun rising above the buildings.

You'll get your wings back when you earn them, the Devil bellowed in his head now that the effects of the beedi had worn off. *If you earn them back at all.*

10

THE WARNING

When Joe emerged from his room the next afternoon, after sleeping off the violence inflicted upon his body, he was not ready for the way everyone barraged upon him. Apparently, they'd been up for some time, the breakfast still laid on the dining table. Amy with paperwork that she needed him to sign to break ground on the construction of The Morning Star's church in New Delhi. Joph with feedback requests for the latest episode of the on-the-road podcast uploaded on TMS's website. Shaun with questions about why they were going to Iraq and not somewhere where they could build a church, because they could most certainly not build a church in a place as controversial and militant-occupied as Iraq. Lilly with questions about where he'd disappeared last night, and why didn't he respond to her calls; she was worried.

"Enough," Joe said, raising a tired yet clean hand. He'd spent an hour scrubbing off dried blood from his body. While Satan might have taken his wings away, he still had most of his other abilities, including healing quickly. The

Joe they all saw standing in front of them was not the Joe who had been wishing for the sweet release of death in his bed after dawn. No. That Joe had gone to sleep, and while he'd slept his body had recovered, sore muscles growing strong, fractures in his bones snapping back into place, torn skin renewing, his blood repleting.

They had no idea what had happened to him last night. Where he'd gone. But there was something in the way Lilly eyed him that suggested that she knew more than she was letting on.

"One at a time," Joe said, reaching out for the documents that Amy was holding out. "The budget's cleared for this?"

"Not just this one. I have a whole stack of approved paperwork for locations in London, Berlin, Sao Paulo, Toronto, Barcelona, and even Moscow. Why Moscow, Joe?"

"Joe, I swear, we're not heading to Moscow," Shaun dug his fingernails into his scalp.

"Relax, we're not going to Moscow, or any of the other locations that Amy's mentioned. I wouldn't put you all through a trip to Moscow anyway. At least not right away. I can visit them once construction's finished on each of the churches and inaugurate them. The rest of you are off the hook. We've just got one more place to visit, and even if you don't want to visit it with me, that's fine. It's my face they want to see. And it's not like I appreciate the support. Whether it was in Switzerland or in India."

"Yeah, but what the fuck, Joe? I packed for a much longer tour! Weren't we going to Brazil and South Africa after this, and then the UK? There was the whole European leg of the tour for which I freaking packed Bermudas! And I never wear Bermudas, so you know how damn serious I was!" Joph aired his grievances.

"I'm not saying that we won't ever embark upon another

tour in the near future, Joph," Joe said, taking a seat at the dining table overlooking New Delhi, helping himself to a glass of orange juice. "But think about optics. One of ours died back in New York. Our headquarters is in ashes. It'd only seem callous if we carried on. Going back would be the accountable thing to do."

"I don't like it when you speak sense. Where's the insane-in-the-membrane Banbury when you need him?" Joph threw his hands up in defeat and stormed out of the suite. "If anyone needs me, I'll be at the pool, getting my tan on while I still can!"

With Shaun, Amy, and Joph addressed, Joe turned his attention to Lilly, who was the only one left in the lounge area, sitting by his side on the dining table, stacking a couple of waffles onto a plate and sliding them in front of him, then pouring some chocolate syrup over them, and handing Joe a fork.

"Thanks, Lill," Joe said, pouring a cup of tea for himself from the thermos.

"Don't think I don't know you weren't here last night," Lill stated. "May I ask where you went?"

"A little nighttime stroll around the city. Soaking in the culture," Joe said, focusing on the plate of omelet in front of him. It looked delicious. He wondered if there was some toast left in the hotpot. Here was a novel thing he hadn't seen back in New York. A hotpot with a sealed top, keeping the flatbread and toast hot and fresh. He reminded himself to get one before leaving. It could come in handy.

As it happened, there were four pieces of crisp toast in it. He took two out and set them on his plate, then made himself an omelet sandwich, and bit into it. Perhaps it was because it was the first thing he was eating after having been beaten to death, but it tasted like the most delicious thing he had ever eaten in his entire life.

"Mmmh! So fucking good."

"Joe. Your nighttime sauntering didn't, by any chance, happen to take you to Varanasi, did they?" Lilly's question was so out of left field that Joe choked on his sandwich. He helped himself to a glass of water to get the toast down his throat, then stared at Lilly with shock-struck eyes.

"Lill."

"I knew it!" She replied. "After I explicitly told you to let it go!"

"First of all, how do you know I went there? Were you following me? Also, what is it any business of yours?"

"It became my business the day you came groveling at my apartment and convinced me to come back and work with you. And since I have your best interest on my mind, I have to tell you that you did the stupidest thing going there!" Since there was no one else in the suite with them, Lilly let her voice go as loud as it could, her fist slamming on the table, spilling Joe's tea on the cherrywood top.

"How do you even know!?"

"Your little friend, Rahul. After I called him from the card you left on your dresser, he told me that he dropped you at the airport. From the way he spoke, you had one too many questions about Varanasi and the Aghoris that resided there," Lilly said.

"He's six foot two, Rahul," Joe said. "There's no way you think he's little."

Lilly pressed her lips and shrugged her face, repressing her anger, eyes closed, one vein in her forehead throbbing dangerously. "What happened in Varanasi?"

"I will tell you *if* you promise to do two things. One, smoke this joint with me, and second, you promise you're not going to be angry with me," Joe said, procuring a hash joint from his pocket, his eyes flashing with roguish intent.

"You're not serious," Lilly chastised, glaring at him, then snatched the joint from his fingers, smelling it. She almost gagged at the rankness of it. "No way this is just hash. There's something profane in there, bordering on black magic. What the fuck have you been up to, Joe?"

"Smoke the joint and I'll tell you everything, I swear to you," Joe said, wiping his hands with a Kleenex, belching, and then taking the joint from her, and waving at the terrace. "Come on. Everyone's gone. Joph's probably down there, sunbathing. Amy and Shaun are not going to come out of their rooms, not with this heat. Besides, they've got work to do. So, you coming?"

"This doesn't change the fact that I am mad at you and I think that you were extremely reckless last night," Lilly chided, following him.

"Yeah, yeah, yeah, you don't know the half of it," Joe said, lighting the joint in memory of the fallen mystic. "Here."

He waited for Lilly to inhale deeply, and then burst out into coughs.

"Good. Now that you've inhaled human ashes, let me tell you something."

He watched her facial expressions growing more appalled as she coughed harder, eyes growing redder, and spit drooling from her mouth. He did not take any pleasure in bringing this upon her, but if he needed to talk without the Devil overhearing what he was saying, he needed to be sure that both of them were high on ash and weed. It was what discretion demanded.

* * *

A dazed Lilly sat with her weed-glazed eyes staring at the sweltering city, herself drenched in sweat, her mouth hung agape. Joe had just finished telling her everything. Well, as much of it as she could handle, and it turned out that Lilly was no lightweight.

"Do you remember when I asked you not to publish the book? Seems like a million years ago," her speech was slurred but underneath the hash-induced slowness, her wits remained sharp as ever. "But this is what I foresaw back then. You dealing with powers you don't quite grasp. Hanging out with the Dreadless. Having your wings torn off by Satan as if you were a fly and he was a budding psychopath in high school. Tripping balls on hash joints laced with human ash. Becoming the antichrist. All of it. I wonder how each of us has served as an enabler in your journey, and if we're wrong for doing that. If there's a history a thousand years later (*if* there's a thousand years later), I wonder if it will remember us as the villains. We could have stopped you. You did not know any better. And yet we didn't. Now, we're here, discussing the Absolute and the Epoch."

"Do you know anything about either?"

Lilly was wearing gym shorts and a sleeveless beige shirt with a deep neck. By now, all of it was drenched and dark with sweat. She put one foot over the other, resting them both on the railing of the terrace, her smooth skin glistening with sweat, waking something up in Joe. Something that hadn't stirred for her in years. But before she could catch him ogling her, he looked away, his addled state blurring and unblurring the urban scenery before his eyes.

"Joe, I think that it's quite ironic that people like us find ourselves pitched in these roles. You were an atheist. I...well, I was whatever I was. And now we're bound by our position to fixate on a narrative involving God and the Devil. I am no expert. You, I feel, while well-read and well-experienced, are no expert either. But neither of us is ignorant enough to straight out claim there's nothing profound out there in the unending cosmos. Maybe there are more universes outside of ours. Maybe Stephen Hawking was right all along about the multiverse theory. I'm digressing but bear with me. Suppose everything we've been taught about God and the Devil are watered-down half-truths. Where's God's wife? Kabbalistic accounts write about the existence of Asherah. Wife of God. Mother of Satan. Where's any mention of Asherah in Christianity? There's not. Where are the female prophets in Judeo-Christian religions? There aren't any mentions of them. Take Lilith. Did you know that the same accounts that speak of Asherah, wife of God, talk of Lilith, the first wife of Adam? There's only one passing mention of her in the entire Bible. And not within the context of Adam's first wife. As a demoness dweller of waste places. Fuck, man. You ask me if I know anything about either. Let me ask you something, do you know all there is to know about the Devil? How much is he keeping from you?"

"A question I keep asking myself lately," Joe brooded. "But do go on. I'd rather you speak, for once, and I listen."

Lilly shook her head, beads of sweat flying in every direction.

"Allow me to benefit from our altered state of mind. Think of God not as some all-powerful being for a moment. Imagine him as a kid in a basement playing a very well-crafted game of Dungeons and Dragons with his brother, Satan. God's the Dungeon Master. Satan's the chief player. But who owns the basement they're dwelling in? Who's the one wearing the pants in that house? Who pays the bills?"

"Who's God's dad?"

"The biblical Jehovah would have you believe, 'I am all

that is and I am all that I am,'" Lilly contemplated. "Why are we so trusting in our faith that we infer God won't ever lie?"

"We're just NPCs in a celestial tabletop roleplaying game? Christ, that's bleak."

"Not really. That was just a metaphor."

"So, the Absolute would be the God above God?"

"The way I see it, and I don't see it one way, God and the Devil are two binaries. For God to exist, He must exist without any badness. And so what happens of all the evil siphoned from the persona of God? That's the Devil. They're one and the same. One entirely good. The other entirely evil. Lords of their domains. One of heaven. The other of Hell. The Absolute would be someone who distilled the good and dubbed it God, filtered the bad and called it the Devil."

"So, more powerful than both of them combined."

Lilly wiped her forehead and threw the accumulated sweat over the railing. She was red in the face, red in the eyes, her skin no longer white but an angry crimson. "You mind if we continue the rest of this conversation inside? I could die."

"So could I."

* * *

Once they were both in Lilly's bedroom and Lilly was no longer wearing her drenched attire but a bathrobe, her hair wet, her body cooled by the quick shower she'd taken to get rid of the stench and heat, Joe sat in what he'd jokingly labeled the 'cuckold chair' in the room. There was one in every hotel room, a solitary sofa in one corner of the room, which, according to Joe, would serve no other purpose than to seat a cuck as he'd observe whatever transpired on the bed in front of him.

As he sat in the cuck chair, so close to a very naked Lilly under the bathrobe, he felt cucked. It was the bathrobe enjoying all the action, rubbing against her nude skin, soaking up her wetness, and he, who had neither bathed nor changed but had instead waited patiently in the chair while she did, was just watching, his cock stirring but rendered effete because of inaction.

Dude. What the fuck am I thinking? Joe wondered and tried to pass it off as his being high, but he knew that wasn't entirely it. Some part of him had always wanted to get back with her. Some part of him had wanted to relive that day over and over again, when she'd sat on top of him and straddled his dick.

"Joe!" Lilly clapped her hands. "Are you still high?!"

"And you aren't?" He stuttered, coming back to the present moment, as hard as that was to do.

"I am. I was just checking to see if you were."

"I'm as blazed as the Burning Man effigy, Lil."

"Cool. What *was* I saying before?"

"I don't know. We were going on about the Absolute. And you said that you could die."

Lilly gleamed toothily, and then said, "Our lives are fucked up enough with one God and one Devil. Do you really want to open a whole new can of worms where there's a universe with a God and a Devil apiece and one Grand Overseer above them all called the Absolute?"

"You're right, that sounds a whole lot like the weed talking," Joe said. It was now his voice that was slurring out of tiredness.

"No more left-hand-path shamans, Joe. I'm warning you," Lilly said. "No Aghori babas, no sheep blood letters in the mountains of Afghanistan, no voodoo mamas in Africa. Got it?"

"A bit racist, jeez, but, yeah."

"And no relic chasing in Iraq. What are you trying to do, get us all killed? Or worse yet, make a laughingstock out of the Morning Star movement and make sure no one ever takes us seriously? It's Iraq, we shouldn't be glorifying it."

Lilly's bathrobe, at that moment, accidentally slipped, revealing her breasts. She hurriedly reached forward to cover herself, but when she saw just how mesmerized Joe was, her grip loosened on the bathrobe, and she let it fall on either side, her wet breasts out in the open.

"Is...this...is this like," Joe was lost for words, his mouth going extremely dry and not because of the hash, his jaw hanging loose as he looked at her naked form seeped in feminine graze. "The carrot after the stick?"

"If you'd rather I followed it with another stick, I have a travel-sized one in my luggage. If that's more your speed, want me to go get it?"

"No," Joe shook his head, and as he did so with such blatant innocence, he no longer felt like the antichrist nor the leader of a religious movement. He felt like a lost boy being guided by a strong, matronly force. His gaze was brimming with vulnerability as he asked, afraid as he'd ever been, "What does this mean? For us? Are we...are we still friends?"

What he failed to bring himself to say, even in such a compromised mental state, in the privacy of this hotel room, was that while he might have felt fondly toward Joph or Tasha, the woman after his own heart from the very start had been Lilly, and he'd never been able to shake her from his system. He'd have pursued it, whatever it was that he thought they had, if not for her rule.

"Would you shut up and come here?" There was an imposing command in her voice as she slowly opened her legs, revealing more of herself.

"Not until I know what this is," Joe gulped. "I am afraid. Of being hurt again. Of losing someone close to you."

Lilly closed her legs and covered herself with the bathrobe once more. She got off the bed and came over to Joe, going down on her knees in front of him, placing her hands on his knees, and looking at him earnestly, a faint smile on her face, hope in her eyes. When she spoke, it was with the utmost softness, "When you and I had our infamous spat, I felt like I'd lost you forever. I was there all along. When you were raising the dead in front of the world, I was sitting in the audience going 'What the absolute fuck!' When the book became an international bestseller and you founded your movement, I was there at your first sermon, thinking 'There's no way this ends well.' And when you came back to me, I was like, leave him Lilly. He's an agent of darkness through and through, and I'd already seen that darkness manifest. I was going to keep my distance."

"Then why didn't you?" Joe leaned back in the chair, letting Lilly lean forward, her lips inches away from his. His heart had never beat this hard, and that was saying something.

"Because you've been trying to come out from under the influence. I feel it. Even if you hadn't come clean earlier today, I knew it. You're reclaiming the person you used to be, before all this mess. And let's just say that I have a soft spot for those who redeem themselves. Satan, despite all his powers, influence, and the time he's had on his hands, has never sought to redeem himself. And here you are, not even half a year after dealing with the literal circus that your life's become, you're trying to do better. I was wrong, Joe. You did not lose your humanity as I thought you would. Somehow, despite it all, you're more in touch with it than most of us. And as much as of an idiot you are, you're an honest idiot. You've decided to put your faith in something better than a God who wouldn't ever reveal himself or a Devil who won't ever let go of you. You've put your faith in us. Those close to you."

"You're close to me," Joe whispered, putting his hands on her naked shoulders, the bathrobe slipping off her body and piling on the floor. "Always have been. I've always been afraid to tell you how I really think of you."

"Then say it now, and make it all okay," she said, her wet hair coolly serenading his hot face, her lips brushing against his cheeks.

"I love you, and I never want to lose you," Joe sobbed.

"Now's not the time you weep," Lilly put her finger on Joe's lips. "No mourning. Not the dead. Not what you lost. Be with me. And I will be with you. Listen to me. I will heed what you say."

"But your rule," Joe, ever the anal-retentive, blurted.

"Fuck 'em. We're in uncharted waters, sitting in India high on dead people. The rules applied to us when you were a writer and I was a literary agent. You're not just a writer any longer and I'm not a literary agent and we ain't in Kansas anymore. They won't do us any good here. Now, why don't you be a good boy and be quiet."

"Yes, ma'am."

The Calm

When she did it, she did it with a gentleness that Joe was not aware Lilly was capable of, her wet hair in a tight bun, her head between his naked thighs, his jeans around his ankles.

Joe moaned.

Her hands reached up into his shirt, touching his scarred torso, her fingers lingering on each healed wound, touching it with affection as she felt his body. He did not dare move his hands lest this was a wild dream and the slightest movement on his part would wake him up.

Yet that did not stop his cock from throbbing in her mouth. She had her lips wound tight around it, her tongue sliding along its length as she lowered her head and swallowed it all, her lips touching his balls, spit slobbering, the deep suction and tight warmth of her throat setting fireworks along the length of his soaked, constricted frenulum.

He could feel her breasts heaving on his thighs as she released his shaft from the grip of her mouth, but before he could have a second to catch his breath, she abruptly lowered her head as far as it could go, pulsating fresh pleasure along his penis.

His addled state of mind was not just a state of mind; it had rendered his entire body sensitive, allowing him to feel more than what was—the slow and heavy trickle of fresh, thick saliva on his dick, the utter softness of the inside of her mouth, the vacuous pull of her throat as she gulped his precum and licked vehemently, her tongue reaching down to his testicles, kindling all the nerve-ends down there.

It was pure madness, this epitomal ecstasy that overtook him, forcing him to relinquish all control to the goddess who held dominion over his nervous system merely with her mouth, causing him to convulse but unable to move under her weight, making him come out of submissive frenzy, his cock throbbing as his ejaculate shot deep into her throat.

Torturous was the way she kept on sucking, her lips clasping tight lest any of his exudence leaked out, the softer inside of her lips massaging his tip as she pulled and lolled and went all in once more.

It had happened before, this rare event where his physiology seemed to forget all about the refractory period, and now it was happening again, with Joe's cock showing no signs of yielding.

Only now, he was done being submissive.

He grabbed onto her wrists, and promptly pulled her up with as much force as could still be labeled gentle and not aggressive. Lilly let him guide her; Joe lay her down on the bed, and lowered himself upon her. Lilly wiped her wet mouth with the back of her hand, welcoming Joe by wrapping her arms around him.

He lay on top of her, both of them purely naked, and reached down to kiss her, tasting a little of himself still lingering on her lips. Lilly traced her hands along his back, and stopped at the place where his wings used to be. She broke the kiss off and pulled her head back saying, "Will you do it in...umm..."

"My demonic form?"

"I wouldn't go so far as to call it demonic, but yeah."

"I don't have my wings."

"Hey, neither do the rest of us. I just want to see if it feels different."

"You'd be my first."

"As I've always been."

Smiling, Joe tapped into his latent form, his skin glowering as it turned from pale white to a deeper color, his tail writhing out of him and slithering along the length of Lilly's body, entwining her. His skin felt hotter, but the coolness coming from her still somewhat wet body felt wonderful on his Hellion body.

He was bigger than he previously was, his form broader,

and the part of him that was soon to enter her felt coarser, thicker, longer. He nudged it gently toward her vulva, and she did the rest, easing it inside of her, accommodating its entire length with ease, her face bearing the radiance of carnal pleasure as he thrust himself inside her.

No matter how hot his skin seemed to burn, it did not seem to perturb Lilly; it only served to increase the pitch of her rhythmic moans as he coiled his leg around her thigh and started thrusting harder, without holding himself back anymore.

Lilly dug her nails into Joe's back and drew blood as she scratched along his length. As much bearable pain this brought on, it also brought forth great pleasure, making Joe pin her hands by her sides as he rode her, his form growing stronger, his tail constricting her harder.

She freed one hand and reached for his face, touched the horns protruding from his forehead, and then hooked her fingers around his neck, pulling him onto her, kissing him on the lips, sucking on his tongue, inviting it deeper into her mouth.

Her raw beauty, the softness of her skin, the heightened sensitivity, the unbridled way in which she moaned upon the apex of each stroke, and the unadulterated affection he could feel emanating from her whole body caused him to relent and lose control of his faculties once more.

He felt her come before he could, squirming and squeezing his whole length tightly. Lilly's eyes went up, her mouth open wide, and seeing her like that was what tipped Joe over. He came as he bit down on her lower lip.

It was not a sensation that confined itself to his penis, for the pleasure traveled everywhere, finding nerve-end after nerve-end, lighting his whole body in a fire that pleased instead of burned, and while Joe was still lost in the throes of sexual euphoria, he felt another extreme sensation burst forth from his back.

"Holy shit," Lilly exclaimed, the lilt of her voice affected by the orgasm she was still experiencing. But it was not his body she was witnessing that made her exclaim; it was what was behind it.

Feeling the sudden weight on his back, Joe pulled back and looked to his left, staring into the dressing table's wide mirror in amazement and post-coital bliss.

They were not the same ones as the Devil had torn.

In fact, there was nothing Hellish about them.

And yet, one could not say that they were angelic in nature, for these were not white wings freshly sprouted from his back but dark gray ones, reminiscent more of a raven's wingspan than an angel's or demon's. Wings like before, that could be hidden from public view, only to appear when Joe needed them.

"As long as I live, I don't think anything will ever top the pure metal nature of what I just saw!" Lilly exclaimed from behind him, her fingers running along his new wings.

"I don't get it. He said he'd return them if I earned them," Joe said, flexing his new wings.

"Maybe they were never his to return," Lilly said, reaching out from behind him and placing her hand on his chest, calming his erratic heartbeat. Joe turned around and kissed her on the forehead.

"Maybe you outgrew your need for the ones that he gave you, and grew your own."

"Let's not let these," Joe said, flexing his wings, "distract from what just happened."

"A lot happened."

"And all of it good."

"Don't you go falling in love with me, Banbury," Lilly grinned, lying back in bed, admiring Joe's form.

"Too late for that," Joe said, letting go, and turning back to ordinary Joe. "I do love you, you know."

"I know," Lilly said, pulling him back in bed such that they lay side by side. "I love you too."

She kissed him tenderly on the cheek, and then fit herself snugly in his arm.

"A few more minutes until we're sober and under his unholiness's watchful gaze again," Joe said, the sudden reminder a symptom of his resurfacing clear-headedness.

"Sleep, Joe, and know some peace for a spell. We have a six-hour flight to Baghdad tomorrow. We're going to need our rest."

"Why are we going to Iraq again?"

"Because when you speak from a pulpit in the cradle of civilization, the world will listen," Lilly said, her voice getting drowsy.

"You should have never quit poetry," Joe commented, himself being lulled away to the province of dreams and desires.

"Who says I quit?"

Before he could investigate on the matter, Lilly was snoring, and the contagiousness of her gentle snores brought on a deep, dreamless slumber for Joe.

11

BILLY HAWTHORNE

The Prophet of Madness

With his throat hoarse from having smoked half a pack of Newports, and the arthritis in his fingers making his joints scream in stiff agony, Billy Hawthorne sat hunched in front of his old desktop, typing away with a smoldering cigarette jutting out from between his teeth, his eyes bloodshot and tired from staring at the screen, and all of his attention focused on the words that flowed from his fingers and not on the corpse of his headless brother standing in the doorway.

It was three in the morning when *The New York Daily's* editor called him, hoping to wake him from his sleep, but Billy had never gone to bed. Most days, he never went to bed at night. If it wasn't work, then it was the vestiges of his unresolved childhood trauma in the phantasm form of Teddy's mauled body sans its head that kept him awake.

It hadn't been his fault Teddy died. It had been his step-father's. And while Billy was sure that his step-father had never known a single night of peace in the maximum-security correctional facility in Franklin, trauma did not merely seek its perpetrators, but also its witnesses, leaving Billy with the lifelong memory of his freshly dead brother lying in the garage, the expressions of fear frozen on his bloodied head a meter away, and the rest of his body lying in a pool of his blood, clutching Mr. Thompson the teddy bear.

Teddy was six when his stepfather, in a drunken rage, decided to take a fire-axe to his neck when he wouldn't stop crying. He'd been crying because he'd been unable to find Mr. Thompson. Billy, twelve back then, had given in to Teddy's tantrum and had helped him find the dusty, missing-eyed teddy bear in the garage, but by then it had been too late.

Billy still had the eighteen-inch scar running diagonally along the length of his torso to remind him of Blake's madness. Tall for a twelve-year-old, he'd held off his deranged stepfather for long enough until the cops arrived, but not without suffering major injuries.

When he came to three days later in the hospital, his mother, who had lost half her weight apparently in the past three days, sat by his side with her hands clasped around his, and much to Billy's dismay, she too bore marks of that night's violence on her face. Her eyes were sunken from weeping inconsolably. One son struck dead, the other in the hospital with fatal injuries.

There wasn't even a trial. They sentenced Blake to life behind bars for murder, attempted murder, assault and battery, and rape charges.

But it was not enough. Not in terms of justice. Not in terms of righting any wrong.

A year later, his mother took her life in the same garage, damning him to five years of foster care and a life's worth of pain that no one human should ever have to carry.

And so, on the nights that he had no work and ol' headless Teddy forgot to haunt his older brother, Billy did fall asleep. He fell asleep to the sight of his oscillating mother, the human pendulum hanging from the rafters by a rope.

It was still a better fate, having to experience the horrors of his past life, than having to take the lethal cocktail of haloperidol, olanzapine, and risperidone and God knew what else his state-appointed shrink had prescribed him for the hallucinations and the depression, because while the meds did curtail the madness, they also jammed his entire system, rendering him an oozing, heart-palpitating, dazed and dizzy slob who couldn't get up from his bed to get a glass of water if his life depended upon it. Such curative indolence did not befit a high-stakes journalist who was the sole reason *The New York Daily* still hadn't declared bankruptcy.

"Not now, Teddy. This is important," Billy snapped, shrugging off his brother's hand from his shoulder, and leaning so close to the screen that if it were a portal, he'd have fallen in. He'd just finished writing the events that had transpired nearly six thousand miles away and had to hit send before the printing press came alive.

The Dead Not the Only Thing Banbury Can Raise

Iraq: No later than a week after a UN-led archeological mission unearthed a statue of the Amorite King Hammurabi in the ruins of Babylon sixty miles south of Baghdad, Joseph Banbury landed in the country along with the upper management of The Morning Star (TMS). While pundits were still discussing if this was a coincidence, Mr. Banbury, self-anointed antichrist and mouthpiece of the biblical Satan, gave rousing speeches in Basrah, Nasiriyah, and Baghdad, calling for interfaith collaboration, coexistence, and the dawn of a new understanding of science, faith, and humanity.

Unfortunately for Mr. Banbury, his actions did not align with his statements, as later that week he found himself at the heavily surveilled excavation site. Around the same time as when Banbury had finished giving yet another speech on the importance of restoring the narratives of old civilizations, a group of vandals, taking advantage of the distraction that was Joseph Banbury's public and televised speech, made their way into the excavation site and sought to destroy the pagan statue, because as per their beliefs, statues were antithetical to the spirit of radical Islam, and a remnant of the false ways of the ancient civilizations.

Six of the vandals escaped before they could be apprehended, destroying the statue with sticks of dynamite. Before the world could have a chance to mourn the loss of such a priceless historical artifact, the remaining member of the vandal's group, in an attempt to escape, unleashed gunfire on the guards who sought to apprehend him. He was shot and declared dead on the spot.

But Mr. Banbury, who also happened to be at the same spot, without counsel and acting out of his own undivine volition, attempted to fix the situation by bringing the dead body of the vandal back to life.

While it was a spectacle to behold for not just the people present at the spot but also for the entire world—since Mr. Banbury's speech was being televised and broadcasted—the resurrected vandal took advantage of the momentary shock and awe, and made a run for it, escaping into the desert.

Later, when the local police force cross-referenced their database, it was revealed that the very man whom Joseph Banbury had raised from the dead was Fawad Ibn-e-

Shamshi, an ISIS captain responsible for several attacks on the civilian population of Iraq and Afghanistan.

As for Mr. Banbury, he has been in the wind ever since, taking zero responsibility for having resurrected a known terrorist. When reached for comment, there was no response from his team or his vast network of TMS members. It would appear that the dead is not the only thing that Mr. Banbury can raise; because he can surely raise controversy just as well.

He knew the entire story was horseshit way before he'd even hit send on the email, but it was what the readers of *The New York Daily* wanted. The fact that he had sold out and published whatever the editor needed him to did not both Billy in the least. At ten cents per word, the four pieces that he wrote daily for the newspaper netted him an even six thousand per month. It was not much by any standards, but two of that six went into the monthly rent for this crap-hole two hundred square foot apartment in Hell's Kitchen, another two went toward bills and utilities, and whatever remained sustained him for the rest of the month. Surviving on cup noodles, stale bagels, questionable hotdogs, and crap coffee from street vendors in under two thousand a month in New York City was an art that Billy had mastered, and when he nodded at the other hard-working, blue-collared, tired-eyed men in line at said coffee stands, he knew that he wasn't the only one who had mastered it.

And just like his blue-collared brothers-in-arms put on their pants in the morning and did something that they hated every day for meager checks, he, too, put on his pants, wrote everything with a lens he disagreed with just so he could get by.

It wasn't in him to be the reporter he was back in the day,

running around with a "PRESS" vest and a dusty camera in warzones, taking pictures, recording videos, and then sending them back via satellite signals. Kabul. West Bank. Baghdad. Benghazi. He had been wherever it was that humanity showcased its worst aspects, and having written them down in every imaginable combination of put-together words, he was done.

It had done a significant number on him, having to watch people get shot before his very eyes, little kids with bombs strapped to their bodies charging at Humvees chanting Arabic, and women in black shuttlecock burqas wielding AK-47s to defend the corpses of their fallen men and children. How he had wished that a stray bullet would have his name on it and he'd be just another victim of war, caught in the crossfire. But for some reason, despite his deliberate attempts at half-hearted suicide, he hadn't died.

Here he was, back in his cockroach-infested apartment in the back alleys between West 47th and West 48th, blinding neon glaring through his windows, his dead mother and headless brother hanging around.

"You know, if you're gonna stick around as much, you might as well pitch in for rent," Billy had joked in their faces from time to time, but when he only got grunts and groans from agitated ghosts in return, he stopped making that joke. What were they going to do, sign up for entry-level jobs at an astral Seven-Eleven? Yeah, he didn't think so.

Five minutes hadn't passed since he'd sent the article when his editor rang him up again.

"Christ, Bill, you seeing the news?"

"I only got the two eyes, Brandon."

"But you gotta fucking direct those eyeballs to the TV. Just look at what's happening!"

"This better not end with me writing another article in

ten minutes, man. Aren't you set to print for the day? I'm not going to write anything else. I'm done for the day."

"Fuck the newspaper, man. Fuck the article. Just watch the news!"

Billy sighed. What had Joseph Banbury gotten himself into now? He had nothing but the deepest sympathy for the guy, and this was coming from someone who'd written no less than a hundred different character assassination pieces on him for newspapers and magazines far and wide. When it was about the antichrist, they bumped his pay. Made it easier to afford the little luxuries.

The way he saw it, he was like Mary Jane Watson from the Spiderman comics that he'd grown up reading in foster homes. In those crusty, ripped, and yellowed pages chronicling the adventures of the Spectacular Spiderman, he'd get to learn that Peter Parker's girlfriend wrote these brutal pieces against Spiderman for the man who hated him more than any other villain in the city. J. Jonah Jameson. Pete knew about it. Mary knew that it hurt him to read his own girlfriend ripping him to shreds in the news, but it was what it was. It needed to be done.

He wasn't even in love with the guy. So it probably weighed a lot less on his conscience than it did on Mary Jane's when he wrote these pieces that he did not agree with. Joe was a New Yorker, and as much as they make it out about New Yorkers being these rude pieces of shit who don't give each other the time of day, in a most literary sense, Billy could feel for Joe as more than just a New Yorker. He felt for the guy, writer to writer.

He had read Joe's books when they'd come out. While Banbury's struggle was different from Joe's, at the end of the day it was a struggle, and if Billy had a soft spot in his heart for someone other than orphans who'd gotten the shit end of the deal in their childhoods, it was people who'd been through the wringer.

He did not envy the position that Joe Banbury was in.

When Billy turned the TV on, he envied Joe even less.

A news reporter stood a safe distance away from what looked like a city in siege, reporting away on the events as they unfolded in real time.

Helicopters flew in the air, circling like vultures around a hotel that Billy was all too familiar with. The Babylon Rotana in Baghdad.

The tempest of people rose and crashed against the hotel's building like crashing waves. The police and the military were trying their best (or were they now? Thought Billy) to curtail the people with batons and riot shields, but what they lacked in numbers and motive, the mob of frenzied people happened to possess. They were fighting the guards at the gates of the hotel, hitting the locked entrance with their makeshift weapons.

Knowing what he knew, Billy was certain it was only a matter of time before these people would ditch their sticks and batons for actual weapons. He had seen this kind of escalation before.

The reporter, a woman with a tightly wound headscarf around her head and a red BBC mic in her hands, spoke into the camera with a shaky voice. "The foreign delegation led by Joseph Banbury has sought refuge from the crowd of angered Iraqis in the penthouse of the Babylon Rotana. The American Embassy has tried to extract them without success. With such a crowd surrounding the hotel, and the sentiments of millions of Iraqi Muslims hurt at the display of Mr. Banbury's allegedly satanic abilities, it's only a matter of time before this rapidly growing mob makes it beyond the hotel's gates and charges the hotel in search of Joseph

Banbury. Honestly, I'm not sure why he came here in the first place."

She intended to speak further on the matter, but someone close by shot a burst of AK-47 fire into the sky, which started a compound effect where everyone who possessed a gun in the mob started to shoot skywards, causing people to scream more agitatedly, and the havoc to exponentiate.

The reporter, a person whom Billy actually happened to know on a first-name basis, ducked rather adeptly behind the news van, continuing her report. Billy changed the channel. There was a good chance that Rashida might get shot on live television, and he was neither drunk enough nor sober enough to watch that unfold before his eyes.

Billy switched to CNN, where a panel of pundits were heatedly discussing the United States's involvement in this affair.

Samantha Robert, a seasoned pundit, pointed her finger at Farah Abraham, stating rather aggressively, "In 2011, when Raymond Davis murdered those two Pakistani men in Lahore, what did the United States do? They got involved. They helped Davis pay 2.4 million dollars to the families of the men Davis had killed, and then they extracted him. They extracted him, because that's what Americans do. We look after our own."

Farah had had enough of Samantha's bull. She had been listening to her fellow pundit with a vexed smile, lips pressed so close together that they might rip from pressure. She raised her index finger threateningly, adjusted her headscarf, and then shook her head. "Davis was CIA. Read a newspaper, for crying out loud, Samantha. Isn't that your entire job? He was there on behalf of the American army. It's clear that Davis was there for wetwork. He got caught. Of course, the government had to step in and rescue him. Joe Banbury, on the other hand, is not operating under the government's order. This whole thing is entirely his idea. The way I see it, he may be a US citizen, but he landed himself in this mess. Not CIA. Not the army. This is his mess. He gets to deal with it on his own."

A rather renowned for his atheistic worldview late-night host, laughed condescendingly, cutting Farah short.

"Farah," the late-night host said. "I wonder if the bias in your contrived statement arises from the fact that you're half-Iraqi, and a full Muslim, as I take it. You had no problems with Joe when he was in Switzerland or India. Hell, I don't think you even know of his journey. The moment he steps on Islamic soil and does something that does not align with your religion's worldview, you get all hot and bothered and detract the original problem."

"Bill," Farah snapped, rolling her eyes, facilitating the quick descent of this talk show into anarchic clownery. "I identify as a Muslim, yes, and I have no problem with Joe Banbury's religious viewpoints. Much of what he says actually aligns with a lot of what my religion states about Satan. So he's right on the money with that. But you don't care about seeing me agree with someone as controversial as Banbury, and that's why you're clueless that I've done a whole podcast series supporting Joe's cause. But to enter the den of a lion and shove a stick up that sleeping beast's butt is a recipe for getting yourself killed quickly. That's what Joe has done, and I cannot condone it. Here, in America, when someone does something that incites public outrage, they're immediately canceled, forced to make an apology, and then have to live the rest of their lives in the shadows, away from mainstream acclaim. What's happening to Joe Banbury is the Iraqi version of getting canceled."

"You might be right, Farah," the late-night host said, consulting his notes. "But in that part of the world, you get canceled, they chop your head off. Would you rather they chop off Joe's head along with the heads of every American who's there with him, and that incites—"

"Let me guess, war in the Middle East?" Farah spat.

"Folks!" Samantha stepped in. "There's another development. Our correspondent in Baghdad has just informed us of what's happening at the Babylon Rotana. Over to you, Sahif."

The screen cut off to Sahif standing outside of the Baghdad Governorate, mic, helmet, jacket, and all. "Thank you, Samantha."

Billy shut the TV off, rubbing his eyes, only to turn it on again the next second. He had to see what was happening. This was like one of those roadside car accidents. You wanted to take your eyes off, but you couldn't.

He switched to BBC again, which was thankfully showing the events and not pundits going for each other's throats. Rashida, the BBC correspondent in Iraq, was still alive, but from the looks of it, it did not look like Joe Banbury would last the night.

"The mob has broken through the gates of the hotel and has charged into the hotel. Presently, the Iraqi military is trying to control the situation with attempts to disperse the crowd, but from the looks of it, there are more people inside the hotel than there are outside."

The mess—for what could you call it other than that? thought Billy—was inexpungible. The same people who had been teetering off the edge of the fence when Joe had been giving his speeches around Babylon now sought to kill him. Billy had lived among these people, was deeply aware of their beliefs. He could make out the chants in Arabic.

"Iqta'u ra's al-Masih ad-Dajjal!"

Off with the antichrist's head.

The conviction in their chants left no room for giving Joe the benefit of the doubt. They had seen him bring an ISIS captain back to life. If everything they had seen before were carefully put-together camera tricks, this was real. Their own media wouldn't lie to them. And so many of them had seen the whole thing unfold before their very eyes.

This man wasn't just dangerous. He was the antichrist. That's what every Iraqi rushing that building thought. Killing him and his associates would be the highest form of jihad. Billy could see it in the eyes of the half-hearted soldiers and police officers that they had no real intention of stopping the mob. They believed in the same thing.

His phone rang out of nowhere, giving Billy a heart attack. Once he was done recuperating from the shock of it, he picked up the call and barked, "What!?"

"Where's the article?"

"What fucking article?"

"The one about the shit happening in Iraq right now."

"It doesn't get printed until tomorrow. Why do you want it?"

"For the newspaper's website! Now, where is it?"

"You think I pull these words out of my ass?"

"I don't care, Billy. I'm giving the readers a play-by-play of this shitshow. I need an article five minutes ago!"

"That's not in the contract. I write four pieces a day. No more."

"I don't care about the contract. Since when have I ever stuck to all the terms in the contract, Billy? I don't pay you according to the contract. Hell, none of the other editors expect me to abide by it. This is journalism. You know this.

Come on, do me a favor. Write me this one, and I'll call it a day."

"It's already a day. The next day. And by the way, you should be careful of what you say on the phone. You never know if the person on the other end's recording the call," Billy, who'd just about had it up to here with Brandon's shit, stated with a sudden coolness flowing down his body.

"Is that a threat?" Brandon stuttered, more so out of confusion than fear. He wasn't the kind of person to take his medicine quietly.

"Yeah. Now. How do you want to do this? I have you on the phone, admitting you don't honor contracts. What's it going to be? You gonna let me off the leash or am I smelling a lawsuit brewing?"

"Billy, you listen," Brandon spoke slowly, his voice rising with his temper.

"No, you listen. I'm not doing this anymore. You clear this month's payment and let me go. I'll look for greener pastures elsewhere. As far as they know, they need journalists to write about potatoes in Idaho. The rent and utilities don't give you a coronary. Consider this my quitting notice."

"I don't have to pay you jack if you quit."

"I know, but I'd rather you pay me my six grand rather than the six hundred thousand that you'll eventually have to pay if I turn this into a class action. There are two dozen writers and five sub-editors under your employment. I don't hate you. I never did. I just hate whatever this thing I'm doing. I'm done sitting on the sidelines. I'm a wartime reporter, Brandon."

"So what is it? Is it wartime reporting or writing about potato yields in Idaho?"

"I don't know."

"Well, when you put it like that, man. I don't hate you

either. It's just business. Tell you what. We don't need to end it like this. You go do whatever it is you want to do, and I'll clear your latest payment with a hefty bonus. Christ, Billy. You're my best writer, man. I wouldn't want you hanging me out to dry."

"What are you proposing?" Billy asked, staring at an apathetic sun's rays crawl above the rooftops, burning away at his retinas. For once, he wanted the sun to lose this game of not blinking. It always ended up being Billy who had to look away with the sun's image burned in his eyes.

"I've known you for a long time. You're always chasing stories. You know what they call you over here at the office?"

"I know," Billy said, nodding, grimacing. He wasn't a fan of it. It was a jab at his mental health.

"I don't think you're a prophet of madness. I think you prophesize the storm and then chase that storm. Wherever you're going, whatever it is you're doing, and I know that you're going to do something. I didn't whiten my hair sitting in the damn sun, you know."

"I know, Brandon. And thanks."

Billy ended the call, knowing full well that Brandon was calling him every swear word in the book, and quite a couple off-book. If he hadn't been so scared shitless to cover his base in the recorded call—and Billy always recorded all his calls—he might have said a couple of those words on the phone, but that'd establish a precedent for hostile workplace practices and add a couple of thousand dollars to the hypothetical lawsuit payout.

So far, Billy hadn't looked away from the sun. Tears ran down his face, his mind repeating the mantra "blink," willing the sun to look away, the sane part of his brain aware that such a thing was scientifically impossible.

And yet.

A fleeting cumulonimbus came between Billy and the sun, declaring the stare-off a stalemate.

"Good enough," Billy grunted and looked away, his patchy vision finding the familiar and far more sweltering sight of his dead brother standing there in the doorway.

Anything was better than seeing him there day in, day out.

"I'm leaving, Teddy. Make sure you tell Mom. I won't be around for some time. Maybe I won't come back at all. But you take good care of yourself and her in the meantime. Kay?" Billy addressed his brother as he packed in quick time. His jeans, t-shirts, camera, laptop, iPhone charger and his PRESS vest.

The corpse's neck went taut and loosened, indicating that if there was a head, it'd be nodding.

"Thanks, kid," Billy said, placing his hand on Teddy's shoulder as he exited his tiny apartment. "I love you."

He took his keys and wallet from the door side stand, turned the knob, and stepped outside, but not before hearing Teddy say, "I love you, too."

His hands shivered as he closed the door on the other side, knowing that there was no way his brother had talked to him for the first time ever since his apparition had appeared.

Billy locked the door and raced down the steps, not looking behind.

They were always there if he looked behind.

The Back Alley Oracle

The first time Billy had laid eyes on the crumpled up, beaten-the-shit-out-of, shit-caked-to-the-seats-of-his-pants, puke-running-down-his-jacket junkie, it had been five years ago when Leonard—the miserable man in question—was being shot at point blank range by two red-masked thugs. Billy had watched the whole thing unfold from the fire escape stairs of his apartment and had stayed put until the thugs had left the scene after stealing something from Leonard.

Later on, when Billy had descended the stairs and administered first aid on the shot man, he'd learned through the inane ramblings that they'd taken the monkey on his back. He needed the monkey back.

Billy, who himself had the same monkey on his back in his twenties, knew all too well how dicey that whole situation got when you asked for more from your dealer and didn't have the money for it. He'd stood on the other side of a pointed gun quite a few times himself, but luckily, hadn't ever been shot.

After gauzing him up and getting him to the ER, Billy had sat there in the hallway outside, waiting for the doctors to fix him up.

The next day, the senile, white-eyed junkie was sitting there in the back alley next to his shopping cart full of his belongings like nothing was the matter and that he hadn't been shot just twelve hours ago.

"What the fuck?" Billy had asked.

"Eh, whatchu gonna do when goons shoot at you? Move? Where? Ol' Nelson lives in the next street over, that's his fucking area. This is my place. Them motherfuckers wanted to own this corner to sling their shit."

"Fair enough." Back in those days, Billy actually went to the newspaper's office downtown every day. He was already ten minutes late as it was.

"Hey, spare an old man a dollar?"

"All right."

"Bless ya!"

"Not lately."

Regardless of whether that dollar-a-day thing blessed him or not, Billy didn't skip a day for the past five years.

Heading out of the back alley, he saw Leonard sitting there, a coffee cup full of quarters by his feet, cigarette hanging from his droopy mouth, his cataract eyes staring into the distance.

"Hey, Lenny," Billy said, putting the dollar bill in the coffee cup. "Doing all right?"

"I am doing just fine, Billy. How's about yourself, son?" Lenny looked up despite being blind, affecting Billy with a familiar smile.

"I just wanted to say goodbye, Lenny."

"You're going somewhere?"

"I don't really know what I'm going to do. There's things that won't let me stay put in that apartment, and I'm all paid up on rent for another month. So, like, if you want to crash there, here's the keys."

"And get there how, numbnuts? I'm blind," Lenny cracked up, throwing the key back at Billy.

"Right," Billy said, leaving for the street. As much as he hated stepping out into daylight, and he suspected it was probably because of his Transylvanian roots, it was good to step out into the day. Day meant no more ghosts.

"But not to your journey," Lenny called out right as Billy was about to turn the corner. His remark made Billy stop dead in his tracks and look back.

"What did you say?"

"I'm not blind to your journey," Lenny said, staring at the brick wall ahead of him, holding his coffee cup full of quarters as if he was about to take a sip from it. He brought it up to his nose and then sniffed generously, then placed it back.

"Smell of pennies. Never quite leaves you when you're a beggar. Ever thought about it? Smells of blood. Every amateur writer uses that expression to describe blood, know what I'm saying?"

"I was once one of those writers," Billy said, walking back to Lenny. Sticking around him for a few more minutes was the least he could do. Who knew when he'd see Lenny next. If he'd see him at all.

"You were once many things. I think you's seen more things than most see."

"And have you?"

"I wasn't always cataracted, if that's what you're asking. I been here. I been there. A little all over the place. I know a lil something something about some things," Lenny stated, lighting a soggy cigarette. The whimsy that had possessed him was characteristic of every high individual ever, and considering that Billy was often that individual on weekends, he didn't need to sniff the odor of rank hash wafting from Lenny's body to know that the old junkie was baked out of his gourd. "And I'm not blind to your journey."

"You keep saying that. What does that mean?"

"It means that I can see that destiny's jizzed all over you, splattering its mark on your soul."

"Pretty sure I didn't consent to fate bukkakying on me, but thanks," Billy commented as he sat beside the junkie, resting his back against the brick wall, taking his own cigarette out and lighting it up.

"There's a war going out there, son."

"There's always a war going on somewhere, Lenny."

"Listen to me," Lenny stated, putting his fingers sternly around the back of Billy's neck and wringing it in his direction. Lenny's eyes slid up his socket, leaving pure white in their absence. "The hour is nigh when one Epoch ends in favor of another. Are you going to be the wind of change or will you be the obstinate who stands in its way?"

"Lenny, what the fuck are you talking about?" Billy attempted to free himself from Lenny's grip, but the old man's grip was hard as an arachnid's pincers, unrelenting, painful.

"No God above God is a lie perpetuated over the centuries like hours by weak men who crave temporary powers. Real power resides within. Wherein? It's not something you find on a whim. It takes you to the precipice. To the brim. And then beyond it. It tests you to see if you really want it. The wager, boy, the wager. The test that tests us all. Polypolarity in a bipolarized world. One world of many where God resides on throne-top and the Devil was hurled. It's relatives and relatives all the way down. Where is the Absolute?"

Lenny was foaming at the mouth, his entire body convulsing, his grip on Billy's neck growing tighter as the old man bled through his nose. When Billy finally freed himself from Lenny's grip, he grabbed hold of the overdosing man and wiped his face clean.

"HELP!" Billy screamed to anyone who'd listen, his shaky hands dialing 9-1-1.

"911, what's your emergency?"

"There's a guy overdosing on West 48th. He needs Narcan!"

"Sir. I want you to stay on the line—"

Lenny, or whoever was possessing his body in this prophetic moment, slapped the phone away from Billy's hand and held onto both his hands, still foaming, still bleeding, still convulsing.

"The madness beckons the prophet of madness and so he must listen before it is too late," Lenny was speaking faster than his mouth would allow, his teeth cutting on his tongue, drawing more blood as he spat a spray of white foam and red all over Billy's white shirt. "The madness beckons the prophet of madness and so he must do before no one can do it. Guide the damned to beyond salvation and damnation. To the precipice where it awaits."

Induced into the reverie that Lenny had been entrancing him in with his oracular words, Billy looked into the blind man's eyes and asked, his voice no more than a hoarse squeak. "Where what awaits?"

"The Epoch."

A group of passersby had stopped at the entrance to the back alley and were looking at Billy bent over the convulsing man.

"I have Narcan!" One of them shouted, racing toward them. He skidded to a halt and landed on his knees beside Lenny's body, shoving Billy aside. "Move over. I'm an EMT."

Billy wanted to move over. But Lenny wasn't letting go of his hands.

"Follow the fire," Lenny whispered, squeezing Billy's hands tightly one last time, then letting go forever.

As the EMT administered Narcan, Billy hoped more than anything that Lenny would come to and sometime later, everything would be back to normal. They'd have a laugh about him going into the fifth dimension thanks to the monkey on his back, and he'd make yet another promise to quit at the end of the year, and that'd be that. On December 31st, Billy would remind him that it was quitting time. Lenny would flip him the bird and say, "Mind your damn business, ya fucking newshound."

None of that would come to pass.

Despite the EMT's timely administration of Narcan, Lenny did not shift, the foam and blood drying around his open mouth, his milky eyes staring at the sun, overhead, winning the staring contest until the off-shift EMT closed them and declared the time of death.

"Jesus, fuck," Billy whispered, his heart squelching arrhythmically in his chest, the pain from its irregular beating traveling to his arm, his lower abdomen, and his neck.

He grabbed a fistful of his hair and tugged at it, realizing fully that it was a self-soothing mechanism he hadn't quite kicked since his toddler years.

Little did it offer him in the way of soothing.

Follow the Fire

There was another location, one which neither Billy's enterprising landlord nor his editor, knew about. At times, even Billy forgot that he had a storage unit at Gotham Mini Storage, one which served not just as a place where he kept stuff that he had no room for in his apartment but also as his office for when things got too loud at his apartment.

It was where he went to regain his sanity. He had never stayed there long enough for the ghosts in his head to become acquainted with the place and haunt it. That had always been Billy's rule number one. This was a safe space, but it was only safe as long as he visited it for no longer than forty minutes. Past the forty-minute mark, his mother conveniently hung herself from the rafter and his brother started a fucked up version of the Easter Egg Hunt, searching for his head in all the wrong places.

Now that he was here, in this place that he considered his secret lair of sorts, not that he possessed any of the virtues to consider himself a vigilante (as per his own assessment of his psyche), Billy turned the lights on and collapsed against the boxes of his old belongings, his throat constricted, nausea traveling up his nasal cavity, threatening to unleash the acidic contents of his stomach.

As much as he wanted to believe that this was a manic episode, he knew that it wasn't. Everyone on the street had seen Lenny die. The EMT kept pestering him about what the old man meant when he said "Follow the fire."

Billy didn't stick around long enough to give the cops a statement. This was New York. Cops seldom came on time to get statements pertaining to the death of junkies. If he'd stayed, he might have had to wait for another hour for anyone to show up and take the body away and jot down witness statements.

The words that Lenny had spurted out in his delirious death throes clung to the surface of his consciousness like bugs on fly paper. Like bugs thrashing away against the domineering stickiness of the paper, the words, too, poked and pinched and prodded, driving Billy crazy.

"Enough," Billy whispered to himself, getting up from the floor, and heading to the back wall of the storage unit where he kept his desk and hung his corkboard. He turned the lamp on and shone it at the corkboard, looking at the meticulous web of red ribbons connecting every facet of Joe Banbury's public life.

From his meteoric rise after the publishing of his first book to his most recent trip to India, it was all there, mapped out on the corkboard. The only missing pieces were ones that had yet to make it to print in today's newspaper.

The oldest newspaper cutouts were almost a decade old.

This side-project had started out of sheer skepticism, and while at first, Billy had laughed at the irony of being skeptical of the guy who wrote *The Skeptic*, the humor quickly redacted itself from the equation as more and more of what Billy started to uncover made him less and less skeptical.

Any cynicism that Billy had went the way of 70's disco when he saw Joseph Banbury raise that little girl from the dead. He was in the audience. There were no camera tricks. The girl was dead. And the second time around, when Joseph resurrected the fanatical Cleric of Jehovah, Billy was there too. He was too drunk to ask any questions at the press conference, but not drunk enough that he couldn't call it as he saw it, and he saw a man who had been shot to death being brought back to life within moments.

There were loose red ribbons all over the corkboard, but the ones that were not loose converged at a single spot.

The Devil.

If Joe claimed that his powers were bestowed unto him by Satan, and had then subsequently proved it to the world, that pretty much took care of any disbelief that Billy had.

Next to the name of the Devil, Billy had scratched out all other questions such as "Is the Devil real?" and "Is Joseph Banbury batshit crazy?"

It took one batshit crazy to recognize another batshit crazy, and according to Hawthorne's expert opinion, Joe was certainly unhinged but not batshit crazy. The Devil in question was very much real, which then broke the back of Billy's entire atheistic argument about God not existing. If there was a Devil, then there was a God. As for what kind of fucked up God it was who allowed little boys to get their heads chopped off by maniacal step-dads and let grieving women hang from the rafter without ever offering an ounce of divine intervention, that was all up for debate, leaning in the direction that God was not all good.

Therefore, if God was not all good, then by the law of association, the Devil was not all bad.

The most recent revelation in this regard brought to him by Lenny the overdosing junkie was that there was a God above God.

The Absolute.

The only thing that had halted Billy in his tracks and had stopped him from dismissing Lenny's rants as inebriated incoherence was how coherent it all was. Lenny had known what he was talking about, and the way he had talked, it wasn't Lenny speaking to him. It was like Lenny was a telephone receiver and someone else was speaking through it. Maybe that's what killed Lenny and not the overdose, otherwise the Narcan would have worked.

"Let's not give into madness, shall we?" Billy slapped himself on the head repeatedly as he stared at the corkboard. The clock on the wall let him know that he'd been there for twenty minutes. Another twenty and the dead would show up.

He didn't have a lot of time to decide.

"Which isn't exactly true," Billy said aloud, holding his hand over his face.

Earlier that day, when Joe had packed his bags and had given his quitting notice to his boss, he'd already decided then. He had decided to chase the storm. To put his wartime reporter hat back on and get into the thick of it. That's why he had left. That's why all his most useful belongings were packed in his luggage.

If anything, Lenny's inanities had further reinforced the idea.

Follow the fire.

He'd been intending to do it for some time now.

Could there be a better opportunity than now?

"And what then, hotshot?" Billy grumbled. "What then? What happens when you uncover the story?"

I retire. The thought came to him instantaneously. This could be the one that wins you that fucking Pulitzer. Puts whatever remains of your skepticism to rest. If it's all lies, smokes, and mirrors, then you get to be the one to take the mask off the whole thing and reveal it to the world. Forget the newspaper. The New Yorker will publish your piece, pay you fifty grand for it, and next thing you know, you're accepting the fucking Pulitzer. The truest mark of a journalist, wouldn't you say?

"The truest of the true."

If it's not lies, then you get to do what you've been wanting to do all along, Billy boy. You get to join Banbury at the right moment. When he's gaining momentum. With you by his side, your wit, your way with words, and your ability to navigate through any situation no matter how FUBAR it is, he could truly be unstoppable, and you'd know, even if the world doesn't ever come to know of it, that you had a hand in it.

"But the—"

Ghosts? Horrors? Nightmares? Madness? What excuse are you looking for? If there's a cure for a condition as terminal as yours, where will you find it? The doctors who've been dosing you up with lithium in hopes of Jack diddly squat? The countless religious clerics from all sorts of denominations far and wide who only told you that the cure was in prayer? Or in the hands of someone who can literally raise the dead? He's already had his Lazarus. Would you then be his leper, that he can cure you? Would you let him cure you? Never see your dead mother and brother again? Never be haunted by the madness that's always lurking around the edge? If God, society, and the medical industrial complex have failed you at large, why not rally to the call of the man who promises to reinvent all of it?

"Stop making sense."

How about all the schizoid nonsense that Lenny blurted before he bit the dust? Concepts you've never thought about before. What's the Absolute? What's the fucking Epoch? Don't you want to know? This is your moment, is it going to be the red pill or the blue pill?

"Didn't you see?" Billy reasoned with himself. "His goose is beyond cooked. It's fucked. By now they've probably already made their way to his penthouse in the hotel. Hell, the next thing I see when I turn on a TV is Joseph Banbury's public beheading. It's too late. And even if it's not, there's nothing I can do about it."

Come now. You can lie to the world but you cannot lie to yourself. We both know that's not true. There's quite a lot you can do, Mr. Wartime Reporter.

"Why me?"

What am I, fucking Gandalf? How am I supposed to know how these things work out? But if I were to say something on the matter, it'd be that matters of madness are best left to prophets of madness. This is not the domain for the meek and sane.

While he was too busy talking to the voice inside his head, Billy forgot to keep check of the time. It was now one minute past the forty-minute mark. And now, the voice that had been tamely residing inside his head found a body to occupy.

The lamps flickered in the cramped storage unit, black ooze began dripping from the corkboard, forming a body that was an identical copy of Billy. But unlike Billy, Other Billy wore the bloodied clothes that his ex-father had worn when he'd clean-cleaved Teddy's head off with an axe. To that effect, Other Billy was wielding an axe and a macabre smile on his face, his leather jacket sporting dried blood.

"Now," Other Billy cracked his neck. "What was I saying?"

"You're not real," Billy yelled, toppling over on the boxes behind him. His mother and his brother he could handle.

They were benign reflections of his guilt. This one, the malignant reminder of his survivor's guilt, always hurt Billy when he appeared.

Other Billy with the completely black eyes and blood-drenched face chortled, swinging his axe around, the axe crashing into the corkboard and causing it to fall off the wall, his years of hard work gone.

"So you always say, Billy boy," Other Billy spat, the deliberate and hot phlegm coming into contact with Billy's face. "But then again, you also say that you didn't kill your brother. Your step-father did. You claim that your mother hung herself, but who tied the noose for her? Who gave it to her and encouraged her to end it all? What do I believe?"

It always took Billy a minute to come to terms with the appearance of this phantasm, but over the years, he'd boiled it down to a simple routine that a priest would call an exorcism and a psychiatrist might dub the sedative effect of an antipsychotic. Billy called it a good old getting even with yourself.

"Believe this," he whispered, yanking out the Glock from his luggage and putting it to his temple.

Other Billy immediately retreated with the axe, stepping back two steps and looking at Billy with resolute dismay.

"You wouldn't."

"One of these days, and who knows, maybe it is today, I will. I blow a hole in the place where you live rent-free, motherfucker. Where will you go?"

"Don't try it," Other Billy bit his lips, his nose flaring, his grip on the axe growing tighter. "Don't."

But Billy was beyond listening. He got up off the floor and put his finger on the trigger. "What happens to my headful of ghosts when I lodge a bullet in my cranium? Do they spill on the floor of this storage unit? You wanna test my theory? Let's put it to the test!"

Other Billy stood his ground, rotating the axe in his hands, then threw it on the ground, and slammed his fist into the concrete wall of the storage unit, unleashing a yell of deep rage.

"That's what I thought," Billy said, stowing his Glock back in his luggage. "And don't follow me or nothing, ya hear? I'm headed to Iraq."

"Leaving your killer instinct behind when heading into the battlefield? We both know you won't last a second without me," Other Billy said, putting the corkboard back where it belonged on the wall, studying it.

"Leave!" Billy said, feigning courage, his pulse accelerating.

"Fine!" Other Billy glowered furiously before eventually disappearing, and Billy couldn't be more thankful.

When at last he knew that he was once again alone in the storage unit, Billy opened the filing cabinet and took out the file stowed in the back. Much of what was written on it was redacted with a censoring marker.

The part that he needed wasn't redacted.

He copied the number in his phone and took a deep breath before he dialed it. The line rang twice before a cold and unyielding voice answered.

"Hello?" The tone was unmistakable—Colonel Westbrook.

"Hawk?" Billy asked.

"Haven't been called by that name in a long time. Who is this?"

"It's Hawthorne," Billy said, steadying his voice despite his nerve ends going haywire.

"As I live and fucking breathe," Thomas 'Hawk' Westbrook drawled. "Jesus, Billy, I thought you'd died somewhere in 'Stan."

"Nah. I'm still kicking. Hey, is it still Colonel or did they finally demote your incompetent ass?"

"It's Brigadier Westbrook now, actually."

"And tell me, does a brigadier keep his old cell number? Don't they give you one of those super high-tech phones with classified numbers?" Billy joked, remembering that Hawk wasn't the hardass that people thought he was. It took him three beers to start talking in fluent Italian and serenading everyone with vaffanculo.

"We get to keep our old numbers exclusively for snicker pusses like you who have reported alongside us well enough and long enough to ask for favors, which I'm guessing you're calling me for, aren't you?"

"Well, *brigadier*, as it happens, I just so have a favor to ask."

"What kind of favor?" Hawk's voice was laced with trepidation. "And haven't you run out of them already?"

"This would be the last one."

"That's what you said last time."

"Tom," Billy said, ditching all pretense. "I need you to get me into Iraq."

There was a brief silence on the other end, and Billy could almost hear the wheels turning in Hawk's mind. Hawk's silence stretched on for a full minute until he finally spoke, his words measured and cold. "Iraq's no playground, Hawthorne, or did you forget about the last time we were there?"

"You didn't let me finish," Billy said, harnessing a little more of that faux confidence he'd put on to drive away Other Billy. "I don't just need you to get me into Iraq. I need you to extract me, too. And I won't be alone."

More silence followed on the other end of the line before Hawk spoke with deliberate finality. "No, can do." In the brief moment during which neither of them had spoken, Billy was certain that one of his staff had filled him in on what was happening in Iraq right now.

"Which part?"

"To all of it. I'm not getting you in there, and I most certainly am not getting you out of there."

"After all we've been through, Hawk?"

"Listen, Billy. I know you're in the know of things, and right now, the whole thing balances on the edge of a fucking knife. One wrong move and a full-out war breaks out. You get me? I know who you seek to extract. Our forces on the ground already escorted Banbury and his associates to an undisclosed location an hour ago. This whole thing, it's out of your depth. Leave it alone. We're figuring out which is the most diplomatic direction. Having you go down there by your lonesome and carry out an extraction mission where you have no jurisdiction nor rank would be akin to a suicide mission, and think of the fucking optics."

"Meet me in the middle, then. Can you get me to them, at least? I'll delete your number and pretend I never knew you after that. Can you do that, at least?"

Hawk sighed. "Suppose I do agree to help you go down there, what is it that you want to do anyway?"

"I'm following the fire," Billy said.

"On your head be it, then. We'll maintain plausible deniability."

"As you always do."

12

ENTER SANDMAN

In 2009, a squad of twelve soldiers was positioned north of Kandahar Airfield. It was a recon mission this squad was on, and unbeknownst to them, where they had camped out for the night was the patrol path of a Taliban platoon. If it hadn't been for Billy Hawthorne, who was outside of Kandahar city, taking pictures in hopes that they'd go well with his latest piece on the war and would earn him a promotion that'd end his long and unlucky streak of wartime correspondence, perhaps that US Army squad would have met their demise. But Hawthorne scoped out the Taliban platoon as it had just left Kandahar, and with the satellite phone the army had issued him for such exact circumstances, he alerted the higher-ups at the Airfield about the oncoming platoon, therefore saving the lives of those twelve soldiers.

One of those soldiers, a private named Thomas 'Hawk' Westbrook, would go on to achieve meteoric heights in the US Army over the next decade. Throughout both their careers, Billy and Hawk crossed paths time and again. Never did Hawk forget that if it wasn't for Billy that night, he'd have been a dead private, and it was because of this eidetic remembrance that he granted him one final favor, the keyword not being favor but final.

After fourteen hours of traveling, switching one C-130 for another, and making his way past the rather rigorous airport security at Baghdad International Airport, Billy had followed the fire some six thousand miles away.

With his luggage (missing his Glock, which he had to give to the pilot of the C-130 for safekeeping) by his feet, he stood at the airport's entrance, Arabic ringing in his ears in the form of the people arguing with each other and the call to Zuhur prayer resounding from the top of the mosque's minaret, feeling the familiarity of Middle-Eastern cacophony washing over him, comforting him.

The pilot—who had been made privy to intel by Brigadier Westbrook—had told Billy that a local contact would take him where he needed to go. His name was Abdul-Basit, and he'd be holding up a placard with the name "Mr. Pasha Khan."

"Why Pasha Khan?"

"Because your Farsi's not half bad, from what the brigadier tells me," the pilot said. "Also, you're going there guised as a Pathan, and they're the only Indigenous group with skin as white as, you know, Caucasians."

"I only know a handful of Pashto."

"That's more than what most Iraqis know, as you know," the pilot told him. "You'll be fine. Just say your salams to anyone who looks your way and wear this."

The pilot gave him a Peshawari hat with a peacock feather at the front. Putting it on, Billy felt awkward as Hell, but given his sunburnt, tired, and grimy face, he felt like he could pull off a passable Pathan impression.

Now, wearing the Peshawari hat, Billy stood remembering the phrases of Arabic that he did know. One such phrase was "La tutlek, ana sahafi," which translated to, "Don't shoot, I'm a reporter." He had *The Men Who Stare At Goats* to thank for that.

A beat-up 1999 model Toyota Corolla, unappealingly painted yellow with a taxi signal atop it stood at the end of the lane, and there, stood a middle-aged man with a placard reading "Pasha Khan."

Relieved that he wasn't deserted in Iraq—as he'd suspected—Billy approached the driver with the white stubble and said, "As-Salam-Alaikum. Anta Abdul Basit?"

The driver's eyes flashed as he considered Billy, then nodded, speaking in perfect English as he said, "Get in, Mr. Hawthorne. I've been expecting you."

He didn't need telling twice. Billy stowed his luggage in the car's trunk and got in the passenger side, strapping himself in.

"Don't do that," Abdul Basit said. "Locals don't use the seatbelt. You want to blend in, you forego safety."

"Fine," Billy said, letting go of the seatbelt.

"We have a long way ahead of us."

"Hey, how do I say, 'I'm not an American. I'm a Pathan' in passable Arabic?" Billy asked, looking for a glint of humor in the man's eyes, but he had none. He jerked his head in frustration.

"Ma ana Amriki, ana Pathan."

"Thank you."

"If the crowd gets ahold of you and yanks your pants to confirm, what then?" the driver asked.

"Well, I'm circumcised, so, go figure."

"Jew?" spat Abdul Basit.

"Hey, I'm not too crazy about this either, just so you know."

"He never told me I'd be escorting a Jew."

"Take me where I need to go and I'll pay you extra. I'm guessing you know my people are loaded with money," Billy said.

Abdul-Basit did not speak for the next hour as they exited Baghdad and headed out on the empty highway. That was fine with Billy, who was taking pictures of the aftermath of the chaos discretely with his iPhone. As they passed the hotel, Billy recorded the video of the burned gates and the bullet marks on the concrete walls.

The mob that had laid siege to the hotel was still out in droves, roaming the roads with wooden sticks and guns, eyeing everyone who drove past them.

"Where did they take 'em?"

"Undisclosed location."

That brief conversation led to another hour-long silence on both their parts, and now the scenery wasn't anything to write home about either. It was just plain desert on both sides of the road with mirages shining in the distance, the sweltering heat making the air above the sand dance like an invisible flame. Twice, they came across a herd of camels traveling along the side of the road. When they reached the third herd that was busy crossing the road, forcing them to stop the car and wait until that slow procession made its way to the other side of the road, Abdul-Basit turned his attention to Billy, who was busy taking pictures with his DSLR now. Some pictures, you just couldn't take with an iPhone.

"Mr. Hawthorne," spoke the driver in an accent that deviated from the way he had previously spoken. "Would you like to resume our last conversation?"

"What, did I suddenly stop being a jew in the last minute, or did you somehow miraculously get past your disdain for my lot?" Billy had been cooking this zinger for the past half-hour on the off-chance that the driver would resume the conversation, and he had.

"I do not see people with these manmade labels, Mr. Banbury," spoke the driver in a distinguished, calm, and familiar voice. "I see you for who you are."

Billy put down his DSLR as the last of the camels crossed the roads, and turned his attention to the driver, only to see that the driver was staring back at him with completely white eyes, vapidity covering his face.

"You?!" Billy attempted to get out of the car, only to find that the door wouldn't budge despite being unlocked.

"Me."

"Listen, whoever the fuck you are, whatever shtick you pulled last time, it caused a man I deeply cared about to die in front of my eyes. So, out with it!"

The driver shook his face, a smile appearing on his lips, as he spoke, "Leonard Whittaker was already dying when I used him as a vessel. Abdul-Basit is a healthy—albeit prejudiced—man who will not remember this conversation when I hand him back the reigns."

"Who are you?" Billy whispered, one hand gripping his DSLR, the other furtively taking out his iPhone and hitting the red record button, the camera pointed at the driver. If this was his madness manifesting itself, there'd be nothing on the video. If it wasn't, then it might be useful to have a record of what this mysterious being masquerading as different people had to say.

"Who I am is irrelevant. What I have to say, isn't," the being spoke through Abdul Basit's mouth.

"Then say it. And while you're saying things, you mind saying where we're headed? The driver's a prick. He's not telling me anything."

"If a similar worldview were perpetrated to you, you'd find that you too harbor the same prejudice and hate in your heart. Is he to blame for how his society has shaped his thoughts?"

"Jeez, man, don't get me started."

"I'd rather you sat and listened as I drive you to Waha, a city north of Baghdad, where an expat American social worker is hiding your soon-to-be friends," the driver spoke calmly, his eyes still white, his face still unassertive.

"Soon-to-be-friends? Why do you say that?"

"Because your paths entwine. For better or for worse, you will soon call some of those people your friends."

"You never said who you were."

"I am not certain you are brushed up on your religious lore to identify me if I were to tell you," The driver said. "But I am not the Devil. Nor am I God. Does that quell you?"

"It barely quells. If only, it creates more questions."

"Then stop asking those questions, and ask the right ones. Why am I here?"

"Why are you here?" Billy asked, more vexed than perplexed at the riddling nature of this conversation. Lines of questioning like these were where journalism went to die.

"To guide you along the path that you are already upon," the driver spoke, turning the car left as they headed down a different road, one leading to Waha according to the milestone marker.

"Can we skip with the riddles already?"

"If you skip with the riddles, then there's nothing left for me to say. Everything that I tell you is so shrouded in riddles and enigmas that it would take the best of both your and Mr. Banbury's brains to crack the code, and even then, I am uncertain."

"Fine. Don't skip with the riddles."

"Thank you, Mr. Hawthorne. Now I shall speak on the matter, listen to me, and listen well. Pass it on to Joseph Banbury."

Billy did as he was told. For the next hour, he listened patiently, not questioning, not challenging. This time around, there was more to wrap his head around than the dying words of his long-time junkie acquaintance.

"What do you know of the cosmic wager, Mr. Hawthorne?" the driver asked.

"Besides what Joseph Banbury wrote in his book and talked about in his speeches? Not much. I still think it's just a clever spin on biblical lore, but that's all I know."

"Suffice it to say, you are only aware of it on a surface level," the driver spoke, his white eyes still fixated on the road to Waha. "The wager is more than just a bet of passion between God and the Devil. It is a framework by which this universe operates. God aspires to see humans act benevolently out of their free will, abstaining from what are described as sins, and pursuing what he's denoted as virtues. The Devil's end of the bet is that humanity will recognize the inanity of this division between sin and virtue, and will instead seek not their ascended selves but their true ones. For some, that true self could be an enlightened self. For others, it could be as base as the people who called Sodom and Gomorrah their home. Both parties have agreed that they won't interfere in this wager other than by way of messengers. Joseph Banbury, at this moment in time, is nothing more than the Devil's messenger. As Jesus was God's."

"Sorry to cut you off in the middle of your monologue here, but you do know that I'm clinically insane, right? For all I know, this is just some elaborate trick my mind's playing on me, and I'm going down the same rabbit hole all schizophrenics and manic depressives go down. It fits the bill perfectly is all I'm saying," Billy said, his face red with the heat, dripping with sweat.

"I am aware of the horrors that haunt you, and should you choose to dismiss me as one of them, I will understand. But you have been recording me on your phone for some time now, and later on, when you replay this conversation, you will know that I am distinct from the visions you see," the driver said, both hands gripping the steering wheel at a ten o'clock angle.

"Omniscient little motherfucker, aren't you?"

"Omniscient, no. But I do possess remarkably periphery vision."

"Do I call you by any name or something? Kinda hard for me to put a name to the face what with their being no face, and no name."

"If you want to call me anything, call me Ynun."

"Okay, Ynun. What's with the infodump?"

"It is prerequisite knowledge for what follows."

"I'm all ears."

Ynun continued, his patience quite commendable. "Have you ever wondered why someone would sanction a wager? If God is the dealer at a table and the Devil is a high roller—am I using those terms the right way? I should think I am—then who is in charge of the casino with hundreds of such tables present?"

"This thought experiment goes to places my mind cannot keep up with. What are you saying, that there's someone above God?"

"I am not saying it. It has baffled me how humanity has ignored the signs of such an existence for so long. God and the Devil are two very relative beings. One cannot exist without the other. The former claims virtue as his domain, the latter sin. There is one above them both, one who oversees all the Gods and Devils in all the imaginable universes, who is not relative to anyone. Outside of all frames of reference. Beyond good. Beyond evil. The Absolute."

Ahead of them, the miles unfurled like a scroll of forgotten fables, and the beat-up, musty-smelling Toyota cut through the hot stillness of the desert, its engine a rhythmic hum against the backdrop of the desert's silence.

Barren, this landscape stretched out in silent reverence, its ochre hues merging with the endless horizon that seemed to hold the secrets of eons past, and above it all hung the sun, a relentless interrogator in an empty sky, shining its stark glare on the undulating dunes rising and falling in rhythmic waves.

Traversing this noonday inferno was no easy feat for the locals, let alone a foreign reporter who was so attuned to the cool temperatures of New York City, but this foreign reporter was more concerned with the contents of the conversation rather than the unbearable nature of the desert heat.

"So, this supreme being or Absolute as you call him," said Billy, feeling the sudden surge of power course through his body upon uttering a word that he had uttered countless times before, but never with the intentionality of associating it with the supreme-most being in the multiverse. "Where does he tie in in this story?"

"He reigns supreme over all. And when I say all, I mean all the Gods and Devils of their respective universes. It baffles one's mind to imagine the magnanimity of the scale, but it is what it is. When, through the process of probabilistic inevitability, a God of a universe makes a wager with the Devil of that universe, it catches the Absolute's attention."

"Let's keep it simple, shall we? Let's stick to our universe, for now," Billy said, his mouth dry and his head aching something terrible.

"Fine. Our universe, it is. When this universe's God and Devil made this wager, it caught the Absolute's attention. There is a cyclicality at play here, Mr. Hawthorne. It's a cycle that has existed for millennia. Across set periods known as two millennium, God and the Devil send their respective agents to bring forth a change. Jesus attempted to tilt the wager in God's favor. Joseph Banbury is trying to tilt it in favor of the Devil. Neither of them knew, because they were never made privy to this information, that there is one above both their deities of choice, and he too has a part in this wager."

"Which is?"

"The Absolute wishes to see if each savior would somehow evolve past God and the Devil and find the one who has not sent any scripture nor any messenger. It's easy to find God, the Devil easier. But what of the one who created them both and confined them to their roles in their universe? If Christ and Banbury are to be perceived as the saviors of their millennium, the Absolute, who oversees the balance between relative good and relative evil, would much rather that they ascended beyond relative good, that is God, and relative evil, that is the Devil, and look for him, the one who is not relative but Absolute in his absoluteness."

"Suppose a savior looks for the Absolute, what happens then?" Billy asked, tapping into his journalistic instinct and treating this thing as an interview rather than a revelation.

"Then they would surpass either and become an all-powerful entity who is no longer in God's image and no longer in the Devil's image but in the Absolute's. Do you understand what I am saying?"

"A world without God, a world without Satan. One deity who rules it all. No burden of virtue and sin behind free will. In such a scenario, free will would no longer be relative free will. It would also be absolute free will. Greed—a sin—won't drive people to amass wealth. Passion, in its place, would instigate them to pursue what drives them. Hope—a virtue—of ascending to heaven won't make someone abstain from murder, but unconditional morality would."

"Right you are, Mr. Hawthorne. You can imagine this new reality all you want, but it all hangs in a very precarious balance. Jesus came and went. His chances of finding the Epoch and ascending to universal Absolutehood are nill. It's on this millennium's savior, Joseph Banbury, to find the Epoch."

Billy groaned, his head throbbing fiercely, the harshness of the elements beginning to break his unyielding spirit. "Now what is this Epoch? You're adding one too many MacGuffins into the equation, Ynun."

"There's only one MacGuffin as you call it, Mr. Hawthorne, and it is the Epoch. A relic hidden in this world that allows its wielder to harness hitherto unimaginable power. Every secret society that has ever existed has done so for the sole purpose of finding such an artifact. Even they don't know of its power. They just know it exists. The Templars. The Illuminati. The Freemasons. They are all blind hounds sniffing away at the scent of something they know exists, but as to what it is, they don't know. You know, Mr. Hawthorne, and there are those who possess secret wisdom who know. Mr. Banbury knows some of it, but I am counting on you to fill him in on the rest of it," Ynun spoke, stopping the car in front of a nondescript two-story house in Waha.

"What happens when he finds the Epoch?"

"Whenever a savior—and this is important that a savior finds it, for in the hands of a commoner, the Epoch is not of any use—finds and wields the Epoch, their mettle is tested. Who they really are. What do they want. The Epoch artifact tests them, gauges their intention. And when it has gauged their intention, it poses the ultimate question. Will the savior go with God or the Devil, or will they break free from both these constructs and seek to repair the fractured nature of this universe, uniting it as a whole under their rule?" Ynun said, gazing at Billy with a warm yet prophetic look.

"Does it follow then, the new reality that I imagined?"

"That is for the savior to decide."

"I'd say thank you, but none of this can be written down in any newspaper that any sane person would read. So what do I do with this information, other than get driven more mad by it than I already am?"

"You can guide Joseph Banbury. He already has a few in the form of friends who are in there with him. You can be another. And you can be more than just his guide. You can be his friend. Remind him of the best of humanity so that if or when he finds the Epoch, he does it with a clear understanding of what's at stake," Ynun said, stepping out of the car.

"How can I remind him of anything like that when I'm so fucked up myself?" Billy asked, tears welling in his eyes.

"Billy," Ynun said, referring to Billy by his first name for the first time in this entire conversation. "It is often those who have seen the darkest of times who get to be the harbinger of light."

Ynun said no more on the subject, and Billy, who stood there sobbing silently, watched the middle-aged man get back into the car and drive off. When Ynun handed the wheel to Abdul Basit, Billy did not know.

He had his attention on the door of this ordinary house. His attention diverted to the window. Someone had been peering from behind the curtains, and the moment Billy locked eyes with them, they retreated behind the curtains.

He looked at both sides of the street to ascertain if anyone had followed him or was spying on him. When he was certain that no one was, Billy knocked on the door of the house.

"Man huwa?" a voice asked in a rather shoddy Arabic accent. They were asking "Who is it?"

"I have been led to believe that I am to be Joseph Banbury's friend. Is he here?" Billy's voice was no higher than a whisper lest anyone else be eavesdropping.

The black iron door swung open, and a hand reached out from inside, pulling Billy in.

As immediately as the door had opened, it clanged shut, and the man who had pulled him in was now locking the door. He was a young black man standing armed with an assault rifle. Having been in this part of the world before, Billy was not fazed at the sight of the rifle pointed at him. It was a custom born out of caution. Instead of feeling threatened, Billy looked around the house. There was a small lawn on one side where two goats were tied under a shade, grazing away at the grass nonchalantly. A Suzuki Alto stood parked in the driveway. Roosters chased each other in circles around the car, pecking at each other's colorful plumes.

"Joseph Banbury?" Billy asked.

"Who are you?" the man asked.

"I'm Billy, the journalist. Are you the expat who's giving them refuge in your house?"

The man lowered his gun and reached out his hand. "That'd be me. The brigadier got in touch with me in the morning. Said some wise-ass would be dropping by."

Billy eagerly shook the man's hand, upon which the man said, "Name's Jeremy."

Jeremy's eyes went from Billy's face to someone standing behind Billy. He nodded, and then went into the alley by the side of the house, leaving Billy standing there with whoever was behind him.

"Do I know you?" a worried voice called from behind.

Billy turned around to face Joe Banbury standing there, his face that of a tired and homesick man.

"Not yet, but I have a feeling we'll get along quite well," Billy said, smiling at this millennium's savior.

It was funny. Standing there in his sweat-soaked t-shirt and baggy sweatpants, anxiety crawling on the frows of his burrow, Joe did not look like the antichrist in the least. He was not wielding any weapon, nor had any hostility in his stance. On the contrary, he held out his hand, a very weak smile on his tired face.

"Good. Because I kinda need all the help I can get," Joe said, shaking Billy's hand with both his, and then gently pulling him toward the drawing room's door. "Say, you wouldn't know anything about how we're leaving this country, would you?"

"I got a couple of ideas," Billy chuckled, following Joseph into the rather crowded and extremely hot drawing room.

13

THE AETERNUM TRIALS

The Drawing of the Sixth

It was a cramped drawing room with large frames of Arabic calligraphy hanging in from all of the walls. White paint had chipped off in big chunks off the walls, showing the dark gray cement underneath. Wherever there weren't patches of chipped off paint, there were big blotches of dried water, signaling that much of the plumbing was leaky in the house.

Two harsh fluorescent lights shone on either end of the room, throwing the topography of the room in stark contrast to everything and everyone present in it. Dark red velvet sofas that had seen better days some decades ago sat sagged along the walls. A long table that could technically qualify as a coffee table (if a dozen people were having coffee at the same time) sat in the center of the room, making it difficult for people to move throughout the room. Underneath, there was a sheer golden and quite grimy Turkish carpet with lots of intricate spirals and designs and just as many muddy boot marks from all the people who'd tracked dirt on it over the years. It had never been cleaned.

Old, wooden shelves with glass windows lined every single wall of the drawing room, and where there weren't books in those shelves, there was crockery and cutlery out on display.

An air conditioner on life support chugged sporadic sprays of room temperature air that only served to make the room more stifling than it already was. It showed on the sweaty and dirt-matted faces of everyone who was sitting uncomfortably in the room, glasses of beverage in their hand. It was a strange red beverage with big black chia seeds swimming like frog eggs.

Billy was offered a glass the minute he entered the room, and one sip from it was enough to make him put the glass down and never touch it again. He asked for water—good old, plain, simple water—and drank the entire bottle dry the moment Jeremy handed it to him.

As disheveled as he looked from his travels, the others looked worse. They bore dirt on their skins, dirt they had not bothered to clean. There was soot on their ripped clothes. Their beleaguered faces were washed in the uniform desolation of tiredness.

The two women and the three men sat awkwardly, neither reclining against the backs of the sofa nor sitting on its edge. They sat mushed together, unmoving, hands clasped, legs cramped against the outlandishly large table.

"Who did you say you were again?" Shaun asked out loud, his graying, balding head a mess of long strands of sweat-wettened hair matting on his forehead and along the side of his face. He was sitting between Joph and Lilly on the longest sofa in the room, and wasn't altogether quite uncomfortable, but he chose to sit in this on-edge stance.

He'd discovered, as had the rest, that if he sat at the back of the sofa, the cushion gave in, swallowing his entire backside. It was hot enough as it was, and he was in no mood to have his ass stuck on a hot, velvet sofa.

"Billy Hawthorne," Billy reached out a hand, and in doing so discovered the same thing about the sofa that others had. It seemed to sink him in, making it exceedingly hard to move. But he relented, pushed himself out, and shook Shaun's hand. "I'm a reporter."

"And this must be the news of the decade for you, huh?" Shaun scoffed, retracting his hand rather quickly. "Lowlifes, all of them. That's what I always say. They come sniffing shit like flies."

"Jesus, man. Would you chill?" Joph shoved Shaun a little too hard, and then stood up. He was the lithest of them all, and despite that, it was getting hard for him to keep seated. After everything that had transpired ever since they'd come to Iraq, Joph felt that sitting on his ass was the most unproductive thing he could do. He paced back and forth by the small drawing room's entrance door, barely able to take more than three steps before he had to turn around and take three back.

"No, no, it's fine. My kind has earned that kind of criticism," Billy said, raising his hands, taking the blame. "But I'm not here in my capacity as a reporter, Mr. Gainey."

Shaun raised his eyebrow. The man had done his research well enough that he was aware of Shaun's last name.

"Do tell," Amy asked. She sat on Billy's right side. Joe sat on his left, staring at the door. "I'm Amy, by the way."

"Amy Banbury, yeah. I know. I've been following the Morning Star bandwagon for some time now."

Amy gave him a gentle smile of acknowledgment before continuing. "Why are you here, Mr. Hawthorne?"

"Billy's fine," he said, addressing the room at large. "I was kind of hoping that Joe and I could have a chat, alone. I didn't anticipate having to...."

"Speak to an entire room? Well, you know that one cliché that gets thrown in every movie ever? The one that goes, 'Anything you want to say to me, you can say to them.' Well, the same principle applies here," Joe said. He was the second to stand up after Josh, but he didn't pace around. There was no room.

"Well, for starters. Seems to me like you guys are stuck. I can help with that," Billy said, unsure of whom to look at when speaking. They were all staring at him unblinkingly. It was deeply unsettling. But he understood their gazes. He'd been stared like that many times before during the wartime. It was always the locals who looked at him and thought they were seeing a messianic figure who would miraculously put an end to the war and save them from their plights. But he could only offer them the granola bars in his jacket's pockets and take pictures of them as he talked to them in broken Arabic. But unlike the instances of his past, he could actually do something of use here, and perhaps that's why they were looking at him so intensely, knowing that he'd have something up his sleeve now that they'd exhausted all the tricks up theirs.

"No, shit, Sherlock. You think we're sitting in this dump because we like the rustic post-war interior décor of this shithole?" Shaun barked, and whilst in the midst of his barking, stood up with deliberate effort that accounted for his lumbering stomach, and then joined Joph by the drawing-room door, taking deep breaths right under the air-conditioner.

"Ignore him," Lilly said, rubbing her forehead. "He's been nothing but a whiny ass bitch this entire leg of our tour."

"Bite me!" Shaun yelped, and threw the drawing-room door open, exiting through it with pounding feet.

Now that he was no longer occupying a huge portion of the sofa, Lilly could sit far more comfortably. Joe, seeing the opening, went and sat alongside her. He did it with a subtlety that Billy was sure no one else other than him had picked up on, hinting at a clandestine relationship. He let it slide. He didn't know the dynamics of this group any more than their official labels.

"How would you help us?" Lilly asked, noticing that Joe had sat beside her, but making nothing of it. She played the discretion game as well as Joe. Playing things close to her chest came naturally to her. She had an amused expression on her face, as if everything that had happened was not a colossal fuck-up but part of a plan only she was privy to.

Upon noticing that, Billy glanced around the room and observed the faces of everyone. They were not worried. These were not the faces of helpless people. Could it be that Billy was only imagining it or was everyone looking satisfied?

Amy scrolling her phone as if nothing was the matter, taking occasional sips from her basil seed beverage; Joph whistling as he checked his daily steps on his Apple Watch; Lilly lounging, one leg over the other, as if she was at a bus station; and Joe staring off in the distance, his face driven, his body poised for action.

"I don't understand," Billy stuttered, looking around. "I thought y'all needed to be escorted out of the country. But it seems like...I'm sorry, am I missing something?"

"Quid pro quo," Shaun said, stepping into the room, a

satisfied smile on his face. “I did it. I fixed the fucking AC. Damn sand in the outer component. Had to hose it. Damn near got electrocuted, but it’s worth it.” He closed the door as he entered the room, bolted it shut, and then put his hand in front of the AC. “Fuck yeah, that’ll get you there.”

Jeremy, the host, entered by way of the other door, the one that opened into the rest of the house. He noticed the sudden change in temperature and raised his eyebrows at Shaun. “I didn’t know you knew how to repair air-conditioners.”

“I got this Italian streak in me, see,” Shaun spoke in a thick accent, his pulled sleeves revealing his hairy forearms. “Course I did an HVAC certification back in the days. Why, what you got in mind?”

“I’ll serve you the best damn mandi you’ve ever eaten in your entire life if you do to the other air conditioners what you did this one. I’ll even score as much booze as I can get my hands on. Seriously. Whatever you want. What do you want? Pork ribs? You want lasagna? Tell a brother.”

“I look that much of a fucking Guido to you, brother?” Shaun raised his voice threateningly, hands on his hips, eyes narrowed as he took aggressive steps toward Jeremy.

“Hey, I didn’t mean no offense, man,” Jeremy said, taking a step back.

Shaun burst out laughing, and clapped Jeremy on the chest as he doubled over. “I’m just fucking with you, man. Course I’ll do it for some good old roasted mutton and chilled beer. Show me the way. Also, do you know of any hot single Iraqi women in the area? I mean, a guy can hope. I’ve been led to believe that Middle Eastern women’s where it’s at."

“Ya Allah,” Jeremy shook his head. “This white boy goan get himself killed.”

The two of them walked out of the room arm in arm, talking about the best way to roast mutton for tonight's cookout. Joph trailed after them, muttering something about "never missing a chance to watch men at work."

Billy couldn't remember where the conversation had trailed off; he was far too relaxed to speak at the moment. The room, now at a much more cooler, comfortable level, was looking far less unappealing than it did when he'd walked in first.

"That's dinner sorted, then," Lilly said, slapping her thighs and heaving herself out of the sofa. "I think I might go and take a bath."

"I think I'll join you," Amy said, getting up from the sofa, and leaving Billy sitting there alone. She then addressed the two remaining in the room. "This isn't Girls Gone Wild. We'll take turns, Jesus."

"Did I even say anything?! Christ, you're my sister," Joe laughed at the absurdity of her statement.

As Lilly was walking past Billy, she reached behind her and procured a fistful of something. Before Billy could understand what was happening, Lilly threw a fistful of dirt at him, covering him in dust, and making him cough loudly.

She leaned in front of him and said, "Welcome to the insane clown posse. We're just getting started.

"Yo, what the fuck," Billy shouted, wiping away at his face.

"I'd highly recommend you don't do that," Joe said calmly.

"Jesus Christ, what is it, some kind of poison?" Billy coughed. "Because it tastes far too bland to be poison."

"It's grave dirt, actually. We each have it on our person. And now you do too," Joe said, reclining on his sofa, unperturbed by how it sank so deeply.

"I'm not even going to ask," Billy said, opening his eyes. The dirt particles still stung his face, but he could bear this pain. It was a solid two on the pain scale. Nothing he hadn't handled before. Though, if it was just dirt, why did it sting?

"You've led yourself to believe that we're trapped here, unable to do anything about it. Do you realize who you're talking to?" There was no condescension in Joe's voice. He was asking it earnestly.

"Allegedly, you're the antichrist. Dajjal, as the Iraqis are calling you," Billy said, spitting out a wad of phlegm thick with grave dirt. Thinking about the dirt made him realize that there must've been some dead body decaying away, in constant contact with the dirt that was now in his mouth, on his face, and down his shirt. He held back the urge to puke, choosing to fixate on Joe instead.

"Tell me why you're here, Hawthorne, and then, if I deem it fit, I'll tell you a story that's very different from all the pieces you've been writing about me," Joe said, finally revealing this vital piece of information.

"You know me," Billy registered.

"When someone writes so prolifically about me, of course, I tend to take notice, myself being a writer first, prophet second," Joe replied tonelessly. The cold nature of his utterance sent inexplicable shivers down Billy's spine.

"Well, if it helps, I just wrote that shit to pay the bills, and I hope you can understand, you being a writer first, prophet second," Billy said, though his tone was full of an earnestness that made him feel awkward. Why was he trying to sell himself to this guy?

Joe was not looking at Billy anymore. Instead, his gaze had followed a direction in the back of the room. He pointed that way and asked, "Do they always follow you where you go?"

Billy's blood froze in his veins as he stared at what Joe was pointing at.

"Y-y-you ca-can s-s-s-see them?" He whispered hoarsely, pain constricting his chest.

"I can," Joe said calmly. "I can also hear them inside your head. What they're saying. They're benign, your mother and your brother. It's the other one that's dangerous, isn't it?"

"How do you know about that? How could you possibly know any of that?" Billy's eyes widened in disbelief as he saw Joe walk over to where his dead mother and his headless brother stood.

"I am the prophet of all that is dark and disconsolate," Joe said, putting his hand on Teddy's headless shoulder. "They speak to me. These memories of yours. They're not just ghosts. They're projections of your own psyche that you carry around with you wherever you go. It's guilt is what it is. And I can understand that you don't want to let go."

"Can you help me?" Billy asked, his eyes stinging, but not because of the dirt. He hastily wiped away at the tears that had appeared before Joe could turn around and see him in this disheveled state, but the way his voice had broken in the midst of his question had betrayed his vulnerable state already.

Joe did a brief and respectful bow in front of Billy's mother, who curtseyed by lifting the hem of her dress and bending her knees. Once he had acquainted himself with the two phantasmal manifestations, he came back to Billy and held out his hand. The moment Billy shook it, Joe pulled him up and locked him in a bear hug.

"You've been through some deep shit, man," Joe said. "I can feel every part of it emanating out of your body."

"Emanating?" Billy chuckle-sobbed. "It's not a word most people use in conversations, just saying."

"And most people don't go around carrying the dead with them. But you are," Joe said, breaking the hug, but still keeping his hands on Billy's shoulders. "I can take it all away if you so wish. The pain. The memories. I can even make them go away," Joe nodded in the direction of Billy's mother and brother. "But do you want me to? Wouldn't it irrevocably change the person you are? Our darkest parts are, at the end of the day, parts of ourselves."

"Parts that make me want to fucking end my life," Billy said, holding onto Joe's arms with a tight grasp. He couldn't describe it in any of the millions of words he knew, but there was something quite deific about Banbury. "I wouldn't mind being normal for a while, you know."

"I know. And it's not with any faux-sympathetic affectation that I'm saying that I know. I do know. I've got a headful of ghosts too. All of Hell dwells in there. I call my head the Devil's loft seeing as how he's there most of the time. Doesn't even pay rent, that motherfucker."

Billy laughed in a way he hadn't done all his life. Despite their saying that they understood, none of the guys in his support group or the shrinks ever really knew what he'd been through. Joe somehow did. And this made Billy want to trust Joe with his life.

"So what do I do? Just live on for the rest of my days with my dead family hanging around?"

"Forgive yourself," Joe said, now holding the back of Billy's neck gently, pulling him close. They leaned into each other, touching their foreheads. "What happened that night was not your fault. I want you to believe it not because I am saying it but because it is true. Pitch any twelve-year-old against a fully grown drunk man with an axe and you'd have the same outcome every time. In fact, you did better than most would have done in that situation. Like I said, you saved yourself. Whether you want to call it fate or the divine hand of some unseen force, you've been saving yourself every day since then. The way I see it, you have two options before you. You can either let go of this burden—and I can help you with that—or you can accept it—in which case, there isn't anything for me to help with."

"What happens if I accept it?" Billy asked, suddenly very aware of the sulfuric smell of acrid grave dirt.

"It's the harder of the two options. You can't expect to accept it in a day. You've got to stop fighting with yourself. You need to have a talk with them. Not just your mother and brother, but the other too. Maybe hear out what he has to say?"

"How can you possibly know all this?" Billy's eyes first went wide out of surprise, then squinted in suspicion.

"As I said, I've got a read on darkness of all kinds, and you, my friend, are an open book with all the black aura you've got about yourself," Joe said, giving Billy's shoulder one last thump. "Now, onto other matters, shall we? I take I you've got something to tell me?"

Billy rolled his eyes, "Can't you just reach into my mind and see it for yourself?"

Joe grinned sheepishly. "I can. But it's a tiring process, and I'd rather hear it from the horse's mouth instead."

"You saying my face is long?"

"Yeah, you've got the longest face. Like, I was being kind with the horse metaphor. Your face reminds me of Squidward from SpongeBob, get me?"

"Well, hey, fuck you," Billy grinned back.

"Now we're talking," Joe laughed, slapping Billy's open palm. "Fuck you too, and have a seat, why don't ya?"

Billy shot one last tentative look at the corner where his ghosts had been standing, only to find that they were no longer there. This was a first. Whenever they showed up at a place, they lingered with the intent to stay. He wondered where they'd gone, and if Joe had anything to do with it.

Billy sat down, far more comfortable now than before, and more eager to have this conversation now that it was just Joe and him. But he had one nagging question he needed to get out of the way first.

"What's with the grave dirt?"

"All right," Joe nodded. "You came all this way, trusted me with some really dark shit from your past, and it seems that you've got some vital information that I need. I'm going to put my trust in you in return. But believe me, as outlandish as it sounds, all of this is true."

"This has to do with the Devil, doesn't it?" Billy asked.

"All of it has to do with the Devil. Including this apparent stranding of ours in Iraq. It's a smokescreen. That's what the grave dirt does too. If you've got it on you, then the Devil cannot see you. I'll tell you how I came to know this. It involves me going down to the Ganges and meeting an Aghori Baba. But it's a long story, and I have a feeling yours is just as long. Instead of sitting here and comparing lengths, let's just get into it, shall we?"

The two sat side by side and had one of the longest conversations of their collective lives. When they were finished, it was no longer afternoon but evening. Outside, Jeremy had assembled the makings of a nice barbeque. Shaun had fixed all the ACs and was enjoying a well-deserved beer. Joph, a grill enthusiast, was helping Jeremy get kebabs on the skewers. Amy and Lilly, who'd both taken turns to bath, were looking fresher (albeit both had a fresh smattering of grave dirt on them for obvious purposes).

Billy was trying to wrap his head around everything that Joe had shared with him. He sat in the courtyard, feeling a little chilly in the desert's night wind. He intended to ask further questions, but not right now. There was a time for everything, and from the general mood of the house, it was time to unwind, have a few drinks, enjoy good food, and talk frivolously about any and all matters that did not pertain to Joe's grand narrative.

Now that everyone knew that Joe and Billy had a conversation, they were more open to Billy, and weren't treating him as an outsider. If anything, they were being candid with him, accepting him as the sixth in their rank.

Joe, on the other hand, was sitting in one corner of the courtyard, beer in hand, mulling over the stuff that Billy had shared with him. It was a lot to digest—a multiverse with many Gods and many Devils overseen by the Absolute. Saviors and Epochs.

He hadn't gotten into this whole mess to supersede God or the Devil. In fact, he had not wanted to get into this mess in the first place. He'd only ever sought to be a writer. What was this, then, this thrusting of responsibility beyond what he was capable of? He was having a hard time dealing with one Devil, a harder time being said Devil's prophet. Now he had to go over Satan's head and find some mythical artifact that would allow him to wield enough power to side with either God or the Devil, or choose his own path and supplant them?

Did Lucifer know about this? And if so, then why the secrecy?

Was it, perhaps, that Satan was afraid?

It'd explain why he'd overreacted back in India, beating Joe to within an inch of his life and ripping his wings off his body.

It also explained why the Devil was being so furtive. He hadn't shown up once to lend a hand, not when the entire mob was upon Joe and his team in the hotel. Not when they were fleeing. And not now, when they could do with a safe escape route.

But it did not explain one thing.

Joe studied Lilly sitting there with a cold beer in her hand, laughing with her whole face as she and Amy swapped dark jokes while sitting in front of the bonfire. A whole mutton was skewered over the bonfire, and Jeremy periodically rotated it so that it would cook uniformly. The air smelled heavenly with the scent of spices and searing meat. Overhead, the sky was clear, all the stars of the Milky Way visible in crisp contrast to the rest of the night.

Lilly saw Joe looking at her and gave him a small nod and a smile.

He nodded back, though, he did not smile.

Whatever knowledge that Joe had come upon, it was so secretive that only two people had dared speak of it to him, and one of them was dead in a charnel house. The other one was sitting there looking disheveled, scared out of his wits.

And yet, somehow, Lilly seemed to have an idea of it.

About the Absolute.

The conversation they had at the hotel's balcony in India came back to him in crisp detail. They were both high, but even then, she'd spoken with guarded words. Joe wondered what else she knew...and why.

What business did a former literary agent have knowing of things that had eluded all of mankind?

As the night grew late, the party turned more rancorous. Shaun was dancing away drunkenly around the bonfire, a skewer of mutton tikka in his hand. He'd do a round around the fire, swaying, then take a sip from his beer, and then bite down on the tikka pieces. Joph, who'd been clapping at

Shaun's extemporaneous display of dancing prowess, had now joined in and was dancing to the beat of the hand drum that Jeremy had procured from inside his house. Jeremy's wife and daughter watched the whole thing from the terrace on the first floor, giggling every time Shaun or Joph would make fools of themselves.

Seeing Amy there, relaxing after two to three days of pure life-or-death toil, made Joe feel a little happy. They were not out of danger yet, and perhaps the hardest leg of the journey was ahead of them, but having her by his side had given him a familial strength without which it would have been difficult to pull this tour off.

He could feel for Billy. Other than one conversation, he hadn't really gotten a chance to get acquainted with any of the others, and so now he sat there by himself. He could understand that Billy perhaps did not want to talk to him more than he already had; that's why Joe was giving him a break.

Everything that had happened since the events in Babylon felt like a fever dream. He hadn't known that he'd be resurrecting an ISIS captain. He didn't anticipate such a visceral reaction from the people of Iraq. When the army helicopter had saved them in the nick of time from the mob, Joe had wondered if coming here was a good idea at all.

But everything that happened after it—from them going into hiding to Billy's sudden arrival—had served to reaffirm Joe's faith in his own plan. This chaos had served as a smokescreen for more than just the Devil.

At this moment, the world did not know what Joe Banbury was up to.

He'd kept his eyes on the news. Those who'd talked about canceling him in the name of inciting religious riots in Iraq had quickly changed their stances in a day. Now they were all worried about the Americans who were stranded in Iraq. Joph had shared bits and pieces from the news as well as messages from the Morning Star's website, showing him that his own movement was going strong. Wherever they had set up bases for the Morning Star, people were protesting for Joe's safe return, for the timely intervention of world governments. In the videos that Joph had shared an hour before Billy's appearance, Joe saw that the people gathered at protests were praying. Not to a God or the Devil, but to Joe himself. They were praying to him that he'd return and resume his mission.

For a while, it had seemed to Joe that he'd started a movement, and had then fucked off on this world tour without making the necessary arrangements. But now, despite all that had happened (including Tasha's death, the burning of the Cathedral, and the retaliation for resurrecting an ISIS captain in Iraq), it looked like that deep tilt of chaos that had gripped him and his movement had found its counterbalance finally.

Counterbalance in the form of people caring for him the world over, people who did not confine themselves to conforming norms. People who actually saw what Joe was doing and appreciated him for it.

Crowdfund donations had poured in like crazy on the Morning Star website. Neighboring countries that were on good terms with the United States had offered to evacuate Joe and the Morning Star team.

But Joe had other things on his mind.

He was making use of this momentary chaos to hide himself from the one who had his eyes everywhere. It helped that they were at a burial site in Babylon, from where Joe had gotten his hands on copious amounts of ancient grave dirt, his instinct being that the older the grave dirt, the more potent it was. And what was older than a Babylonian burial site?

It was enough dirt to last him and his friends a few days.

Convincing them to splatter some of that dirt on their bodies had been a task unto itself. Again, it brought to mind Lilly, who had been all too eager to take the dirt and smear it upon herself, convincing the others on behalf of Joe to do the same. She'd even somehow convinced Jeremy and his family to do it so that they could all remain hidden from the watchful gaze of Satan. Jeremy and his family, being orthodox Christians, were all too eager to believe her, even if they did not believe in her cause.

It made Joe think differently about her.

What did she know?

Who was she, really?

"Joe! Come on over. Food's getting cold!" Jeremy called out from behind the grill, waving a skewer at him.

Joe put his thoughts and musings to rest, eager to join the others in feasting, drinking, talking, and dancing. The world might come to an end. The Devil may see Joe to an early grave. But that was all in the future. Tonight, he could unwind.

Tonight, he deserved to.

The Dive into the Abyss

Billy threw up blood.

It splattered on the Eastern toilet, the sight of which made him more nauseous, and this time around, it wasn't just blood he threw up but the entire contents of the rather lavish dinner he'd enjoyed earlier that night.

"Jesus Christ," Billy groaned, holding his stomach with both hands, bent over the toilet, wondering how it was possible for people to just sit there and squat on such a broad thing without busting their knees every time.

More blood, followed by a long strand of drool and sick that stretched from his mouth to the seat of the toilet, clinging firmly to both ends. Billy swiped it off with the back of his hand, his insides squirming, making it feel as if someone had poured burning lead into his intestines.

Right on cue, black grime appeared on the bathroom's brick wall and out from it stepped Other Billy, the manic one with murder in his eye and the axe in his hands. However, he did not look like he was concerned with Billy at this moment. Hawklike, he stared around the bathroom, axe gripped fiercely in an offensive stance.

"Something's bloody off, Billy boy," Other Billy said, his tone serious, lacking all manner of snideness.

"Why the fuck are you here?" Billy groaned.

"Are you blind, numbnuts? We're in fucking danger over here," Other Billy barked, standing next to the door. "Something's coming."

"I meant, why are you looking out for me?" Billy's voice was weak, but the inflection of concern in it was anything but.

"You've been following his trail like a bloodhound, clinging to every word like it's fucking scripture, sustaining yourself for more than a year by writing exclusively about him, but when Joe Banbury finally says something that's sensible, you forget it? Don't you remember what he said about us? About me? About mom? Teddy!?"

"There's no you," Billy sat with his back next to the brick wall, holding his stomach, knowing that this was it. This was what death was supposed to feel like. He'd done his job. He'd relayed the message to Joe Banbury, and now, inexplicably, he was dying.

"There's always me," Other Billy strode up to Billy and grabbed his head with a fistful of hair. "Who do you think took over when good old step-dad was about to fuck you up with the axe the way he'd done with Teddy? It was me, motherfucker. I'm not some figment of your imagination. I'm your goddamn survival instinct. Always have been. And I'm telling you, something's fucking off. We're being overtaken. Hacked, more like it, and not with an axe this time around. It's a possession, Billy, and I don't know how to stop it."

"Is it the Devil?" Billy asked, his eyes closing against the relenting force of the intrusion of some unseen force, an unseen force that made his whole body sear with pain and his head feel like it was being split open.

"It's not the fucking Devil. I'd know. I've seen him before at work. This is something else, and that's what scares the fuck out of me," Other Billy snapped. He sat beside Billy and stared at the shrinking walls of the primitive bathroom.

"Glad to know that something scares you. All this time you've been the one haunting me," Billy chuckled, spurting more blood from his nostrils. It fell on his shirt, smudging alongside all of the rest of the dark maroon blotches.

"What kind of a fucking idiot fears his own instinct?"

"The same kind of fucking idiot who's choking on half-digested kebabs in Iraq, about to have his faculties hijacked by some cosmic interloper," Billy gasped, struggling with his words. It was getting exceedingly difficult for him to stay awake. Whatever was descending upon him had struck its landing, and now, Billy could feel someone else in his mind, besides Other Billy, his mother, and his brother.

We meet again, Billy Hawthorne.

"Ynun?"

Yes. Please tell the fragments of your psyche that I come in peace, despite how grotesque it all seems. I am sorry about the convulsions and the blood. You are difficult to possess as compared to others. Your defenses are...stronger.

"Hear that, Other Billy? It comes in peace. You can relax now," Billy heaved in a deep breath, as those were the only kinds of breath he could take, what with the crushing pressure on his chest.

"Ask this motherfucker why it's here!" Other Billy shouted in Billy's face, wielding the axe close.

I come to guide the savior to the precipice. To the Aeternum Vow.

Billy was no longer there. His body lay limp in the bathroom, very nearly completely possessed by the being who called itself Ynun. Other Billy stood up, watching Billy's eyes glow oracularly.

"You better not hurt him, or I don't care who you are, I'm going to find you, and I'll wedge this axe up your ass," Other Billy addressed the being possessing Billy's body.

"It won't come to that," Billy spoke hazily, his tone reflecting the voice of Ynun. "You and I, we are on the same team. We want the same thing for Billy. It's just that this next part requires me to meet the savior. I have tried to meet him before, but it has not worked out in either of our favor. Now, though, I hope to talk to him at length. Will you let me use Billy as a vessel?"

It was strange that this timeless, almost omniscient being was addressing William Hawthorne as Billy. Other Billy chuckled, swinging his axe, and said, "I'll let you use him, but be aware that we're also lurking in there. One wrong move and we take over. Try talking to the savior or whoever the fuck you think Joe Banbury is without a vessel."

"Rest assured. It will not come to that."

"On your head be it, then."

It was not a dream. None of them were dreams. For them to qualify as such, Joe would need to be asleep. These days, he barely slept at all. When he felt tired, he descended down into an astral state, his body still aware of what was happening, his spirit soaring restlessly, trying to uncover the mysteries that eluded him even after everything.

Following the barbeque party, Joe had retired to his room. They had accommodated him with a room of his own, and since his relationship with Lilly wasn't official or anything, she had not slept with him. She'd whispered in his ear that once everyone was asleep, she might drop by, but Joe had told her not to do that. Tonight, he did not feel bound enough to the mortal coil that he wanted to indulge in human relationships.

Tonight, he felt anything but human.

Strands of the gold substance hung suspended around him like celestial streamers, reaching all the way up to the sky. He could see farther than the clouds, beyond the stars, thanks to his astral state, and doing so allowed him to recognize these strands for what they were.

The threads of destiny of all the people who were in this house, in this city, in this world. Each of these threads had exhaustive documentation upon them in a writing that Joe could not recognize, but from what he could infer, each thread spoke of what the person had done up to this point in their life, and what they would likely do based on how they'd lived their life. Speculations, patterns, routines. Old mistakes repeated anew.

The strands sometimes touched each other, coiled around like double helixes, and then went their own ways.

To get a better view of things, Joe's astral form flew out of the room and landed on the roof. Now that he was no longer beholding this sight holed up in his room, he could appreciate it for its true scale. Hundreds of millions of strands in view, all of them weaving every which way. New words wrote themselves along the lengths of these strands as people performed actions in the past.

It did not feel predetermined. On the contrary, it seemed as if the thing known as destiny or fate was like a real-time, self-learning algorithm that adjusted to things on the fly rather than predetermining them. No such thing as bad luck, thought Joe. Only a bad attitude.

He mused on the wager's terms. It seemed like the ones who'd set the rules weren't kidding about free will being free will. Joe wondered why most people, then, didn't realize just how good of a gift they had, this ability to do anything.

You could kill someone in cold blood if you deemed, but you could also save someone's life. You could plant a tree or rip them out by the forestfuls to feed your factories.

There didn't need to be a divine or unholy hand at play to fuck things up for human beings. They were equally capable of doing that on their own.

A few minutes earlier, Joe had sought to pursue the strand of his fate as far as it would take him, regardless of the direction, but to his surprise, he couldn't find his own strand. It wasn't hovering over his body as everyone else's.

"Where's my fate?"

He felt naked standing there without it. As if he'd been let go by the collective universe and any and all authorities that oversaw it. Go. You're on your own.

Is this the part of me that's becoming less and less

human with each passing day? Joe wondered. Is this why I can see such a profound thing unfolding before his eyes. He could see Lilly's cerulean-colored strand coming out of the room she was sleeping in. He felt a warmth toward it, wanting to touch it with his hands and tell her that he loved her.

Instinctively, he walked over to the strand and reached out, undecided if he should touch it or not.

Unable to help himself, he touched the strand with his finger.

It was like terabytes of data was downloading in his psyche instantaneously. He could see himself in the visions but from the eyes of Lilly. Lilly on her knees with his cock in her mouth. Lilly lying naked alongside him in bed.

But then he saw things that he wasn't sure he should.

Lilly sitting in the middle of a magic circle made from chalk, bleeding herself from the wrists, eyes gone up, reciting Latin fluently, herbs and bones in the periphery, black flame candles lit on each end of the magic circle.

Lilly in a pointed hat and a black robe traversing a Victorian, cobble-stone paved street with a tome in her hand. Lilly touching a dead tree and bringing it back to life.

Lilly dancing naked in the forest, her body slowly lifting off the floor as she chanted arcane chants.

Lilly's body bathed in blood as she lay in a bathtub, communing with spirits of the damned.

Lilly in a small town in Massachusetts, sitting rather placidly in a circle of egotistical middle-aged housewives.

Before he was violently pulled away from the strand and thrown on the floor, the last thing that Joe saw was a little girl crying in a forest, backed against a tree, a wolf approaching her, its maw hung open.

He wondered if this little girl was Lilly.

Someone had pulled him away viciously from the strand he'd been holding.

Joe looked around and saw, to his surprise, Billy standing there, his eyes shining white, his face angry.

"It is a most defiled act, Joseph Banbury, to pry upon the fates of others!" Billy spoke. "It makes me reconsider thinking of you in a positive light!"

"Billy?" Joe asked, flying back to his feet. No. This was not Billy.

"Do not tamper or touch the fates of others. The balance of free will is delicate. Everyone deserves to follow their own will without interference. That includes spying on others," Billy—or whatever was possessing him—said. "To interfere is profane."

"Have you looked at me? I embody the profane," Joe said, raising his arms self-defeatedly. "I'm as damned as damned gets. Get with the program."

"You think lowly of yourself. More importantly, you think of yourself in the same binary way as has been forced upon you and every single human being, dead or alive. There are modalities beyond just good and bad, consecration and damnation," Billy spoke. He did not speak in the same accent as earlier. That, and the way his eyes were ablaze with white light, made it evident that Joe was being visited by someone possessing Billy's body.

"I've been getting unsolicited visitors lately. Do I know you, friend? Or are you a foe?"

Billy chuckled. "There is that binary modality again. I am neither. I do not know you well enough to call you a friend. I do not have any other agenda against you that would dub me as your foe."

"You speak awfully like a guy I knew in India. Are...are you him? Are you Kali Aatma?" Joe asked, stepping forward.

The strands of fate that had been overwhelming his senses moments prior all disappeared, leaving the night vacant of any light other than that coming from the stars.

"*He's* a friend of mine," Billy said a smile on his face. "Most of us tasked with Watching are more or less each other's friends. The Spirit of Time, or, rather, Kali Aatma, is just one of the Watchers."

"Watchers? As in the Fallen Angels?"

Billy laughed. It was strange for Joe to see Billy laugh in a way that did not match his Bronx affectation. It felt like the kind of awful dubbing you saw in foreign movies with English voices.

"There is it again, that binary that you've not rid yourself of yet, Banbury. Fallen Angels? Who's perpetrating that rumor? We're not angels nor are we fallen. We are the Watchers. We watch the Elements that are under our domain. Kali Aatma oversees the linear flow of time in this universe, and no, that little stunt the Devil pulled didn't kill him. You cannot kill time, even if you're the Devil."

"I'm glad to know that he's well," Joe said, mustering up a small, customary smile. "And, so, you, who are you supposed to be?"

"I am the one that Billy spoke of. I am Ynun."

"Madness," Joe said acknowledging.

"You catch on quicker than your friend," Ynun said, holding his arm out. "This next bit requires you to forego sanity. Will you take my hand?"

"Jesus, take me out to dinner first," Joe said, casting a look at his body in the room. He sat there on the sofa, lifelessly gazing ahead. He didn't feel comfortable being in the astral form anymore. Whatever Ynun was proposing, it felt... *wrong*. He was not ready to be whisked to some other dimension or plane of existence. He'd had enough of that for one lifetime, thanks to Satan.

"We, the Watchers, have been watching you, Banbury, deciding if we should help you in your journey to find the Epoch. We are aware of what you have done and the influence that you're forced to act upon. But thankfully, you're free of that influence even if it's temporary. The Devil's not here to hold you back, is he? He's finding you in all your old haunts and cannot. Grave dirt is powerful like that. So is madness. I offer you a gift. Take my hand. Let go of the very thing that you've been clinging so firmly to all your life. Sanity only takes you so far."

"Okay, Mad Hatter. What's this about?" Joe asked, bracing himself.

He took stock of his surroundings one more time before he'd take Ynun's hand. The desert air was cool, quiet. Beyond the small town, there was desert sand all around with its dunes and depressions. Not a single thing moved in the stillness that had gripped the night. No one made a sound.

"This is about the Vow," Ynun said, his hand still hanging suspended in the space between him and Joe's astral body.

"I'm not looking to get married, thank you," Joe joked, but the joke fell flat, getting no reaction from Ynun, making him wonder if Ynun was indeed who he said he was; knowing what he knew of madness, madness had a sense of humor.

"You have been married to this since the moment you became the Devil's prophet. You are this millennium's savior. It falls on us, the Watchers, to guide you to the Epoch. Alas, we can only guide. You have to find it for yourself, for even we do not know where it is. Are you not going to be the savior this universe needs? Do you not wish to—"

"You know what I wish for?" Joe shouted, knowing full well that his voice wouldn't carry over from the astral realm into the real one. "I wish for a fucking normal life. I wish that none of the shit that happened to me happened to me! I didn't want my mother getting ass-fucked by Satan! All that Christian bullshit that I was choked with till I was chockfull of it. I didn't want that. I wish my mother wasn't Hitler growing up. I wish that I'd never seen, never endured all the horrors that I did. Can you grant that wish, Ynun? If not, then don't fucking ask me what I wish for." Forgetting that he was in his astral form, Joe pushed Billy by the shoulder and was taken aback for a second when his hand went through the lanky journalist's body.

"There, there," Ynun said, his voice dripping with sarcasm.

"Yeah, well, fuck you," Joe said, wiping sweat from his face. "I never set out to achieve any of this. Do you know why my fate's not there with the rest of the people? Because it was already sealed even before I was born. Is that fair?"

"I am not the Watcher of Fear that you beleaguer me about the horrors you endured, nor am I the Watcher of Fairness that you pose questions about fairness to me. I am Madness. And I extend an invitation for the final time. Do you wish to undergo the trials of the Aeternum Vow?"

"Pray tell," Joe said, reflecting the same sarcasm. "What is this Aeternum Vow?"

"The Aeternum Vow is a code of ethics older than this universe. It is a guiding principle created by the same Creator who created me, my Watcher brethren, the Devil, and even God. Unlike all the different variants of Watchers and Gods and Devils across different universes, the

Aeternum Vow is the same across the multiverse. You pass the test, you fulfill the Vow. You fulfill the Vow, and you discover where the Epoch is. I come to take you to the Trials. Will you relinquish your sanity for delirium and hysteria?"

"Is that part of the test?" Joe asked, finally taking Ynun's hand.

"I'm not at liberty to say."

"You pretty much said yes."

"Do you? Say yes? Do I have your consent?"

"You do."

With one hand, Ynun grabbed Joe's forearm fiercely, and with the other, he pressed his palm upon Joe's forehead, breaking the thin barrier in his mind that kept insanity at bay, flooding Joe with all the demented thoughts in the world.

Right as Joe's state of mind turned manic, Ynun pulled him vigorously, toppling him over, both of them falling through a void that appeared on the roof.

"Is this how Alice felt going down the rabbit hole?" Joe yelled, laughing like a lunatic. Ynun, who had bore witness to the familiar mad cackle of every lunatic who had ever existed, smiled satisfactorily.

His job was done.

14

THE TROLLEY PROBLEM

The two men stood by each other's side like two astronauts who'd just landed on an alien planet. It was new, even for Ynun, who hadn't ever been to this realm. Wherever this was, the sky was not lit by a sun but by some spectral source of light that shone through perforations. Like cavern mouths on the roof of caves. With its strange flora that bloomed with bioluminescence, and animals the likes of which did not simply exist on earth, this place was not a barren wasteland but a thriving ecosystem in some distant part of this universe. Gravity did not operate here the same way as it did back on the planets humans called home. There was less of a pull, and as a result, the waterfalls did not so much as fall over the craggy cliffs as much as they loitered lazily, ebbing down with no urgency. Gigantic trees swayed slowly, their leaves resembling batwings and the connective tissue between cartilages shaking and stirring up this subterranean savannah with sentient whispers.

Whatever dwelled here had eyes everywhere, and it peeked as these two men, one possessed by madness, the other possessed of madness, walked further into this darkly beautiful realm.

Joe grappled with his newly inflicted insanity, trying to keep the thoughts at bay but failing at doing so. That was madness, wasn't it? When you failed to keep the intrusive thoughts at bay and started acting on them. It was all so very clear to him, everything. The universe was just one of many great jokes. Existence was nothing more than a farce. It was fucking weird how people had adapted to the most craziest of things and had considered them normal for thousands of years.

Defecating. Urinating. Copulating. Eating. Sleeping. Dying. These were all insane things that people had somehow made their peace with. Your anal sphincter relaxes and out oozes something brown. You put part of yourself in another person and some time later, a new life form emerges from the same part that you'd so passionately fucked. You closed your eyes and your mind went in one direction, your soul in another. At the end of it all, you closed your eyes forever, not knowing where you went.

Everyone was living out insanity one human life at a time, one crazy thing at a time, and yet people failed to see it as the jest of infinite proportion that it was. Which God in their right mind had created such a comical set of rules and then sought it fit to bind everything by these rules?

Joe was only slightly aware of Billy/Ynun walking ahead of him, showing him the way through the forest, past the thickets of brambles and overgrown bushes, down the slope of a hill populated with hundreds of tombstones. In the great distance, there was a crumbling castle, remnant of some old civilization that had once called this place home.

A tall bridge reached this castle from the highway up the mountains. The bridge, like the castle, had crumbled, with only its foundations left standing. Carnivorous birds of giant proportions flew over the turrets of the castle, clawing and biting at each other, drawing blood mid-flight.

They kept walking past the ruins of ancient temples, following the cobbled and overgrown pathway, Joe paying heed to the pontifications of madness, Ynun leading down the path, knowing that whatever trial they were here for lay at the end of this road. On either side of them were waylaid trolleys and carts, their contents scattered on the dark brown grass, abandoned for centuries. Rusting metal equipment. Shipments of wines and olive oil.

"Do you know what this place reminds me of?"

"What."

"Menzoberranzan."

"I am not acquainted with the intricacies of your culture well enough to recognize that place. Where is it?"

"It's not real," Joe said. The more he spoke, the more the madness ebbed away. It was like a bad high finally going down, leaving him feeling disdainfully sane. He did not know for how he'd been walking with Ynun, but somewhere along the length of the long road unraveling through this Underdark-like realm, it had stopped giving him Hell. "Menzoberranzan is a fictional city in Dungeons and Dragons. I used to play this tabletop game all the time with my friends. I wonder what my friends are up to. There was Mike. Oh, man. The last time I saw Mike he treated me like I had leprosy. He wouldn't look me in the eyes. Do you know what I mean? Mike was always this good little Christian boy. He acted like he'd grown out of it, but I know better. People think I don't know better, but I know better. I can see them all like books on a shelf. I can read 'em like that too. Mike didn't even shake my hand when I reached out to shake it, you know? I mean, what the fuck. He's poised to become the mayor of the city in a few years."

"…"

"I'm still batshit crazy right now, aren't I?"

"You passed the first test, if that's what you're wondering."

Joe stopped dead in his tracks, whatever madness instilling mad thoughts in his head stopping dead in its tracks too. Seeing him pause made Ynun pause. Ynun sighed, began nodding his head, and said, "This Vow, the trials that it entails, they're not ordinary. You're questioned at every turn. You don't even know if some of the tests are tests or something devoid of meaning. When you dove into the abyss, you embraced madness. That was the first test. To see whether you would accept a reality beyond reason, and not have your own senses to rely on. Somehow, you not only forewent sanity, but you also traveled the entire length of this field with me, proving that you can reason even when you're robbed of the very faculty of reason itself."

"That's pretty cool and all, but when does this end? Am I going to come out of it or will it stay with me forever?" Joe asked, his heart palpitating as a fresh barrage of deranged thoughts attacked his consciousness.

"It stays with you for as long as it does," Ynun said, then turned around and carried on.

Joe followed him until they came to a stone viaduct held in place by a series of hundreds of arches.

"Are we meant to cross this on foot?" Joe asked.

Ynun did not reply. He only walked. Joe walked behind him, wondering how much time had passed back on earth, if it had passed at all. From the looks of it, this was another dimension, and different dimensions, as per his experience, had different flows of time. Back at the Devil's house, he'd spent days upon days working on the book, and when he'd come out, only moments had passed on earth. Perhaps the same principle applied here. Perhaps not.

After another hour's worth of walking, they came to the end of the viaduct, and now stood at the gate of Cathedral. The castle, ever looming, was behind it, resting on the elevated plain between the mountains. It did not look like they were going to head to the castle at all.

Ynun knocked on the Cathedral door.

Joe stood there wondering why this cathedral resembled the Von Barreth Cathedral. Was it possible that they hadn't traveled anywhere other than his own subconscious? He did not dare ask this question lest it meant that he'd fail one test or another. But from the looks of it, it seemed more and more likely that they were indeed traveling within his subconscious.

Spectral banners hung on either side of the Cathedral, marking it as a place of importance. As the door opened, the banners waved.

Joe gasped, seeing the woman standing there, dressed in white robes, a most somber look on her face. She wasn't happy to see him. He, on the other hand, was weeping where he stood.

"Tasha?"

She nodded, then let him in.

The inside of the Cathedral was entirely different than real ones. Here, there were no pews nor any altar. There was a white marble floor and a domed ceiling, and at the center of the room was a lever. On one side of the lever were the gallows with five ropes hanging. On the other side was a display that looked less like a screen but more like a viewing platform.

Joe hadn't gotten over the initial shock of seeing Tasha in

the Cathedral. She looked beautiful, her cheeks blushing red, her eyes round and large, her hair parted in the middle, long tresses flowing down her shoulders. The pastoral garb did not suit her, yet she wore it with firm authority, just as she wore the sadness on her face.

"Joseph Banbury, the Trial of the Savior commences now," Tasha said. If there was ever any familiarity between the two of them, it had long since died, like Tasha herself had died. She did not even seek to recognize who Joe was or what he'd meant to her. This version of Tasha was apathetic at best, cruel at worst.

"Bring them in," Tasha said, raising her arm.

Joe looked around and found Ynun nowhere in the Cathedral. In the hallowed white glow of the Cathedral, he was alone. But not for longer. A nondescript door opened in the back of the room, and five rigid guards with stony expressions and brawny bodies walked in five people wearing black bags over their faces. Joe did not need to know whose faces were there under the bags, for he recognized each of them by their physiques.

They were Lilly, Joph, Amy, Shaun, and Billy.

One by one, the guards brought them up to the platform, made them step atop the hatches, and put the nooses around their necks.

Then, at the same time, they yanked the black bags off of their faces.

The soon-to-be-hanged shot looks aghast in each direction until they found Joe standing there at the center of the room.

"Joe! What the fuck is happening!?" Shaun yelled. "One minute, I'm sleeping in Iraq of all places, and then I wake up here. If this is about my performance, I'll do better. I'll stop whining. I swear. Just don't kill me, man. I swear. Come on!"

Amy did not say anything. She only cried, looking at Joe with a betrayed look.

Joph was catatonic with shock, and was staring at the rope around his neck going up to the wooden post. His mouth was hung open, dried tears forming streaks down his cheeks. "I guess I should have known it would always end like this."

Billy, who was seemingly no longer possessed by Ynun, shrieked, "Every fiber of my being told me not to find you. But I'm fucked in the head, see. And this is what happens to fucked-in-the-head-men who don't listen to reason. They get hung by the very people they idolize. Never meet your heroes, am I right, fucktard?"

Lilly reached out with her hand, whispering, "I thought we loved each other."

Tasha coughed to clear her throat, bringing Joe's panicked attention to the other side of the lever where the viewing platform showed the world. On the surface of the planet were noticeable orange dots, some of them aloof and afar, others in clusters.

A number appeared on the surface of the screen.

768,981,504.

"This is the number of your adherents, people who have ascribed to the beliefs of the Morning Star movement, people who look up to you as their prophet, their lives forever changed by the impact you've had on them. More than seven hundred million people call themselves members of the Tribe of Morning Star. A baffling number," Tasha spoke, waving her arm at the screen, which zoomed in on the planet, showing a slideshow of all the people who had faith in Joe as their leader. Teenagers laughed as they talked to each other and clapped each other's hands. Middle-aged, sheer black-haired women with thick mascara kneeling in front of Satanic altars in Morning Star temples, praying to Joe. Men dancing around in fire circles, holding each other by the arms, hailing Satan, hailing Joseph Banbury. Rallies in the streets of Madrid. Protests in Rio De Janeiro.

Sit-ins and flashmobs in Chicago, New York, LA to bring Joe Banbury safely back from Iraq. Charity drives and soup kitchens being run by Morning Star tribe members in Philadelphia and Detroit.

"Stop it. This is sick beyond measure," Joe whispered, his throat dry, clawing for breath. He had never before seen his impact on such a scale and at such a speed than he'd done on this ephemeral screen.

Despite his saying so, the screen kept playing snippets from the lives of his tribe members. It showed the newly constructed temple in India being visited by Indian Morning Star members, praying in Hindi. Then, the temple in Geneva, where a lesbian couple was getting married, officiated by a temple cleric saying, "In the name of all that is unhallowed, in the name of Joseph Banbury, I pronounce you woman and wife!" The two women kissed fiercely as they hugged each other in the temple packed with cheering friends and family members. The scene cut to a temple in Newcastle where there was a children's after-school program happening. Little kids accompanied by their parents were being taught by volunteering tribe members. They looked happy, getting to learn about things like ethics, philosophy, and the occasional nerd stuff thrown in to retain their interest.

"Before you is a lever," Tasha said, waving her hand at the lever standing perpendicular to the platform it was on. It was a sharp, brown, one-foot-tall piece of wood tied to gears. "You have a choice. You can either pull the lever and doom your friends to death by hanging. Or you can push the lever and save your friends, but in return, seven hundred million souls perish as a consequence of your choice."

"Is this real?"

"Why don't you ask them?" Tasha pointed to the five people teetering on the edge of the platform, their hands tied, the noose around their necks pulled tight.

"I-I never meant for this to happen," Joe said, holding fistfuls of his hair, pulling at them, not knowing what was happening, and if this was still happening in his Menzoberranzan subconsciousness or in real life. Truly, this test did not involve killing seven hundred million people.

"Jesus Christ," Amy whispered. "I wouldn't want to be in your shoes right now. There's no choice here, Joe. You gotta save...the people."

"But you're my people!" Joe argued fervently, walking over to the platform so that he could be near to his loved ones.

"So are they!" Lilly reasoned. "Seven hundred million people call you their messiah. Think of it. Five people for seven hundred million?"

"Fuck thinking!" Shaun said. "Joe, you can always get new followers. What you don't always get are ride or dies who've been with you since day one. Don't fucking reward our loyalty with death, man. Save us."

"Why? Billy asked Shaun. "Why would he save us? We're flawed, imperfect people, each with our own baggage. I don't know you all well enough, but I'm not the only one with a demon on his back. I can see that you've all got yours. At this point, are we actually helping him or are we the ones holding him back?"

"You shut the fuck up," Joph yelled. "Who the fuck do

you think you are, not even a day old and already making audacious statements!?"

Joe reached past the platform and touched Lilly's leg.

"You know me better than most. What do you think I should do?"

Lilly smiled a teary, wet-faced smile at Joe and said, "Alas, but this is not my Trial. It's yours."

"You're right," Joe said. "It's a Trial. And the universe, in all its infinite wisdom, could only bring forth the most basic of tests. The trolley problem. A problem designed not to have any favorable outcomes. It's a lose-lose in both scenarios."

He could see it very clearly now. It did not matter if this was real or not; what mattered was that he'd cracked the code. He had a choice, as this version of Tasha had said, and it was a no-win scenario. Of all the things that could come to his mind at this moment, the only thing that stuck in the tempest of madness blowing in his mind was Star Trek.

More specifically, Kobayashi Maru.

Captain Kirk had changed the conditions of the test to come out on the other side as a winner.

"Props to whoever designed this test," Joe said to the Cathedral hall at large. "You really threw me off my game with Tasha over here. She's not Tasha, is she? Tasha's dead and somewhere where I can't follow. This is a ruse. And that is too!" Joe pointed at his friends, ready to be hanged. "Kudos on that screen. It was really fucking immersive. Thanks for showing that to me. Here, I'd been disconnected from my movement. But I can see that it's going full steam ahead."

"What choice do you make?" Tasha asked, her tone robotic.

"How about this?" Joe sneered at Tasha, grabbed her by

the back of her head, holding onto her flowing hair with his fist, and then brought her head down on top of the lever with all the brute force he could muster, impaling her skull through the still perpendicular lever.

Blood gushed out of her head as she hung dead with her head pinned by the lever.

Feeling really confident that he'd outwitted the trial, Joe stepped back satisfactorily and beamed at his friends.

They did not reciprocate his smile.

The hatches gave away from under them, and all five of them hung by their nooses, thrashing, gasping, their legs kicking, their eyes growing redder and redder, their faces turning purple.

Lilly was the first one to go limp after she died. Foamy spit oozed out of her mouth. Blood poured out of her nostrils, coagulating over her lips.

Amy hung bent-neck, the look of betrayal still in her lifeless eyes.

Shaun, the fattest of them all, hung there for a minute before the rope gave in, snapped in half, and made his corpse crash through the wooden platform.

Joph looked like a pale mannequin, his lithe form rotating, his face waxy, his eyes closed. Somehow, it looked like he had accepted his fate rather easily.

Before he could look at Billy's hanging body, the screen blared red on the left.

He went over to it, and saw that each of the orange dots on the planet were marked red now. The counter that showed the number of his adherents started to go down.

650,030,180.

The newly opened temple in India, caught on fire, hundreds of people running out, screaming, caught on fire. Those who were unable to escape the fire burned inside, melting away, becoming one with the intricate stonework.

575,234,126.

The little kids in the afterschool program collectively throwing up blood, their parents wailing as they witnessed the death throes of their children helplessly.

341,002,731.

A plane crashing out of the sky, falling on the Geneva temple, the looks of pure bliss removed from the newly married lesbian couple, replaced by pure fear as they watched the plane descend upon the temple, soon to crush everyone under its crashing body.

99,432,112.

Mass shooters surrounding a street full of Morning Star protestors, shooting them down with assault rifles. A bloodbath resulting in an entire avenue filled with corpses holding placards and banners.

3,056, 172.

A cataclysmic flood in Chicago, accompanied by a tornado, killing everyone at large, Morning Star protestors and civilians alike. A woman was trapped under the water, collapsed railings blocking her path. She choked underwater, her hands letting go of the railing, her body going limp and floating against the surface of the water.

631,992.

Religious protests breaking out in Italy. Protestors trampling Morning Star members in the stampede that ensued.

45,353.

Joe forcefully steered his head to the right and saw the stone-faced guards taking his dead friends off the gallows and dragging their bodies out of the hall by way of the same nondescript door.

9,386.

He looked at the screen and saw the numbers had dipped below thousands.

511.

A group of Gothic women knelt in front of the altar, their eyes closed in anticipation of the terror, all of them holding each other's hands, the door of the temple beginning to strain against the brute force of those who stood outside. A window crashed open as a grenade flew into the room. The women looked at the grenade, then at each other, and before they could react, the grenade exploded, ripping their bodies to shreds, blood flowing on the pristine hardwood floor, limbs and viscera splattered all over the ornate walls of the temple.

Joe blinked and saw the counter go down to 1, and then 0.

Tasha, paler than ever, and her white gown now covered in her own blood, shifted from death and pulled her head over the lever that had impaled her. She stood facing Joe, a hole in her head, crimson splattered over her face and shook her head.

"What does this mean? Did I pass? Did I fail? What happened!?" Joe asked. Having seen what he'd just seen, his friends die, all his followers perish, had completely broken his spirit. The question in his head was no longer whether this was real or not. He just needed to know what would happen afterward.

"You had a choice. You *chose* to be clever. There is a difference between wisdom and wit. You are not aware of it. And so you had to witness both consequences," Tasha stated. "Would you like to move forward to the next trial?"

"Wh-what do you mean? Where's Ynun?"

"You disposed of him mere minutes ago. Ynun won't be joining you on the rest of your journey."

Joe stood there, feeling as if he'd been doused in ice, his limbs going numb, his body losing the last remnants of its strength. Tasha opened the door in the back of the Cathedral and beckoned him to follow her.

He looked at the screen one last time. It had turned off and showed nothing anymore.

Joe sighed and followed Tasha into the next room.

Flashpoint Paradox

The next room was not a room but a vacuous space. Although Tasha had opened the door for him, and he had followed her, she was nowhere to be found.

The vacuous space started to fill in with definition. He was standing on the surface of still water. The tranquil surface of this unending ocean spanned infinitely in each direction. Overhead, a blood moon hung low, seemingly dipping into the ocean.

Not sure what he was supposed to do, Joe walked toward the blood moon, watched it get bigger with each step he took.

When he had walked for an hour, he came to a stone fountain that resembled the bird bath in the back of Father O'Hara's church, in front of which he and Joe had sat for a long time and talked about the Devil.

Someone tapped him on his back.

Joe wheeled around to find Father O'Hara standing there in the flesh.

"Father?"

"Joey, my boy," Father O'Hara replied kindly, his face breaking into an affectionate smile, making him squint his eyes and stretch his wrinkled cheeks.

Having experienced death and cataclysm at both a personal and global level, Joe sought to repair his fractured psyche by throwing himself at Father O'Hara and hugging him fiercely. Father O'Hara hugged him back, patting his back.

Joe wept inconsolably, heaving long breaths as he held Father O'Hara firmly.

"My boy," Father O'Hara said, putting his gentle hand on Joe's head. "I wish I could help you. I wish it more than ever now, now that I see what you've become. If only we'd talked more directly that day. Maybe I could have said something that would have helped you on your journey. I'd have swayed you somehow."

"And then what would have happened?" Joe asked, wiping his eyes. "Would none of this have come to pass?"

"You can find that out yourself," Father O'Hara waved his hand at the fountain spouting some silvery waterlike substance. It was thick and viscous, opaque. Joe looked inside, and at first only saw his own haggard reflection staring back at him.

"What's this?"

"A way out. You can opt out of this entire thing if you go inside. It will take away all the challenges that you faced growing up. You'll be born again in the same household, to the same mother and father. Satan will not have sired you. Your own father will have. Your mother will not have met the Devil at all, and therefore won't resort to a life of religious extremism to make up for her grievous sins. It will be a very happy, normal, and peaceful life. You'll thrive as a happy child, and then pursue life on your own terms. No longer fated to become the antichrist. You will forget any of this ever happened. Didn't you wish for the very same thing earlier this night? That you wished for a do-over without all the messed-up things that happened to you?" Father O'Hara asked as he circled the fountain, dipping his hands in the liquid.

Joe looked into the fountain, only this time he did not see his reflection but a very well-kept house in the suburbs of Red Bank, New Jersey. Unlike his actual house, which had been decrepit and run-down even back in the 80s, this was a very prim and maintained residence. A garden in the front. Flowers neatly growing in the flowerbeds. A sprinkler irrigating all the flora. Joyce standing there with the brightest smile on her face, awaiting someone. She was joined by her husband, Tommy. Tommy was smoking a pipe, his gaze following both sides of the street. He had a hand around his wife's waist, something that Joe had never seen his actual father do.

Helplessly, Joe looked up at Father O'Hara.

Father O'Hara nodded. "You can try it before you buy it."

"What happens if I buy it?"

"Then you become a permanent fixture of that reality, absolving yourself from your present one. A shot at a normal life. No more hauntings. No more nightmares. No Hellish tomes to write. No reigning over Hell."

"And what happens if I don't, seeing as how that's the way to pass this test?"

"This test is not so polarized. None of these are. You don't win or lose, pass or fail. If you choose to stay, the one who designed this test will understand and bear you no ill will. No prophecy will ever come to pass. The burden of responsibility will be lifted from your shoulders. The world will do what worlds do best. It will move on."

"It cannot be that easy," Joe pleaded.

"It's not. That's why it's a trial," Father O'Hara said matter-of-factly with a smug grin on his face.

"You're enjoying this, aren't you? Is that what you've been in your afterlife? Administering tests?"

Father O'Hara clapped Joe on the shoulder and laughed.

"Wherever I am, I am fine. Don't you worry about me, my boy. Now, before the water level rises, hurry up, and take a dive in this fountain. It will introduce you to a new reality, and should you decide that you want it, you can stay in there. I will wait here. If you come out, I'll know that you've decided to carry on."

"Well, here fucking goes," Joe said, knowing that he was not ready for what was to happen, but still choosing to dip his head into the fountain.

He fell headfirst into a new reality, screaming at the top of his lungs as his body reached terminal velocity.

* * *

It was different from what he had hoped.

Joe had anticipated finding himself in the body of his eight-year-old self and experiencing how it felt to be a kid from a normal family, but that did not happen. He was still himself and was observing this unfolding scene as an observer.

For some reason, it struck him harder, seeing a healthy-looking eight-year-old cycling up the street with the basket of his bicycle filled with comic books. Not used comic books being covertly snuck into his room; these were brand new, still in their plastic covers, and his eight-year-old self looked quite proud of the haul he was bringing home.

Joe stood across the street watching the well-adjusted parents talk to each other.

"I get a little anxious, you know? He's just eight. And Mikey's nice and all, but going all the way downtown to buy comics? Isn't he a little too young for that?" Joyce asked, slipping her arm around her husband's shoulder.

"It's just your maternal instincts kicking in. Back in my

day, when child labor laws weren't so stiff, I used to lug milk bottles on my bike, deliver 'em to homes," Tommy replied, looking proudly at his kid cycling to a halt in front of the driveway.

Eight-year-old Joe beamed at his parents, waving his hands at the comic books in the front basket. "I got 'em all. The ones I set out to find. X-Men, Spiderman, and the latest Justice League issue where they fight Zod. Cost me only two bucks, can you believe it!?"

"I sure can," Joyce said. "These books are getting more and more expensive each day."

"Pshaw, mom!" Little Joe laughed. "I earned my money fair and square."

"He's got you there, Joyce," Tommy laughed. "Mowed the lawn and all."

"Can I go in and read them, Mom, please!?"

"You can, but after lunch. I want you to go in, wash your hands, see what your sister's up to, and then call her downstairs. I've cooked up a mean brisket that I'd hate to see go to waste."

"Did you make sides?"

"Did I make sides? What do you think?" Joyce grinned. "Mashed potatoes and broccoli."

"That's a major eww on the broccoli, Mama Bear," Little Joe said as he parked his bike in the driveway, carefully taking the comics out and holding them close to his chest as he walked inside.

Joyce and Tommy watched their son head inside, themselves still standing on the pavement, Tommy smoking his pipe, Joyce with her hand on her hip.

"Can't be too careful when you're a parent, you know?" Joyce said.

"But you gotta let 'em grow, babe. It's like—"

"Tommy. The other day I saw a kissing scene in one of his Spiderman comic books. I mean, I didn't know what to say," Joyce whispered.

"It's a kissing scene, Joyce. Kid's probably seen dozens of couples do that in real life. Heck, you've pecked me no less than a hundred times in front of him. A couple years later, he's gonna be a teenager. He might introduce us to his first girlfriend. They won't be playing gin rummy when they're by themselves if you catch my drift."

"You know, Tommy. Sometimes, just listen to a woman. Don't have to make perfect sense every time," Joyce chuckled.

"Yeah, because that's your job, right?" Tommy laughed.

Hand in hand, they walked inside the house now that their son had come home safely.

Joe, who'd been standing there listening to every word, paced behind them and called out a loud, "Hi there!" before they could go inside.

Pleasantly surprised, the both of them turned around and looked at him.

"Hello there," Tommy said, still smoking his pipe. "How can I help ya?"

"That's a strong handshake there, da—" Joe said, shaking Tommy's hand, almost spurting out the word 'dad' before quickly changing it mid-course, "darn."

"Oh, these hands? Thirty years at the factory kinda gives you an iron grip. It's either that or arthritis. God saw to it that I didn't get the other," Tommy smiled care-freely, his skin relatively wrinkle-free. Disease free. This was a face that had never seen cancer.

"You must be Joyce," Joe said, shaking his mother's hand.

"And who might you be, may I ask?" Joyce shook Joe's hand warmly, the warmth extending to the rest of her body in the form of her relaxed pose and her graceful smile. He had never seen his actual mother look so at ease. The hand he held in his hand was not calloused from hard work. It was a soft hand, one that had known nothing but luxury and rest.

"I'm Joe...er... Joe Hawthorne. I'm the guy who bought the house across from you fine folk," Joe pointed behind him, hoping that in this reality, the house across the street was also abandoned.

"Mrs. MacMahon finally found someone to sell it to?" Tommy asked, shaking Joe's hand. "I'll be damned."

Joyce did not reproach her husband for his language. Joe noticed that this version of his mother wore no cross on her neck either. Her hair was not in a bun; it flowed long and silky down her back. That dress was not one that she'd salvaged from the Salvation Army. It was prim.

Joe wondered how.

"And you must be..." Joe directed his attention at Tommy.

"Seeing as how we're going to be neighbors, you can call me Tommy. And I won't be forgetting your name anytime soon neither seeing as you share the same name as my son," Tommy said.

"That's wonderful," Joe said, holding back his tears. Growing up, this was what he had wished for—a well-adjusted family that did not resort to booze or Bible to cope with whatever demons haunted them. Parents who actually loved their son and did not bear him as a burden. As a cross. "And what do you do, Tommy?"

"He's a senior production manager at the Glenson Hardware Factory!" Joyce said, hand on her husband's puffed chest, a proud gleam on her face. "Started from the floor, he did!"

"Well, that's the good old American hustle, isn't it, Tommy?" Joe said, smiling at his father.

"You betcha. And what is it you do, Joe?"

"I'm a writer. And before you go on giving me that look, trust me, I ain't no commie," Joe joked, making them cackle candidly.

"Say, my wife here cooked a nice lunch seeing as how it's a nice Sunday. We've got room at our table for one more. You wanna come in? It'll be like a welcome-to-the-neighborhood kinda thing," Tommy said.

"I hope you like brisket," Joyce added.

The two of them stepped inside the house, hoping that Joe would follow, but when Joe stood his ground, they turned around and gave him an inquisitive look. Folks in Red Bank were some of the most friendly and hospitable that you could find all over the state of New York.

"Oh, guys, look..." Joe tried to reason with himself, knowing that following them inside the house would cement his fate, and make him fail the test. And yet, it was the most tempting sensation he'd ever experienced in his life. If he followed them inside, he didn't know what would happen. Would his consciousness somehow shift into the body of his alternate reality eight-year-old self or would he get a fresh start from scratch, rebirth and all?

As tempting as it was to think about the what-ifs and why-nots, Joe stood his ground, shook his head, "...you seem like lovely folk. But...there's this matter that I've got to see to. Maybe in another lifetime?"

He stifled a sob, covering his face casually so that they wouldn't notice.

"Another lifetime!?" Joyce laughed. "Don't be silly. You live across the street. Drop by anytime."

It broke his heart as he smiled one last time at his

parents, but what truly sent a fracture line traveling down its center was seeing bright-eyed, eight-year-old Joe running up to his parents and jumping into his father's arms. Tommy kissed his son on the cheek. Joyce ruffled his hair.

But young Joe's gaze was fixated on the stranger standing in the driveway.

He waved at the stranger.

The stranger waved back.

"Have a great life, kid," Joe whispered, his voice breaking, eyes welling up. It was the hardest thing, turning around and stepping away from the house, but he managed to do it.

He might not have lived a perfect life—in fact, it was a life that was as on the opposite part of the spectrum from perfect as could be—but he'd lived a remarkable life nonetheless. Or so he told himself to console his aching heart. He didn't believe a word of it. That kid, the one in his father's arms, holding onto the fresh new comic books, he'd live a remarkable life. A boringly predictable and remarkable life with all the right things happening at the right time.

It was time for Joe to return to the mess that was his life.

* * *

His face covered in the silver substance, Joe finally pulled himself out of the fountain, taking deep breaths. It hadn't seemed so, but that prophetic liquid was actually quite suffocating. Joe sank down on the floor as he tried to ease the burning in his lungs, wishing more than anything to smoke a good old Marlboro right about now.

Father O'Hara sat down by his side, and to his surprise, took out a cigarette from his pocket.

"Light up, son," Father O'Hara said, procuring a lighter, letting Joe have his oral fixation.

Joe quietly smoked, wondering if it was too late to go back into that reality where his mother's face was not marred by the scars of age and his father was a successful and healthy man.

"I can't go back, can I?"

"I am afraid it's too late for that. You already made the decision to come back. If there's one thing that the Absolute deals in, it's absolutes."

"Kind of like the Sith," Joe chuckled. This cigarette tasted like death.

"Not exactly. With God and the Devil, you'll see that there's a sense of bargaining. With God, no matter how many times you sin, you can always bargain for forgiveness. With the Devil, it's the same way. You turn down his temptations and he'll come back with better and better temptations, bargaining with you to come over to the dark side," Father O'Hara stated, his back resting against the concrete pillar of the fountain. "But when it comes to the Absolute, there aren't any grounds for bargaining. You either pull the lever or push it. There's no room for a third option. With this test, too, you either relinquished everything and stayed in that alternate reality or you came out. There's no other choice."

"I seem to be doing pretty fucking shitty at these trials," Joe said.

"I wouldn't say that. As I said, the Absolute deals in absolutes. No percentage connotes failing or passing. You either pass or you fail," Father O'Hara said.

"Does it blow your mind, this realization that there's someone above God, someone called the Absolute? All your life you preached the word of God, and now, you're talking about an entity that's bigger and more powerful than God. Does it not make your mental faculties crack?" Joe stood up, and doused the stub of his cigarette in the fountain, pissing on any sanctimonious that this place possessed.

So fucking Avant Garde, he thought as he stared at the pristine fountain tampered by the smoldering cigarette stub sticking to its surface like a greedy fly caught on the surface of a vanilla cake.

"Not really," Father O'Hara stayed put where he was, shaking his head. "Neither Satan nor God are separate from the Absolute in my mind. The Absolute sought to interact with the world he created. With the worlds, I should say. And so he created two manifestations. One divine. The other unholy. Yin and Yang. What does it matter if I'm talking about God or the Absolute? To me, they're one and the same."

"But they're not, though," Joe argued. "The Absolute in their absoluteness embody both good and evil. Your God's all good. Your Devil's all vile. By your own metric, you should be talking about the Devil with the same reverence as you do about God!"

"And did I not?" Father O'Hara raised his eyebrow. "I talked of the Devil with the same amount of condemnation as I did of God with reverence. I taught my followers to fear his snares. Warned them of fire and brimstone, the domain of Satan. God demanded reverence. The Devil demanded despisal."

"Suit yourself. If they're reflections of the same entity, why the polarity in the first place?" Joe scoffed, his lifelong anger at the nonsensical nature of organized religion resurfacing.

Now, Father O'Hara rose up and stretched his back. When he was done, he placed his hand on Joe's shoulder.

"Would you believe me if I told you that it's the Absolute's primordial way of playing good cop, bad cop?"

"At this point, I don't know what to believe. But this Absolute sure seems like he's got a sense of fucking humor. It'd explain why he put the male g-spot inside the asshole."

Father O'Hara chortled, looking in the distance.

"You have one last test ahead of you."

"It can't be any more difficult than the ones I've already been through," Joe sighed. "Or did I just fucking jinx it?"

Father O'Hara looked behind Joe, nodding solemnly.

"He awaits you."

Joe didn't turn around. Whoever had appeared behind him had such an intimidating effect that it turned Joe's back to ice, raising his hair on edge, rooting him to the spot. Around him, everything started to dissolve. The water disappeared, leaving there nothing in its absence other than pure blackness. No moon hung in the sky nor any light emanated from any source, trivial or large.

Father O'Hara began to fade as the other approached, his steps echoing in the nothingness.

"Who's he?"

"The Equalizer."

"Great!" Joe said sarcastically.

"The great equalizer, my boy. And it is here that I bid you farewell. It was pleasant seeing you again."

"Don't leave me alone," Joe called out to Father O'Hara's disappearing form.

"In the end, the great equalizer sees to it that we're all alone. Every mortal has to taste death, Joe."

Joe gulped raw air, standing in the utter dark, the presence behind him now standing right behind him, his cold presence causing Joe's bones to become frosted.

"Hello there, Mr. Banbury," a baleful voice spoke behind him.

"Who's there?"

"I have been called the full stop at the end of every sentence. The finality of seem. Your priest called me the great equalizer. That was nice of him to put it like that. Everyone comes to know me quite intimately. I am the one who snuffs the light at the end of the tunnel."

Joe rolled his eyes and wheeled around, coming face to face with Death.

"You do realize that was the most cliché monologue in the history of monologues," Joe said.

Death, who did not stand in front of him black-robed and scythe-wielding but in a black, impeccably tailored suit, had a handsome face resembling a young Hugo Weaving, sharp features and all. With hawklike eyes he gazed at Joe, his very gaze killing a little bit of him. There was some bit of strange comfort in those eyes.

"I wouldn't know," Death shrugged, unsmiling. "I've usually killed people off before they've had a chance to tell me if I'm being cliché or unhackneyed. I'm not here to wag tongues and trade clever aphorisms. I am here to take your life, Mr. Banbury."

Ego Sacrifice at the Altar of Self

While Joe was still coming to terms with the fact that Death had shown up not in the capacity of a Collector but as someone who was going to end Joe's life, the scenery around them changed.

This time around, they did not have to walk anywhere. All Death had to do was clap his hands and a tall altar rose from nothingness.

"Quite immaculate," Death admired his handiwork, stepping on the stairs that led up to the altar, leaving Joe standing there in disbelief, wondering what kind of test this was if it involved Joe dying. Who would find the Epoch if he died? Would the universe in its infinite wisdom wait for another thousand years to pass before posing the same test to some other shmuck?

Was this perhaps the reason why there hadn't ever been a savior so far? Because the Aeternum Trials killed off whoever struck it out till the very end? Was there even an Epoch at all?

Death clapped its hands, making a warm orange-yellow glow fall upon the altar. It was made of stone—carved stone with intricate patterns and dead languages etched to convey a message that Joe already knew; this was where he died. At the center of the altar was a slab with a deep grove in it, presumably where Joe would have to put his neck.

Behind the elevated slab was a statue in the likeness of Jesus, only instead of Jesus, Joe Banbury hung there, his meticulously carved body hanging by the cross.

"Welcome, Banbury, to the Altar of Self," Death spoke, mincing no words. "This is where you have to kill yourself."

"Why?"

"Why, what, precisely?"

"What's the fucking point? Why do I have to kill myself?"

Death sniffed the air, adjusting the creases that had appeared on his white shirt. Then he buttoned down the front of his jacket and descended down the steps to where Joe stood.

"Because the Absolute has deemed it so. This test. All these tests, as a matter of fact, are meant for a savior who can right the wrongs, bring balance, and unify the universe. What have you done that remotely resembles any of what I have spoken? Nothing. You are an agent of chaos, a servant of Satan, and all you have done in your life is tilt and topple every balanced thing in your path. You covet life. You crave power. You consider yourself the sole intellectual to have ever walked the earth. Even your attitude here and along your tour has smacked of an egocentric maniac who gives little rise to anything but himself. Everyone else seems like cattle to you. Menial mules and bulls plowing fields and pulling weights. The Absolute has passed his judgment, and it is this. For this world to thrive, for there to be another savior another two thousand years later, you must die. Relinquish your right to the Epoch. Kill yourself," Death stated, producing a cleaver out of thin air, its blade sharp and curved, its handle ornate and black. He handed the cleaver to Joe, who wielded it in both hands apathetically, and then stepped away.

Joe climbed up the steps and stood in front of the altar. He had missed a lot of the sacrificial depictions from below. At the base of the statue's feet were books. The statue was crushing them. On the right side of the statue, the forces of God were bracing for a fight, angels with halos, crusaders with giant swords, and heavenly entities descending in a bid to smite the unhallowed. On the left side of the statue, there was an armada of the damned led by someone familiar. Satan stood at the head of a ship, wielding his trident, yelling orders at his legions upon legions.

Joe was the barrier between them, hung with a crown of thorns, nails impaling his palms and his feet in place.

"You've brought the world to the brink of a religious war. If you are not stopped, you will push the world beyond the precipice. The end of times, as you know them, will usher, and blood will flow freely in the street of every city in the world as men of God and men of the Devil murder each other in the name of their patron deities. Nothing of the sort transpires if you end your life and spare this world. Perhaps, in the next cycle, a truly deserving savior can pass this test and wield the Epoch to unite the universe in the image of the Absolute, because you," Death spat, looking disdainfully at Joe, "are not capable enough to do that."

"Jesus Christ, I get it. It's overkill. Are you compensating for all the clichéd shit earlier?"

Death ignored Joe's words and issued the order. "Joseph Banbury. Take your life. Or it shall be taken from you." Upon saying these words, Death transformed from the impeccably dressed man to his real form—that of a Collector, standing there taller than the altar, wearing the black night as his robe, wielding its all-powerful silver scythe, his eyes no longer softly gazing but glaring redly, his skin turning to white bone.

"I don't get a choice?"

"No. You are too volatile to be offered a choice. Make it easy on yourself. Die."

With his hands shaking under the weight of the decision and the blade they held, Joe knelt in front of the altar. The stone the altar was made of looked blood-starved, its porous surface whispering, calling for blood. His blood.

Joe brought the blade to his neck.

He smiled, relieved.

This was the end, wasn't it?

No more Devil haranguing him. No more leading the Morning Star movement. No lovers to be held accountable to. No people to let down anymore. No one else would die because of him. His death would equalize all that was wrong with the world. Maybe his body would wash ashore on earth and people far and wide would see their dead messiah. They would lose faith in his message. Insanity would be abandoned in favor of sanity. Satan would have to wait for another thousand years for another savior.

If by his death he could make all that happen, avert the apocalypse, and put an end to this madness, then all of this was not in vain. His torture would end, and with it, so would the world's.

"Do I go to Hell after I kill myself?"

"Where else do you think the likes of you are sent to?"

Instead of his heart sinking, Joe smiled. "It's fitting. Besides, that's where all the good music is." Before he slit his throat, Joe looked up at Death's dispirited skull and asked, "All that shit you said about me, it was pretty fucking bleak. Surely I must have done something right in all my life?"

"In the face of all that you have done wrong in your life, it pales in comparison," Death brooded.

Joe took a deep breath, his breath cold, his fingers numb, and then lifted the blade once again to his neck. He closed his eyes against the pain, finally doing something that he had ideated all his life.

In all the different ways he'd fantasized about talking about his life over the years, he had never imagined it to be something as ceremonial and official as this.

Finally, with what little strength he had left in his hands, he sliced the blade across his neck, anticipating the pain. It came in a frenzy, the sensation of this throat being ripped open, the tendons and muscles cutting, gushing blood. It felt like there was a black hole in his throat, sucking away all the life from the rest of his body. His arms felt limp, as did his legs. He was no longer kneeling in front of the elevated slab, but on the floor, thrashing, writhing, guttural sounds rising involuntarily out of his gashed neck.

In the few more seconds he stayed alive, Joe was very aware of all the blood that had oozed out of him and was now pooling under him, clinging to the back of his head, soaking up in his clothes and making them wet and cold. He was cognizant of his waning strength quickly evacuating his body. As painful as this sensation was, it also brought forth great closure to Joe, which was the last thing he was expecting. Ever since he had published The Skeptic, Joe was aware of the momentous change he was an agent of. Most of the time, he ignored the magnanimity of it and kept himself busy in life; however, when, on the few occasions, that he had to come to terms with it, Joe felt existentially terrified at what he had done. How callously he had influenced millions without ever thinking how it would affect their lives. Now, he would never do that again.

And what a beautiful thing that was.

A quite hopeful last thought to be snuffed out to.

No more hauntings.

No more guilt.

No more pain.

His breath caught up in his ripped throat one last time, and it was at this time that his life force slipped away, leaving his body soulless, sacrificed at the altar of self.

* * *

"Every mortal must taste death," Death spoke to no one in particular, "And now that Joseph Banbury has tasted death, he is no longer a mortal."

The scythe he wielded brimmed with a pure white light. Death brought the scythe's tip down to Joe's dead body and poured the essence into his slit throat.

"Arise, therefore, Deathless One."

The shimmering light glinting off the scythe solidified at Joe's throat, sealing the place where he had cut himself fatally.

"Arise not in the name of any God or any Devil but in

the name of one who rules Absolute above all. Arise, savior, and claim what is rightfully yours. For you have passed the Trials of the Aeternum Vow. Arise, Ascended. Arise free from all influences but your own. Your life your own. Death ne'er to darken your doorstep again. Arise and do what thou wilt, for that is the law. Your law."

Joe stirred back to life, his hands finding his throat, aware of the alien sensation that had sealed the gash shut. It was not noticeable in any way other than by a cool sensation that was waning fast. In another moment, even the sensation was gone, leaving Joe there sitting, wondering what had happened, his ears ringing with the words of Death.

"What just happened?" Joe asked, blinking blankly as he looked around confusedly. "Why am I back? There was so much peace where I was!"

"Because your task here is not yet done. By sacrificing your ego at the altar of self, Joseph, you have passed the last of the trials of the Aeternum Vow," Death spoke, and as he did, he transformed himself from his menacing self to the mild-mannered one in the crisp suit. "Congratulations."

Joe shook Death's hand, still confused.

"So, all that stuff you said?" Joe asked.

"It was part of the test. To drive your ego to the precipice of desolation. And then kill it. Which you did remarkably well. How long have you been holding back the urge to kill yourself?"

"I've lost count of the years," Joe replied. "I...you said all that stuff about me being Deathless and Ascended and whatnot. I don't feel different. I still feel...Joe."

"Well, *still* Joe," Death grinned cheerily. "You only passed the tests. You have yet to wield power. You overcame the most sinister of malfeasances, madness itself. You made an impossible choice possible. You relinquished your right to a life of luxury. And finally, you conquered death. You passed not one, two, but all of the trials."

"Now what?" Joe asked.

"Now that my job is done, I hand you back to your friend, Ynun. He will explain the rest. As for me, well, goodbye forever, Mr. Banbury. We shan't ever meet again."

"I was just beginning to like you."

Death smiled, a brief reflection of sadness in his eyes. "Do you want to know a secret, Mr. Banbury?"

"Shoot."

"I have witnessed your toil from the first day. Your mother, knowing that you were the son of the Devil, sought to strangle you in your crib merely an hour after you were born. I was there, ready to take your sinless soul. But she stopped. I don't know why she did, but I did not get to take your soul that day. When the demons visited you each night, so did I, not knowing which night they'd finally kill you. When Satan showed up at your doorstep, I was told to remain on high alert, what with Satan being so ill-tempered and impulsive. I have not kept watch over another soul in my entire lifespan as I have yours. And you have lived an arduous life. You have my utmost respect, Mr. Banbury. It is not in my nature to have friends. But if it was, know that you would have been my friend."

"Thank you, Azrael," Joe said. "Should things change and you find yourself in a capacity to have friends, you know where to find me."

Death embraced Joseph with a hug he had not felt before, surprising warmth, seeping his body with comfort, nourishing him with strength. As he transferred this angelic energy into Joe's body, Azrael whispered, "This is a little pick-me-up from me. No one told me to give it to you. This I give of my own volition, your strength renewed, your mind fortified."

Joe no longer felt frail and drained of blood. With a jump in his step, he got to his feet and yelled loudly, "Whoo! Jesus Christ, that was like a doze of coffee made from Red Bull!"

"I am glad, and this is goodbye."

* * *

In the madness of dimension hopping that followed, Joe was only aware of a hand on his wrist. He trusted that hand. He let the hand guide him through the blinding lights and the brilliant display of colors until they came to a sudden stop atop a rooftop in Waha.

Billy, still possessed by Ynun, stood next to Joe, a look of deep happiness and satisfaction on his face.

"What gives?" Joe asked, his astral body adjusting to all the traveling they'd done by way of queasiness. But the moment passed, and with it, so did the nausea.

"I am most impressed by you, Joseph," Ynun said. "You passed the trials of the Aeternum Vow. And now, I get to share with you the location of the Epoch."

"Just like that? I was hoping there'd be sort of a ceremony for me passing the trials," Joe grinned.

"The ceremony, Mr. Banbury, comes after. There is still the task of retrieving the Epoch, and that is no small feat. Take it seriously, Mr. Banbury. Neither is what comes after it," Ynun said, raising his hand and placing it on Joe's forehead. He pressed his thumb deep into Joe's skull, embedding by way of telepathy the location of Epoch.

"Hey, I know this place!" Joe exclaimed as the image formed clearly in his head.

"As does everyone, but no one knows that the most important artifact in the entirety of this universe is stored here."

"I just bade Death a touching farewell, and between you and me, after everything that's happened tonight, I'm quite drained. Can we just call it a night without, you know, cranking things to an eleven in the emotional department?" Joe asked, taking stock of his surroundings. The night was just as still and quiet as it was when he had left. In fact, from the looks of it, it seemed like no more than a couple of minutes had passed since he'd gone.

"Mr. Banbury, unlike Death, I'm not going anywhere. We may end up meeting again. But for now, now that I have performed my task, I have to abscond. No long farewells," Ynun nodded, shaking Joe's hand.

"See you when I see you," Joe said.

"Indubitably. Now, I will return this body to its host. And I bid you do the same."

Joe watched as Ynun, still possessing Billy, headed down the rooftop stairs, giving up control of the body sometime after. He could hear Billy asking, "What the fuck just happened?!" but he was too exhausted to head down after him and fill him in on everything. He would do that the following morning.

Joe waded back to his corporeal form and occupied it, waking up to find Lilly standing there, frowning at him, arms on her hips, a look of sheer worry on her face.

"We need to talk," Lilly spoke, her words bereft of any love that she had for Joe.

15

THE WITCH

Something Wicked This Way Comes

Once upon a time, the universe shifted, and a witch was born. Such was how all witches were born—a consequence of a vacuum. They were not sent on a holy mission by a patron deity nor did they rise out of Hell to heed the call of a dark master; witches simply were—and they were there to serve as an antidote to most of what was wrong with the world. Their powers and the innate wisdom that they carried allowed them to holistically seek the off-kilter and bring it back to balance.

A kitten got its legs crushed by a speeding van? A witch was there to fix it with a dose of her magic.

A land struck by draught, its inhabitants dying of thirst and starvation? A witch would summon the clouds.

As proactive as the universe was in sending witches wherever witches were needed, the sad truth of the world was that there were problems aplenty and only a handful of witches left to deal with them.

For magic was not an infinitely renewable source. There was only so much of it in the ether, and only so many people who could tap into the ether. When the world got wise to the ways of the witches, instead of revering them as the matron deities that they were, the world burned them at stakes, dissolving any faith that the universe had in the world. It did not altogether stop but severely limited its sending of witches lest they grow in number to become noticeable enough to be mass-burned at stakes or hunted by narrowminded men of the clergy.

The universe had gotten wise to the ways of the world, and only the world suffered for it.

But whenever there was a big disparity, the universe forwent its rule and sent a powerful witch to deal with a powerful problem.

Lilly Thurman was one such witch, and her thumbs pricked something awful.

* * *

While she had successfully hidden her true self from the rest of the world—even from Joseph Banbury, whom she had recently gotten into a relationship with—she felt that she could not do so anymore. Joseph Banbury had uncovered her secret.

She had performed a spell in secret, a spell called 'The Casting of Fate,' so that she could read the destinies of those who were close to her. Chart out the right way for them to leave Iraq and go safely back to the United States. But she had not anticipated that Joseph Banbury would be standing there in his astral form on the rooftop of the house.

She sensed his presence on the rooftop, her Third Eye being wide awake and staring around in every direction, and had tried to stop her spell in time, but failed. Joe had already touched the fabric of her fate, and in doing so, had discovered that she was not some mere mortal but a vessel of magic.

In the brief window during which Joseph Banbury was escorted to the deep depths of the Astral Realm, Lilly wondered how she would break it to him that she was a witch all along, from the time she was a little girl and got lost in a forest only to be rescued by a pack of wolves to the time when she wrote his homework assignment for him back in college and transported it into his locked room. There was no easy way to reveal this, and so perhaps it was a good thing that Joe had come upon this information on his own and rather intrusively so. It was a profane act to touch another's weave of fate, a profane act that witches were pardoned from, but not ordinary people.

Joseph Banbury was not ordinary people. Joseph Banbury, as Lilly knew well enough, was the antichrist, the Devil's prophet who had recently learned about the existence of the universe's most profound secret—the Epoch.

How Lilly knew about the Epoch and the Absolute was a long story, one that involved her divining the mysteries of the universe under the tutelage of her coven's madam sorceress, who spared no effort in equipping her pupils with all manners of spells and the wisdom behind each of them. On off days, the madam sorceress would speak on meditative matters, matters of introspection, and matters of mystery, prefacing each conversation by saying that each witch was free to believe in whatever she wished, for that was the holistic way.

In time, Lilly forgot about those lessons, the ones that spoke at length about the creation of the universe and matron deities like Asherah and Lilith and Hathor and Hecate, all the while still channeling their energy. She remained true to her purpose, holistically solving problems of imbalance in the world.

Her specialty, in terms of the magic she wielded, was words. She could weave poetry out of thin air, and that poetry wouldn't just be a combination of fanciful words; those words would contain within themselves enough power to alter the course of someone's life.

Once, she had recited a poem in front of a young and impressionable Joe, a poem that had bolstered his spirits and had kept him true to the course of writerly pursuits.

Later, when it was revealed to her that Joseph Banbury was communing with the Devil and writing an apocryphal book based on the life of Satan himself, she had not seen it as the opportunity it was but the biggest imbalance she had ever witnessed in her life. If this thing tipped the other way, it would result in the world coming to an end.

The end of days.

Apocalypse.

For he wasn't just the Devil's scribe; Joseph Banbury was the son of Lucifer, the antichrist himself. She had read plenty from sources far and wide (and not just biblical) to recognize the antichrist when she saw him. Every religion, cult, and creed talked of a being who would bring forth Armageddon. The Norse knew him as Surtr, the Muslims knew him as Dajjal, the Christians called him the False Messiah, the Hindus identified him as Lord Vishnu's final avatar Kalki. He was the one constant that all the diverging belief systems of the world agreed upon. There might've been hundreds and thousands of gods in all those religions combined, but when it came to the Heralder of the End, they all agreed that it was one person.

Joseph Banbury.

Lilly's recent discussions with Joseph had revealed to her

that he was being guided by the universe—the same force that guided Lilly—to find the Epoch, an artifact placed in this realm by the One Above All, the Absolute, as the ultimate test of free will. After talking to him, Lilly traversed the Axis Mundis, past the Collectors realm and on to her Madam, who asked her to revise what she had told her about the Epoch.

After a long conversation with her mentor, Lilly could not help but agree with the parting words.

"If Joseph Banbury is indeed who you think he is, and if you're asking me about the Epoch, then know this, child," the madam bade, "Under no circumstance should he ever find it. This is a man who has already sided with the Devil. If he wields the Epoch, he will bring ruin to this universe. But I shouldn't be too worried about that. The universe, in all its infinite wisdom, has devised tests. I am not confident that he will pass them. The Trials of the Aeternum Vow are many things, but they are not easy."

This conversation had only served to unnerve Lilly further, as she knew what Joseph was capable of. He might be a man who had sided with the Devil time and time again, but he was the only man she knew who had gone toe to toe with the Devil and lived to tell the tale. Her madam sorceress did not know what Joseph was capable of.

Lilly did.

She scried at night—a practice deeply prohibited—to see where Joseph was, and found him in the deepest recesses of the Axis realm going through the Trials of the Aeternum Vow.

If he failed the tests, that would be the end of the matter, and they could go about living their lives as intended. But if somehow, he passed, then it was all down to Lilly to ensure that Joseph did not get his hands on Epoch.

While he was still in the astral realm, Lilly snuck into the room of the man she had been charged to oversee, a man she was deeply in love with, and stood there waiting for him to surface, knowing that what was to follow was not going to be easy for either of them.

But if it would save the world, then it did not have to be easy.

It would still be worth it.

The Hour of Crows

Steeped in black, standing tall in bare feet and wielding her hands imbued with deep magic, Lilly Thurman, magic incarnate, faced the antichrist, her heart hammering arrhythmically with trepidation.

"We certainly do," Joe said, standing up from the sofa, kicking his legs around to get a feel for them. Having perfected her own version of astral projection over a lifetime, Lilly was well aware of the toll leaving your body took on you once you came back to it. That's why you never astral projected for longer than an hour. Otherwise, your muscles atrophied and your basal body abandoned sanity for insanity after wondering where its occupant had gone. Joe was getting reacquainted with his physical body after traveling goddesses knew where.

"You first," Lilly said, forces that she had so far kept at bay seeking a channel for escape by way of her eyes (they crackled with the electricity of oracular prophecy, probing into Joe's soul to unearth any secrets hidden therein), by way of her fingers (their grip tightened on the wand she had concealed in the sleeve of her robe), and by way of her mouth (for her tongue was begging to recite a poem powerful enough that it might kill Lilly after speaking the last word but at the same time seal the fate of the universe by stopping Joe dead in his tracks). She kept those forces at bay and sought to reason with the love of her life by way of simple, unenchanted words.

"Me first? You're in my room!"

"You can drop the act right about now, Joe."

Fury flashed across his face as he, just as powerful—if not more—than her, affected her with a judgmental gaze before softening his features and looking at her not as a trespassing interrogator but as the woman he had opened his heart to. This could be an opportunity for them to grow closer to one another if he reasoned well enough with her.

"I never had an act to drop in the first place, Lill. You, on the other hand....I *saw* who you were in the weaves of fate," Joe said. "How come you never told me you were a witch? Do you know how that drives the average guy crazy, to have a thick, goth magical mommy as their girlfriend? I'd have let you tie me to a pentagram and do whatever you wanted. Real missed opportunity, babe."

Lilly resisted the urge to laugh. In the face of the gravity of it all, she dared not laugh.

"I kept that part of my life concealed, and it would have remained concealed if you hadn't been astral projecting when I was performing my spell earlier tonight," Lilly said.

"Why were you performing that spell, if I may ask?" Joe asked, sitting back down on the sofa now that he'd reacquainted himself with his body. Thanks to the touch of Death, he did not feel as exhausted as he should have been. He was also quite in control of his rage. This was a conversation that he could potentially navigate without resorting to anger.

"Because I was worried for us. I've been safeguarding us with covert spells and charms since the moment we landed in Iraq. That miraculous appearance of the helicopter in the balcony of the hotel? That was all me. If that chopper had been one minute late, we'd have been stampeded upon by the mob," Lilly pleaded. There was some relief in her tone. Now that her secret was out, she could talk more freely about what she had been doing underhand all this while. "I only did the spell to foresee my own fate and check to see if I'd make it back to the States in one piece. You weren't supposed to touch my strand."

"Oh, come now. I've touched more than your strand," Joe grinned sheepishly.

"Can you stop being so juvenile for five minutes? This is serious," Lilly covered her face with her palm, her fingers digging into her forehead to drive out the vexation. But there was no hex nor jinx she knew that could eliminate vexation; if at one point she knew about it, she had forgotten the exact spell for it way back when.

"Okay. In the interest of transparency, and since I already saw yours, I'll show you mine," Joe said, then shared his story with her. He told her all about tonight, including the trials, and when he was done, he said, "There. I'm not hiding anything anymore. Nor did I intend to hide it from you. I would have told it to you the first thing in the morning. Well, no harm no foul. Now you know."

Lilly, who had listened to his entire story with a look of horror on her face, just sat there with her mouth hanging open. This was not as the madam had foretold. Joe had somehow passed the Trials of the Aeternum Vow. This made matters worse than she had anticipated. Half the speech she had prepared was for the occasion where Joe might have failed the Trials and she'd have consoled him, told him that he could go back to his old life or even start a new one with her. But she discarded that speech in a mental trashcan and brought forth the other one, the one she had hoped she wouldn't have to give.

"I presume you want to know more about my being a witch?" she asked, sitting down on the edge of the bed, revising what she was going to say in the meantime.

"I am a little taken aback that you'd hold back something this huge about yourself from me," Joe said, reaching out to hold her hand. "And I'm sorry. I didn't mean to pry. I've been since then told that it's a blasphemous thing to do, touching someone else's fate-strand like that."

"Joe, the life I lead as a witch is a very secretive one. No one, not even the other witches, knows what I've been up to just as I don't know what they're up to. We're not the front-facing reception desk agents of the world. We're grunt workers, doing back-end stuff that no one sees or cares about. We nurture and nourish, tend and befriend. And whatever we do, we have to do it in secrecy, or do I need to remind you of the last time witches went public? The very grounds of Salem are still bitter with the ashes of all the witches burned there," Lilly said. She could feel herself growing even lighter now that she could share this deepest and most secret part of her life with Joe.

"You could have trusted me with it. I wouldn't have told anyone," Joe said.

"I think we're going off on a tangent from the bigger picture here," Lilly said, trying to get the conversation back on its original subject matter, that of the Aeternum Vow.

"Stay with me on this tangent a bit. I love you, always have, and I care enough about you to want to know more about your life."

"I love you too, and perhaps that's why instead of casting a forgetting spell on you, I'm sharing it with you," Lilly smiled, the creases of her smile showing just how vulnerable she was being.

"Then share more. For instance, that day when I woke

up in my locked-from-the-inside dorm room, was it you who wrote my assignment? All this time I've been thinking the L stood for Lucifer," Joe said, now holding onto her hand even more firmly.

"It was me," Lilly smiled back. "I couldn't help it. Couldn't you tell? I'd developed a crush on you in the few minutes we'd talked."

"Finally that mystery resolves," Joe breathed deep. "Jesus Christ, here I'd been going crazy wondering who did that. Now I know it's my witchy boo who did it."

"Stop," Lilly blushed, looking away. She looked back at him, thinking something, only to ask it seconds later. "You could have been deeply mad with me just now. Why aren't you?"

"Because between slicing my own throat open at the altar of self and this...I'm still processing the former. Kind of puts it all into perspective. It wasn't the only death I saw tonight. I saw you die during one of the Trials. It broke me bad. Seeing you here, alive, well...it's everything."

Joe reached over and kissed Lilly softly on the cheek. She responded by holding onto his collar and pulling him close, reaching forward, and kissing him on the lips.

"In another life, where I wasn't a witch and you weren't the antichrist, we'd have made a great couple, and I could have told you that I love you without you thinking that I had an ulterior motive in mind," Lilly said, sudden tears trailing down her face. "It doesn't matter if I say that I love you a thousand times over, you won't ever believe me, will you?"

"Where is this coming from?" Joe hugged her tightly. "I know you love me. Babe, I love you too. What are you talking about?"

Her face wet with tears, strained with sadness, she

asked, "You don't think that I'm leading you on so that I can stray you from your goal? You don't think I'm a distraction?"

"If anything, babe, I think that you're my true north, steering me in the right direction. I haven't ever doubted that you'd do such a thing. And even when we fought and parted ways, I knew deep in my heart that you had my best interest in mind. I was just too coked up on Devil juice to see straight."

"Don't say Devil juice," Lilly chuckled, her face still wet from the tears that her vulnerability had made come out. Joe, giggling, dapped her face with the edge of her black robe, drying it.

"What are you not saying?" Joe asked sincerely.

"If I say it, you will hate me for it."

"I think we've established that I am deeply in love with you for that to be true."

"Know that my love for you is just as true, but the responsibility upon my shoulders demands that I say what I have to say."

"Then let's unburden your shoulders. Say it. I'll listen to everything you have to say."

Lilly looked at the man who was kneeling in front of her, and could see that a part of him had returned changed from the astral realm. She wondered if it had changed enough that she should abandon her worries and let him pursue the Epoch.

In that moment, she tried to gauge just how much of Satan's influence Joe was still under, and after peering into him, she found none of it.

But still she worried, and so she shared what she deemed was right.

The harder of the two speeches.

Lover's Remorse

"Every so often, a witch gets assigned a task of great significance. It does not matter who does that. To be honest with you, it's rather holistic, this bequeathing, but back when I first met you, I was given your charge. I did not know why exactly I was appointed to oversee you, guide you, and help you where I could, but as time went by, it became clear. Nowhere did it say that I had to be your consort. I did that myself. But the rest of it, from guiding your manuscript to the right hands so that it could be published to shunning you when you wouldn't listen to reason, it was all premeditated," Lilly began, uncertain of whether Joe would still love her by the end of her speech, but so far he was still very amenable, listening to her words with an understanding look on his face.

"Remember what I told you back when you were seeking to publish your second book?" Lilly asked.

"That nothing good could come out of it. And you were partly right. I am sure you remember that I was punished by the Devil, and rather severely so. He had me trapped in Hell until I cried uncle," Joe said. "My arm had been wrung as tight as it could have. I did not have a choice."

Lilly clasped her hands around his and pulled him closer, her words earnest as she said, "But you have a choice now. Now, you get to put it all behind you and just...stop."

"Why?" Joe asked, pulling his hands away from her grasp. "Why would you say that? Did you not hear me recount the entire Aeternum Vow and everything it entailed? First I saw those close to me die, then I saw all my followers die. If that wasn't bad enough, I was tempted with a life of normalcy, a chance for a do-over. You know what stopped me from taking that chance? You did. I could see your face. I could see Joph's face. Amy, the actual Amy that's my sister and not some alternate reality version of her. Real people who have touched my life and have made it very real. How could I have been so selfish as to ditch them and seek a new life entirely? Finally, Lill, when all was said and done, Death himself ordered me to kill myself. Ask yourself this. What selfishness or pride or ulterior purpose would I have left in me after I killed myself? The Joe that's in front of you is a changed man. One who's taken a long time to break free from the influence that Satan had over me so far. After such a long fucking time, I have a new purpose, one that isn't riddled in the murkiness of evil or bathed in the blinding glow of God's hallowed goodness. I get to do something that affirms my belief in the fact that it does not matter if you believe in a God or not because belief in and of itself is not relative, but absolute. You can't believe in God one day when you're feeling devout and then discard Him like a used condom when you don't feel like vibing with his beatitudes. You have to be absolute in your faith. And what I saw, what I felt, it was nothing short of Absolute. It affirmed all the beliefs that I'd learned over time. Multiverse theory. The great filter. The inconsequential nature of organized religion's superimposed sense of good and evil. The Absolute does not confine themselves to concepts of good and evil. There's no duality. Do you get it? Nietzsche might have said that he we've killed God but the fucker's very much alive and kicking somewhere out there. This.... this gets me a chance to make things right."

None of the words that he had spoken brought her relief. Instead, her panic worsened as she realized that there was no swaying him from his stance.

"What do you intend to do with the Epoch should you find it?" Lilly asked, not wanting to know the answer.

Joe studied her face with wisdom beyond his years and then replied, "You're worried that I might side with the

Devil, given my history with the guy. You think that I think that he's right. Well, allow me to allay your anxiety by telling you that I've outgrown Satan for quite some time now, as I'm sure you can tell."

"Joe, I need you to understand," Lilly said, kneeling in front of him and attempting to hold his hands again. He let her, but only tentatively. "The artifact that you're searching for, it doesn't just change one or two events in time. It changes the course of this entire universe forever. That's power as no one has ever imagined it. Who do you become when you wield that much power?"

"What do you mean?"

"Why do you think there were so many Trials of the Aeternum Vow? What overarching message do they convey?"

"Can I have a night to sleep on it and think about it, jeez? I just underwent the trials. I haven't really gotten into the transliteration of every single step of the trials," Joe scoffed, his old self resurfacing, anger glinting in his eyes once again.

Lilly defeatedly shook her head before saying, "It's not about who you side with. That's not what I'm worried about. Knowing you, I understand your heart is in the right place. What happens, I wonder, when you wield power that grants you complete autonomy, allows you to steer the course of the universe in whichever direction you want? Do you bring about the end of days, as is prophesized in every religion ever? Or do you do something even worse?"

"Why is it that you always think so condescendingly of me? Why can't you, for once, trust me to do the right thing!?" Joe finally snapped.

"Because, possessing as much knowledge as I do, even I don't know what the right thing would be for someone in your position? Can you say the same? Can you claim to know what's absolutely right and what's absolutely wrong? Or are you simply window-shopping for newer and hipper deities to follow? When you were a kid, it was God; when you grew up, you associated yourself with Satan; and now, when evidence of another has presented itself in an irrefutable form, what are you doing? You're pursuing the Absolute! Why?"

Joe lowered his head in somber silence. When neither of them spoke for a long time, and when both of them had regained their composure, Joe looked out the window, witnessing the dawn of a desert sun. "You think I don't know that the Epoch holds immense power? You think that I'm not aware of how it tests the savior's true intentions? I know that it challenges one's sense of free will by posing the ultimate choice in front of the savior, which in this particular case, is me. I did not seek out the role of the savior. I was fine being a nobody in a grimy New York apartment. I was also okay with being a damned vessel of Satan. But I've been sought by someone, something that I've been seeking all my life. The answer to all the unanswered questions in my mind! You're worried about whether I'll side with God or the Devil, I'll tell you something else. The artifact poses another choice to its wielder."

"What?" This part, Lilly did not know about. All her discussions about primordial artifacts with the madam had been speculative at best, including the one about the mythical Epoch and the choices it offered. Lilly was not aware that there was another choice. For once, she listened without the intent of responding.

"There's another choice, as I've been led to believe," Joe said. "You don't have to side with God and turn this world into some virtuous utopia. You also don't have to side with the Devil and bring about the New World Order. You could transcend both."

She wasn't aware of this revelation, and now that she did, her whole body quivered at the implication of such a choice.

If, somehow, Joe was to wield it, what would it mean for every living being in this universe?

After her conversation with him, one thing was clear to her.

He wasn't going to be swayed by anything that she had to say.

It was time for her to ask for intervention. Any kind would do at this point.

Divine.

Unholy.

She'd ring all the numbers and hope someone in charge would pick up the phone, tell her what to do, because as of this moment, Lilly did not feel love or admiration for Joseph.

She felt fucking petrified.

16

THE ABSOLUTE

The Way Home

The next morning, when everyone woke up from their sleep, it was to find Billy Hawthorne in the drawing room, a spring in his step, a calm resolution on his face. He was more than happy to share the news with the others. Brigadier Westbrook, in Billy's words, had come in clutch and had finally sent a plane to a nearby abandoned military base to pick them all up.

Lilly and Joe did not talk much on the drive to the abandoned military base. Instead, Billy and Joe, who sat in the open back of the pickup truck, filled each other in on what had happened last night. Joe told Billy about Ynun, their travel into the astral realm, and how he overcame the Trials of the Aeternum Vow. Billy told Joe a very different story where he finally saw the haunters inside his head not just as haunters but as his protectors. Following his possession, and regaining control of his body, he had a long and fruitful talk with the ghosts of his mother, his brother, and the fragment of his own psyche called Other Billy, and found closure with them.

Joe was glad to know this but was cautious enough to ask if Billy remembered any of the conversations that Ynun had with Joe while Ynun had been possessing Billy's body. To that, Billy replied in the negatory. He remembered nothing of the night except passing out in the bathroom and then coming to the base of the rooftop staircase.

Jeremy, the sleeper agent who had given them sanctuary in his house, got them to the airstrip just in time for them all to get on the military plane and leave the troubled and roused country of Iraq behind.

After a thirteen-hour flight during which they had to land once to refuel, the six people whose lives had been in constant jeopardy finally touched down on American soil.

While his friends were rejoicing that they were finally back home, Joe knew no such comfort. There was an image seared into his mind, a place at the center of which hung suspended a cross with a pentagram superimposed upon it. He alone had to be the one to retrieve it from its resting place.

Nevertheless, he waved at the crowd of his followers gathered at the airport, gave a brief interview to one of the reporters, and bade everyone that they would host another press conference soon.

No longer bound to one another by being in another country, each person took a cab and headed their own way, parting from one another without much words or acknowledgment, knowing that they'd meet again sooner than later. There was much work to be done, after all.

When he reached his Chelsea brownstone, Joe took a long shower, washing away all of the travel off of him, trying to bring himself back to a sense of normalcy, but what normalcy could he have after the journey—both extrinsic and intrinsic—he'd had.

After wiping away the last of the grave dirt off of him, Joe prepared for the Devil's arrival, bracing himself for the mother of all horrible confrontations.

But the Devil never showed up.

Not even when Joseph Banbury called out to him by name.

After a sleepless night tumbling and shifting in bed, Joe got up early and headed out into the city on foot. Nothing better to wash away the PTSD than a walk in the city. The dawn sky was still settling around the relatively quiet city, and whoever moved, moved with purpose. The homeless guy pushing his cart had somewhere to go. The lone cab on the street had a passenger in it. The sidewalk was exclusively occupied by fitness freaks jogging away, measuring their caloric burns on their smartwatches. Pigeons cooed in code, conveying news from other parts of the city.

The city was a breath of fresh, fumy, and polluted air that did Joe's metropolis-accustomed lungs some good. He'd gotten quite unnerved breathing all that clean, natural air on his tour. This...this was where it was at.

He bought a cup of coffee from a cart—plain ol' black Americano—and walked along the lengths of the streets, smoking a cigarette, drinking his coffee, enjoying the breakfast of champions.

An hour later, and after much meandering, he found himself standing at Park and 106th, beholding a sight that had been kept secret from him.

He had hoped to see the burned remains of the Von

Barreth Cathedral, but in its place was a fresh, funky building with a rather sleek, Icelandic design that screamed futurism. Long towers merged abstractly with the central oblong block, all the windows tinted a reflective black from the outside. There was a wrought iron fence around the new building of the Morning Star HQ, and a couple of security guards were stationed at the ornate, intricately patterned wrought iron gates, both of them wielding pump action shotguns.

It wasn't the sight of the new building or the impressive, rose-bush-covered iron fence that caught Joe's eye but the flowers by the entrance of the building. Hundreds of them, and by the looks of it, all of them. From lilies to wisteria bouquets, it was a vibrant display of every color in the spectrum, all of them lying by the base of the entrance. Candles that had lit to their very end lay solidified on the concrete. Pictures of Tasha were placed along the fence. The biggest picture of her, a very candid shot taken by some photographer friend of hers, had a wreath of white tulips around it.

Joe stood mesmerized at the display of thoughtfulness, smelling the deep scent of the flowers, momentarily enjoying the change of the smell from the sulfuric stenches of the city to the sudden floral aromas.

"To Tasha, A Morning Star Martyr."

Joe looked at the hand-crafted plaque placed at the base of the pictures and gave it a silent nod. They got that part right. She was a Morning Star Martyr.

Joe walked past the gate, nodding to both security guards as they let him in, and read the commemorative stone slab placed in the miniature garden in front of the HQ's entrance.

The Morning Star Temple—A humble, crowdfunded

effort by the Tribe of Morning Star to show Joseph Banbury that he is not alone. For every person who seeks to shred and tear down, you shall find a hundred who are eager to rebuild. As this temple stands stalwart, we let the world know our faith stands resolute in the face of all that is dark and uncertain.

The first thought that crossed his mind after looking at all this effort was, *They've got this from here.* It was true. No matter what'd happen to him in the coming days, he was certain that the people, *his* people, could take care of each other. All seven hundred million of them. Come what may.

Ever since Ynun had shared the location of the Epoch artifact with Joe, Joe had been gripped by uncertainty. Who would take care of the people if something were to happen to him? But seeing this monument that was a testament to the tenacity of the Tribe of Morning Star, Joe felt comforted, knowing that even if something were to happen to their messiah, they would be able to carry his movement forward.

He turned away from the newly constructed temple, resisting the temptation to walk inside. Today had been enough. He had walked through the city he had always loved. Strolled through all the streets he had once trod without a worry in the world. If there were worries back then, they did not seem as worries now. And wasn't that life? Whatever you thought was big-picture panic-inducing stuff in your past never really amounted to much, did it? The Joe of old might have had horrors haunting him every night, but he did not have Satan to worry about, did not have to think about his fate, and how the universe's destiny hung in the balance.

His final walk through New York City, one where he admired all the 24-hour bodegas and delis, gazed at the sleeping city shifting from its slumber and waking up to meet a new day with the same affection as a father does a child, and treating his feet to the beat-up sidewalks of the cultural capital of America, had done him good.

Now he could leave without anybody knowing where he was going.

As he headed back to his Chelsea brownstone, Joe took the scenic route, the one that wound through Central Park. As he enjoyed the vivid scenery that this beautiful park had to offer, the Devil, God, the Absolute, and Epoch were the last things on his mind. He stood atop the Gothic Bridge, admiring the view of the reservoir, feeling himself in a similar state of placidity and peace as the surface of the still water. A flashback of Elias Tomlinson ringing in his telepathic mind.

The early morning orange glow on the towering lengths of the city's skyline seemed to be bidding Joe a farewell of its own, the light reflecting from all the glass panels of the buildings, shimmering through the miasma of low-hanging clouds and smog alike.

Farewells

He had meant to bid a similar farewell to everyone he knew and cared for, starting with his parents. Ever since his ego sacrifice at the altar of self, Joe, even after trying to muster up his old feelings of hatred toward his parents, could not see them in the same loathsome light as before. He pitied them. Having seen what kind of life they could have lived, he no longer bore them the same ill as before. In fact, he downright felt terrible for having had that screaming match with his mother in the locker room. He hadn't even checked up on either of them since.

He intended to remedy that.

There was no telling if he'd come back from this voyage. He did not know what would happen. Maybe, just as this was the last time he was seeing Manhattan, this be the last time he was seeing all his friends and family members.

He started with the easiest one.

Joph.

Joph was taking a long day off after his travels, sleeping in, and naked at that. Seeing him standing there buck-nude at the door of his loft, Joe grinned.

"Sup, and mind the erection. Ryan Reynolds featured heavily in my dream again," Joph said, letting Joe in. Joph wrapped an apron on his body on the way from the kitchenette, standing there looking comical as Hell.

"Is everything okay, Joe?" Joph asked. "Haven't you grown tired of staring at my ugly mug? I'm not sure I'll ever get that grave dirt from all the many crevices of my body."

When Joe, overcome with emotions, did not say anything, understanding finally dawned on Joph.

"Oh," Joph said, an anxious hand raised to his head, another covering his face. "You're going somewhere, aren't you?"

Joe nodded, pressing his lips together. If he spoke a word, he'd break down.

"And we're not coming along with you this time around, are we?"

Joe shook his head.

"Will you be coming back?"

Joe said nothing.

"Joe, you cannot be doing this to me this early in the fucking morning, Jesus, I haven't even had my coffee!" Joph caved in first, tears spilling from his wide, reddened eyes.

"You've been the friend that I always wished to have," Joe said. "Whatever happens to me, I want you to know that."

"Don't say that," Joph squeezed the sides of his head with the palms of his hand. "What is this, some sort of suicide mission?"

"I don't know what this is," Joe said. "But before I went, I just wanted to say thank you. For being a part of my life. For being there in the trenches with me. For pulling me on my feet when I was...fuck."

"Hey," Joph moaned, wiping his eyes. "No. I'm not having it. This isn't goodbye. You listen to me, motherfucker. You go and do whatever it is that you need to do, and then you report to the HQ first thing Monday. Got it? *Got it?*"

Joe nodded, his tears spilling.

Joph brought up his hand for a pound shake. Joe clasped his palm to Joph's, pulled him in, and hugged him while holding tightly to his hand.

"Morning Stars for life," Joph hiccoughed. "Ain't nothing gonna change that, no matter what happens."

"I'll see you Monday," Joe winked.

"Monday it is, comrade," Joph nodded back, the deep sorrow of loss etched into the lines of his face.

As he parked in front of his old home, he was surprised to see Amy's car in the driveway. It had been less than a day since they'd come back. What was she doing here?

He let that thought go as he knocked on the door.

It was Amy who opened the door.

"Joe?"

"Ames."

"What are you doing here?"

"I just thought...well, I...what are you doing here?"

"I'd been gone so long, I figured I needed to check in on Mom and Dad and see how they were doing," Amy said, letting him in.

"Yeah, I'm here for that too."

"Hey, you can't copy my reason. That's cheating," Amy chuckled. "Come up with your own."

His parents were sitting where they always sat in the living room, Dad in front of the TV with a beer in his hand, Mom with knitting needles in her hands as she knitted away a scarf. They both looked up in shock to see their prodigal son standing there.

"Hey, mom," Joe said, waving at her.

"Joe," His mother whispered. He could tell in the way she spoke she was more afraid of him than anything else. If there was any matronly love there, it was buried deep under layers of fearful anticipation.

"Hey, Dad," Joe waved.

His dad only cast him a scowling look, then reverted his attention to the match on the TV.

"Well, that's that, I guess," Joe said, taking a step back. He wasn't sure why he'd decided to come here second instead of going to Shaun or Lilly's.

"I saw the news," his dad spoke out of the blue. "It'd have been a damn shame if you'd have gotten yourself killed there. What the fuck were you thinking, son?"

That word. Son. Spoken by the guy who was his father in every way but one. And did it matter, really, where the seed had come from? Or was it in the gardener's hands that the plant nourished? Joe had been a tough plant—no thanks to the seed—but hadn't this guy done everything in his meager power to raise him as his own boy, put food on the table, drive him to school some mornings, help him with the homework when he was feeling like it, and occasionally take him down to the park to play a two-man, father-son game of baseball? He'd never been a perfect parent. But he had been a parent. An actual presence around the house who in his own stoic way had seen to it that Joe grew up in one piece, went off to college, and then did his own thing. Here was a man who'd fought terminal cancer, toiled away at the factory all his life for minimum wage, and barely had anything to show for it other than an old rusty car and a run-down home.

"I'm sorry, Dad," Joe said, his head bent low. As he stood there, taking his scolding from his father, he wasn't the antichrist, the leader of a global movement, or a bestselling author. He was his father's son, getting a dose of tough love by way of good old reproachment.

"Sorry don't cut it. If you do anything reckless like that again, there'll be Hell to pay," Tommy said, his voice firm, showing no signs of aging or disease. As he rose from his sofa, standing towering over Joe by half a foot, he looked down on his son. "I don't care for any of that satanist shit you're pulling, thinking you're hot shit, but at the end of the day, you've only got the one life. Take it from someone who nearly died from cancer before you were ever born. Don't squander it. And goddammit, don't ever put your sister in danger like that again."

"I promise, I won't," Joe said, his head still low, which was a good thing. It did a good job of keeping the tears at bay.

Tommy placed his giant hand on his son's shoulder and said, "Good. Well. That's good, then. Did you get a kick out of going to Iraq, stirring shit?"

Joe looked up at his father and saw him smiling ever so briefly.

"Yeah, I gave 'em Hell," Joe smiled back, extending that smile to his mother too. "And I'm not into that satanic shit anymore."

Amy raised her eyebrows at Joe, but it was his mother who showed the most expression. She broke down into tears, her voice frail and high-pitched. Who knew how long she'd been holding that sorrow inside?

"I was so worried," Joyce cried, sitting there on her sofa, her knitting forgotten, lying at her feet.

Joe went over to her, knelt on his knees in front of her, and held her hands. "I'm sorry, Ma."

"Christ's sake, you worried the heck out of your mother!" Tommy barked from the kitchen, fetching fresh beers.

Amy wept uncontrollably, unable to help herself after seeing this reconciliation between mother and son.

"I've been a difficult son," Joe said. "I know it. I...I don't know if I have it in me to forgive you or if you have it in you to forgive me."

"There's nothing to forgive," Joyce said. "It couldn't have been easy for you."

"It couldn't have been easy for you either," Joe whispered, making sure this part of the conversation was just for the two of them. "But you protected me as best as you could."

"I tried."

"Trying is all it takes. Look at me. In one piece."

"You're really done with all that devilish propaganda?" she asked, her voice fraught with caution.

"I.... whatever rebellion there was in me that propelled me in that direction, I've let it go," Joe said. "Or so I think."

"Better late than never," Joyce said, placing her palm on her son's cheek.

"You...you know," Joe struggled with his words. From the

corner of his eyes, he saw Amy leave the room and head into the kitchen. "It wasn't really your fault, all that happened. I want you to know that. Temptation is his craft, and he's an unmatched master of his craft."

It was in no way a direct apology or forgiveness, but it was good enough. After a long time, Joyce smiled at her son.

After drinking a beer with his father, Joe bade them both a brief goodbye. If he'd have made it longer, it would have been all the more difficult for him.

Amy came out of the house after him, asking, "What the fuck was that? What's happening to you, Joe?"

"Ames. I'm...this is the end of the line for me, it seems. I'm off to the last leg of this journey, and I'm afraid I must go at it alone."

Her lower lip quivered as she too, like Joph, understood what he was talking about. Neither of them knew the full picture, or that he'd found out where the Epoch was hidden, but they knew that there was a finality to whatever it was he was planning to do.

She hugged her baby brother fiercely, holding him close to her.

Joe kissed her on the forehead before leaving.

"Like I told Joph, see you Monday," Joe said, getting into his car, waving at her as he drove off, leaving Red Bank for the last time in his life. His sister grew smaller in the rearview mirror, waving her entire arm in goodbye as she watched her brother drive away, some part of her knowing that she might not see him again.

"Was it something that I said?" Shaun asked worriedly. They met at a Starbucks downtown. "Is this like a talk all the rest of you had? You're letting me go? Christ, Joey, it's only been a day since I came back. Come on, man. I grant you I wasn't on my best behavior overseas, but I did fix the fuck out of those ACs, man."

Joe chuckled. He'd expected Joph's farewell to be easy, and yet it was this one that felt the most effortless and natural.

"Shaun, you're a sick son of a bitch," Joe said, shaking the man's hand. "And that barista you've been eying like a bloodhound's barely eighteen."

"Hey, come on. She's the one winking at me, that foxy thing," Shaun said, biting his lower lip as he waited his turn in line, depravedly flirting with the barista. "Anyway, what's this about? Where are you headed?"

"To Lilly's. That's why I called you. Wanted to meet you while I was on the way to her apartment," Joe said.

"So what's this about, then? You're not firing me, are ya? Cuz it'd be a total dick move if you do. I don't have any other job to fall back on at this moment. Who's the fuckwit? Is it Billy you're hiring in my place? What's going on?"

"Your job is safe, man," Joe said. "No one's out to get you. I just wanted to tell you that as heinous a man as you are, you're one of the good ones."

"Well, thanks, partner, put her there," Shaun said, extending his hand once again. "They didn't diagnose you with cancer or something, did they?"

"I'm fine."

"So you say, but you're missing that pep."

"Goodbye, Shaun."

"Joey?"

Shaun followed Joe out of the Starbucks, forgetting that it was his turn to place his order in the crowded shop.

Inside, the barista was looking around for him, wondering where he'd gone.

Joe stopped outside the Starbucks and was surprised to see Shaun had followed him out.

"Joey, are you okay? We've never talked like this. Is this like, what, your fly-into-the-sunset sort of moment?" Shaun looked worried. In all the time that Joe had known Shaun, he had never pegged him to be the guy with more than a teaspoon's worth of emotional intelligence, and yet here he was, astutely assessing the situation.

"I'm just taking a break from this whole thing for some time," Joe said, realizing that it was not as effortless to say goodbye to this man as he'd thought.

"Who leads Morning Star in your absence? What are you talking about, man?" Shaun asked. "Without a leader, I mean..."

"They'll be fine. So will you. So will everyone. You take care, yeah?"

"Joey? You're breaking my heart over here, being awfully cryptic," Shaun said, following Joe down the sidewalk. "At least tell me that it meant something."

"What?"

"All that we did, Switzerland, India, Iraq. The tour. Everything else in between. Tell me it meant something," Shaun said. "I may not seem like it, but I'm a purpose-driven man. It's one of those things that I keep real close to my chest. See, people can't know that you've got dreams and aspirations, or else they seek to crush them. But somewhere along the line I dreamed that this thing we're a part of, it'd end up meaning something big. Did it?"

"Of course, it did, Shaun. Of course, it *does.* This is not over. And you played an important role in it. I couldn't have done it without you," Joe said.

"Well, jeez. Thanks, man. It means much to me," Shaun said, standing there confusedly, not knowing what was happening, his eyes wounded the way of puppies in dog shelters.

He didn't need to know.

None of them did.

It'd save them the pain.

"You take care," Joe said, smiling at him.

"And you, stay golden, my friend."

JOE KNOCKED HESITANTLY on Lilly's door. They hadn't had a reconciliatory talk after their conversation following his adventures in the astral realm. The last thing she had asked of him was to drop the whole thing, to which he had replied that he could not do that. Not after having come so far.

He rapped thrice on the door in addition to pushing the bell.

Lilly opened the door, her hair haggard, her face bearing the vestiges of sleep.

"Joe?"

"Lill."

"It's too damn early in the morning for....er...what time is it?"

"It's twelve in the afternoon."

"Oh, shit. I slept for twenty hours?"

"You needed the rest."

"Why don't you come in?

"Why don't I?" Joe chuckled and followed her inside. Her luggage was open in the living, the stuff inside thrown out without much thought. The whole place was a mess of sweaty clothes, smelly socks, and dirt-ridden shoes.

"That's one way to unpack," Joe commented.

"Oh, shut it, Marry Poppins," Lilly groaned, rubbing her eyes.

"Lill."

"What?" Lilly yawned, struggling to keep her eyes awake. Joe could not help but take in the sight of her nightgown-covered body. It was a blue, silk nightgown with its fabric so thin that it was almost transparent. "Joe..."

"I came here to tell you that I'm going to find the Epoch," Joe said, not knowing what was the right way to say such a thing, and therefore winging it. Now it was out, the ball in her court, the weight of revelation off his shoulders and hers to deal with.

"I know," Lilly said. "And I also know that there's nothing that I can say to stop you."

"You're giving up just like that? Taken me for a lost cause after all?"

"Not a lost cause, Joe," Lilly said, wrapping her arms in front of her chest, hiding her bosom from him. That slight movement made it clear to Joe what Lilly was on about. In her mind, she had already parted ways with him. This conversation would only cement it into words. "A cause beyond my paygrade."

"Come again?"

"Whenever I've tried to shepherd you, you've retaliated with such brutality that it makes me wonder if you see me as a person at all. I'm twice shy over here."

"I didn't come here to let you sway me into staying with any reverse psychology or your magic," Joe said defiantly. "Just so you know."

"And I'm not going to stop you."

"Fine."

"Fine."

In that moment as they stood tense, the divide between them was greater than the mere length of the living room. The two couldn't be further apart. She was someone charged with maintaining the balance of the world. He was someone destined to throw out the scales.

"We did love each other for a hot minute there, didn't we?" Joe asked, his hand on the doorknob.

"Did? You idiot. I still love you. Which makes it even more difficult for me to let you go," Lilly cried.

His hand trembled on the doorknob. All the will he had mustered up to face her and stand his ground faltered.

"I do not wish this pain upon any woman who walks this earth. To be in love and to be rendered incapable by that love of doing the right thing. With a snap of my fingers, I could smite you off the face of this earth. They'd scour the depths of Hell and they wouldn't find you."

"And you think me so effete that I'd let you do that?" Joe turned around, unleashing his wingspan, embracing what remained of Satan's powers inside him, glowing red and grey.

"Don't you get it!? When it comes to you, I am fucking powerless! I cannot change your mind. I can't even stop you from leaving through that door! Might as well do all your bidding and let you do what you will, because isn't that what you do best?"

"Goodbye, Lilly," Joe said, returning to his normal form, and stepping out the door.

"Why did you come here!?" Lilly screamed in agony from inside the apartment, then burst into mournful wails.

"To ask you if you'd come with me," Joe whispered from the other side of the door, these words not meant for her but for him.

~

An emotional wreck, Joe stood in front of a dingy door in a ramshackle apartment complex in Hell's Kitchen. He'd gotten the address from Billy back in Iraq. He was glad that he did, because this felt important. They might not have known each other for long, but there was no denying the impact Billy had on Joe's journey. He deserved a farewell too.

Joe hadn't even knocked on the door when the door opened. Joe peeked inside, expecting an apartment in disarray, but found himself quite surprised to see the place spick and span.

Billy stood inside, covered in sweat, dark circles in his eyes.

"I knew you were coming," Billy said, smiling, a wild madness in his sleep-deprived eyes. "I've been cleaning my place ever since I got back. I mean, it reflects well on one's mental health, doesn't it? Part of my misery was self-inflicted, know what I mean, man?"

"You doing okay?" Joe asked, stepping inside the tiny, old, yet organized apartment, admiring the amount of literature on the bookshelf. A man after his own heart, it seemed.

"It's all very Fight Club-esque if you can believe it. I sleep, and Other Billy takes over. Man, I spent the longest time trying to resist him. What a waste. He's only ever looked out for me. Guess what he's been doing while I've been conked out?"

"From the looks of it, you guys are taking turns cleaning the place," Joe said. "Don't stretch yourself too thin. You're two people sharing one body. Sooner or later, you'll collapse."

"Hear that, OB?" Billy called out to no one in particular. "We gotta dial it down."

"Hey, Billy, as much as I'd love to play shrink, now's not the time for it," Joe said, pulling Billy by the shoulders. "I need you to listen to me."

"No. Un-unh!" Billy shook his head. "OB told me this would happen. That you'd come to me and give me that old fond farewell and be off on your journey. No sirree, Bob. I'm not letting that happen. Not on my watch. Wherever you go, I go."

"Dude, you didn't even give me a chance here," Joe said, a little irritated. "I..."

"I know what you're going to do. You're going to find that artifact. And when you do, it's all on you to do what you think is right. But I ain't letting you go on that journey alone. You're gonna need someone to look out for you. My name might be Billy, but I'm a total Sam. Geddit?"

"Huh?"

"Samwise Gamgee. Sam Winchester. Popular sidekicks in fiction. Christ, you call yourself a writer?"

"Oh," Joe felt a little stupid for having missed that reference, but in his defense, he had other things on his mind, things along the what-happens-when-I-wield-the-Epoch variety. "I don't know what happens when I go down there. I'm not about to put you in the blast radius."

"Who says there will be a blast radius at all? Maybe the whole affair's a really quiet one," Billy said. "Maybe nothing bad happens. Ever thought about that?"

"I cannot afford to hope that nothing bad will happen," Joe said.

"That's your mistake. One can always afford to hope, despite how dark shit seems."

"What would even do?" Joe asked, worn down by Billy's relentlessness.

"I've got like fifty ccs of crazy pumping through my bloodstream. Something tells me you're gonna need it. Besides, didn't I already get you out of your most recent sticky situation? Come on, man. Take me with you. I'm expendable anyways."

That stung Joe. He held Billy's elbow gently and pulled him close. "Who's telling you that?"

"I don't know," Billy said, his eyes wet. "All the rest of your friends have full lives. Purpose. Well-adjusted adults with things to do. Movers, shakers, all. I die, who cares? Some editor of a declining newspaper?"

"I'd care," Joe said. "You're not expendable."

"Thank you for saying that, but it's my badge of honor. It's why I made an excellent journalist in the first place. I didn't care if I lived or died. And despite all the crossfires, bombs dropped, and buildings collapsing around me, I made it out in one piece. I believe that I was being saved for a greater purpose. Let this be my greater purpose, I'm asking you," Billy said.

"This is not a death wish, is it?" Joe, who was no stranger to mental torment, asked.

"I could ask the same of you," Billy laughed. "You're not thinking of undergoing cosmic euthanasia, are you? Tell me this doesn't end with you dead."

"I do not know," Joe confessed, his emotional faculties in shambles. "And it scares the fuck out of me!"

"Then let's do it together, you and me. Who better to decide the fate of the universe than two madmen? You and me. Thelma and Louise style, we're gonna fucking drive our car off the edge of the universe. I'll go with you as far as you'll take me, and that'll be enough to call my greater purpose."

Joe stood there indecisively. Of all the things that he'd accounted for, this was not it. He hadn't expected Billy to make such a strong case.

It would mean one thing—that he did not have to do this alone after all.

"Okay," Joe said finally, making Billy pump his fist in the air. "But you're not going to pull any reckless shit."

"Oh, I'll be a good old boy scout," Billy said, crossing his heart.

"So I guess we're going across the pond, then," Joe said, readying himself for the final journey that lay ahead. "Who'd have thought that the gateway to the Epoch would be the Stonehenge of all the places?"

"It crossed my mind once or twice," Billy said. "I mean, what is it, besides a formation of rocks? It's five thousand years old, and no one knows what it's there for."

"I mean, we do," Joe grinned.

"Yeah. Here's to solving one of the oldest mysteries of the world. The Stonehenge is a multiversal portal," Billy nodded slowly. "When are we leaving?"

"Today."

17

LITANY OF DEATH

Grave dirt or, in some parts of the world where instead of burial corpses were cremated, the ashes of the dead, like a child's fear or the blood of a virgin, was one of the most powerful and profane ingredients in magic. Wielders of arcane power were advised not to experiment with these ingredients, for the consequences—whatever you do unto another shall come back unto you times three, one of the bigger ones amongst them—were dire.

Lilly had rarely, if ever, dabbled in dark magic. She saw herself as a holistic witch, one guided by nature and the need of the universe rather than contempt or material drive. But when the moment called for it, she had to, for the sake of everyone close to her.

It was right along the time when Joseph Banbury had gotten the beating of his life and had come out of that fight scathed and insightful. Grave dirt was a powerful devil repellant. Lilly, who already knew of this in some deep part of her subconscious, realized that sooner or later their reserves of grave dirt and the ash of the dead would run out.

In secrecy, she performed a rite called the Litany of Death, harnessing what power she had into a little sieve, poured in the ashes of the dead that she procured from one of Joe's beedis, along with a hair apiece from everyone who had embarked on the world tour. Once sealed, this spell protected the enchanted from the Devil by obscuring them from his view in every way. She did not share this information with Joe or any of the others, for none of them at that point knew that she was a witch.

Even when Joe discovered that she was a witch, she did not tell him that the reason they had been evading the Devil for so long was her most powerful ritual yet. She held onto it. When Billy showed up, she even took one of his hair and added it into the sieve to ensure his protection.

Now, with Joe gone, and her apartment trashed in a fit of remorseful rage, Lilly stood disheveled, holding the stopped sieve in her hand, staring at it. It was not an easy decision she had come to, but if there was anyone who could stop Joe, it was the Devil himself.

And she needed him to stop Joe, because both God and the Devil, like herself, were beings of balance. One maintained the plateau of virtue while the other oversaw the depths of sin. God, for all she knew, given that he had never answered any of her callings, was dead, his corpse rotting away in the garden of Eden or wherever it was that God had croaked. If he had croaked. He hadn't ever responded to her pleas and prayers, so why would he respond now?

The Devil, on the other hand, had always been quick to respond. When he didn't respond himself, he sent emissaries in the form of demons to do his bidding. That was why black magic was dominant over any other forms of magic. Holy magic was only a farce at this moment, with a handful of actual clerics practicing it, and for what banal purposes? Exorcisms? Baptizing children?

Lilly knew in her heart that she did not need any forgiveness for what she was about to do. This was her decision, and it was the right one. She hadn't stopped Joe the last time, and not a day went by that she did not regret it. If she did not stop him now by any means necessary, there would not be anything to regret over.

He might singlehandedly cause a cataclysm that would wipe out the entire universe, and the ironic part of it was, he might do it thinking it was the right thing—to recreate the universe in his image and rid it of all the flaws it contained.

Lilly crashed the sieve on the floor and watched with bated breath as its contents scattered all over the floor.

Wherever the Devil was right now, he wasn't blind to the six of them.

And the Devil being the Devil, quick that he was, appeared almost instantaneously in front of Lilly, and not in any of the avatars that he had ever appeared to Joe. The Devil who appeared to Lilly was the God of dark magic itself, seethed in black, rage as his heartbeat, fury his gaze, fire his claws. With Hellion, slitted eyes he glared at the woman who was responsible for obscuring his own prophet from him, and threw his bestial arm forward, grabbing her mercilessly by her throat, intending to crush her neck.

"Speak witch," The Devil hissed with his forked tongue, his immense horns jutting dangerously close to her as he pulled her toward him, his broad, brawny, animalistic yet grotesquely humanoid body standing tall in the room, the flames of Hell licking his flesh red. "Speak of your actions before I douse your light."

"He knows..." Lilly choked, making no effort to free herself from the Devil's grip. She had already been driven to the point of such melancholic misery that death, even by the Devil's hand, felt like sweet relief. No longer did she wish to partake in the ways of the world and bear the burdens of others. Wherever it was that witches went after death, she looked forward to her journey there.

Lucifer's hand loosened around Lilly's neck when he heard her speak. She crashed on the floor, certain that her knee-first collision with the marble floor had shattered both kneecaps. She squealed in pain and retreated against the wall, cowering in front of Satan.

"What does he know?" Lucifer roared, producing his trident out of thin air and placing its sharp fork against her neck.

"About everything. The Absolute. The Epoch," Lilly gasped, struggling to breathe against the still-fresh pain of the Devil's crushing grip and wincing as the tip of his trident prodded past her skin, drawing blood.

In a fit of rage, Lucifer retracted his trident and then brought it forward with all his force.

The trident dug deep into the wall right next to Lilly, leaving her relatively unharmed.

The Devil ushered another maddening scream, his booming voice resounding in the apartment.

"He's headed down there right now," Lilly said.

"Where?" The Devil growled.

"I don't know!" Lilly squealed as he sought to thrash her with his clawed grip. "But I lifted the spell, so you can find him wherever he is!"

"Bitch, if he's already past the threshold, I cannot get to him, and it is already too late!" Satan bellowed, digging his nails into the flesh of his skull.

"Then you best stop wasting your time with me," Lilly croaked, holding her bleeding throat in her hands. It wasn't a fatal amount of blood leaking from the gash Satan's trident had left, but it was still an alarming amount.

"Don't think this ends here, witch. You will earn your reckoning when all this is over."

Flames billowed from the floor of her apartment, scorching the hardwood floor, and setting ablaze everything in the living room. In the wake of those flames, Satan left, leaving Lilly to a fate of being trapped in her burning apartment while bleeding out.

18

STONEHENGE

It was nine o'clock on a Wednesday in the middle of March when two men got off the train at Salisbury engine. These men wore ordinary summer clothes, and other than the two, rather strange strings with pouches around their necks, they seemed like ordinary folk headed to Wiltshire to admire Stonehenge at night under a sky full of stars.

"Good thinking on the grave-dirt pouches," Joe tapped the pouch around his neck. "I'd almost entirely forgotten about that."

"Needs must when the devil...you know how it goes," Billy said, smoking a well-earned cigarette after being on an airplane and a train for so long.

"Drives. Needs must when the devil drives," Joe finished for him.

"Where you laddies from, then?" the cab driver asked, peering behind. "Is the two of you married or what?"

"Nah, just *mates*, as you call 'em around these parts," Joe said.

"Americans," the cab driver said. "Figures."

Joe did not pay any attention to the cabbie. He was fine, allowing them to smoke inside his cab with the windows drawn down. Joe did not know the routes nor cared enough to look them up on his phone. He enjoyed—as much as he could, given the circumstances—the cool night air, a little concerned about the rumbling clouds overhead.

"It better not rain," Billy said.

"Why? Afraid to get wet?" Joe asked.

"Afraid to catch a cold in another country, more like," Billy said.

They traveled the rest of the way in silence, each thinking their own thoughts, Billy about the impending rain, Joe about the monumental nature of his undertaking.

The cabbie dropped them off at the parking lot.

From there, they made it up to Stonehenge with its pillars and columns.

"I believe they're called lintels and trilithons," Billy said, looking at his phone. "Wikipedia says there's an outer ring of vertical sarsen standing stones, topped by connecting two horizontal lintel stones. Inside is a ring of smaller bluestones. And those that you see further inside, are the free-standing trilithons. Joe?"

"I don't see any of that," Joe whispered. The sight he beheld was altogether different than the one he had seen in pictures or the one that Billy was describing.

The night above was covered in total starless darkness because of the clouds. However, inside Stonehenge, in the places where there would have been empty spaces between the stones, Joe could see into different dimensions. Each hollow space was occupied by a different window displaying vivid colors of other universes. A brilliant galaxy doused in deep purple swirling away in the abyss of space. A colorful waterfall splashing over cosmic waters. A corridor of unending stairs leading into nowhere. As he walked closer and looked through each of the windows, he saw a separate vision every time, as if the Stonehenge itself was alive and shifting with each step Joe took toward it, anticipating his steps, welcoming his arrival.

He could see the utter, blinding, fascinating brilliance of other worlds than this one, silhouettes of people from other dimensions carrying on in their daily lives.

He saw it all. Everything that he could ever imagine. New universes being birthed through big bangs. Heat deaths of old universes as they imploded upon themselves.

Ephemeral visions of past lives of people, the lives people would come to live, and the lives of people as they were now—Joe could see these clearly as he came to a halt right in front of Stonehenge.

"What do you see?" Billy asked.

"It's...beautiful....unlike anything that I could have imagined. A multiversal convergence. A flux point of cosmic proportions. A nexus of all realities," Joe whispered, entranced by the very sight of infinitude itself. He did not notice the rain as it fell upon his body, drenching him within minutes.

He could only walk forward, eager to step in through one of the portals and come to another realm. After all, this was no test. This was not a trial. He had been shown that the Epoch artifact lay cradled at the center of Stonehenge. He had taken the necessary measures to ascend via the Aeternum Vow to be able to see what no one else could.

That this megalithic structure was a gateway to somewhere where the Epoch was stored safely.

"Joe!" Billy yelled from behind before Joe could take another step toward the Stonehenge.

The trance broke for a moment, allowing Joe to look back and see the Devil descending from the sky, burning despite the rain.

Panicking, he grabbed at the pouch around his neck only to notice that it was empty. The torrential rain had dissolved the dirt and had washed it from his body.

He could stay. Fight for his life and save Billy. In fact, he intended to do exactly that.

But before the Devil, bathed in fury, could land, Billy raced forward and grabbed Joe's shirt.

"I knew what I signed up for. Go, then. I'll hold him off," Billy yelled, and pushed Joe into the Stonehenge.

Before he fell into another place entirely, Joe saw the Devil strike his landing and pounce maniacally upon Billy, seeking to rip him to shreds.

And then, no longer able to control his fall, he fell. Fell down a deep depth as constellations, galaxies, star clusters, and altogether different universes whirled past him, taking him to a place where it lay within hand's reach.

Joe landed upon his feet, standing on elaborate stonework seemingly suspended in the middle of nowhere. There was absolutely nothing around him, above him, below him. Only this square platform at the center of which there was an ornate stand.

Housed upon the stand was a large cross with a metallic pentagram coming out of it.

"Joseph Banbury," a voice called out, followed by the appearance of a form that Joe recognized.

"Sam?" Joe asked.

"Samuel, I believe is the name I gave you last we met," the man, if he could be called a man, said, dressed no longer in any earthly attire but a robe devoid of any substance, shape, or color. It was as if he was melting away into his surroundings. "I believe you know enough now that you can call me by my name."

"The Absolute," Joe whispered, to which the Absolute nodded in kind, responding with a warm smile, extending his hand toward the artifact.

"I have waited a long time to have this conversation," The Absolute spoke. The being who was the beginning of everything and the end of all shifted its form, no longer resembling the human that Joe had once seen in the Devil's abode, but a form that embodied the title more fittingly.

Silver-haired, sharp-faced, white-eyed, with an immaculate and short beard on his face, this pale-skinned manifestation of the Absolute now walked toward Joe in a gray robe. "I am, if anything, nonredundant. I only appeared in that familiar form so you may recognize me."

"Whoever you are, you possess such grace that even if you hadn't introduced me to yourself prior, I would have recognized you," Joe spoke, awestruck. "Part of me wants to bow in front of you."

"Please, by all means, don't," the Absolute grinned. "I never made myself evident to anyone strictly because I abhor worship of myself. Worship. Such a derisory act. Who can dictate in absolute terms that they deserve to be worshipped? And why? I wouldn't want you to worship me for the same reason you wouldn't want me to worship you."

"I am so lost," Joe said, his entire body feeling frail and vulnerable in the presence of this being of infinite power and wisdom.

"Would your worship of me grant you Godly boons? Would you yourself become a God? No. Would my worship of you rob me of my Absolutehood and turn me into a mortal man? It would not. Worship should be extended toward something that one can aspire to become, and no man alive can ever become more than himself. So if there is anyone you should ever bow to, it should only be to yourself. They're both within you, these constructs of hallow and Hell. You contain God in your mind as you do the Devil. What power do these irreverent fanatics, one obsessed with virtue, the other a craven sin seeker, possess other than what people have bestowed unto them with worship?"

"Then what is the point?"

"Of deity-hood? Worship?"

"Yes. What's the point of it all, and why has it turned into the fulcrum by which our world turns? You're either a believer or a disbeliever. If you're a believer, you devote yourself to a life of worship. If you're a disbeliever, you spend all your life wondering what's out there, if there's anything. And once you make up your mind that there's nothing out there and write a book about it, guess who shows up? The Devil. Next thing you know, you're....argh," Joe became overwhelmed with the metaphor that had gotten out of his hand.

The Absolute circled around the Epoch artifact and came to a standstill, one hand resting atop the relic, the other hand moving with his speech to emphasize the points he was making. "Whenever someone asks for your allegiance, whether it's a higher power whose religious order demands worship and alms or a politician who asks you to align with their vision and give them your vote, it is a power play. In all the universes that I have created, and I have created them beyond count, I have observed the same phenomenon. Whether they're power-hungry people or deities obsessed with their stature, they need the vote of faith from their followers. Without that vote, they have no power. Without his billions of worshippers, what is God but a three-lettered word? If one day everyone stops believing that Satan is the source of all wickedness in the world, do you know what happens? The Devil loses his influence. I will indulge you by asking you a question. Strip away everything, and what remains?"

"What? I'm sorry, Your Absoluteness," Joe stuttered.

"Free Will," The Absolute explained calmly. "It is the most powerful force in the entire world. It is one that I created. It is one that both God and the Devil—in every universe—seek to manipulate. If someone, by their own volition, chooses to believe in one or the other, it grants them power. They have their little wagers, these Gods and Devils in these different universes, where they see who can harness the most amount of free will."

"You think of the wager as petty, despite all these many lives hanging in the balance?" Joe asked, feeling a little angry, perceiving the Absolute to be apathetic.

The Absolute, on the other hand, shook his head.

"I do not see it as petty. That is why this is present in every universe," The Absolute tapped his hand atop the Epoch artifact. "This is my intervention. A safeguard, if you will. Should someone from humanity ascend past these binaries and seek truth, reconciliation, higher purpose, and free will in its purest form, this is the vessel that allows them to do it. One savior per each two millennium gets a chance to wield it. And would you be surprised that in this universe, you are the first one about to do it? No one has ever made it this far. Dozens have tried. They have failed. As I said earlier, I have waited a long time to have this conversation."

"It does feel rehearsed. You've been practicing in the mirror?" Joe asked.

The Absolute smiled, saying nothing.

"What happens now? I have a friend outside of wherever this is, and right about now, the Devil is beating the living shit out of him. Any way I can grab that thing and save him?"

"Where we are, we are outside of time and space. Nothing is happening to your friend at this moment, for this is no moment at all."

With that tension alleviated, Joe looked around more intrepidly.

What he had first perceived as absolute darkness was not darkness but a deep pattern of dim light weaving in and out of nothingness. It illuminated the platform they stood upon. As for the platform itself, it was twenty feet by twenty feet, five pillars on each side, arches running along the length of those pillars, connecting throughout the platform.

The Epoch artifact hummed with its own energy, inviting Joe to step forward and take it.

"It cannot be this easy," Joe whispered.

"What about your life has been easy?" The Absolute asked. "And you are right. It is not. There is one more test. The ultimate one as far as you and your universe are concerned."

"Why do you emphasize that, the universe bit?" Joe asked, sitting down on the floor to contemplate his upcoming decision.

"Because I am the creator of all the universes. I specify your universe because I have had this conversation with saviors in other universes. Though, not as many times as I had hoped," The Absolute said. "And most of the time, the saviors ended up making the unexpected choice. I would not call it the wrong choice, but if I were to use that term, 'wrong,' it would be the wrong choice for that universe. Some universes are so overthrown by their Devil that the savior is required to align themselves with God. In others where God reigns supreme leaving no room for human trial and error, the savior must see to it that they bring in the counterbalance for free will to exist. And then there are universes like yours, where the wager is still anybody's game. And that, Joseph Banbury, is your final test," the Absolute finished.

"Side with God or side with the Devil?" Joe asked.

"Or destroy them both," The Absolute added.

"Which choice, if any, saves the universe?"

"That's a first," The Absolute mused.

"What is?"

"Of all the saviors I've met across different universes, I have never had one ask me this question," The Absolute said. "They think they know which choice saves the universe, which dooms it to its death. Many of them make the choice that results in the death of their universe. The answer is different for each universe, including yours."

"So what do I do?" Joe asked helplessly.

"Wield the Epoch."

The Absolute stepped down from the elevated platform and watched as Joe lifted himself off the floor and took slow, calculated steps toward the Epoch.

He stood there for the longest time, his hands inches away from the relic, wondering to himself, thinking that this was the point of no return. If this place outside of time and space were to be bound by time, then perhaps Joe might have stood in front of the relic for years, decades, an eon, an epoch.

As he stood weighing his decision, the Absolute stood behind him, patiently.

"Here goes nothing," Joe said, reflecting on his entire life, all of it flashing before his eyes in vivid detail, from the first moment when he'd called his mother "mama" when he was nine months old to his most recent heartbreak when he had to part ways with the woman he loved.

He picked up the Epoch and nothing was ever the same again.

19

THE FINAL CONFRONTATION

The First and Final Summoning of this Universe

Yet, nothing changed.

Undoubtedly, the Epoch was a relic charged with unfathomable power, and Joe Banbury, once an ordinary wet-behind-the-ears boy from New Jersey, now stood wielding it, but nothing changed. There were no cosmic fireworks. No implosions. Nothing sudden.

"There is truth spoken, and truth acted," The Absolute said, clapping his hands together. "Now that you wield the Epoch, you will speak true, act true, your true nature revealed, and will perceive truth in its absoluteness. What do you have to say, Joseph Banbury?"

"I am the Truth."

"Then so be it," the Absolute responded. "I rid you of the falsehood of doubt, lies, uncertainty, guile, deception, and any and all ruses. You are laid bare. You cannot feign. Truth shall move your tongue as we hold the first and final summoning of this universe."

"What do I have to do?" Joe asked.

"Decide the fate of this universe as you see fit. Summon

God. Summon the Devil. Confront them as you see fit. I shall oversee it yet I won't partake. This is a matter that needs to be resolved by the constituents of this universe, its God, its Devil, and its Humanity represented by you. As the judge of the matter, you hold complete autonomy and authority," The Absolute said, raising his hand and closing his fist, dissolving the suspended platform, and bringing an end to the dimly lit darkness all around them. "You yield free will. Your decision decides whether this universe thrives or dies."

"Tell me, Absolute," Joe, propelled by forced honesty, asked, "Do you care that this universe lives or dies?"

"Even I don't interfere in matters of free will. If by free will this universe lives, so be it. If it dies, it dies" The Absolute said, creating a new scenery around them, one inside a pristine interior that resembled a cathedral, a courtroom, and a large ceremonial hall all at the same time. White its walls, white its floor. Light flooded through the many windows of this chamber, reflecting off of the smooth floor, but it was not light so intense that it would blind. Joe, already freed from the burden of lies, could feel himself becoming purer, stronger in this light, his resolve fortified, his will emboldened enough for what lay ahead.

"As for your question, do I care?" The Absolute continued, walking with his arms behind his back, his footsteps echoing in this great hall. "I care. Why else would I place the Epoch in each universe? But I only care so much. There are countless universes, and I have to oversee each one, facilitate the birth of new ones, guide the dying ones across the threshold. I care about each universe, but I do not let my care interfere beyond a certain degree."

"You realize that this does not in any way relieve the pressure that I'm feeling right now," Joe said.

"You're meant to. This is the final test. Its result final. I would be perturbed if you weren't feeling pressure. It would indicate that there was something wrong with my procedure of choosing a savior, and I, as the Absolute, make no mistakes."

"Explain the existence of suffering, why kids suffer from terminal cancer, why..."

"Let me stop you right there," The Absolute said, raising his hand. "I did not create the construct of pain in your universe. Neither did I come up with cancer or suffering. Your universe's God did. And it's high time you called God to the stand. And the other."

Joe held the artifact in both his hands, summoning them both at the same time. With the Epoch in his hand, it was as easy to summon them as it was to breathe, to blink, to think.

Satan barged in through the door at the end of the hall, wreathed in fire, eyes aglow with fury. He stomped his feet, bringing all his dark aura in with him, blackening the otherwise pristine place with his inauspiciousness. He wore no suit nor held back the intensity of his form by way of appearing humanoid.

Tall as he was broad, brooding, sneering, gripping his trident firmly, his tail swirling around behind him, he affected the two presences in the hall, Joe first, the Absolute second.

It was only after he saw the Absolute standing there did Satan quell his inferno and halted his stomping. He regained whatever composure he could muster up, and began to walk toward them slowly.

At the same time as the Devil walked up the hallway, a different shade of brilliant light—golden in its vividity—shone through the windows of the hall and God descended out of that dazzling luminescence. Olive-skinned, and feminine in her features, God possessed an intensity on her face that juxtapositioned itself with the warm benevolence also present in her features. She looked amused and irritated at the same time, this being with her long blonde hair flowing down her back, and her subtle golden robes flowing all over her immaculate body. The beings presented themselves, as the Absolute did, in a form that would resonate with Joseph.

Joe gazed at God with awe and disbelief. He looked over at Satan, who sneered, "Weren't expecting that, were you?"

"I have never been summoned," God stated with authority as she strode forward to meet Joe.

"You are summoned now," The Absolute responded dryly. "This is the culmination of your existence, and depending upon the decision of the Savior, this could be your consolidation or your end. The same goes for you," The Absolute laid his gaze upon unruly Satan, who stood there possessing what little defiance he could without appearing insubordinate. "I would advise you both to be keen as you make your statements to him, for he decides the fate of this universe."

"My Lord Absolute," God curtseyed, lifting the hem of her robes.

"Absolute," Satan did a smaller bow than God, one that barely acknowledged the Absolute.

The Absolute nodded to them both, then waved his hand in Joe's direction.

God beamed upon Joe with open arms, coming toward him, saying, "If it isn't Joseph Banbury, erudite author, braver of toil, my worthiest warrior."

"Excuse me?" Joe asked. "Up until a moment ago, I did not even meet you. Where have you been in the midst of all this?"

"Don't bother waiting for an answer from her. She's going to peddle his whole 'I operate in mysterious ways bullshit," Satan spewed.

God only smiled and shook her head.

"I have been watching you, Joseph. Observing your every move. Throughout your life, the courage that you have displayed has been a testament to the sheer tenacity of humanity. I created you in my own image, and seeing that resolve reflected in you..."

"You didn't create me. He did," Joe pointed at Satan. "In case you missed the memo, being wherever you were, doing whatever you were, I'm his son." Joe could see through God's guise of saccharine appeasement, and it did not impress him one bit that this, this diplomatic politician with the calculated words and bureaucratic poise was The Father In Heaven—in actuality not even a Father—every Christian prayed to. Standing in the presence of the Absolute, who witnessed this proceeding silently and from afar, God did not dare step over her bounds, otherwise he would have. Joe could see all that and more now that he was the Truth.

"You tell him, junior," Satan sneered, ditching his menacing form in favor of the one in which he had always appeared to Joe.

Joe ignored his witticisms and walked over to the end of the room and sat down on the solitary chair there. On either side of the chair were two stands.

Joe beckoned them both to take the stand at the same time.

God and the Devil shared a brief, perplexed look of annoyance and disdain before nodding to each other as they each took their place on the stand, and stood there.

"I wield the Epoch as ordained to me by the Absolute," Joe spoke, nodding at the Absolute, who sat on a single bench in the far distance. The Absolute nodded back. "And today, I gather you here so that each of you may present your arguments for the future of the universe. I, in my capacity as the Savior, the vessel of Truth, reserve the right to make a judgment as I see fit. Though, I will preface it by saying this, gentlemen. Neither of your track records with me has been good enough to sway me in either direction. But my personal disagreements have been taken from me, and in its place, I remain, Objective Truth."

"That's good to know," The Devil derided, "because it makes it easy for me to tell you that I burned your witch whore and rendered the madman's flesh till nothing but bones remained. Still feeling impartial there, or are you barely resisting the urge to end my existence?"

Joe smiled. "You know, this lets me sift through the lies in your words." He raised the Epoch in the air, waving it at Satan. "I can see what's true and what isn't. You did not kill them."

The Devil glowered, his bargaining chips gone.

"You're a creature of habit, but for your sake, I hope you can speak the truth today, Lucifer. Speak it like your life depends upon it," Joe ordered. The artifact pulsated in his hand, showing him visions of Lilly recovering in a hospital's ER, and Billy being taken down to a medical facility in an ambulance. While he may have done a number on both of them, even the Devil was not foolish enough to harm those close to Joe now.

20

THE DUALITY CONUNDRUM

Within minutes of the commencement of the trial, both God and the Devil had taken rather heated positions in the debate opposing each other. Realizing that it was a matter of their existence, they both argued as earnestly as they could and Joe listened.

"You're always going on about the Great Filter, Joe. You wanna see the Great Filter? Look at Mother Bitch over there. She's the one who has been singlehandedly holding back humanity's progress. Sodom. Gomorrah. Sumerians. Atlanteans. Babylonians. Romans. The Greek. Look at every civilization that spanned across history and see just how close each of them got to true progress, and then take stock of what God did. She smote them all down before they could reach their true heights. Were it not for her, everything that the world lacks today, it would not have lacked in the first place. Who better to know it than you? Who better to understand this than the man with whom I have held long talks over the matter!" What anger the Devil had against Joe was smothered temporarily under the growing concern that with the snap of his fingers, Joe could annihilate him. Now more than ever, the Devil was aware of it. Only now, he was helpless against it. His legions of Hellions could not come to his rescue, nor could any of his schemes.

"He drove me to the point of annihilating them," God pointed a blaming finger at Satan. "Were it not for him and his incessant compulsion to drive humanity to the precipice of evil, I would never have had to exact my judgment upon those he mentioned!"

"Judgment," Joe remarked. "What, I wonder, became of the love you claimed to have for all of humanity, when you exacted said judgment? Or are you a God incapable of love? What went through your head as you buried those civilizations? I wonder if it wasn't a selfish impulse, one that would tilt the wager in your favor."

God was no longer smiling benevolently, for she had come to the same conclusion as the Devil. Her eternal silence had cost him severely. She had no bargaining chips in this conversation nor did she have any way with which to assuage Joe. Not while the Absolute was watching. Not while Joe wielded the artifact.

"I am your God, creator of your world, progenitor of it all, the first Cause. I do not need to explain my actions to someone who was a mere mortal a few moments ago. Five minutes into power, and you dare question my necessary means?"

"Perhaps if I were still in possession of my humanly limitations, I would have quivered in fear at your ire," Joe spoke. "But my stature as the magistrate of these matters has relieved me of any such limitations, even if temporarily. So, yes. I dare."

"Don't let her self-righteousness fool you," The Devil snarled. "She would go to every length imaginable to justify her actions, even if it means banishing me from Heaven, or smiting entire populaces to prove a point."

"I am God. I owe no answers to anyone, least of all the Devil and his prophet. Do you really think that you can do a better job of serving this universe than I do?" Any faux benevolence God had displayed earlier was replaced with stern wrath, a more accurate representation of the biblical God, one who banished with great satisfaction, punished with gratification, and terrorized the world with her suffocating rules.

"You might not owe any answers to the Devil or his prophet, but I am neither. I sit here not at my own behest but upon the order of the Absolute, just as you are summoned by his order. You owe all answers to me, and I can see how cravenly you wish you had been less of an asshole to me and to the billions you've wronged, but it is too late for that now. Even God and the Devil are not exempted from judgment, and this is yours," Joe said. Throughout this procession, the Absolute sat still and watched, not interfering, not revealing any expression.

"Joe," the Devil spoke, his voice lacking its recent coarseness, possessing the same charisma that it did when he first appeared to Joe. "I have been a fucked up parent to you. Worse yet, I am as everyone sees me. The worst of the worst. There's no epitomic metaphor worse than the Devil to connote evil. I realize that. But take stock of your life, and see how closely linked I am to it. Speaking of metaphors, if I have been a violent, maladjusted, and altogether bad parent to you, then God's the cosmic equivalent of the parent who fucked off to get some milk and never showed her face around the house again. Where was she in all this? Mass murders, Massacres, where has she been? Heed my words. You know them to be true. Whatever I did, and I've done plenty, at least I was the one who showed up."

There was no lie nor any sycophancy in the Devil's declaration.

"You showed up because your base purpose calls for it. Where I seek to guide them right, you set them astray each day anew. Every civilization that you mentioned, their decline is on your hands. Had you not waylaid Sodom, Gomorrah, I would not have had to crush them. Had you not driven the Babylonians to the maddening depths of ambition, I wouldn't have had to take away their power. You bring empires to their decline. I have only ever cleaned up after your messes!" God boomed, her cheeks flushing with color, her eyes glowering, her body increasing in height.

"My messes!? The second humanity kicks back and chills, you show up as the police, confiscating my contraptions. No wonder humanity has never once progressed beyond the menial in these thousands of years. With a dictator such as yourself at the helm of it all, no wonder they're still in shambles!" Lucifer directed his fury at God.

"I illuminated their minds with knowledge corporeal and ephemeral! Factual and philosophic! Without me, they —" God began, but Joe held up his hand.

"You illuminated, God? Name one instance where *you* did that. Credit hogging ill fits you. Whatever knowledge humanity came upon, it came upon its own," Joe said. "Your scriptures do not teach the intricacies of mathematics or the wondrous phenomenon of metaphysics but abstinence from one's own needs, desires."

God pummeled her fist on the stand and yelled, "I am responsible for every system this universe has in place. Each moment, I carry it forward! Would you be able to do the same? I think not."

"Lie," Joe snapped, rising from his chair and stepping toward God. "You take credit for the work of others. Systems in place? Are they your systems or are they the Absolute's, who has such systems in place across all universes? You carry forward nothing. The universe operates automated. You perch upon your throne, idle, while those below wonder if God's dead or if she was there at all to begin with. Responsible? Irresponsible, if anything. Have you once come down from Empyrean to see how an average person lives their life down on Earth? In the suffering that you've devised?"

God spat vilely at Joe's feet. "Suffering is the yardstick by which I measure the courage of those who believe in me."

"Oh, bullshit," Satan jumped in. "Admit to him what I already know. You're just as sick and twisted a fuck as I am. You get off on watching them writhe in pain. You like it when they die in the throes of old age. You relish the screams in cancer wards as terminal patients cave into the metastasis collapsing their bodies. It's not any yardstick but your personal form of sadistic entertainment."

"You're one to talk, beast," God retorted. "Your suffering is just as heinous. Hopelessness. Sloth. Greed. Pride. I did not create those. You did. Those are your snares by which you've trapped them."

"ENOUGH," Joe said, standing at the center of the room. "I did not bring us here to have us squabble. There is a point to this proceeding. If either of you at any point ever cared about the fate of this universe, now's your time to present your case for the future of the universe."

The Devil coughed to clear his throat. "You already know my case. I just want humanity to be free from the bounds she's kept them trapped in. They follow their own path, a path—"

"—paved with sins of your devising! Over my dead body," God said.

"Don't you get it?" The Devil addressed God with a malevolent smile. "That's the entire point." Then, directing his attention back to Joe. "End this façade, Joe. You and I both know what you want. We've been aligned in our visions from the first day, haven't we? A world free from the influence of God? We're finally there. Let's do this, you and me."

Joe ignored the Devil and looked at God.

"Well? What is your plan for the future of this universe?"

"Isn't it clear?" God seethed. "My plan has always been the same. Judge humanity at the end of this universe's lifespan. Reward the virtuous with paradise eternal. Burn all those who stood in defiance to me."

"That's not very benevolent of you," Joe said. "You've given them little to go on, and if they don't believe in you for their whole lives, which isn't more than a couple decades at best, their punishment extends for eternity? Forgive me, but that does not sound like a plan for a well-adjusted universe. It's macabre."

"To you, maybe. It makes perfect sense to me," God stated. "The universe was fine before you came along. You're fetid like your father, fleeting like your mother. The universe will be fine after you're gone."

"Any closing statements from you?" Joe asked the Devil.

The Devil, perhaps seeing that this was the end, let go of the anger he had been holding onto ever since his fall. He smiled as he dug into his coat and brought forth a cigarette. With the edge of his index finger, he lit it and dragged deep, smiling somberly at Joe.

"She might be too conceited to see it, but you're my son. I saw it in your eyes the moment you summoned me. You've already made up your mind. Whether this was formality or an earnest attempt at giving us both one more chance, I cannot say. I do not wield the Epoch. You do. As the Devil, I knew my cause was a doomed one from the first day. Yet when I came into your life, I tasted something different for the first time. Hope, if that's what you can call it. I foresaw your greatness. I like to believe I had a hand in shaping you into the man you are now. As the Devil, I cannot begin to express my disappointment at how this whole thing has turned out. You and I were supposed to do it together, by each other's side. But you did what God did to me. You cast me aside. I hope that can make you understand my recent annoyance with you."

Lucifer's hands shook as he held onto the stand, smoking his cigarette. His voice broke ever so slightly as he said, "As your father, on the other hand. I..I am proud of you in my own way, you know? I didn't make it any easy for you, and neither did God. It speaks to the tenacity of the human will that despite everything, you stand here, the most important decision of the universe thrust upon you."

Joe could sense no lie in the Devil's words. He spoke this from his heart, meaning each word.

"I'd wished that we would shape the universe in our image together, but if you see me as part of the problem, I get it. I am, by my nature, problematic. So is that fucking bitch over there!" The Devil pointed at God. I would be a hypocrite if I stopped you now from doing what you think is right."

Joe smiled at the Devil.

The Devil smiled back grievously. "Hey, how about one more interview for the road?"

"I think we've had enough interviews for a lifetime, you and I," Joe said.

Before they could talk, God interjected by bellowing, "What in the fuck is this?"

Joe turned around, taken by the fact that God had ditched all remaining pretense and had descended down to the same level of perturbation as any ordinary human.

"Don't tell me you're buying this," God said. "He's the Father of Lies. This is what he does."

"Not today he isn't," Joe said. "He's my Father. And I am the Truth."

"Oy vey," God said.

Joe went back to his chair and sat down, looking at both of them, then at the Absolute, who had observed this all with silent patience.

"Having heard from both of you, I am tempted not to change anything. You're both flawed, and maybe our flawed universe requires us to acknowledge humanity's flaws and embrace them instead of seeking perfection. Who better to lead the flawed than a flawed God and who better to waylay them than a flawed Devil?"

"Speak for yourself," God scoffed. "I lack all imperfections."

"Isn't that by its own definition the biggest imperfection? That you lack any? Who can ever relate to you if you don't have any shortcomings? Have you seen how they talk of you down there? They cower in fear. Any love they have for you derives from that fear. Fear that you're perfect, they're not, and you will punish their flawed nature with an eternity in Hell. All their lives they try to perfect themselves according to the doctrine you've laid down. And for what? For heaven? Is it worth it to ascend to heaven if doing so changes your very flawed nature?"

God looked away, her expression full of scorn.

It was the Devil who finally asked, "So, what's it going to be?"

Joe looked at the relic in his hand, noticing the cross in all its intricacy, and the pentagram shining its metallic sheen against the dull wood.

"The answer," Joe whispered. "Has been in my hands all along."

21

THE END OF DUALITY

Joseph Banbury, having heard both sides of the argument, walked over to the Absolute, the relic in his hands.

"I have made my decision," Joe said, very aware of the gazes of God and the Devil fixated on him from behind.

"What is your verdict?" The Absolute asked.

Joseph Banbury shared his verdict with the Absolute.

After much thought, the Absolute looked up at Joe and asked, "Are you sure this is what you want?"

"Yes."

"So be it."

Joe headed back to the center of the room, facing both God and the Devil as he held the Epoch firmly in his hands.

"In order for this universe to thrive," Joe said. "I have decided that there is no more place in it for either of you. You counteract each other's moves, and at the end of the day, humanity suffers for it. We have not advanced as well as we should have. This cosmic cognitive dissonance has been the cause of most of the conflicts on earth. For once, I would like to see just how far humanity goes without the encumbrance of either burden."

When neither of them said anything, Joe lifted the relic over his head, and channeled his power into it.

The white hall shone brighter than before as light beamed from the Epoch.

God stood there, gape-mouthed, struck by disbelief as the relic absorbed her. The Devil, doing the same and having come to terms with his fate, parted ways forever with Joseph Banbury with the last words, "Give 'em Hell."

The relic burned in Joe's hands as it absorbed all the hallowedness of this universe along with all of its darkness.

Joe held onto it, despite the relic searing away at his flesh. He screamed as flames billowed forth from the Epoch, enveloping Joe's own body in bright hot, silver-white brilliance.

As he burned, he looked for the Absolute one last time before the light became too blinding for him to see anything. The Absolute was nowhere to be found.

The power of both absorbed beings flooded through the Epoch which sought a conduit, a source that would store it, sustain it, and harness it.

Joseph Banbury held on for dear life, his screams echoing in the disappearing hall, himself disappearing with it, leaving nothing but bright brilliance in his wake.

EPILOGUE

In the beginning, there was nothing, and then a voice said, "Let there be light."

His old body had perished by way of the flames that had erupted from the Epoch. First, the relic shattered, and then, Joe with it.

When he came to at long last, it was to the familiarity of his own consciousness in a different body. A body brimming with the life force of the universe, a body serving as a transcended vessel for the united polarities housed within. Those polarities did not exist as separate entities within him but as a part of him.

Joseph Banbury, no longer human nor a God or a Devil by any definition, opened his eyes to find himself standing on a green pastured hill. The light that he had sought shone from the sky, illuminating the countryside, shimmering along the length of the rivers that flowed, reflecting off the leaves of the deciduous trees in the valley below, and illuminating the hilltops all around him. It was not a place on earth, that much he knew for sure.

However, wherever this was, it was a fresh start.

Home.

With crystal clarity, Joe had supplanted God and the Devil, and, now, with the mere clap of his hands, he collapsed the old Universe.

He took a step on the pastured hill, feeling the coolness of the grass under his feet. On his body.

He looked down, rediscovering that this was not the battered and scarred body that he had been acquainted with over his old lifetime. This was an immaculate vessel, emanating a silver aura. A very naked aura.

"Here," a voice called from behind, robing Joe where he stood.

"Thanks."

Joe tied the robe around his torso, no longer naked, and acknowledged the presence standing beside him.

"Where are we?" Joe asked.

The Absolute chuckled to himself. "This expanse I have created is so large that I often find myself asking myself the same question. Where am I? And then I realize, I am wherever I want to be. So are you. You decide where you are."

"Wherever it is, it's quite nice," Joe said.

"You created it."

Joe admired his creation with all its alpine trees lining the hillslopes, the mountains towering one above the other in the distance, the pasture rolling below endlessly as far as his eyes could see.

"Reminds me of the Pacific Northwest," Joe said.

The Absolute looked around, nodding. "That it does."

After they both stood there for a long length of time, not talking, just looking around, Joe finally asked, "Did I do it?"

"Did what?"

"Save the universe."

"Only time will tell. There are no rules as of this moment save for the ones by which the universe is now operating. You, Joseph, hold all autonomy."

"It's strange. I don't feel like it. All this power surging through, me, this sense of endless potential, and I still feel the same old," Joe said, looking at his hands.

"Perhaps that is for the best," the Absolute responded. "The journey you are on now requires you to remember all the lessons you learned in your old life. You contain multitudes within you now. Your universe lacks a God. It also lacks a Devil. You're all that it has now. To do with as you will, what you know now will guide you and your people to new destinies."

"I feel connected to all of them. I see them connected to each other. I can hear their thoughts, their dreams, their ambitions." Joe smiled.

The Absolute's energy fluctuated, resonating with the complexity of their discourse. "This universal consciousness, as you call it, is the foundation of the cloud complex, what the old mankind called the Great Filter. The Filter acted as a barrier, a threshold that civilizations must transcend to achieve higher states of existence. It is not merely a physical obstacle but an epistemological one. To bypass the Great Filter, one must grasp the underlying principles that govern the quantum realm. But tell me, Joseph, why now? Why not let mankind evolve under your guidance organically?"

"I'm afraid it wouldn't have worked," Joe continued, "I saw it, time and time again, mankind in its old state was doomed to repeat its mistakes and ultimately, all I saw was destruction. They won't know any difference, I made sure of that. They'll wake up in their new world and in time, as they traverse the cosmos, they'll realize they are the only planet in this universe that has survived. God and Lucifer held quite the arrogance and it's apparent now."

"Very good," the Absolute continued, " I am sure you are well aware of the intricacies of quantum entanglement and its implications on the Filter. As you know, entanglement allows particles to be interconnected across vast distances, instantaneously. It defies earthly mechanics and has profound implications for the fabric of reality."

Joseph nodded, his eyes reflecting the depth of his understanding. "Indeed, the non-locality of entangled particles challenges our perception of space-time. The collapse of the wave function upon measurement reveals a hidden layer of reality that exists beyond our conventional understanding. The interconnectedness of all particles suggests a universal consciousness, a web of information that transcends the limits of their sensory perception. I can see it, it's beautiful."

Joseph's mind raced, connecting the dots. "The Great Filter represents a convergence of quantum mechanics and evolutionary biology. Civilizations that fail to understand and manipulate quantum entanglement are doomed to stagnation. The collapse of their potentialities into a single, deterministic reality seals their fate. Only by mastering the probabilistic nature of quantum events can a civilization unlock its true potential. While a millennium is nothing to us, I couldn't watch them implode on themselves."

"Joseph," the Absolute stated firmly, "the Great Filter was not placed arbitrarily. Its purpose is deeply intertwined with the nature of existence and the evolutionary trajectory of intelligent life. The Filter acts as both a challenge and a safeguard, ensuring that only those civilizations capable of true enlightenment can advance beyond certain thresholds."

Then, its voice resonated with a sense of calm. "Quantum entanglement is the key to breaking free from the deterministic chains of classical physics. It allows for superluminal communication and the synchronization of consciousness across vast distances. By harnessing it, humanity can achieve a level of collective awareness that transcends individual limitations."

Joseph's eyes gleamed. "Yes, indeed. The Great Filter, then, is a test of a civilization's ability to transcend its own limitations. It is a crucible that forces them to evolve, to expand their understanding of reality beyond the macroscopic. The manipulation of entangled states would lead to breakthroughs in energy transfer, information processing, and even teleportation."

The Absolute's form shimmered with approval. "Precisely. The mastery of quantum mechanics will enable humanity to overcome the constraints of the physical universe. By collapsing the wave function in a controlled manner, they can navigate the multiverse, accessing parallel realities and alternate timelines. This is the path to true ascension, to becoming beings of pure consciousness."

Joseph's mind expanded with the possibilities. "And by doing so, they can ensure their survival and progression to higher states of existence. The entanglement of their collective consciousness will allow them to perceive and interact with the fundamental fabric of the universe, and themselves to rewrite the laws of physics."

The Absolute's energy pulsed with a sense of finality. "This is the ultimate goal, Joseph. To guide humanity to a point where they can transcend the Great Filter and become masters of their own destiny. Your role is to shepherd them through this transition, to ensure they grasp the quantum nature of reality and unlock the infinite potential within."

Joseph nodded, his purpose crystallizing with every word. "I will lead them to this understanding, to this transcendence. Together, we will navigate the quantum landscape and reshape the universe in ways that defy imagination. The Great Filter will be but a stepping stone on our journey to the stars and new worlds."

The Absolute's form shimmered with approval, and together, they gazed upon the newly formed universe, contemplating the infinite possibilities that lay ahead.

Joseph, now the transcendent being, stood with the Absolute on the verdant hill. As the landscape shimmered with ethereal light, Joseph's curiosity about the greater cosmic design grew.

~

"ABSOLUTE," Joseph began, "why did you place God and the Devil in this universe? Was it a test to see if humanity could transcend the worship of deities?"

The Absolute's form radiated a thoughtful glow as it prepared to explain. "Yes, Joseph. The presence of God and the Devil was an integral part of the cosmic test. In almost every universe, it's required at first. They represent the dualistic nature of existence—order and chaos, creation and destruction, good and evil. Their roles were not merely to be worshipped but to serve as catalysts for growth and self-realization."

Joseph's eyes sparkled with understanding. "So, humanity's journey was never about blind worship but about evolving beyond the need for external deities."

"Precisely," the Absolute affirmed. "God and the Devil

were embodiments of fundamental principles that shape the universe. They provided a framework for humans to understand the complexities of existence. However, the ultimate goal was for humanity to recognize the limitations of these dualistic constructs and to seek a higher understanding of the Universe."

Joseph pondered this revelation. "By transcending the worship of deities, humanity could achieve a more profound connection with the cosmos and their own inner potential."

The Absolute's energy pulsed rhythmically. "Yes. The presence of deities was meant to spark philosophical and ethical contemplation, pushing humanity to question, explore, and ultimately transcend the simplistic dichotomy of good and evil. It was a way to encourage growth through the struggle and to inspire the pursuit of higher truths. Religion played a much larger role in this world than any of the others I've witnessed. Humans had five million years to advance on this planet, but something was different. God and Lucifer were in a fierce competition with each other, playing on mankind's weaknesses, keeping them down. So whilst you think it's only really been two thousand years, humans in other Worlds advanced after the first million years or so."

Joseph's thoughts turned inward after chuckling with the Absolute, contemplating the path humanity had taken. "In many ways, the conflicts and challenges posed by God and the Devil forced humanity to evolve, to seek deeper meanings, and to question their place in the universe, I guess it just happened later."

"Exactly," the Absolute said. "But you're not wrong, this World would have imploded on itself before they reached their potential. The journey through the realms of belief and doubt, faith and skepticism, was essential for humanity's evolution. The presence of God and the Devil provided the context for this journey, but the true test was always about moving beyond them."

Joseph nodded, a sense of clarity washing over him. "And now, with both God and the Devil no longer in their previous roles, it is my responsibility to guide humanity towards this higher state of consciousness, free from the confines of dualistic worship."

The Absolute's form shimmered with approval. "Indeed, Joseph. You have transcended the roles of God and the Devil, embodying the unity of these principles. Your task now is to lead humanity towards an era of enlightenment, where they can embrace their true potential and understand the intricate balance of the universe."

Joseph's resolve solidified. "I will guide them wisely, ensuring that they move beyond the limitations of worship and towards a deeper understanding of existence. Humanity will learn to navigate the complexities of the quantum realm and the ethical dimensions of their journey."

The Absolute's energy pulsed with affirmation. "Lead them well, Joseph. The future of the universe depends on the wisdom and compassion you impart."

Joseph took a deep breath, considering the enormity of the task ahead. "I understand that it will still take time for them to catch up."

"Correct," the Absolute agreed. "Humanity must evolve at its own pace. You've created a new universe overnight, and now you can accelerate at a faster rate. The journey to higher consciousness is a gradual process, requiring time and experience. Your role is to set the stage, to provide the opportunities for growth and enlightenment."

Joseph looked out over the verdant landscape, feeling a sense of purpose. "I've created the conditions for their evolution. I will guide them gently, ensuring that they have the freedom to explore, to learn, and to grow."

The Absolute nodded. "And in time, they will transcend their current limitations. They will come to understand the deeper truths of existence, the interconnectedness of all things. But for now, they need you to be their shepherd, their guide."

Joseph smiled.

With that, the Absolute faded out of sight and Joseph stood looking down on Earth, ready to embark on the next phase of the cosmic journey.

AFTERWORD

When I first embarked on the journey of writing this trilogy, I had no idea just how deeply I would become intertwined with the world I was creating and the characters who would inhabit it. "Interview with the Devil," "Resurrection," and now "Epoch" were initially conceived as a way to explore profound questions about existence, free will, and the nature of power. However, as I delved deeper into Joseph Banbury's story, I found myself falling in love with the characters and their journeys in ways I hadn't anticipated.

Each chapter I wrote opened up new dimensions and possibilities, making it impossible to fit everything I wanted into just three books. The more I wrote, the more I realized that there were countless stories left to tell, threads left to weave, and depths left to explore. This trilogy became not just a series of books, but a living, breathing universe with its own life and energy.

While "Epoch" concludes the initial arc of Joseph's journey, there are many more tales waiting to be told. Characters who have captured my heart will continue to evolve and their stories will unfold in future works, including "The

Witch" and "The Collectors." These spin-offs will dive into the lives of other key players in this vast universe, offering new perspectives and adventures.

Moreover, for those who have been captivated by the intricacies of this world, I am also planning to release an unabridged version of the trilogy. This comprehensive edition will include expanded scenes, additional insights, and the richer details that couldn't fit into the original releases.

As I move forward, I am excited to continue sharing the magic, mystery, and profound questions that this universe inspires.

Joseph's journey will continue too, at some point. Promising new adventures and deeper mysteries in a universe still unfolding

I challenge every reader to find their own Epoch. As tomorrow is a new day, and what a time it is to be alive.

Michael

Made in United States
Cleveland, OH
06 November 2024

10468044R20184